ETERNALLY CURSED

JANUARY RAYNE

This is a work of fiction. Shallow Cove Dimensions is a world I have created. Unless otherwise indicated, all the names, characters, businesses, places, events, and incidents in this book are either the product of the author's imagination or used in a fictitious manner. Any resemblance to actual persons, living or dead, or actual events is purely coincidental.

Formatted with Vellum

Also By January Rayne

Shallow Cove™ Dimensions

The Eternally Series:

Book 1: Eternally Hers

Book 2: Eternally Damned

Book 3: Carnival of Creeps

Book 4: Eternally Cursed

Book 5: Eternally Rare

Book 6: Eternally Lost

Dead Man's Ranch Series:

Book 1: Kentucky Nights

Shallow Cove™ Dark Dimensions

The Monster Stalker Series:

Book 1: Honeysuckles

Book 2: Snapdragons

Book 3: Hollyhocks

Book 4: Nightshades

DEDICATION

To all the ladies out there who have good boys.
Make sure you tell them every chance you get.
They love a good treat.

DISCLAIMER

This is a work of fiction. Shallow Cove Dimensions is a world I have created. My imagination ran wild and will run untamed with no reins. Only whips and spankings when asked for.
Unless otherwise indicated, all the names, characters, businesses, places, events, and incidents in this book are either the product of the author's imagination or used in a fictitious manner. Any resemblance to actual persons, living or dead, or actual events is purely coincidental.

Author's Note

There is going to be knotting (if you don't know knotting, research it, or take a chance and dive on in. I can't promise weird photos won't come up). There will be heat. There will be biting, blood, primal kink, pregnancy, pegging, breeding/praise kink, a bit of rough play, a bit of sub-action from the male character, CNC, mention of child death, and lots of shmex. A LOT OF THAT. So, if you're reading and you say, "Oh my gosh, there is so much shmex." Well, yeah. I told you so.

It's werewolf corno. There will be a huge giant eggplant a swingin' and this is your W-A-R-N-I-N-G.

Family, family friends, friends of friends who know my family, Mom, Dad... just don't even read beyond this page. Turn around. Go back. Pretend I still think boys have cooties. Love you.

Prologue

ANWYLL

Fifteen years old

The smell of smoke is everywhere, and the flesh of my loved ones are burning. I cover my ears as the screams pierce the air. Tears blur my vision, hot like molten lava, as I dart my attention around the village.

What remains of what used to be my home.

I curl into myself, burying my face in my knees, and wrap my arms around my legs. This will all be over soon. My pack will be okay. We will run under the stars tomorrow, and all of this will have been a bad dream.

I'll wake up any minute.

Any second.

"Please," I whimper to myself, a heated tear dripping from my face to the dry dirt floor. "Please, please, please." The ground rubs against my butt as I rock back and forth, the pebbles tugging on the thin cloth of my pants.

Another bomb explodes, shaking the earth under me.

The white noise of grains of dirt slinging against the bodies of the trees surrounds me.

I'm hiding between thick bushes and banana leaf canopies we made to camouflage our werewolf forms while we hunt. We don't have to hide when we hunt. We're the apex predators, but sometimes, we like to play with our food.

Not even our werewolf forms are strong enough to beat whatever force is at play here. Before mom shoved me into the bushes, I saw the electric firebombs sparking through the air before landing on someone or something.

The electricity is black, inky with long fingers waiting to grab whatever is in its way.

It makes my stomach feel funny—like I'm going to be sick. A man controls it. Mom and Dad told me stories when I was little about warlocks and how usually the ones who weave magic are good.

But then there's one line of warlocks, the Halls, who want nothing more than to cause pain, destruction, and death wherever they go. They are powerful. Stories have said the warlock family got their name from walking the halls of Hell itself, making a deal with the devil to take and own as many souls as possible.

Halls is a plain, boring name, but knowing why it was given to them always reminds me that there is always more to the unseen.

I don't know how they walked through Hell, and I don't want to know, but after seeing the darkness of the magic they wield firsthand, I believe it.

A howl rips through the air, and my breath catches when I recognize the call. I fall to my knees as others answer my mom's call.

She's dying.

The ache causes me to change into my werewolf form. My bones stretch, my skin morphs to grey, and I bolt for the tree line, dropping to all four paws to lengthen my stride, ready to attack. No restraints, no more hiding, no more control. I'm ready to fight for my family.

Ready to kill.

Ready for vengeance.

Ready to die.

"What the hell are you doing?" a harsh, exhausted voice snarls from my right. An arm stretches out and a hand folds over my snout, gripping it tightly, forcing my jaws shut.

I narrow my eyes at Aziel, my brother, and he applies more pressure as he tightens his grip. I whine.

"Don't look at me like that." Aziel lets go of my snout and curls his fingers into my neck, clutching the baby skin I still have since I'm not full-grown in this form, and he picks me up like I'm a pup.

He looks around, blood and soot smeared on his cheek.

"Look around for more young wolves! I don't give a fuck how long it takes. I want an army."

Aziel's eyes round, sweat dripping down his face as he tries to think of a plan. He sets his sights on the closest village cabin and runs into the woods, holding me in his arms as he does.

He is light on his feet, sidestepping every fallen branch and plant there is. When we get to the cabin, the back door is hanging from the hinges.

"Shift back," he mouths, gently placing me on the dust-covered floor.

I do as he says and shiver in fear as I look up at him through the shaggy ends of my hair.

"Aziel?" My voice cracks as I watch him creep through the house. He tosses a rug away from the floorboards and opens a trapdoor by clutching an iron ring embedded in the door. "Aziel, what's going on?" My chin wobbles as I try to fight my tears. I'm trying to be a strong werewolf, a fighter, but I'm failing. "I'm scared."

He lifts his head when he hears those words admitted by me. In three big strides, he is gripping my face with his hands. I look away ashamed, and he brushes a tear off my cheek.

"Look at me." He is so quiet with his words, no one else would be able to hear if they were in the room.

I drag my attention away from the floor and stare into his tired face.

"It's okay to be scared," he says, reassurance causing a slight bend to his brows as his face softens. "Being afraid doesn't make you weak, Anwyll. It makes you strong because you want to survive. Being scared is the fine line between a coward and a man. It's up to you to decide which side you want to take a step toward."

I nod, taking a deep breath to calm my nerves.

"We don't have much time. We're going to hide under the house. I promised mom I'd do everything I could to protect you, but we are out of options." He drags me to the trapdoor, and I jump down into the hole.

The space is cold and damp, the ground hard yet wet at the same time. I sit down, and cobwebs cling to my hair. Aziel quietly drops in next, with barely a thump from his feet as he lands. He shuts the door with a soft click, the rug folding back down over the door, leaving us in near darkness, the only light sneaking between the cracks of the wood.

I gasp when I hear footsteps in the distance, my werewolf senses kicking in.

The enemy is closer.

My heart pounds, throbbing inside my chest with every beat. It hurts.

Aziel sits behind me and silences my heavy breathing by holding his hand over my mouth.

"There's a good chance they will find us. Whatever happens, I'm not ever going to leave you. Everything is going to be okay. I'll protect you until my dying day, baby brother." He leans his head against mine, and I squeeze my eyes shut when the door to the cabin opens.

The only sound that follows is the slam of the door against the wall.

I grab Aziel's free hand while his other becomes wet with tears.

"I smell werewolf." The warlock begins to whistle, calling us like dogs. "Come out, come out wherever you are."

"I have a bone for you to bury," someone else tries to bait us. He laughs.

They walk above us, each step vibrating the dust and dirt loose. The debris falls on us, but even with the irritation in my eyes, I can't look away from the shadows of the intruders crossing over the floorboards.

"I can give you all the bones, all the meat, everything you've ever wanted and desired. All you have to do is come out of hiding. Your friends, your family, what do you call them?" The warlock snaps his fingers. "Ah, yes, pack. Your pack is safe. They have agreed to my terms."

I turn to look over my shoulder, needing confirmation from Aziel that this man is lying.

He gives a slow shake of his head, giving me all the answers I need.

"The terms are simple. You serve me until I get what I want. After that, you're free to do what you want."

Aziel holds my hand tighter, sweat slicking our palms as it gets warmer in the small space. It hits me then, as the temperature becomes so hot my lungs can't fully take in a breath, and my eyes begin to sting, I'm going to die here.

There's no way we are getting out of this.

"I really only need you for additional strength. We have the same enemy, the vampires."

Aziel's body tenses from the word, his breath somehow evenly puffing against my neck, but I can feel how much weight each exhale carries. The pressure nearly suffocates me.

"Come on. Imagine the strength I can give you, the power, the freedom!" he shouts, the heels of his shoes grinding against the floor as he spins above us.

The light fades between the cracks of the wood from the shadows of the warlock's body.

"We can be the team that the vampires fear. I know how much you love tearing them limb from limb. I've witnessed it. Your need to kill outweighs anything and everything else."

That's not true.

For many years, at least that's how the story goes, we have been trying to come to a truce with the vampires. Our kind, the werewolves, become riddled with this thing my kind calls 'sickness.' We don't know what it is or what the cause is, but we believe it happens when we need our fated mates.

Vampires mate for life, and my kind are no different. When we don't meet our mates, we become hungry to kill, for death, for the taste of blood.

We hunt.

We hunt anything and everything that gets in our way of finding our one true mate.

We hunt until it kills us or until we find our mate and kill them too.

Werewolves who get to that point can't be saved. The sickness turns their veins black, and when the color gets to their hearts, everything is downhill from there. They are too far gone. Werewolves want their mates so bad at that point, we literally tear them apart because we crave them so much.

I've heard from the stories passed down from my father and his father that when a werewolf kills their mate in a fit of feral want, the haze clears. A sadness overcomes the animal—regret and pain.

It's too much for us to take. With our sharp claws, we dig into our chests and rip out our own hearts since we tore our purpose for living to shreds.

And we don't know why.

The kills we make when we are with sickness are why the tension with vampires exists.

Werewolves have killed a lot of them, and in return, they have killed us. They think we are bitter about being anomalies, but we aren't.

We're aching with agony, and our hearts can't take it.

It's something my dad used to say.

"What if I told you, you could have the one thing your heart desires?" The warlock baits. "What if I told you, I could snap my fingers and your werewolf would never pine again because they would have what their nature needed?"

Aziel's body tenses again, but I feel the slight turn of his head as if he wants to hear more. I shake my head desperately, needing him to realize having a mate isn't as important as living. He's older than me, so the urge to find his mate is stronger. I don't have a want for her yet. I have the ability to think clearly.

I squeeze his hand with all my strength, and his body relaxes. Leaning his head against me, he nods and doesn't fall for the lies the warlock weaves.

The warlock sighs in annoyance. I imagine he has his hands on his hips, gazing around the room in confusion.

I slowly tilt my head up when his boots scuff across the floor and stop right above us. A cloud of muck bursts from the rotten groves, tickling my nose and threatening a sneeze. My eyes burn and water. My throat tingles.

Swallowing the need to sneeze, I fight my body's instincts so we can remain hidden. A hot tear breaks from the outer corner of my left eye, rolling slowly down my cheek.

I'm so scared.

I wait for the warlock to make a move, to do or say something, but the cabin becomes quiet. I don't hear his boots kick against the floor or the impatient huffs of his breath.

It's so quiet, my internal thoughts are whispering.

Boom.

Boom.

Boom.

The wild thump of my heart slams against my chest, hoping our enemy can't hear it.

The screaming dies down outside. The chaos coming to an end. Worms slither across my hand from the dirt. A black spider scurries along the wooden beam, adding final touches to its web.

The strong stench of sweat fills the air, adding to the musk of dirt. My skin begins to itch.

I want my mom.

A loud crash comes from above us, glass breaking, and the weak planks above us cracking. "You'll fucking obey me or so help me, I'll rip the skin off your bones, you damn dogs!" he yells, ripping the trap door open above us, blinding us with scattered light coming through holes in the roof.

He leans down, a wicked black storm crackling around him as a wicked grin scorns his face. "Aren't you a sight for sore eyes?" he says in awe, staring down at us as if we are the answer to all of his problems. "Just beautiful."

Aziel throws me to the side and shifts midair as he jumps through the trap door, attacking the warlock. A murderous snarl has the hair on my arms standing straight. I scurry to my hands and knees, squeezing the dirt between my fingers. Jumping, I grab the edge of the floor and pull myself up.

"Ah, ah, ah, remember who you're fucking with." The warlock shakes his finger left and right, tsking at Aziel.

He has Aziel suspended in the air, controlling his body with magic. The warlock smiles and cocks his head at Aziel, finding my brother's attempt to save us humorous.

How is he able to control a grown werewolf without so much as a flick of his fingers?

"Aziel!" I call out his name, and his eyes cast to the side, his arms limp. I struggle to pull myself onto the floor, but I manage.

I'm forced to slide across the ground until I'm at the warlock's feet. One hand wraps around my throat, and his poisonous magic sinks through my skin. I feel sick, weak, and at his mercy.

"Look how cute. So protective of your puppy, aren't you?" he hatefully asks Aziel, and a low, weak grumble vibrates through my brother. "You have no options. I have either killed the people you love or have put them under my control. You will follow me, or I'll kill this pup right in front of you." His hand tightens around my throat, and I can do nothing but take it.

I want to fight him. I want to shift, but he has paralyzed me somehow. I can't move.

Something so strong shouldn't exist. To take over another person's being, their animal inside them, it's too much power for someone to have.

"I'll snap his neck right in front of you. I'll skin his hide and wear his fur as a coat while you serve me if you don't agree."

I'm able to lift my tired gaze to Aziel's. One tear breaks free, darkening the gray fur on his face.

I hate when I see Aziel give in. He shifts into his human form, and the warlock drops him from the spell that bound him in the air. Aziel lands on his knees, gasping for breath, hair damp from sweat, and he stretches his arms as soon as I'm free.

"I knew you'd see it my way. I'm Brenden Hall. I'm sure you've heard of me."

Throwing myself in my brother's arms, I hide my face in his shoulder, not wanting to see what fate has waiting for us.

"We've heard of you," Aziel's tired voice gravels as he continues to catch his breath.

"Good. Introductions aren't needed then."

"How long do you want us for?"

"Until what I want is mine," Brenden answers.

"My brother will be safe?" Aziel asks again.

"Everyone will be. You won't have to worry about a thing. Do we have a deal?" His face reminds me of a boogeyman lurking in the darkness, wanting to make a deal for peace, but really, he brings death.

We've always been warned not to make deals with dark

warlocks. They thrive off their debts, the souls they collect, and the damage they cause. What's worse, their lifespan gets longer with every life they take.

He'll get to live forever.

Brenden grips the tops of our heads with his hands, a current blanketing my mind as I drift away from myself.

I see everything, but it's not me in control.

"There's some fine print you didn't know about," he bends down to whisper. "I control you."

He walks.

We walk.

He runs.

We run.

He wants us to kill.

We kill.

We're numbed. We're paralyzed.

What's worse is that I see everything I do.

And I'll never forgive myself.

Chapter One

ANWYLL

Present Day

I remember everything I did while bound by the spell of the warlock. Every person's face. The blood. The screams.

To be locked inside yourself and not have a way out is a curse that will always imprison my soul. My heart is bruised, and my bones are fractured, but that's okay because I deserve the everlasting torment of what I've done.

Being a prisoner in your own body is torment. The only thing I can compare it to is being right under the water's surface, so close to catching your next breath, but instead, you drown. No matter how hard I pushed at my mind, no matter how loud I screamed, they were futile attempts that never worked.

My conscience was buried too deep to be heard. I killed so many people. Innocent people.

Children.

The elderly.

Animals.

I killed everything in my way, but there is one person out of the thousands who sticks with me.

A little girl. She was maybe eight years old. Brown hair, brown eyes, and so afraid of me. I snatched her from her mother and made the little girl watch as I mauled her guardian.

My conscience that was shoved away cried and begged for me to stop, but the spell was too strong.

I cared, but the beast didn't.

That little girl wailed for her mom, fought, clawed, punched, and then spat in my face. Her tears were hot against my claws, and there was a moment when our eyes met where I was sure my werewolf was confused as to why we had an innocent girl in our arms.

The confusion was short-lived.

Like a fog rolling in on a humid morning over the lake, the spell snapped back into place, and I broke the girl's neck, slinging her limp body to the side as if it were nothing.

I don't deserve to live. Why couldn't I fight that spell? Why wasn't I strong enough? Maybe my soul wanted to kill. Maybe I'm not a good man after all. Maybe I am just like that warlock, sick and sinister with evil cloaking me.

Guilt twists my stomach. I'm not sure if I can live with the horror of what I've done much longer. The regret, the memories, the heartache, it all makes me want to die.

Burying my face in my hands as I sit on the edge of the bed, I weep. I do this every morning and every night. Crying is a cycle. I get tired. Go to sleep. Have nightmares. Wake up screaming. Cry again.

Sleep again.

Dream again.

The screams of that little girl are loud in my mind, rattling my core, gripping the veins in my heart so it stops beating.

"You're in pain."

I can't catch my breath. The weight of what I did crushes my lungs.

"You're always in so much pain." Rarity, the coven master's sister sits next to me on the bed. She weighs so little that the mattress doesn't dip.

None of the vampires here have warmed up to me or Aziel, not that I can blame them. The master hasn't kicked us out of the coven, but no one is welcoming.

Except for Rarity, which always astonishes me because my kind killed her mother. She's a beautiful, unique-looking vampire. Albino skin, white hair, violet eyes, and yet her soul, her heart, is nothing but kindness. How she can manage to be in the same room as me, how she can talk to me after what I've done, how she can forget werewolves killed her mother, I don't know.

She takes my hand, and the pain eases. I inhale a sharp breath, filling my lungs with the air I've been craving. It's one of her many gifts.

One she uses every morning to take my pain so I can feel relief.

Why does she think I deserve it? Add that to the questions I'll never get answers to.

"Are we friends, Anwyll?"

I turn to look at her in confusion. She searches my watery gaze for hope, and her hand squeezes mine to reassure me.

Friends? What is she talking about? Why on earth would she want to be friends with me?

"Well, are we?" she pushes, huffing with impatience.

"I don't know," I answer honestly, my voice rough from the time spent crying. I'm a grown man over six feet six inches tall, but I've never felt so small in my life. I wish I had died that day when the warlock found my brother and me.

Men are supposed to be strong. We aren't supposed to cry, but at this point in my life, the ability to be a man was taken from me. I'm a shell of what I hoped to be when I was fifteen.

That dream, that man, that hope, is gone.

"I think we are. And I want to tell you something that maybe you haven't heard yet. I know it's been an adjustment here. Everyone is learning. Vampires and werewolves living together will take time for people to get used to. I don't mind living with werewolves, and I want you to know—"

"—Why?" I interrupt her, my tone harsh and short. Her kindness makes no sense to me. "Why don't you mind? Your mother, so many of your coven, are dead because of my kind. Let's not forget Atreyu, your brother, is in a coma, probably until he dies. And you don't mind?" A chuckle, borderline sardonic and sad slips from me. "I don't believe you." My bare feet pound against the floor as I stride away, stopping at the bench below the window. Taking a seat, I stare out of the UV-protected glass, and the familiar hurt in my heart returns.

I'll say this, this house, this land, it is beautiful.

And I feel like I've tainted it with my presence.

"Did you kill my mother? My coven? Did you bite my brother?"

My attention locks on the sunflower field. They are in full bloom and tall due to Maven's magic, the impressive witch.

"Did you?" she pushes, taking the opposite end of the bench.

So persistent.

A sigh deflates my chest. "No, but—"

She lifts her hand. "Stop. Yes, werewolves killed so many I loved, but *you* didn't. I don't blame you."

"Then blame me for all the other murderous things I've done."

"Anwyll." She scoots closer, taking my hand in hers once more, and gives me a small smile. Her long, snow-colored hair falls over her shoulder as she cocks her head. "You really haven't been told, have you?" Her brows pinch and her lips frown, something along the lines of disappointment showing in her angelic features.

"Been told what?" My voice breaks and I clear my throat, glancing away in embarrassment.

"All of those horrid things, the actions that haunt you..."

My breath catches again when I hear the little girl's screams. I shut my eyes. I can't look at Rarity. I can't have her see me so weak.

That's what I am.

Weak.

A sorry excuse of a man, of a werewolf, of a person.

Her hand lands on my cheek, her thumb brushing away my tears. "Look at me," she urges while keeping her tone sweet and soft.

I force my eyes open and peer at the vampire through wet lashes.

"What you did, the atrocities you committed, the beings that are dead, are not your fault. It is not your fault. Do you hear me? You were under a spell. You weren't in control of yourself. You were forced to do those things; things I believe you would never do given a choice. You are not to blame. I do not blame you. You aren't at fault. And if it helps, I forgive you."

My lips part as unstable, broken breaths escape me. More tears fall, and this time, I'm sobbing with relief. I did need to hear those words. They won't fix me. I have a ton of healing to do, and I still feel guilty.

Rarity, a vampire, someone who should want nothing to do with me, offers me words of solace I had no idea I needed.

She's a friend.

My first one in all my life.

I yank her into a hug, wrapping my arms around her tight, and she reciprocates. Her body is kind of cold, and I shiver. If she were human, I would have crushed her with my strength.

There's a small part of me that wishes she were my mate, but alas, she isn't, and that's okay. The last thing I deserve is a mate. I will live for a long time, slowly aging, and will remain young-looking for thousands of years.

One day, I'll have someone when I deserve her.

"What's this?"

A deep, commanding, powerful, and curious tone pierces the moment. I yank away from Rarity as if I've been burned and wipe my eyes before staring at her brother, Master Monreaux.

Fucking great.

If he didn't want me dead before, he will now.

He leans against the doorframe, arms crossed, ankles over one another, and a glint of a fang showing as he curls his lips. "You aren't to be alone with men in their rooms, Rarity."

Wait. Is that it? Not because I'm a werewolf?

Rarity rolls her eyes. "Get over it, Lexy. Anwyll is my friend, and he needed me. Don't be such a bloodsucker."

Master Monreaux grins at his sister's insult. "Just being protective. Is she your mate, Anwyll?" he directs the question towards me, and I forget how to act. I haven't spoken to anyone besides Rarity in weeks, not since I was snapped out of the spell.

I fall to one knee and bow my head. "No, Master Monreaux. Rarity is not my mate. She's my friend and helped me when I didn't know how to help myself." I swallow, realizing then he could kill me.

End the misery.

He strolls into the room, his expensive loafers stopping right in front of me, blocking my burning stare into the floorboards.

"Stand, Anwyll," he orders.

On my shaking legs, I do as my Master says and continue to keep my eyes cast downward.

"You're a big wolf," he notices.

"Yes, Master Monreaux. My brother is too." I need to go check on him. I wonder how he is doing. We have a tendency to lock ourselves away and never see daylight when we are troubled.

"I need to speak with you in private."

I nod, putting on a brave face, but I'm nervous.

"Everything will be fine." Rarity gives me one last hug. "Meet me downstairs when you're done. We will go grab some food." She narrows her purple irises at her brother. "Be nice."

"I'm always nice," he grumbles, tugging on the sleeves of his suit as if the words bother him.

She scoffs and heads out the door, giving me a thumbs up before she closes me and the Master inside my room.

I'm bigger than him. I could kill him.

I don't want to. I'm tired of fighting. I'd let him kill me because I'm just... done. Done with hate. Done with revenge. Done with war.

Simply, done.

Master Monreaux rubs a hand over his mouth and exhales, opens his mouth to speak, but closes it again. He crosses the floor and sits down in a chair placed in the corner. He unbuttons his suit, and his sleeves shorten as he leans over, placing his elbows on his thighs. Alexander Monreaux is impressive.

While powerful, I've noticed how he lets his beloved lead more times than not. He is a strong vampire, wealthy, and one of the few who have ever been awakened from a coma.

Anyone would be a fool not to be afraid.

If he kicks my brother and me out, I don't know where we will go. I'm assuming that is what this conversation is about.

"I'll tell my brother we have to leave at once. I am forever grateful for your hospitality." I sit down on the bench again and run my fingers through my hair, wondering if Aziel and I could jump in the portal. Go somewhere new and start over.

"What? No, I'm sorry. Please, that isn't what this conversation is about. We do not want you to leave." He locks his icy blues with mine, and I let him have my mind. I can feel him rummaging through it, and if I'm not mistaken, his eyes become misty before he turns away. "I can't imagine how hard life has been for you. Your life was taken at fifteen years old. Nearly fifteen years of being a slave to someone, you must feel so many emotions."

I remain quiet, not wanting to get into all of my feelings.

"I know it's been an adjustment, and it will be for a while. I've noticed your actions. You aren't a threat to me, my family, or this coven. It's hard to have my prejudices against your kind disappear after so many years of believing you were the enemy. All this time, your free will was taken from you. It's been an internal battle for me to accept you."

"I understand."

"I'm here to offer you and your brother security positions. You'd get paid. You'd become official members of the coven. Everyone has agreed, and some are reluctant, but I believe in time, we will be a family. Prejudices aside, if that is what you'd like."

Hope bubbles inside me, but my past is stronger. "I'm dangerous. The things I've done... they are unforgivable. I understand your hesitance."

"You aren't the only dangerous creature in this house, but I know you did those things because of Brenden, not you."

"So I've heard."

"So I say," he corrects me, a final tone in his words warning me not to argue. "Do you want to be a member of this coven, Anwyll? Do you want to join me in moving forward with our futures instead of letting the past haunt us?"

Do I?

My past will always haunt me, but this is my chance to prove I can be worthy and have a family again.

"I'll need to speak with my brother." Is what comes out instead of the obvious answer.

"I expect you to report back to me later. And I mean

later today. I'm not a patient vampire, Anwyll. And stop submitting to me, we both know you are not submissive. You're an alpha. You have nothing to prove to me."

I'm trying to prove something to myself too. I want to show myself I can be gentle, agreeable, and kind.

"Yes, Master Monreaux. Thank you."

He eyes me before giving a curt nod, and a flash of disappointment echoes across his face. That leaves me a bit dumbfounded as he leaves the room.

Does he really want this to work? Thousands of years of killing one another, and now there is hope for the war between us to come to an end. The pressure is a lot, but I truly want to put in the effort.

My attempts are the least I can do after the agony I've caused.

With a new pep in my step and hope flaring in my chest, I take a left down the hall out of my room to search for Aziel.

"He isn't here." Greyson, a vampire who has recently been freed from the portal, stands in the middle of the hallway, tugging on his shirt.

No one has really talked about their time in the portal, the places they have seen, or the place they were stuck. They called it the in-between, but it's a dark cloud in the room no one ever mentions. Master Monreaux is the one who immediately shuts the conversation down when it is brought up. He doesn't want to acknowledge he lost so many years with his family. It's a truth he hasn't come to terms with yet. No one dares to bring it up now, so the master doesn't get upset.

"Do you know where he is?"

"He seems out of it, like he is searching for something. I saw him go outside."

My hackles raise, the hairs on my arms stand, and my mouth dries. Aziel is at the age where he needs a mate. It can't be the sickness, right? It can't be.

Greyson stops fluffing his collar when his bedroom door opens and a small man with dirty blonde hair steps into the hall. Greyson freezes, and I can hear the kick of his heart speeding up.

"Thanks for the good time, handsome." The twink stands on his tiptoes and kisses Greyson on the cheek.

I glance away, staring at literally anything else but Greyson. I don't do awkward well. God, I'm nervous, and this moment isn't even about me. I pretend to look at my wrist to see the time, on the watch that I do not have, and scratch the back of my head.

"You'll forget this happened," Greyson says, and I snap my eyes from the chandelier to him mystifying his one-night stand. "You had fun, but you got drunk, and you can't remember a thing. Don't worry, we were safe. I'm clean but forget me. I'm not good for you."

The younger man strolls by me with a blissed-out look on his face and blown pupils. I don't miss the pinprick marks on his neck.

Greyson buttons his shirt and, in five quick strides, stands in front of me. "I'm asking you not to say anything, please," his tone desperate and pleading. "Please, keep this between us. They... no one knows," he whispers. He surveys the room to make sure we are alone. "I risked bringing him here, I know that, but it's easy to sneak in and out with vampire speed."

"You don't have to explain—"

"—Just don't say anything."

"I won't. You have my word."

His shoulders sag, and he blows out a breath. "Thank you. I appreciate that."

"Aren't vampires..." I create a waving motion with my hands. "Sexually... you know, uncaring of what gender they like?"

"It isn't about that, and keep your damn voice down."

"What's it about then?"

He grips me by my shirt, my brother long forgotten, and Greyson opens his bedroom door, shoving me inside. I trip over my own feet, then slam my hip against the edge of the wall.

Mother fucker.

Greyson peeks his head out before shutting the door. He runs his hands down his face before tugging at his hair, leaving it standing in wild spikes.

"Listen, I didn't mean to walk in on you and your hookup. I don't care. I really don't give a fuck. I need to find my brother to talk to him about something Master Monreaux offered. So, I'll just..." I point to the door and walk forward. "Go."

He grips my bicep. "No vampire in this coven, in this family, has ever been with the same sex. Yes, it's heard of. Yes, vampires are fluid, but no male here has ever been with another male. And I don't want to be the first. I don't know if I'm ready for the questions and the odd looks. I've been gone for so long; I just want to be... for now."

I nod, watching him stare out his window, dark circles under his eyes. He swallows and releases the tight grip he has on me. If I were human, he would have crushed the bone; lucky for him, I'm as strong as he is.

"Sorry for being rattled."

"It's okay." I pat his shoulder. I take a step, then pause to look back. "You know, it's okay to be the first. There might be others who follow you. I don't think anyone here will care. Just be happy."

"And are you? Happy? Being here must be hard. What you've been through..."

"You mean what I've done."

"No, I mean what you've been through. The past has no business here, Anwyll. Both of us have a new start in life. Let's do it right."

A howl interrupts our conversation, and it's one of mourning, pain, and heartache. So much fucking heartache.

"Was that..."

I'm gone before Greyson can even finish the sentence. I'm stripping off my shirt as I run down the hall, tossing it on the floor. When I get to the steps, I jump, morphing into my werewolf midair. I land at the bottom on my elongated feet, and Master Monreaux is at the front door with the coven behind him.

I try to shrink my size, so I don't look so threatening while I flick my gaze from the door to Master Monreaux.

Will he allow me to leave?

"The ones who can step into the light are right behind you," he says, swinging the door open.

I throw my head back and howl, the strength shaking the paintings on the wall. The elf, Reuel, covers his ears, and Luna, the fae, begins to dance as if she hears a song.

Falling to all fours, I sprint out the door, leaping over the porch stairs, and with giant strides eat away the distance between me and my brother.

Another painful howl agonizes the sky, and I whimper, almost slowing as his pain becomes my own.

I slide my eyes to the left, seeing Rarity beside me. Her stark white hair is bright against the umber of the trees.

My giant, humanoid paws grip the dirt, flinging it backward as I run. My claws rip the ground, unforgiving and relentless. The fingers growing on the branches scrape through my fur and scratch my skin. It barely hurts.

Pain is a constant that numbs the ability to feel anything else.

My chest is heaving, my breath is fogging the air with every harsh exhale, and I skid to a stop in the middle of the woods. Leaves and dirt fan around me, and the vampires who can still go out into the sun stand next to me.

Another wave of guilt hits me when I'm reminded how Master Moreaux and any other vampire who decides to bond to the coven can't step into the sunlight.

Because of my kind.

Is there anything good about my species?

I shift into my human form, my tattered sweatpants barely hanging on my hips.

There's a rundown barn between the trees, the sun baring down on my brother's back as he lies on the ground in his werewolf form. He has wounds everywhere, and by the looks of the barn and how half of it is spread out in pieces, Aziel took his heartache out on the abandoned building.

"Aziel?" I hurry to his side, kneeling on the ground beside him. "What's wrong? Talk to me." The breeze quickens, and a sweet scent captures my attention. I forget I'm with my brother and I'm peering into the woods, wondering where the delectable smell is coming from.

In my next breath, in my next blink, the smell is gone, and whatever drew my interest away from Aziel has vanished.

Aziel shifts, and his skin is soaked in sweat; the slight shivers trembling his body snap reality into place. I forget about the fleeting scent and focus on the matter at hand.

"What the hell is going on, Aziel?"

"You have to lock me up, Anwyll. Lock me up. Chain me up. Fucking put me down because it's happening, I'm sick..."

I shake my head. "No. We will figure it out. You'll be fine." Aziel protected me at a time when we lost everyone we loved. It's my turn.

He groans as he sits up, sore and bleeding. He sways from exhaustion.

"Whoa, I got you." I catch him, and his fingers dig into my shoulders.

"Promise me, Anwyll. Promise you won't let the sickness take me. Don't let me die like that. Don't let me kill innocent people. Don't let me kill her."

I stay silent and glance at the barn, thinking of ways I can save him.

"Anwyll." He grips my chin, forcing me to look at him. "Promise me."

"I can't do that."

"You will because I'd do it for you."

The familiar, sweet, fleeting scent hits me again, reminding me of something greater than the life I live.

I suppose anything is greater than this moment.

"I promise." The words are sandpaper across my tongue, and the scent haunting me falls to my tastebuds, bursting like caramel droplets. My mouth waters at the same time my heart breaks.

Then, the mind-twisting aroma of salvation disappears, and I'm left with a trigger in my mind wanting to be pulled.

Heartache

A slow spiral to damnation where death is the only savior.

Chapter Two

RU

Àdh: Planet name meaning luck.

I'm addicted.

There isn't anything like it. I get excited every single time. I can hardly stand still. My fingers itch to grab it. I know it's wrong to do it so much, but I can't help it—I have to.

"How many?" an unamused, unfazed man asks, not surprised to see me again so soon. He blinks, yawning so large I can see the gold filling in his teeth from cavities in his molars.

Gold.

I love gold. I love anything that shines.

"Twenty—no—thirty. Yeah, thirty." I wipe the bead of sweat off my top lip and begin to bounce on my feet, impatient as he counts.

Huffing, I cross my arms over my chest and inhale, calming when I smell the new loaf of bread O'Molly's sandwich shop just put in the oven. A woman with a grumpy frown and flaming red hair snaps her fingers at the guy standing at the counter. She's a small woman, wearing a ton of rings varying from gold to rose gold to silver. Some have a ton of gems, sapphires, diamonds, and emeralds… I'm envious.

Leprechauns, once they find their luck, they like to flaunt their success. Some leprechauns like jewelry, some like cash, some like cars, actual gold, hell, I've seen some that want a ton of fresh meat.

Finding your luck as a leprechaun is everything to us. It's what gives us power, 'luck,' if you will. We have until we are twenty-five years old to find it or bad fortune will follow us forever. We are unlucky all our lives until we finally find our jackpot, and if we don't, we live with an evil fate of being forever banished to the part of Àdh that no one ever wants to go to. Not only does bad luck live there, but so does death. People who get banished to the Unwanted Lands have to fight to survive every day. I hear it's dark and gloomy. The sun never shines, rainbows do not exist, and no one ever finds their gold.

Luck doesn't live there.

We search forever for our destiny to find us. We get addicted easily to certain things, and when that happens, it's in hopes that it is because that 'thing' is our destiny.

Being a leprechaun is a bitch sometimes.

I'm twenty-three.

I only have two years left before I'm royally fucked.

"Dude, are you done yet?" I snap, tapping my nails on the counter.

Freaking Luricawne Leprechauns are the worst. They are lazy, take their time with everything, are short, slimy, and they all love hoop earrings in their ears.

"Shite, was that sixteen?" He tugs on one earlobe and clicks his tongue. "Looks like I have to start over, Dote."

Dote.

Another freaking thing I can't stand. I don't know what it is about leprechaun men calling women Dote, but I hate it. I don't want to be called cute and adorable, especially by him.

"Oh, for the love of chauns." I reach over the counter and snatch the strip away from his sweaty sausage fingers. "Don't call me, Dote."

He leans his elbows on the counter, the hair on his arms gleaming auburn, and he gives a flirtatious smirk. "Come on. You know you like it. I'd give you a good luck rub down." He licks his lips, eyeing my body as if I'm the treasure he has been waiting for his entire life.

I press my hand to my chest and gasp. "I'm clutching my non-existent pearls right now because I don't know what makes you think you can talk to women like that and expect them to actually like it." I shiver at the thought of his hands touching me. The spiced coffee I had earlier threatens to creep up my throat.

Folding my purchase up, I stuff them into my back pocket and glare at the man. He nearly has tusks, his top lip hidden behind his massive underbite.

"Your loss."

"Yes, I'm sure I'll feel the pain of it for decades to come." I keep my words flat and joyless. Slapping sixty chauns on the counter, I head out the door, the scratch-offs nearly burning a hole in my pocket.

I want to see if I won so badly.

I swear on all the luck living on this planet, I will win my jackpot and be the luckiest damn leprechaun that's ever lived.

So what if I have wasted thousands of chauns on scratch-offs? It will all be worth it one day. I'll win it all back—plus some. And it isn't technically gambling. It's more of a hobby like reading; my climax just consists of finding my luck instead of the protagonist getting his revenge or getting laid.

"Ru, babe, I think you might have a problem." My best friend sing songs, whom up until now, I completely forgot was standing next to me.

"Mannix, I'm dying to find my luck. I only have a few more years, and then I'm banished. That's it. I'll be in the Unwanted Lands. I don't care how much of a lunatic I will look like—" I whip out my scratch-offs from my back pocket "—This is my only chance."

"Ru, what if your luck is elsewhere? What if you're wasting your time with this?" Mannix, my gorgeous gay best friend says gently, taking my hand as we cross the road to the beach. "I think there is something else out there you could set your sights on."

I sigh in frustration and stop walking when we get to the other side of the road. He doesn't understand. Mannix found his luck when he was fifteen, young for someone of our kind to find it, and he has forgotten what the feeling is like.

You're empty. You crave it. You need it to thrive, to live. Every day you can't think or dream about anything else. The closer one gets to twenty-five, the stronger the urge becomes to be... what nature fully intended.

Leprechauns are more than lucky; we grant wishes. We hold a sort of power that people are envious of. People would pay with their souls if they could get their hands on a wish a leprechaun could grant.

I want that. My soul craves it.

Slipping off my shoes, my toes dig into the pale clover colored sand, and I stare off into the baby pink ocean. The waves crash against the shore, the shells of bright blue and lavender rubbing together from the movement of the tide.

The shells are Mannix's luck. They are why we are here. He wants more to add to his collection. He's able to put a spell on them and sell them. Each one a native buys will lead them to true happiness, whether it is for a moment, hours, maybe weeks, or months; he helps other Àdhinians feel better about life.

How beautiful is that?

Happiness is so hard for people to find, and to be able to give it so freely, so purely, willingly, is beautiful.

Mannix is a good man, a good person, but it's he who hasn't found his happiness in his luck. When will it be his turn?

The sky becomes a dark shade of midnight green, and the three moons hang high, each one glowing subtle shades of the rainbow.

I bend down and take a broken shell in my hand, turning it left and right as we walk along the water's edge. Foam from the broken waves crashes against the rocks, sprinkling the slightest amount of water onto us, creating a dull mist that whispers across my skin.

Mannix bends down and grabs a shell, his magic lacing around it and giving it a euphoric luminescence for a second. If you blink, you'd miss it, but it truly is fascinating to witness. A calmness comes over him too, a peace, like he is exhaling a breath of stress he had no idea he was holding in.

"Well, are you going to scratch them to see if you finally won or what?" He elbows me in the side, yanking me out of my jealous thoughts.

I surprisingly don't feel like it right now. Scratching them will just make me feel disappointed when I notice I didn't win, and I won't get my luck.

Two years before I become a nobody, fighting to survive in the Unwanted Lands.

I change the subject, kicking a few shells as we walk, passing a gorgeous cove nestled between the rocks. Pausing mid-step, I stare at the glittering water, hearing...a howl? I think.

"Ru?" Mannix stops up ahead and turns around. "You coming?"

"I just thought I heard something coming from the cove." I can't tear my eyes away from the circular pool cradled between misshapen rocks that come to tall, angular points.

"I don't hear anything," Mannix says, his eyes sliding over the water. "Just the waves. Sirens aren't singing just yet. It isn't dark enough."

"No, it wasn't that. It was—" There! There it is again, a distant howl. "You don't hear that?"

"Ru, are you okay? Is the stress of not getting your luck bothering you that much? Babe, I'm telling you, you're going to be fine. I believe that." He turns me by my shoulders, and his thumb brushes my cheek. "Hey, what's with the tears? Ru, it's going to be okay."

I hadn't noticed I was crying, but the sound of the howl, the longing, the loneliness, the ache matches my own. I sink into Mannix's arms and take a deep breath, tasting the sugar in the air from the ocean.

"The closer I get to twenty-five, the worse it feels. You don't understand." I push away from him and step into the sea, the shallow depth reaches my ankles, and the waves softly caress my skin. The wind blows through my hair, no doubt tangling the strawberry blonde ends. "It's beautiful, isn't it? We live in a gorgeous place." The stars twinkle against the green sky, and the pink tint of the water is nearly sheer. I can see to the bottom until it reaches the cove surrounded by rocks.

It looks like a never-ending black hole.

"I don't ever want to stop looking at this view." There are mountains in the distance with snow-covered tops. Along the sandbar to the right, there's tall clover growing, swaying with the beat of the current.

Heavy pounds of hooves have me turning around, and Mannix follows my line of sight to see unicorns running through the sand. They are protected by Àdh. No one is allowed to touch or keep the unicorns as pets.

One unicorn spreads its wings, fluffing and stretching them before neighing.

Gorgeous creatures.

The leprechauns who are banished seek to slaughter the unicorns for their horns. They are worth a lot of money and hold a temporary amount of luck, enough for the unwanted to feel powerful. It's fleeting though, and since we become addicted easily, those leprechauns need a unicorn again.

It's a vicious cycle.

"I don't want to be like him, Mannix," I whisper, gazing at the cove once more. "I can't."

"Ru, you're nothing like him." Mannix stands beside me, placing a shell in my hand, and for a moment, happiness swims in my mind instead of worry. "Your father has never been as kind, gentle, sweet, or thoughtful as you. Your father always had malicious intent. No one was surprised when he didn't get his luck. You are so much better than him."

I take a step forward, the howl in the distance getting louder, echoing in my ears, and I can't help but sink a little deeper into the water. "What if bad luck runs in the blood? What if I am just like him?" My fingers play on the surface of the water. "What if these next two years are all I have?"

"Then I'll make enough shells for you to make sure you experience nothing but happiness, but I'm telling you, Ru, you might be related, but your blood is built differently. We'll find your luck; I swear to you." Mannix reaches for me, and his finger curls into my back pocket. "Don't go any deeper. You know we don't know anything about the cove. It isn't normal. You can't see through it, and it isn't pink, Ru. Stay away from it."

How can I stay away when it is calling to me? I've never been so close to the cove before, but I can feel something in it telling me to jump in. No one has ever dared to go into the cove.

I keep walking, and Mannix's finger tightens in the pocket, but he manages to pinch the scratch-offs. They slide out along with his hand, and I hear his annoyed groan.

"You know, you wanted these so much, and now you aren't even using them. Don't worry. I'll keep them safe," he calls out after me.

I don't even care about the scratch-offs anymore. Nothing else matters besides this cove.

The water is to my waist now, then my chest, and I begin swimming to the rocks, the waves sloshing sweet water into my mouth. My ears are full of the sea, and the painful howls are stronger under the ocean's surface.

Inhaling a large breath, I sink my head under and stretch my arms out in front of me, opening my eyes to see the green sand beneath me. The rocks form ahead, gradually getting bigger. Reaching out, I grip the edge, the sharp edges digging into my palms. Kicking my legs, I rush to the surface, gasping for breath as soon as my head breaches the waves.

"Ru! You about gave me a heart attack. Get back here. The water is getting rougher, and it looks like a storm is coming in."

I spit the extra water out of my mouth and turn my chin on my shoulder to see Mannix pointing to the sky. Dark, ominous black clouds roll in, forming in the blink of an eye.

"I need to know," I shout over the wind blowing violently.

"Know what? That you're insane? I get that. Get your ass back on shore, damn it. You know I can't swim if you get sucked under by a wave."

He's right. I'd be screwed, but something inside me is telling me to risk it.

"Come on, Ru. You're freaking me out," he shouts.

I lock eyes with my best friend, climbing the jagged rocks. They are slick from water and algae. My hand slips, and the hard stone slices my elbow as if it is butter. Blood washes into the sea, fading into the sheer pink of the water.

The discomfort doesn't stop me from climbing. I ignore Mannix's protests, his voice getting lost in the growing storm.

That's the thing about Àdh's storms, they come on quickly and out of the blue, dangerous with the fury they bring.

I have to be careful, one wrong move, and I could be lost to the tumultuous current, the storm seizing me in its catastrophe.

Something tells me my life is worth the risk.

Wiping the water from my eyes, I take a deep breath and look around. The waves are growing larger, and black raindrops begin to fall, turning the beautiful bubble gum shade of the ocean to a blooming dark red.

I continue my climb, my clothes sticking to my skin, cold and wet. I can't stop. The howling becomes louder, my heart aches more, and tears drip down my face, getting lost in the mixture of the rain.

Stopping isn't an option when I'm so close to easing the pain. Why do I suddenly feel like this? I was fine fifteen minutes ago, but this call I hear, it's for me. I know it is.

When I get to the top of the rocks, I peer down into the cove. To me, it reminds me of a crater, like a meteor fell from the sky and made a perfect circle. What if that is why it's never ending and an abyss of ink?

I grip a slender, long rock, tall and skinny like a rod, and it comes to a sharp point as I lean my body over the edge to get a better look.

"Ru! I swear on my luck, I will cast you to the Unwanted Lands if you don't get your ass back here. I'm going to call Àdh Parachauns if you don't get down here right now, Badru Bellatrix Byrne!"

Wow, full name usage. That's when I know I'm in trouble.

It doesn't matter.

The longer I peer into the cove, the more I notice how unique it is. While the ocean rages and the rain falls from the sky like melted licorice, the water in the cove doesn't move. It's still.

There isn't a ripple upon the surface. I'm able to see my reflection, a mirror, a sheet of perfect glass that's daring me to jump in and break its peace.

But the more I stare, the image of myself begins to change. The howls of despair make me cover my ears, the man in the picture clutching someone to his chest. He tosses his head back, his skin a beautiful slate grey, his teeth sharp, and howls. It doesn't last before he sniffs the air, whipping his head around as if he is looking for something.

And I swear, he stares straight at me.

It steals my breath, and a gust of wind blows against me so hard that I lose my footing. I balance myself on the crater's edge, arms stretched out and afraid to move. My heart slams against my chest. Fear coils around me like a snake.

"I'm calling for help! For the love of all the luck, don't fucking move, Ru."

"Obviously," I whisper, knowing Mannix can't hear me.

Time seems to slow as the air leaves my lungs, and I stare at a huge set of waves curling toward me. The first wave hits the rock, the foam spraying against me, and I can't help but watch the second one slam against the rock's wall, the water falling into the depths of the cove.

It's the third wave that solidifies the fact that I'm going to die. I tilt my head back to stare at the top of where it crests. I barely have time to inhale my last breath when the momentum of the tide hits me, sucking me into its insides. I swallow a massive amount of water, tumbling and rolling in the most dangerous part of the wave.

Flipping and turning, I can't see anything. All I can think about is dying. My life isn't flashing before my eyes. I'm not thinking about what it would be like to have my luck, my parents, my first high school boyfriend—none of that.

Just the howl.

Just the creature who led me to the cove.

The wave finally falls, slamming me inside the crater. My body twists, and I try to find my way to the surface as my lungs burn. My head feels like it's about to explode. I use my arms to push the water down while kicking as hard as I can, fighting to get air.

I breach the surface, sucking in water but air too. I choke, spitting out the now bitter taste of the ocean since it is raining. It's no longer as sweet as sugar, but as rancid as spoiled milk.

It's revolting.

I barely have time to catch my breath when another giant wave crashes on top of me, sending me into a rolling barrel in the water. The force slams me against a rock. My head snaps back, cracking against the hard surface, and my body falls limp. My eyes hood, but not before I see millions of bubbles in front of me. The current takes my body, pushing me further into the cove, into the void no one has ever dared to enter before.

Closing my eyes, I feel weightless, happy, and at peace.

Bad luck, good luck, none of it matters now.

The howl becomes louder, and I smile, relishing in the lullaby the ocean uses to put me to sleep— forever.

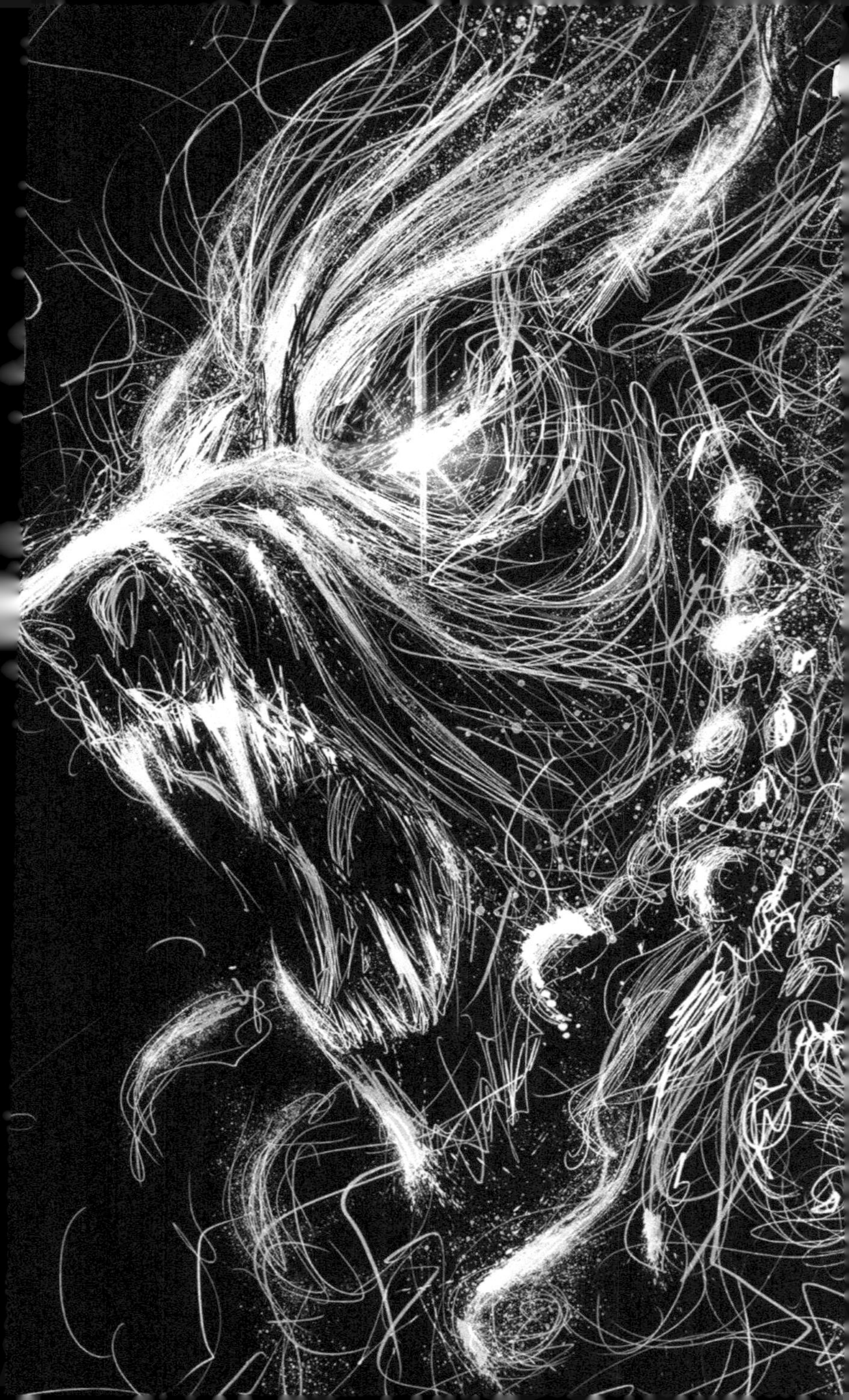

Chapter Three

ANWYLL

I want to hunt.

The sickness hasn't taken me like it has my brother, but it's there, swirling around in my chest, waiting to take me... It wants to break free. I'm on edge, my fingers twitching from the build of adrenaline, and I have no idea why.

"There has to be something that can help him. We can't keep him locked in the catacombs and chained to a wall. It isn't humane." Master Monreaux rubs his hand over his face, clearly exhausted. His face is pale, and a faint pink hue has taken over his eyes. I wonder if he has eaten today.

"You have to keep him down there," I say, tapping my fingers against the long table of the conference room. I peer up after staring at the same spot since this meeting started. Everyone is looking at me.

Luna, the fae who came from the portal, is staring at me intently, along with her elf friend Reuel. Drayce, the Viking vampire, sharpens a blade as he waits for me to say more.

Zaffre, another vampire, lifts his feet and places them on the table, leaning back to relax. He reaches inside his pocket and opens a pack of cigarettes, but Master

Monreaux wraps a hand around the newcomer's throat, baring his fangs.

"Don't you fucking dare light that in my home, or I'll rip your lungs out from your body. My beloved is pregnant. Or have you forgotten?"

"Lex, it's okay," Maven whispers, rubbing both hands on her stomach. "The smoke wouldn't bother me. I heal, remember?"

"We don't know what the smoke could do to the babies. I won't risk it." He bends Zaffre's hand back until the vampire groans in pain, eyes wide and alert. "Have I made myself clear?"

"Yes, Master Monreaux."

With a sneer, Master releases him with a hard shove. "Anwyll, you were saying?"

I sigh, pinching the bridge of my nose as I try my best to stay seated. For some reason, I want to break the table in half and run outside, shift. The feeling is nearly feral, a need clawing at my insides.

"Anwyll," Luna's voice is soft, holding a tint of something magical from a faraway place. It eases me.

"Are you okay?" Rarity is on my left in an instant, taking my hand. "My god, Anwyll, you're burning up." Her palm touches my forehead. "Are you sick?" she tries to whisper so no one can hear, but we're in a room full of paranormals—they can always hear.

"No." I begin to gasp, breathing becoming impossibly difficult. I wipe my face with my shirt and then slap my hands on the table. My nails shift, long talons digging into the wood. I clench my teeth when my eyes shift next and try to speak, "You have to leave him down there. The sickness is taking him. His heart will die, change, in some way. All I know is it will turn black, and he will be different, and he will begin to kill everyone, without remorse." I open my eyes, and Amberella, a vampire that came from the portal, gasps. "He will kill your mate and your unborn children without a care in the world, Master. He will murder us. He will rip the hearts out of everyone's chest until he finds the one meant to be his— then kill her too. And don't you think he won't kill me, he will. You cannot release him from those catacombs. If you truly love your life and your mate's, this coven, then you'll leave him there."

Master Monreaux's jaw is tight, and I can tell he is fighting the urge to rip me to pieces after giving him a mental image of what my brother could do to his mate. It had to be said though.

"He isn't that far gone yet," Maven chimes in, her delicate tone sinking into the space around us. "This sickness, whatever it is, it's new. He's still him."

I slam my fist on the table and stand, the chair flying against the glass wall behind me. "He won't be! Don't be so naïve as to think he can be saved. One minute, he can be fine, and the next, he will bathe in your blood while feasting on your fucking bones. Do not trust him. The sickness is unpredictable. We don't know a lot about it."

In a flash, Master Monreaux throws me against the wall, talons gripping my windpipe, fangs bared. His eyes flip to a murderous red, and the werewolf inside me threatens to stretch my skin and emerge. I'm an Alpha, through and through, a damaged one, but an alpha nevertheless. Any threat to me, I want to fight, but Master Monreaux is different, so I continue to fight the shift.

I don't know what's going on with me, but I feel hot, like my insides are boiling. My sanity seems to be on the brink of snapping, and that's why I lost my temper with Maven.

"I should strip your skin from your bones for talking to my mate like that. I should drain you of your blood, put it in a jar, and have her curse it so you never know what heaven is like."

"My love." Maven's hand rests on his arm. "He isn't himself. Something is wrong with his beast."

I close my eyes and toss my head back, screaming as my fangs lengthen despite my best efforts. It's always painful to deny a shift, but since I don't know why I need to, I can't risk hurting anyone. I don't trust myself right now.

"Anwyll, what's going on?" Master Monreaux's voice changes from wanting to kill me to being concerned. He releases his hold on me and cups the back of my head. "Talk to me. I can't help if I don't know what's happening." Alexander Monreaux is the kindest, most selfless vampire I've ever met. He can switch from a murderer to the most understanding man in an instant.

He and his beloved make a powerful team. He's vengeance, and she is grace.

"He is a werewolf. He probably wants to kill us all," Finnick grunts from the corner, the stab hurting me more than I wish it did.

Master blurs to Finnick's side and punches him across the face so hard, Finnick flies through the air and smacks against the wall. He groans as he tries to stand, but Master is there before Finnick can right himself. He breaks the leg of the chair off and spins it in his hand, pinning Finnick against the wall by aiming the makeshift dagger at his heart.

Everyone in the room holds their breath.

As for me, I feel confused as to why he would threaten a coven member's life, and not just any member, another vampire, for me. Why would he defend me?

My stomach begins to cramp, and I fall to my knees, clutching my midsection. Sweat stings my eyes, and saliva drips from my fangs onto the floor.

"Don't you dare insult him when he has done nothing but protect us. Remember, you lost your ability to walk in the sun, Finnick. Everyone has pledged their allegiance to me as of last night. Anwyll and his brother included, but guess what? It is he who protects us during the day when we can't protect ourselves, and you dare insult him in my home, in front of me?" Master leans closer and hisses, "The audacity." He ends his sentence with a bite, his teeth clanking together. "I should lock you in the catacombs for a night with Aziel and see if you survive."

Another roar leaves me, only this time, it's the growl of my beast, tearing me from the inside out.

"Anwyll, talk to me. Maybe I can take the pain? I'm so sorry, I don't know more about your kind. I will do everything I can to change that." Maven's hand lands on my back, and I flinch, crawling away from her.

"Don't." I squeeze my eyes shut, sweat soaking my hair. "Don't touch me. I don't know what I'll do. I'm not... I don't know what's happening. I've never been in this much pain." My feet change next, bursting from my shoes, lengthening to a gigantic size. "Oh my god." I bend to the right and vomit; the coffee I had earlier pooling on the carpet. "I'm so sorry, Master Monreaux. I'm sorry. I don't... I don't know what's wrong with me. Everyone should leave. I don't know how much longer I can contain myself." My eyes burn from the heat inside me, and I watch as fur sprouts along my hands, my vision hazy as I begin to lose consciousness.

"Everyone out," he orders. There are a few people who are reluctant to leave but listen to their leader.

Greyson stays behind and shuts the door while Maven

takes my hand in hers, the tingle of her magic seeping into my palm. I sigh in relief, the pain lessening, so it allows me to breathe.

I open my eyes and force my tongue from the roof of my mouth. "Thank you," I tell her. "But you need to go. Master, please, get her to leave. I'll never forgive myself if I hurt her and your children." I drag my left hand across the wood, my nails leaving scratches on the floor. "I couldn't live with myself."

"I don't want to leave you like this."

"It's okay." Rarity comes through the door with a glass of water and a cloth in her hand. "I'll take care of him. He is right, Maven. You can't stay in here."

"I agree," Master Monreaux states, picking up his pregnant mate. "Keep us updated. I won't be able to help until nightfall. I apologize for that."

Peeking up at him from the floor, I can see how much it bothers him. He gives me a tight smile, with flexing cheek muscles. Before I can say anything, he spins on his heel and walks away.

"I am not a bag of rice you can just throw over your shoulder. I'm going to poison your food later." She hits his back as they stroll through the doorway.

He chuckles darkly. "You are my food, My Sweet."

It's my turn to laugh now, but the movement only makes my stomach hurt more. My hands shift and I cry out, falling to the floor, back bending to the point I know it will break.

"How can I help?" Greyson kneels next to me, hands hovering over me.

"Undress"—I bite out—"me. Don't want to ruin...my clothes." The last word comes out deeper, rougher, the voice of my wolf.

Greyson nods and unbuttons my pants, stripping them down my legs. The cool air hits my skin, but it does nothing to reduce the heat dancing across every inch of my body. Next, he works my shirt over my head.

"I hope you don't care that I see all of you… I'm not…" He bends down to whisper in my ear, "I'm not trying to ogle you or whatever. You aren't my type."

"I don't give a flying fuck about that, Greyson," I laugh again. "I really don't care!" I shout again, bones cracking and morphing.

"Your eyes," Rarity gasps, sounding shocked. "They are glowing green."

That's new, and it makes no sense. I've never heard of a werewolf's eyes changing color.

She wipes my forehead and splashes water on my face. "Don't fight it anymore, Anwyll. Let go. Figure out what your beast wants. Give in."

"Listen to her," Greyson urges. "You're only causing yourself more pain."

Rarity's hand lands on my chest. The anxiety fades, my breathing slows, and she croons, "There you go. Relax. You're okay. You're safe."

But are they?

I rake my nails against the wall when another wave hits me, contorting my spine. I growl a thunderous sound that has my two vampire friends taking a few steps away from me. Flipping to my stomach, I give in to my beast, my legs growing longer—bigger—my muscles bulging, my torso elongating, and my skin changing to the common slate grey. My hair morphs to a dusting of fur, and when I'm done changing, I'm more conscious in my mind than ever before, and maybe that's because being in this form without that warlock controlling me still feels so new.

I'm learning how to be a man and a werewolf for the second time in my life. The first was stolen from me, and one day, I'll become everything I truly want to be.

I hope.

If the warlock, the regret, the guilt, and the blood on my hands don't haunt me for the rest of my life.

Taking a minute to myself, I inhale a few deep breaths. The wood creaks under my massive weight. Two other heartbeats pound against their chests. My claws drag across the floor as I straighten to my full height on my hind legs. Greyson and Rarity inch their way toward the door, their escape plan, but if I wanted to attack, they'd never make it out of here alive.

"Anwyll?" Rarity's voice shakes as she says my name.

I ignore her, letting my werewolf take control. I glare out the window, my eyes searching the quiet forest.

There's something out there for me to hunt.

To protect.

To make mine.

I don't understand this feeling, but my heart is about to explode, and panic begins to well.

Something is wrong.

With a sneer, I charge through the wall, the thick glass shattering from the impact. A few shards cut me, opening a wound across my nose, but I don't care. I need to be in the forest. I need to follow my heart.

It's been so long since I've felt anything that I'm not sure if I trust what is happening to me. Trusting myself after all the blood I've shed seems like a betrayal to everyone I've hurt. I don't deserve to find whatever my werewolf is hunting, but if I don't, no one will be safe.

I'm already on the verge of sickness. I felt the darkness tugging in my mind after I got a whiff of something that smelled so delightful. That's when I turned into a ticking time bomb.

Leaves crunch under my massive feet, and I scratch my nails against a nearby tree, leaving an imprint to last forever. I lift my snout, sniffing the air, searching. A sweet smell has my cock jerking between my legs.

What is this sensation? I've never had an erection. I know what they are, but being trapped inside myself for so long, the urge for sex wasn't there.

Tilting my head back, I howl, letting my desire be known. Dropping to all fours, I sprint, letting my nose take me to my fate.

I recognize the area. I smell the magic Maven has bound to Shallow Cove. I feel it. It's a cloak over my skin, and I slow, cold air causing my breath to puff into small clouds as it bursts from my throat.

Licking my lips, my toes dig into the dirt as I stand upright, and I drop my arms to my sides. A low growl continues to hum through me the closer I get to the water. It looks different from the last time I saw it.

It's bigger, the grass around the hole is greener, and big purple flowers are blooming around it. The water begins to ripple, and I fall to all fours again, a growl of excitement turning into whimpers.

Peering into the abyss, the new shade of green of my werewolf's eyes reflect back at me. The more I stare at myself, the more I wonder who could ever want to be with a monster like me.

And I am.

I'm the monster that haunted people at night, killed them, and destroyed their lives.

I don't know why I'm here, but I know I can't leave.

Leaving would kill me.

I'd deserve that too.

The cove holds answers to questions so many have, and if my wolf senses led me here, then there is a reason.

Dipping my head further toward the water, the ripples begin to grow, and I think I see something floating to the surface. I would say that's impossible, but with so many coming through the portal, I don't think anything would surprise me.

The closer the object becomes, the more curious I get. What looks like dead grass comes to the surface first. I reach in, soaking my arm, and I brush it out of the way to see a pale face.

A person.

A woman.

Mine.

A wave of fire possesses me, desire, love, possession, it overtakes my mind when I see her. I smell her, even through the water, but the one thing I can't hear is a heartbeat. With a roar, I dive my entire body into the cove and pull my fated mate close.

Once I have her in my arms, her strawberry blonde hair smells of caramel, and instead of rejoicing at having my mate in my arms, I whine, mourning that it is too late.

My heart is shredded, not that I don't deserve it.

Fate would bring me my mate to tease me, to give me hope, and to yearn for happiness. Then, Fate laughs at me, delivering my dead mate to me in retaliation for all the other mates I've killed.

I deserve misery.

I deserve the pain of trying to bring my mate back to life.

I deserve the cruelty of Fate.

Slapping my paw on the soggy ground, I dig my claws

in and lift us onto the grass. Using a long black nail, I push her hair away from her cheek and revel in her beauty. She's gorgeous. Hanging my head, I begin my mournful howl, a tear breaking free. Whining, I slip my arms around her and pull her to my chest, cradling my one and only as gently as possible.

I'll die.

There's no point in living now.

I lean back, her lips are blue from the cold water, and suddenly, anger takes over me.

Why was she in the cove? Why would she put herself in danger? Why? Fucking why can't I have my chance at happiness?

Snarling, I shake her, her hair tumbling around her shoulders.

Wake up, damn it! Breathe. I need you. I need you so fucking bad.

I shake her harder, then lay her on the ground when it doesn't work. I try to shift, but I can't. I'm locked inside my beast now.

Until I die.

Because she is dead.

Bending down, I press my ear against her chest.

Waiting.

Hoping.

Nothing.

With a sob, which sounds more like a sneer, I lift my fist and punch it against her chest.

Angry. I'm so fucking angry. I want to tear her apart for leaving me before I ever got a chance to experience her.

Wake up!

I hit her chest again.

Breathe!

Her sternum cracks with the force of my next hit.

You have to breathe. There has to be good in this world, or I'll never hope for anything again. Come on, Baby. Breathe for me. Breathe.

I don't know how much time passes. It feels like hours, but it's only been seconds. Time is relative when your heart is breaking.

Pressing my forehead against her chest, I relish in the fact that I got to hold her. A tear falls onto her skin, and I lift my head, grazing a claw softly down her cheek.

I love you, and I haven't even gotten to hear your voice. Thank you for finding me, mate. In the best way you could.

My werewolf won't stop crying, the whines are getting louder, but there's nothing I can do for us. I can only mourn with him.

Lifting her into my arms, I nuzzle her cold cheek and inhale, squeezing my eyes shut as a fresh wave of pain slices into my soul.

The slice that belongs to her.

It's forever dead. No one else can ever revive it.

I begin to walk back to the estate, my feet dragging through the mud and leaves. Finding the strength to carry her is hard when my soul is unraveling, but she deserves a proper mate's funeral.

A small, choked gasp startles me, and I glance down, watching as my mate spouts water from her mouth. Eyes widening, soul repairing, I kneel, turning her head so the water can get out of her system. A low growl trills in my chest for her, only for her, hoping it soothes her pain.

She sags against me, gasping for breath. My mate groans, and I lift her to my chest, hoping she feels my warmth on her cold skin. Tossing my head back once more, I howl again, a happy sound that echoes for miles. When I peer at the gorgeous stranger, her eyes are still closed, but her chest is finally moving up and down.

I maneuver her in my embrace. Only now that I'm not blinded by heartache, I smell her blood. Curious, I lift her and follow the scent, growling when I see a big cut on the back of her head still bleeding profusely.

Her blood is all over me.

My newfound happiness is short-lived, and I begin to run, clutching my small mate to my chest. She's so fragile, so short. I can hold her with one arm against my body as I run.

She grumbles, and I slow, looking down at her face. Her lips are still blue. She's still so cold, but she manages to flutter her eyes open, showing me irises of bright clover. While Maven's eyes are dark green, like the forest, my mate's are a true green, just like a four-leaf clover.

Like my werewolf's new eyes...

"You're real," she croaks, a tiny smile tilting her lips.

I try to grin the best way I can in this form, but she's unable to see it before she passes out again.

Not wanting to waste more time, I book it to the estate. I call on my human form, but still, it's quiet, and I don't understand why. With a determined roar, I clutch her safely to my chest, my claws digging into her back. My large paws fling the dirt, grass, and leaves behind me as I sprint. The cold air nips my lungs, the sign of winter closing in.

My mate is already freezing. She can't handle a cold front coming in.

When I see the estate, I roar, howl, anything, and everything to warn them I'm home and coming in hot.

The sun is setting but not enough for them to meet me outside. I run up the steps, ruining the new porch with deep claw marks. Not slowing down or decreasing my momentum, I shoulder through the door, busting it down without care. Pieces of wood splinter everywhere, and one of the vampires hiss from the sun coming in.

Maven rushes to the door, forcing roses to grow from the floor, vines, and kudzu blocking the harsh UV rays.

"Are you fucking mad?" Greyson snaps at me from the corner.

I whine, showing the woman in my arms. I let my eyes get bigger, spinning around, I beg the best way I can to show Maven she needs help.

"I need you to shift to explain," Maven answers my silent plea.

I shake my head and shrug my shoulders the best I can.

"You can't?"

I shake my head again.

She takes a step closer and presses her hand against my mate. "She needs Luna. I can warm her, take her pain, but Luna is better at healing. I still have so much to learn. Greyson, take her and—" I growl in a menacing way, crouch low, and turn away from Maven, grasping my mate tighter.

No one can take her from me.

No one.

"Oh." Her lips form a perfect circle before she smiles, her lips curving slightly to the left. "I see."

"Let me take her," Greyson pitches in. "It's okay." He reaches for *my* mate, and I snap my jaws at him, lifting my lips to show all my fangs.

"What the hell, Anwyll?"

"Greyson, that's his mate. You can't touch her. Especially if she is in danger. She's injured. He won't shift. He'll protect her while she heals. He's stronger in this form." Master Monreaux comes down the stairs in a sharp suit with a red shirt that's unbuttoned at the collar. He grins at me. "I'm happy for you. Congratulations. We'll make sure your mate gets the best care. Maven, show him her new room—"

Another growl erupts from me.

Master chuckles. "Apologies. Anwyll, take her to *your* room where Luna and Maven can help. I'll make sure all men are not allowed to visit."

I bow my head, trying to show my appreciation. Crouching again, I leap, jumping over the stairs to the top. I rush to my bedroom, dragging mud over the floor. I don't care. My purpose is to only think of my mate from this moment on.

Lying her on the bed, she moans in her sleep, a painful sound. Her brows pinch and a whimper escapes. I reach my monstrous hand out to cup her cheek and sit on the edge of the bed. The mattress dips low, and the frame groans from my weight.

But she sighs happily from my touch and nuzzles my palm.

My werewolf's palm.

"Okay, we have to get her undressed."

I snap the air with my teeth, directing them at Luna.

"You can snap all you want, Wolf Boy, but she's cold. She's hyperthermic. So be a gentleman and turn around to let us work, please?" Luna asks, her hair glittering with magic.

A pathetic huff leaves me, but seeing my mate naked without her knowing feels wrong. I get up to turn around, closing my eyes as Luna and Maven work. It takes so long that my limbs become restless, and I begin to shift my weight on either leg. I sigh, annoyed.

"Stop whining. God, you're worse than a puppy," Luna mumbles.

I grunt out a breath, turning my nose up in the air.

"She's got a really bad concussion, but she's in dry clothes now, I've warmed the blankets with magic, and she's got some cuts and bruises, but she'll live."

I spin around and launch myself at the two girls, pulling them into a hug. They both laugh, slapping my back.

"It might be a while before she wakes up. Don't get impatient."

I shake my head and crawl onto the bed, lying right next to my mate, my large humanoid hand on her chest. My entire palm takes up the width of her torso, my talons curling around her ribcage. I'm so inhuman compared to her.

"Ah, be careful. Her chest is cracked."

I whine to show regret at Luna's words, hoping she understands it is my fault. I've only caused my mate more pain.

Maven's hand presses against my cheek. "Don't feel bad for saving her life. We'll check back in later."

I press my nose against my mate's neck, inhaling her scent, hearing her heartbeat, and watching her chest rise and fall.

She's alive.

Sleep should come easy but it won't.

I can't sleep.

I'm too focused on her and watching the door.

Protecting her is what I live for now.

Chapter Four

ANWYLL

She should be awake by now. Something has to be wrong. My beautiful mate hasn't opened her eyes, not once; she has barely moved a finger.

I place another paw over her chest so I can feel the steady thump. My fear of losing her eases. I truly am sick, only in a different way than my brother. I'm already obsessed with this woman, and I don't even know her name.

I've stared at her endlessly, hours upon hours. I haven't slept in fear I'd miss her move, hear a sigh, or her waking up. Sleep is for the souls who need rest, and my soul is restless. I've memorized the structure of her face, the bridge of her nose, and the arch of her eyebrows.

Her lashes are blonde, long, and curly as they fan over her cheekbones.

But the one area I can't look away from, the one desire that has ignited lust for the first time in my body, is her lips. I've had a constant erection since I brought her to my bed. I'd never do anything about it, not while she's lying here, not that I'd know what to do anyway.

I feel insufficient now. What if she is disappointed in me as a mate? What if I can't satisfy her wants and needs? I'd want to learn. I'd want her to teach me. I want to do whatever she wants me to.

She sighs, and I'm riveted to her lips once more as they purse. The curve of them, the indent in the space below her nose, I've mapped to memory. I'll dream of her mouth on mine.

I'm hypnotized as they press together, every breath leaving her I inhale, fucking obsessed with just the air she breathes. Crawling over her, I tilt my head as I watch her sleep, my attention never leaving her lips.

What would it be like to feel them? I've never kissed anyone before. Here I am, a grown fucking man, an alpha werewolf, and I feel like a teenager trapped all over again. How will I find myself?

Leaning down, I run my nose through her hair and inhale the scents of salt water. There's an underlying sweetness that I can't put my finger on. It's delectable, and it's making my mouth water.

The pulse in her neck has me licking my fangs, my instincts telling me to mark her, to make her mine, to claim, to own, to have, and to fucking take.

I want to rub my scent all over her and make her smell of me so every creature in this house knows she belongs to me.

"Well, that doesn't look creepy."

I hang my head when I hear the sass in Dottie's voice. I've never been so glad to be in my werewolf form so she can't see the blush of embarrassment creeping along my neck.

Gaining my courage, I turn my head to look at the sharp-lipped woman and fall to the side of my mate.

I guess it was a little creepy hovering over her like that.

Would it change the situation if it was creepily romantic? In a good way? It's not like I was going to eat her.

My eyes roll to the back of my head when I begin to imagine that.

I *could* eat her.

For days.

For weeks.

I'd never satisfy the craving I have for her.

Once she's sated, maybe then I'd stop feasting on her.

Maybe.

A low rumble builds in my chest as I lick my lips, the hot, tormenting sensation burning my cock.

"Okay, one, put that damn thing away. I don't want to see it. Why are you naked? Don't werewolves clothe themselves? You look human enough. Give her some space, Anwyll."

I don't want to give her space. I've had so much space my entire life, and now all I want to do is latch on to my mate, the one person who is supposed to love me.

Flashing a bit of fang, I yank the blankets up to cover my body. I guess I should figure out clothing when I am in my werewolf form. The last thing I want to do is scare my mate when she wakes up.

A rumble fills the room, sounding from my chest.

"Don't get growly with me. I came to check up on you. I haven't seen you downstairs in a few days. You have to eat, Anwyll. If you want, I can watch over her while you hunt or see your brother."

This time, I leap from the bed and land with a hard thump right in front of her, forgetting who she is as a coven member and friend. Right now, she's an enemy wanting to take my mate away from me.

She's mine.

I growl, lifting my top lip to show my long, thick fangs. Mine aren't like a vampire's. While theirs are dangerous, they are made to sink into the flesh so they can drink.

Mine are different. Mine are meant to kill, to rip, to tear flesh, to shred anyone who gets in my way apart. And unlike vampires, my fangs aren't just on the top, but the bottom too.

Dottie straightens her spine, her eyes glowing a bright gold as her mysterious creature takes over to protect her from me.

My face is mere inches away from hers. No doubt she can feel my hot breath against her face. Electricity crackles around her, building for a fight.

I snarl, taking a small step forward. I forget who she is entirely now. My instincts take over as I wrap a paw around her throat, lifting her off her feet, baring my sharp teeth at her once more.

"No one is trying to take her from you," the threat says, but her voice is distant, yet refined to the slight gravel of her beast.

I toss the intruder to the left, and she smashes against the wall. Standing protectively by my mate's bedside, I roar, the bellowing sound of my anger leaving my lungs.

Surrounded by a golden shadow, the woman stands. The wicked curve of her lips tells me she isn't backing down. She lifts her hand into the air and conjures a glowing rod, similar to a bolt of lightning. Spinning it in her hand, she twists and turns, using it as if it is a sword.

She'll have to cut me in half to get me away from my mate.

Something flicks from behind her, a long wave snapping in the air, and the human's face begins to change into something sharper and more defined. Before I can decipher what it is, she lunges, the rod in her hand beaming brighter.

Not wanting my mate to be harmed, I attack, wanting to fight to the death. Flashes of my past remind me of what I used to be, and my mind returns to the dark. The smell of blood, the screams, and the feel of flesh giving under my claws transform the fear I've been experiencing into the monster I've become.

The glowing creature is knocked out of the way, and she lands on the floor, rolling before she leaps to her feet in a crouch.

A vampire stands in front of me, fangs bared, and his eyes a neon red with hate and murder. His long hair is braided to the side and without fear, he challenges me.

"Stand the fuck down, Anwyll. Before you kill someone or before they kill you."

"I don't need your help, Drayce." The woman who was trying to hurt my mate throws the bolt, slicing through the Viking's shirt and nailing him to the wall. "Dottie won't need protecting. I protect her."

"I'd believe that if I knew what the fuck you were and if I knew you truly meant her no harm." Drayce struggles against the lightning rod, unable to get free.

"Her and I are one. Harm will never come to her. She's my soul just as I am hers." The blur of a beast keeps its true nature hidden and turns to me, Dottie following a moment later as if she's possessed. "Your mate is safe, wolf." With one last look at my gorgeous mate lying in bed, my anger fades, and I recognize Dottie leaving the room.

Drayce falls from the wall, the glowing rod disappearing once Dottie leaves the room, taking her magic with her. The Viking vampire stares out the doorway, a smile on his reddened face as he rubs his shoulder. "She's fucking amazing, right? I love me a woman who can fight her own battles."

I growl again, not agreeing or disagreeing with him. I want my mate to need me. It's a fierce, overwhelming emotion. Maybe it's because I was locked away inside myself for so long wanting to protect the people I killed so much, that now I need someone to rely on me.

It's a traditional mindset, I know, but I can't help that I need to feel useful.

A whimper escapes from the bed, and in a flash, I'm at her side again, hating to see her brows pinched in distress. I wish I could change into my human form, to hold her how I really want, but instincts won't allow me to leave her unprotected. As a werewolf, it's easier to kill someone who would want to steal her from me.

"I'm going to leave so you don't think I want your mate, but you should know your brother needs you. He's struggling, Anwyll. You need to see him." Drayce hovers for a moment, waiting for me to acknowledge him, but even with my adrenaline-beating heart coming down from the previous fight, I can't let him see the fear in my eyes.

I can't look weak in front of a Viking warrior. And if I do turn to look at him, I might want to start a fight all over again.

A huge sigh escapes him before he shuts the door, finally leaving me in peace.

Another whimper escapes her, her lips parting to inhale air as if she's struggling to breathe. I bend down and rub my cheek against hers. A vibration of pleasure builds inside my chest because I'm marking her, but also because a relieved sigh relaxes her body.

She notices me.

She knows I'm here even if she's asleep.

I'm here, mate. I'm here for you. I won't leave your side.

Closing my eyes, I trail my nose down her neck, filling my lungs with her scent that was made for me, calls to only me. This woman, this beautiful creature beneath me, was created to fill the gap in my soul.

Oh, how I want you to love me just as much as I already love you.

What if she wakes up and doesn't want me?

I wrap my arms around her and lift her to my chest, holding her close just in case I never have the opportunity once she's awake. I don't know a thing about mating. I was too young when the spell took me. I don't know how to please her.

What do I do? How do I convince her to be mine when she opens her eyes?

A knock at the door sounds and I lie my mate gently on the bed. Wrapping my long nails around the knitted green blanket, I tug it just below her chin, so she stays warm.

No one here will hurt her. Remain calm.

Standing, I open the door to see Master Monreaux there. Arms crossed and a look of annoyance on his face. After the battle with the warlock who tried to steal his beloved because of a contract the evil wizard made with his grandfather, he has bloomed into a confident, fair, and understanding leader.

"Anwyll." He is curt and doesn't elaborate on why he is here, but it doesn't take much to guess. I did throw Dottie against the wall.

I owe her a huge apology.

"I know wolves can't be away from their mates, but I'm asking you to go see your brother. He is slowly getting worse, Anwyll. I don't want you to regret anything. Your mate will be safe while you're gone. I swear it. I'm here to watch her myself. I'm mated, remember? I am no threat to you or your mate."

While I know he is being kind, I can also tell he isn't asking me. He is telling me to go. I can't deny him, and I don't want to. His eyes harden when I don't answer right away. My wolf wants to challenge him, the alpha daring to break loose.

Curling a fist, my deadly talons sink into my palm as I control the natural urge to rip Master's head from his neck.

After a few minutes of a staring contest, I give a curt nod, but before I leave, I head to my mate's bedside and stare at her as if I'll never see her again. My eyes dart over her features, lingering on her blonde hair. There are stripes of light red, no not red, a pink, a natural color that I've never seen before. There's a small scar above her lip, and rage swells inside me when I see she's been injured. I want to find the person or object that left their mark on her.

I'll destroy them.

I'll destroy anything in this world that harms her.

Even me.

She pouts, and I rub a talon gently across the plump bottom lip.

God, I want to taste her if she'd allow me.

I'll be anything she wants me to be.

I'll bow to her every command. I'll let her use me. If she wants a toy, I'll be the source of the pleasure she seeks.

If pleasing her means having her control me, then I'll give all my strength, all my power, all my force, and let her use it against me as she sees fit.

I glance at Master Monreaux, and his eyes are soft. His hand lands on my shoulder and gives it a squeeze.

"I know it hurts to leave her like this, but I swear on my life, on my tears, Anwyll, she will be safe."

Vampire tears are sacred. Master explained everything to me and Aziel when we decided to pledge our loyalty to the coven. Hunters believe that in order to gain pleasure and immortality, they must harvest a vampire's fangs, but Alexander explained it isn't in the fangs at all, but their tears.

They heal the worst of diseases, give enhanced lifespans, and increase libido, but no one knows. It's a secret I treasure. A secret I'll gladly take to my death.

And yet, I still don't move from my spot next to my new mate. I take her hand in mine, the odd humanoid soot-colored paw with long talons seems so out of place against her opal skin.

It's as if I'm a demon coming into contact with an angel, wanting to drag her to my darkness while letting her use her wings to fly us from hell—saving me from an eternity of torture.

"I'll sit right there." Master points to the chair across the room, far enough away from her that I'm not threatened. "I won't touch the bed, so your scent remains intact."

The thought of another man's scent in this bed, surrounding my mate, has me digging my nails into the mattress and dragging them through the dense material. Just the thought of smelling another man on her skin, in my bed, heightens the need to kill.

Werewolves have much higher senses. We feel every emotion so much more than other paranormals. Love? We surpass it. We become obsessed, infatuated, and borderline insane.

It's why when the sickness takes, it takes us easily because we're halfway sick, to begin with.

"Calm yourself." The order from Master Monreaux is

accompanied by a threatening squeeze to the back of my neck, one meant to control me.

I don't like being controlled by anyone.

Not anymore.

"I'm not here to hurt you, Anwyll. Breathe. I know you want to kill me. I feel it. I hear it in your mind but open up the coven bond. Feel my intention to help you. Your energy is bothering your mate. She's falling quickly into a nightmare. The rage you're pouring out is seeping into her mind."

My eyes widen in horror, not wanting to believe him, and whip my head around to look at Alexander.

I grip my mate's hand, whining at the thought of hurting her.

"She's running in a dark place, a dead place. The grass is brown, the dirt is black, the skies are an endless void of death, and there are no signs of life. She's screaming as she looks back at her attacker. Hmm, she knows him."

A wicked sound escapes me, and I yank myself out of his grip, holding tight to my mate's hand.

Please feel me. I'm sorry. Please, come back. I'll do anything.

He flashes a fang with a curl of his lip, displeased with me. "You are so young still because of what's happened to you. You haven't experienced life how it should be, which is why I'll let you get away with snarling at me. You're young in more ways than one, Anwyll."

Don't remind me.

"Learn to control yourself. Don't think about killing me for no reason because it *would* be for no reason, I'm no threat to her. Think of how happy you are she's here, Anwyll. Control your rage. Let me teach you how to finally be the wolf you are meant to be."

Alexander knows my struggle. He knows in so many

ways that while I am a man, there are aspects of which I'm stunted emotionally and intellectually. There are things I just don't know.

Like sex. No one can teach me that.

Or how to handle my emotions. I still feel like a fifteen-year-old in that sense, like everything is urgent, everything means to harm, and I overanalyze a moment, a conversation, and blow it out of proportion.

How will my mate want me?

"Trust the alpha inside you, Anwyll. Listen to him and listen to me—*your* Alpha."

I've never heard him say that to me before, but I didn't know how much I needed to hear it, to feel like I truly belong here, because Master Monreaux... that title is for vampires. Let's face it, I'm not one. I'm the thing vampires hate the most. Hearing him give himself the title of Alpha, everything in my body relaxes, and I slip to the floor, my knees hitting with a hard thud.

I bow my head to show submission to him, letting him know I trust him.

A satisfied sigh comes from my mate next, and I swear the relief settles in my bones.

"Is that what you needed this entire time? I had no idea the title would be so important to your wellbeing, Anwyll. I apologize." His sharp talon lifts my chin. "From now on, you only call me Alpha. Okay?"

I nod the best way I can in this form.

"I'm proud of you for listening to me. It's a step forward, Anwyll. In your growth. Give yourself time. Now go to your brother. Your mate is safe with me."

I stand on shaky legs and sit on the bed again, the frame unable to contain my monster's weight without creaking.

Taking her precious hand, I bring it to my mouth, kissing her knuckles the best I can, and stand.

Leaving her behind burns every instinct I've ever known and begins to flame around my soul. Fuck, it hurts. I pause at the doorway, watching Alexander stride to the corner of the room. He sits in the chair as he promised. He gives me a reassuring nod, the cufflinks glistening in the sun's rays peeking through the UV-protected window. He can still feel the warmth, he just won't burn.

He wouldn't have to worry about burning if my kind didn't bite him and curse him into a coma for 121 years.

"Go, Anwyll."

His voice is laced with exasperation.

Stealing one last look at my mate, I force myself away and leave my heart behind. From the tops of the steps, I jump, smashing onto the floor when I land on the main level.

The living room is empty, and the only sound is the crackle of the fireplace. Winter is closing in, and with Maven pregnant, Alexander—Master—I mean Alpha, always keeps the house warm so she isn't cold.

My loud, heavy steps thunder across the floor, shaking the wooden planks. The lamp on the nightstand flickers from being disturbed. When I'm my beast, I'm nearly eight-feet tall and have four hundred pounds of solid muscle.

I'm shocked the floor can hold me.

On the other side of the room, the door next to the library mocks me. I stare down at my feet, a few stories beneath me, my brother agonizes. If I see him, he'll ask me to kill him, and I can't. He's all I have left of my pack. He protected me. He sacrificed himself so I wouldn't die when the warlock took us all those years ago.

Killing him would be like killing me.

"He's been asking for you."

I peer down at Rarity, holding a jug of water and a bag of what smells like food. She holds them out to me expectantly. Reluctantly, I take them.

"He hasn't eaten, Anwyll. He's giving up."

My chest hitches, and Rarity's hand lands on my furry arm.

This time, she can't ease the pain.

The hurt is too great.

I pull away from her dainty hold and bound to the door. I expect to hear his screams when I open it, but it's quiet. Dark. The smell old and musky of an unused basement. I've never been down here. I've been ignoring it because this is where my kind cursed Alexander and his brother—who still sleeps until his beloved comes.

Panic begins to set in when I step into the darkness, remembering being trapped in my own body for fifteen years.

Deep breaths.

Be better.

Don't panic.

You're safe. You're in control.

"Hey." Greyson's voice brings me back to the real world. Sweat is hot all over my body, and I've never felt more pathetic or weaker in my life.

I want to laugh when Alexander calls me an alpha.

Yeah?

Where? Where is he? Because I've never felt more submissive in my entire life.

I'm a disgrace.

"I'll lead you down, so you aren't alone. It's spooky down here. Gives me the creeps."

I know he's just saying that to make me feel better, but like a child, I follow him.

Let's keep adding to the ways I'm still a teenager.

A bookshelf opens, and a glow pumps out of black roses lining the walls.

"Maven keeps them here so it's never dark. You should see Atreyu's mausoleum. It's beautiful. She makes sure the flowers fill the dreadful place, so he is surrounded by beauty."

Yeah, that sounds like her.

The tunnel is cleaner than I imagined too. I expected cobwebs and insects, but I suspect Maven and Alexander had something to do with that too.

My heightened night vision lets me see into every nook and cranny. I'm able to see the door down the hall, and when Greyson opens that, it's nothing but a quick slip down a trapdoor in the floor for me to hear the cries of madness coming from my brother.

They range from a vicious roar to timid howls, to him scratching his nails along the floor and walls.

As a werewolf, hearing another in pain makes me want to comfort him. He howls next, the one that calls for me. I run, turning the corner so hard I slide, slamming my shoulder against the opposite wall.

And there.

I see him.

He's at the end of the hall, chained like a fucking dog, iron around his neck. He wanted this. He asked to be put down here so he wouldn't hurt anyone. His neck is red and bleeding from chaffing against the collar and the walls are ruined with deep scratches from his claw marks— a few stained with blood.

When he sees me, he shifts into his human form,

collapsing on the ground. The flame of the torch on the wall reveals the sweat and dirt covering his body. He is gilded by the hands of death.

"Anwyll." My name is a tired breath coming from him.

I slowly make my way toward him, reaching to pull him against me in a tight hug. Even in this form, I feel my eyes burn with tears.

I'm really losing him.

He pulls away and gives me a tired smile. "You came," he slurs with exhaustion, his eyes surrounded by black circles.

Guilt eats away at me for not seeing him sooner. I bow my head and place the water and food on the floor, right next to his mattress.

"Shift, brother. I won't stay like this long. I'd like to talk to you."

"He can't." Greyson's voice echoes at the end of the hall. "His mate is unconscious, so he won't shift until she's safe."

"Your mate?" Aziel's eyes round, and then a big smile that doesn't belong on his face takes over. "Your mate? And you didn't tell me? Well, not that you can. I understand why you haven't come to see me. She's so much more important. Oh, I wish you could tell me what she's like or how you met." The happiness begins to fade, and he tugs on his collar, wrapping his dirty fingers around the iron. "I hope I last long enough to hear your story, Anwyll. I hope"—he swallows, then licks his cracked lips—"I hope I get to meet her before it's too late." He glances at his hands, and that's when I see it.

The markings of sickness. His fingertips are black.

No. I can't lose him like this. I refuse.

He leans against the wall, his head snapping to the left and the tendons pulsating.

Reaching out my hand, I take his, and this time when he sees me, it isn't him at all, but the eyes of an infested wolf—pure black.

"You were supposed to kill me!" his yell reverberates off the walls. "You promised you'd kill me." His tone is replaced with a deeper tone. "You're a fucking liar, aren't you, Anwyll? A weak, pathetic liar. Always the one needing to be saved. Your mate deserves better." He lunges at me, arms stretched out, and I step back before he can wrap his hands around my neck.

He'd kill me in this state.

He's stronger, inflicted with the strength insanity brings.

"I should have left you when I had the chance." He half shifts, his skin a light grey, his eyes onyx, and his fangs lengthen. He grows taller too, wider, and he pulls against the chains binding him again, shouting in fury when they won't release him. "I'm going to fucking kill you when I get out of here." He snaps his jaws, venomous saliva dripping to the floor.

"That's enough!"

I hold my arm out to stop Greyson from doing anything stupid. Even if he is immune to a werewolf bite, I don't know if a bite is different when the wolf is inflicted with sickness.

A disease so much harsher and crueler than love could ever be. I give a slight shake of my head.

It's the disease talking. Nothing else. My brother isn't hateful.

Aziel cackles next, staring straight at me. "I'm going to make her my mate. I'm going to have her fall in love with me. She'll be mine. I deserve that! I deserve love, and I'm going to take yours!"

Before I can stop myself, I hit Aziel so hard in the face with my fist, he flies back, smashing against the wall. Falling to all fours, I snarl at him, daring him to talk about my mate one more time.

He shifts back and cries. "Fucking hell, Anwyll. I'm so sorry. I'm sorry." His feet slide along the floor. "I'd never do that. Ever. Fucking kill me, please. Kill me. You swore you would. Please, don't let me turn into... into a monster."

Inching forward, I grip the back of his head and press our foreheads together. He grips my shoulders, his blunt nails digging into my tough hide.

"Please, brother," he begs.

I shake my head, not wanting to discuss this again.

"We need to go," Greyson says. "Master Monreaux thinks your mate is waking up."

I'm about to ask how he knows, but now that the coven is linked, Alpha can communicate through the bond if he needs to.

My heart thuds in my chest, the one she owns and doesn't even know.

Aziel chuckles and squeezes me tighter. "I'm so happy for you, baby brother. So fucking happy." He pats my back and leans away, sagging with exhaustion.

I don't want to leave Aziel while he fights this. Leaving him alone is something I never wanted to do in the first place, but he made me promise him I would.

I'm torn. I know I need to go to my mate, but my brother needs me too.

How do I choose between the person who is meant to be mine from the person tied to my blood?

Love isn't supposed to have ultimatums. If I leave Aziel, he struggles. If I abandon my mate, I'll fall with sickness next.

I already had the tiniest of tastes of it when I smelled her. It wasn't enough to drive me crazy, but enough to keep me on edge.

"Go to her. You only get one mate, Anwyll."

And I only have one brother.

"It's too late for me, but it isn't for you. I know you love me, Anwyll. Don't fret over that." His head turns again, and the bones begin to snap. "Fucking go! Get out. I don't want you here." He shifts and falls to all fours, trying to get to me by walking, but his feet drag from being bound to the wall.

My heart breaks knowing one day I'll have to kill him because I can't stand to see him like this.

"Come on. Let's go," Greyson urges, stealing one last glance at the rabid wolf. "I'm so sorry, Anwyll."

I punch the wall with my fist, a chunk breaking and crumbling to the ground.

"It will all—" Greyson's sentence comes to a halt when a high-pitched ring has us both covering our ears.

A scream pierces the air, reminding me of a banshee signaling her warning, only this sound is full of fear.

Mate.

And she's in danger by the sounds of it. I sprint, jumping through the trapdoor, then give in to my nature and run on all fours. The quicker I get to her, the faster I can protect her.

I might be learning how to live again, but there is one thing I'm never afraid to do.

I'll kill.

Becoming a monster is easy; it's being human that's hard.

Chapter Five

RU

The first thing I notice is that my entire body hurts. My head feels like a troll smashed it with its club. Squeezing my eyes shut, I attempt to move my body starting with my arms, legs, and then wiggle my toes. Nothing is broken.

Shockingly.

I'm on something soft. It's comfortable. I'm warm, and the blanket I'm wrapped in smells earthy, like grass after it rains, and I'm obsessed because it's my favorite smell. Before I open my eyes, I bury my nose in it and inhale as deeply as I can until there is no more room left in my lungs.

"Good. You're starting to wake up. I was worried you wouldn't and was going to call Luna, our healer, to come check you out if you stayed unconscious much longer."

My eyes snap open at the commanding voice, a deep tone that's filled with authority.

I don't recognize it.

I bolt upright, and there's a figure sitting in the corner, an air of danger wrapping the room in a cloak.

I do the only thing I know to do.

I scream. I scrabble back, kicking away the sheets, and press my back against the headboard. Running out of room to sink into the frame, I stand on the mattress. It's unstable, but I'm freaking the fuck out right now.

Where am I? Who is he?

Oh man, am I in the Unwanted Lands?

Over my dead, unlucky body.

Bending down, I pick up two pillows and toss them at my kidnapper, slapping him right in the face.

He grunts, then sighs as if he is annoyed with me.

With me! I'm the one in a stranger's bed.

"Will you please stop throwing the pillows? And stop screaming—" he quiets when a savage, deafening roar vibrates the house "—Damn it, he just may kill me." He doesn't seem alerted by this revelation. "Stop screaming. You're safe, and you're making my ears hurt. And he is pissed. You realize this? I'm going to have to fight after I calmed him down once already." He pinches the bridge of his nose and unbuttons his blazer.

"Anwyll! Don't!" A voice tries to stop the reckoning coming toward the room, and a loud smash follows next.

"Anwy—" the person doesn't even get the chance to say this person's name before a loud shout sounds, followed by glass breaking.

Earth-shattering steps boom, trembling the picture on the wall until it falls crooked.

I gulp.

Maybe it is a troll.

The door bursts open, pieces of broken wood fly everywhere, and I duck, barely dodging the sharp edge of the door handle.

Another ear-piercing roar sounds, and the beast in the doorway takes my breath away. I freeze, mouth wide open in pure shock when I see him. He has glowing green eyes that match mine—like clover—and he has to duck his head to get into the room. This creature's muscles ripple with tension, and when he looks at me, fear is the last thing I feel.

The moment is cut short when he tears his eyes from mine to stare at the person at the foot of the bed, the handsome man in an expensive suit.

He still doesn't look fazed.

"Anwyll, she's fine. She woke up scared."

Anwyll.

I let the name roll around in my head. I like it. It's so different. I find myself wanting to speak his name to get his attention, but I still can't seem to move.

Anwyll lets out a bellow, fangs glittering in the light, and he charges, slicing his talons in the air just inches away from the stranger who was watching me.

The man dodges Anwyll's blows effortlessly, moving as a blur as if he anticipates the creature's next strike. A stomach-turning growl makes me whimper and curl into the bedpost as Anwyll gets the upper hand, slicing the kidnapper's cheek.

But a second later, it heals.

I rub my eyes, wondering what universe I must be in. Did I smoke too much clover? Am I dreaming this?

No, that can't be it. I haven't smoked clover since I was sixteen.

A crowd of people comes flying into the room next, watching the scene unfold as the massive eight-foot-tall creature fights the other man. Red eyes flash and fangs descend. My body trembles when I realize I'm surrounded by the unknown.

I don't know where I am.

I don't know these people.

"You have to stop him. Hey, look at me. You're safe, okay? I swear you are, but you need to stop him. The only person he will listen to is you." A woman with snow-white skin and violet eyes is next to me, hands cupping my face as she wipes away my tears.

I didn't even know I was crying.

"Why? Why would he listen to me?" I whisper, swallowing to try to coat my dry throat.

"I can't tell you that, but please, stop him. Master Monreaux is strong, but he isn't a werewolf-on-the-verge-of sickness strong. He has a mate and twins on the way, please," she begs. "He's my brother."

The last word is choked as if she is scared he is about to die, but the man is holding his own. He bends the werewolf's arm back, and the wolf howls in pain, my heart surging with protectiveness.

"Stop," I barely force out, my tongue sticking to the roof of my mouth.

No one hears me.

They are locked in battle.

The werewolf— which I can't believe they are real— turns around and smashes his palm in the middle of the stranger's chest, sending him flying backward.

"Enough Anwyll!" the man tiredly orders, gasping for breath as he wipes the blood off his cheek. "As your Alpha, I command you to stop."

The werewolf has his hand up above his head, readying to give a killing blow when he pauses, his breaths coming out in harsh huffs.

I jump from the bed, my feet tangling with the blanket, and fall onto the floor.

Face freaking first.

I push myself up and hurry to the werewolf's side, my safety be damned, hoping he listens to me.

What hold do I have over a giant creature I never knew existed?

His gorgeous muscles tremble with the fight to listen to his leader and to kill. This werewolf is so far gone in rage, he senses nothing else around him.

With quaking fingers, I touch his arm, and warmth encompasses me, just like the blanket I was wrapped in moments ago. A shock consumes my being next, a feeling of rightness, and home settles in my bones.

He gasps, jerking his head down to finally break the spell that had taken over him. This... man? Beast? Whatever he is, he's incredibly sexy. I can see human-like features in his face. High cheekbones and full lips barely cover the large fangs. His nose is human too, not too much of a snout, but elongated, and his brows move with expressions I can relate to. His stone-colored lashes blink at me, long and luscious, and dare I say I'm jealous of them?

He is beautiful.

Slowly, ever so slowly, he drops his arm, and without warning, he wraps it around me, tugging me to the heat of his chest. His heart pounds in a fierce rhythm, banging against my cheek. So much power, yet so much tenderness.

Who is this werewolf?

And why do I feel like there is so much more to him than the violence he displayed?

"Finally," someone groans. "I'm so glad to see you awake. Anwyll has been unbearable."

"Yes, he has," snips the man with blood irises as he fixes his suit, narrowing his eyes at Anwyll. "We will discuss this later. We need to give them a moment. Everyone out," he demands, and everyone vanishes in the next breath, leaving me with an animal that could kill me before my lungs exhale.

I reach my hand to his face, unable to touch him since he is so tall, and he bends down, nestling himself into my palm. His shoulders ease, and I finally take a moment to look at all of him.

Pushing aside my fear and that voice in the back of my head ringing like an alarm, *"Stranger danger! Run away!"*

I simply can't. My feet are cemented to the ground, and I'm locked in a trance of staring at the most gorgeous creature I've ever seen. My eyes roam down his body, and I gulp as I take in the statuesque form. He is carved out of the toughest rock. Unable to stop myself, my hands take control, and I ever so gently skim them down his impressive pectorals. His skin is rough, like how sandpaper is after it's used too much.

I like it.

There's a dusting of hair, soft and fine, and I find myself wanting to lose myself in the silkiness until I fall asleep.

What would it be like to sleep with a werewolf?

My mouth dries when my fingertips touch the block of abs made for fine dining. I'd eat every meal off his body, and I bet the food would taste even better from his hard abdominals.

I'm caught in a trance, continuing to trace every defined line I see, including the V along his hips.

A resonating rumble is felt through his skin as I touch, skim, and appreciate—a sound that finds a way to cause a throb between my legs. Without thinking, I continue lower, the hair on his body growing coarser until a thick base makes me freeze.

Eyes wide, I yelp when I see the massive cock swinging between his legs. It's the biggest damn thing I've ever seen. The beast—and not the werewolf—is long, heavy, and thick. He is solid, the head flared and girthy to match the stalk. The veins protrude on either side, pumping blood through the massive muscle so it stands at its fullest.

And saying it is standing is being generous.

It's so heavy, it is weighed down, the slick rubbing against his lower thigh.

Oh, I want to touch it. I bet it feels strong in my hand, solid as a boulder, and indestructible.

I'd be lying to myself if I said I didn't want a chance to attempt to destroy it.

The swinging eggplant jerks, and I'm forced out of my admirable haze, stumbling back and out of his arms until I hit the bed. I lift my eyes to his face.

Then down.

And up.

Fuck me, I don't know where to look.

Another growl sounds, and I nearly fold over, wanting to give him everything, but my brain is somewhat working now. I won't be blinded by the biggest, most mouth-watering cock I've ever seen. Even his sack is large, two giant orbs that would overflow in my hands, full of come.

I bet he'd make a mess.

A needy whimper builds in my throat. I'd want to clean up any mess he made.

Oh, snap out of it, Ru!

What the hell is wrong with me?

Okay, breathe. It's fine. I'm fine.

He takes a step forward, and I hold out my hand to stop him. "Don't. Don't come any closer." Or I'm afraid I'll lose all my common sense.

If it's possible for a werewolf to look sad, he does. His arms drop at the sides, and his mouth curls downward. His head drops so low, he falls on all fours.

"I need some answers. Can you help me?"

He glances up, hope once again shining in his lucky-colored eyes, just like mine. So odd. Anwyll nods eagerly, and his body begins to change. The gargantuan beast vanishes, and a man replaces him.

"Oh my luck." The words escape me on a surprised breath when I see the man crouched before me.

When he stands, I have to crane my head back. He's still tall in his human form. I feel like I barely come up to the middle of his chest, which is an exact replica of his were-wolf form.

Chiseled.

Wide.

Defined.

I swallow to coat my dry throat, my tongue stuck to the roof of my mouth as I take him in. His shaggy hair is the color of ash, his eyes different in this form, a cinnamon-colored brown with flecks of red and gold. Anwyll's jaw is square, and his shapely brows sit low.

The V on his hips are whittled handles, setting perfectly on either side of his torso. I could grip them as he fucks me.

Oh no, don't go there. I don't know this man.

I'm not a virgin, but staring at him has me wondering if I'd know what to do with a man like that.

Climb him like the tree he is, for one.

He blushes and snags the blanket from the bed, then wraps it around his waist. The material tenting from his erection. He tucks the corner of the blanket in, then covers his weapon—because something that big has to be considered dangerous—and gives me an awkward wave.

"Hi."

I grin at how bashful he is. "Hi."

Anwyll runs his hand through his hair. "I'm sorry about my beast. I didn't mean to scare you. I'm very protective of you."

"Why? Why am I here? Where am I? What happened? Why does my head hurt?" I reach a hand to the back of my skull where pain pulses.

Anwyll's eyes thunder with worry. "You are in pain? Do I need to call for Luna or Rarity? Maybe the Alpha Mate?" He stands right in front of me, close enough that I can feel the heat from his body against my chest as he moves to only a few inches away.

"No, I need..." I almost said I needed him, but how does that make sense? "I need to know where I am. I need answers."

Anwyll's gaze is full of love and obsession as if looking at me won't ever be enough. His palm cups my face, and the rough pad of his thumb glides across my cheek. I sigh in response, sinking further into his touch.

"I felt you nearby. I couldn't contain my shift because you're my fated mate. The soul meant to make mine whole. I ran to you and found you in the cove, not breathing, and it was..." his words hitch while he tries to catch his breath. "It was the most devastating feeling I've ever had and believe me when I say I have known the worst kind of devastation in my life. My beast tried CPR, which is why your chest probably hurts."

I touch the ache in my sternum and hiss.

"Don't." He takes my hand instead, and I can't remember anything I was concerned about.

All I want is him.

All I want to feel is him.

And according to my heart, all I need is him.

But I've never been good at listening to my heart.

Vague memories begin to return of walking with Mannix on the beach. I heard a howl…

"Where am I? And what's a mate? Leprechauns don't have mates."

His eyes round in surprise. "You're a leprechaun? That's amazing. I didn't know you existed. My Little Lucky Charm," he croons, dragging his finger on the edge of my jaw. "Do you feel a pull in your chest to be close to me?"

I nod, my eyes hooding as I become drunk from his touch.

"We can't live without one another. You're made for me. I am yours. I'll never want or need another. You're my cure."

I don't know what he means by cure. I'll ask later.

"As for where you are, you're in Salem, Massachusetts."

I blink at him in confusion. "Where's that?"

He cocks his head, and his eyes dart all over my face. "America."

I wait for him to elaborate, and I shrug my shoulders. "Where on Àdh is that?"

"What is Àdh?"

My panic begins to make my heart stutter in a different way. "The… the planet I'm from."

His jaw drops in shock. "What's your name, My Little Lucky Charm?"

I like that. "Badru, but Ru for short."

"Ru." His eyes drop to my mouth. "You're on Earth. My planet."

"You mean…" My vision blurs, and I stumble when everything I see goes sideways. "You mean I'm not on my planet?"

"No, Ru. You're not. You're safe here, though. I'd never let anything happen to you."

I don't even know what Earth is. Or where it is.

Oh chauns.

My eyes roll back when darkness edges my vision. My body goes limp, and I fall.

I just hope I don't fall into another dimension.

Chapter Six

ANWYLL

My involuntary shift ignites from the inside quicker than a flame lighting a match, and I catch my mate in my arms. Is something wrong with her? Did she hit her head too hard on her journey through the cove?

The thought of something wrong with her head has me whining, nestling my nose against her cheek to rouse her, but she doesn't move. I rush to the balcony and roar, trying to speak my concern.

I lie her down on the bed and watch her closely, my Ru. My Leprechaun. I'm fascinated and I can't wait to learn more about her and where she is from. I love her intensely already, but by the way things are going, it's going to take some work for me to get her to fall in love with me.

That's okay.

I'll do whatever it takes to have my mate love me.

She's so beautiful. Her hair is blonde, but I'm obsessed with the light dusting of rose through it. Dropping my eyes to her lips, the plump red clouds cause a rush of something unfamiliar to course through me.

I glide a talon along the bottom lip, wishing I could feel her mouth against me.

What's that mean?

My nail has a mind of its own, lightly scratching the surface of her skin, and I pause when I get to her chest. My eyes land on her large breasts, and with every inhale, they stretch the material of the shirt she's wearing, her nipples hard underneath. My mouth waters, saliva dripping down my fangs, and the buzzing of the unknown feelings heats my body, flowing south to my cock.

I want...

I want to tear her apart.

With a shake of my head, I take a few steps away from her. Why would I want to harm my mate? No one has ever told me about this. Mates are supposed to be sacred.

"Anwyll?" Luna's melodic voice yanks me from my thoughts. "What's wrong?"

I never take my eyes off Ru, and my chest rises and falls quicker with every passing moment.

"What happened?" Luna sits on the side of the bed and holds her hands over Ru's chest. A pink glow forms under her palms. "She's okay. She's passed out, but she'll be fine." Luna stands at the same time Rarity enters the room.

Friend.

She's my friend.

I don't feel the need to tear her apart.

I'm a bad mate.

I'm a horrible person.

The horrors of what I've done slam through me, reminding me I don't deserve happiness. The murderer inside me lives.

And it wants to hurt Ru.

"Anwyll?" Rarity's hand lands on my arm, but her touch feels wrong.

This is all wrong.

I bat her hand away, my attention falling to my mate's chest again.

The feeling won't go away.

Tears brim my werewolf's eyes, the screams of the little girl echoing through my mind. I'd never do that to my mate. Would I?

I dash out of the room, leaping over the balcony, and land on all fours in the living room, my nails digging into the hardwood floors.

Again.

Maven isn't going to be happy.

I burst forward to run out the front door when my Alpha blurs into my path. The momentum is too strong when I try to stop. I slide across the floor, doing my best to slow down. Alexander plants his feet on the ground, twists his body, and his shoulder slams against my chest.

I fly backward, the strength of his attempt overshadowing my own.

"So that's what it's like to fully embrace my power? I barely felt a thing." He dusts off his suit and strides toward me, confident and without a hint of fear. Alpha crouches beside me. "No more running from the unknown, Anwyll. I'll help you. Your coven—pack—will help you. Now shift so we can talk."

"He can't shift. She's unconscious again!" Luna shouts from upstairs.

"Well, that's inconvenient, but you know what Maven just informed me of?"

He waits for me to answer, and I chuff. He knows I can't speak in this form.

"I can force your shift since I'm your Alpha. I hear it hurts, but you'll have to put up with the pain so I can ask you questions."

I shake my head and scramble to my legs, begging him silently not to force me against my will.

"I'm sorry, Anwyll, but it's the only way. Maven has looked into your kind, and I think we can help you." His eyes turn the color of blood, and his fangs lengthen. Alexander's power has my skin rippling. "Shift."

I fight it, snarling at him with disobedience.

"Do not make me drag you by the fucking fur. I said shift!" His voice deepens to a sardonic bellow, and the crystal drops of the chandelier clank together from the vibrations of his voice.

The order, the strength, the bond I've pledged myself to with blood forces my beast to shrink under my human skin. My bones ache with my werewolf. He wants free, but the command to obey my Alpha is stronger than the monster inside me.

The magic, while it makes me human, it does not take away the pain. Sweat drips down my forehead, and my body begins to shiver from the agony.

"I'm so sorry, Anwyll. This needs to be done. Can you stand?" His tone is different, gentle, and calm. Surprisingly, the care and tenderness eases the ache in my skeleton, and I'm able to breathe.

I nod. The force making sweat drip from the ends of my hair to the floor. He wraps an arm around my waist and holds most of my weight. The show of how strong he is reminds me how superior vampires are compared to werewolves.

"I got you, Anwyll. You're okay. Uncle Luca! Get a blanket and some tea." He calls for his second. We haven't seen much of him since he has been in the catacombs, guarding my brother.

"You got it. Give me two shakes and a squeeze," Luca responds.

"You could be classier, brother," Severide slaps him on the back of the head.

"That's what you're around for. If I wanted a stick up my—"

"—Silence. The both of you. My mate is in the room," my Alpha and their Coven Master commands.

It must be hard for Severide to take orders from his son, but when I see his lips fighting a smile, maybe he is happy not to have the responsibility of coven master.

Alexander is being a great Alpha, better than the one I had growing up—which was my own father—and I find myself wanting to be stronger for him and the coven.

If only my alpha wasn't buried under fifteen years of fear, abuse, and nightmares.

He sets me in the chair, the cushion giving easily under my nude body. Maven is at the end of the conference table, flipping through a book without looking at me. I still feel exposed. I'm not used to anyone seeing me naked. I was supposed to grow up with being at ease with nudity, but I never got that chance.

Just like everything else, it was stolen from me, and now I have to learn at my own pace.

I cup my cock, hiding it from others, and Luca wraps the blanket around my shoulders while Severide sets down a blue mug full of tea. The steam billows, and I inhale, sighing in contentment when I smell hints of citrus.

"Thank you," I say, wrapping the blankets around me like a burrito. When I'm comfortable, I clutch the blanket tight with one hand and hold the mug with the other. A tremble courses through me every few seconds from my shift being submerged, but it doesn't hurt as bad as it did.

Being in this form feels unnatural when my mate is in a vulnerable state.

Mate.

Remember, you want to tear her into pieces.

My talons lengthen and scratch grooves into the mug.

"Relax." Alexander places his hand on my shoulder and the tension in my muscles eases.

Maven finally looks up from her books, a large smile on her face while one hand cups her growing belly. "Hi, Anwyll." She is so genuine. Her kindness always makes me feel better.

"Hello, Alpha Mate."

She waves the title away. "Please, call me Maven. Anyway, so I've been doing some light reading with the books from the library—"

"—You call books that weigh more than ten pounds light reading?" Luca mumbles, and Alpha elbows him in the gut. He groans, doubling over. "Sorry," he wheezes.

She glares at him for a moment, narrowing her eyes into slits. "Like I was saying before I was interrupted, I've been studying up on werewolves. There's actually a Veiled library located in the in-between this plane and the other realms, according to my grimoire, and I really want to go. Apparently, they have books on every creature ever known and potions and cures and evils and—" She blushes when she begins talking faster and ahead of herself. "Sorry, I just got so excited to know there's so much more to learn about."

"Don't apologize, Beloved. I love your newfound appetite for knowledge." Alpha eats away the distance between them, wrapping an arm around her waist until his palm cups her pregnant belly. "It makes me want to teach you all the things you're hungry for, Maven." He kisses the side of her throat, and I turn my head away, feeling like I'm intruding on a personal moment.

It also hurts to see because I'll never have that with my mate.

I'll kill myself before I kill her.

"Alexander Monreaux. Stop distracting me."

He grins, a wicked delight spreading his lips, and the tip of his fangs glisten. "Fine. I know there are other things to discuss." He straightens, their arousal thickening in the air, which doesn't help my state of mind.

"Anwyll. Can you tell me how you feel about your mate?"

My beast hums inside me, happy to talk about the one made for us. "Her name is Badru. She likes to go by Ru. She's so pretty. She says she's a leprechaun. She's from another planet called Àdh. When she found out she's on another planet, she passed out again." An urge to run to her and protect her while she sleeps hits me, and my body shudders, fighting the shift again.

"No fucking way! I didn't think leprechauns actually existed," Luca says with a burst of excitement. "That's really cool."

"Another planet? This is fascinating." Maven flips through her books again.

I'm not done talking about my mate though. "She's beautiful. I love her already. My werewolf is very protective."

"Then why did you run from her room?" Alexander probes, splaying his hands on the table as he leans forward.

I lick my lips, not wanting to tell the truth. I'm too embarrassed. "I was watching her and... this feeling came over me." I stare into the mug in my hands, watching the steam swirl and vanish into the air. "I wanted to hurt her, I think. I wanted to tear her to fucking bits," I growl, the rush of heat engulfing me again, and the thought of giving in has my cock growing hard beneath the blanket.

"Are you sure that's what you're feeling, Anwyll?" Maven questions, a knowing smirk on her face. "What do you know about werewolves? The need to claim? Sex."

Like a teenage boy, I glance away, unable to look at her when she speaks of such things. "Not much." I clear my throat, my damn cheeks heating, showing my fucking innocence.

How embarrassing.

I begin to panic. I want to be anywhere but here right now. Everyone must think I'm so pathetic, being thirty years old with no experience. The walls are closing in, and Luca squats next to me, leaning his head until he is in my vision.

"Hey, there's no judgement, buddy. Do not be ashamed. You were spelled for fifteen years. How could you know when your will was taken from you? It's okay, Anwyll. You're with your pack. There's no judgement here."

"Can you tell me what you do know?"

I exhale and tear my eyes from the mug, not wanting to be a coward. "Werewolves don't learn about sex until they're seventeen, since we don't mature until we are eighteen. It was taboo for a werewolf to know anything to do with his or her body until they were 'of age.'"

Maven tilts her head, and it isn't with pity, but understanding and love. "I'm sorry no one was honest with you, but werewolf culture must be different. I can tell you about your anatomy if you want. What you're feeling... What happens when you find your mate. Do you want that?" Her voice is so calming, tickling a memory of a song I heard when I was younger. A lullaby, perhaps.

"Yes, please. Anything. If it means I won't tear my mate apart, I'm willing to listen to anything." I freaking beg.

"Great. So… hey, drink your tea." She points to the mug, then to my face, and I listen immediately.

I sip the tea happily, smiling around the rim when she seems satisfied. She's going to be a good mom.

"Good. Okay, if anyone is uncomfortable with what we are about to talk about, you need to leave," she warns.

Luca, Severide, and Alexander do not move, but Severide does pull up a chair and sits right next to me. Luca follows suit, and before I know it, I have two friends supporting me through this.

"Okay. Welcome to Werewolf Sex Ed." She clicks a button, and a page from the book comes up on the TV. "Okay, so the good news is, you don't want to kill your mate. You want to ravish her."

"Hurt her?" I question, staring at the image of a werewolf that came from a book. It's weird. My werewolf doesn't like it.

"No," she shakes her head. "The rush, the heat you're experiencing, when your penis—"

Luca snickers.

"Really? Would you rather I say cock?"

Luca stops laughing, and his nose scrunches. "No, it's just been a while since I heard the exact term. Sorry, continue."

"You want to mate, Anwyll. You want to claim her, meaning you want to have sex with Ru. When you do, the base of your penis will swell, and that's called a knot. It locks your…uh…sperm…inside her. To breed."

The heat returns, and I lick my lips.

"A knot?" Luca asks.

"Yes." She clicks another button, and I sputter my tea when a hard version of my cock appears on the screen with a huge base.

"Fucking hell, Anwyll. That's a damn baseball bat. Will he hurt her with that thing?"

I sneer at his question. "I'd never hurt my mate."

"And that's why the feeling you have is not dangerous, Anwyll. You want to please her. And then you'll bite her, marking her right here." Another picture appears, and teeth marks are drawn on a sketch of a neck.

A grumble of delight courses through me, thinking of marking my mate.

"Sounds like you like the sound of that," Maven teases.

I nod, leaning forward, wanting to learn more. "What else? Is there more?"

She winces. "Yes, and I'm afraid it isn't great news. We know werewolves are prone to sickness when they don't find their mate, but this book also says if a werewolf doesn't claim their mate when the female goes into heat, and when you're in a rut—"

I stop her with a shake of my head. "What the hell is a heat and a rut?"

"I'm so sorry. I should have explained. A heat is when the female is ready for you to breed. She'll be beyond thinking clearly. And you'll get thrown into a rut, the urge to just constantly have sex until her heat is over. Until it is successful in completing the mating and she's pregnant."

While I want all of that, all I can think about is my mate. "And if she doesn't want to mate? I won't force her."

She rubs her stomach, and her eyes look away from me. "Then the sickness will take you until..."

"Until?"

"Until you force her to mate, and you'll end up killing her." She clicks to another page, and what I see has me standing so fast, I bump against the table, the tea spilling across the wood.

The picture is of a werewolf, he's crazed, fucking his mate while she cries, and he slashes her. Wounds cover her entire body.

Maven clicks to the next picture, and the beast is red from head to toe.

Another picture appears, and the room goes so quiet, I can hear the heartbeats of the twins in Maven's womb.

The werewolf is ripping his heart out.

"I won't...I won't rape my mate. I won't kill her. I won't." My eyes brim with tears. Why is Fate so fucking cruel? Why would this be the consequence? "If she denies me, kill me. I won't fucking kill her. No." I shake my head, and the tears spill down my cheeks. "Why is this our nature? Does the book say that?"

"No, but I promise to look for answers."

"How long before her heat is triggered?"

"The next full moon which is in two weeks."

"Two weeks?" I yell. "No. That isn't enough time to let her choose me. Her kind doesn't have mates. Can't you put a spell on me? Can't you fix this?"

"I can't fix biology, but maybe I can slow it down with a potion? I'll have to research. I'm sorry, Anwyll."

I turn around, giving them my back, and press my head against the wall. "She'll never choose someone like me."

"Why would you say that?" Alexander questions, each word louder as he comes closer.

"I'm too fucked up. I'm weak. I'm—"

"—Healing from something terrible happening to you

and if she is meant to be your mate, then she will understand that," he states, and he sounds so damn confident.

I stare directly into my alpha's eyes. "Promise me you'll kill me before that happens. Promise me."

"On my tears, Anwyll." He grips my shoulder.

"Thank you," I croak.

As much as I want to run to my mate, learning all this information makes me want to stay away from her.

All I've learned is that werewolves are monsters. I see why the warlock chose us. Our endings are the same no matter what path we take.

I'll have a hole in my chest, but it's my mate who will always have my heart.

Chapter Seven

RU

My head hurts again, and this time, when I sit up, I'm alone.

Why does that bother me so much? Anwyll said he was my mate. Didn't that mean he didn't want to be away from me?

And why do I care? I hardly know the man, but I wish for his presence. The sun is peaking through the windows, and I wonder if it's the same day.

"I've really fallen down the rabbit hole." I throw my legs off the bed, and my stomach rumbles, reminding me I haven't eaten in...I can't remember how long.

Standing, I take a look around, seeing if there is anything personal that can tell me about my werewolf.

My... mate.

I don't hate the sound of it, but I'd like to get to know him a little before I jump into bed with him. Even though I really *really* want to.

But I have control over my body, and I can wait a few— just the thought of waiting makes my stomach hurt— and I feel sick.

I'll have to learn more about that later, but I'm assuming it's this mate thing he was talking about.

"You're awake."

I scream and hold a hand to my chest when I see a beautiful—yet interesting—looking woman stands in the doorway. "Holy chauns, lady. You can't just come out of nowhere and scare me like that." My heart thuds rapidly against my palm, and my other hand grips the dresser that's as tall as me.

She grins, showing two pointy teeth.

"What are you?" I ask, frozen in fear.

"Oh my god, you really don't know?" Her white lashes frame her violet eyes, and a cold shiver slides down my spine.

The cold isn't a bad feeling, more like the temperature dropped a degree.

"I don't know where I am. How am I supposed to know what you are?" I can't hold back the bite of sass, and I rub my temples with my fingers. "Sorry, I'm starving, and it's still hard to believe I'm on another planet. On top of that, I have a really hot werewolf mate, which I have no idea what to do with. Where is he?" I try not to sound too curious, but I can't help but wonder if he is with another woman.

Oh, the thought makes me want to throw unlucky shells at him.

The strange woman takes a step forward, and I take a step back because—stranger danger—and she has fangs. I'd be an idiot not to be trepidatious.

"No, don't apologize. I can't imagine all the confusing things you must be feeling. I'm Rarity. A vampire." She points to her long, pointed cuspids, and I can bet they sink into flesh easily.

I gulp.

Maybe sweat a little too.

"And your mate, he found out some things about himself when it comes to you, and he wasn't happy. So, he is currently...indisposed."

I open the drawer and peek inside, seeing a bunch of folded up T-shirts, so I grab one before tossing her a disbelieving look. "That's what people say when the person they are asking about doesn't want to see them. I might have been born on another planet, but I wasn't born yesterday." Well, there it is again, the unnecessary sass.

Rarity places her hand on my arm, and I inhale swiftly, her ice-cold hands stealing my breath, but at the same time, my anxiety begins to fade. Her violet eyes stare into mine, and I get lost for a moment, in a trance of pure peace.

"Listen to me when I say this: he wants to be with you. More than anything. Anwyll...he has a really bad past and I can't get into that. That's something for you two to talk about as mates. He's downstairs with his brother right now, that's all you need to know."

"Can I see him?"

She shakes her head, her hair fluttering around her shoulders like fallen snow. "No. He asked that you don't come down."

"Oh." The disappointment is evident in my tone. "I see." The drawer slams harder than it should. I blame the mechanism that causes it to slide shut, and definitely not my attitude. "Figures," I chuckle ironically. "If I didn't have bad luck, I wouldn't have luck at all, which really sucks because leprechauns need their luck. I follow a howl, show up on a new planet, discover I have a mate—which I only ever learned about in mythology class—you guys"—I circle a finger at her—"aren't supposed to be real. And my mate is rejecting me. I mean, a date would have been nice." The floors creak when I begin to head towards the bathroom, the sunlight piercing through the glass and showing the freckles of dust drifting through the air.

"He isn't rejecting you. Are you kidding? He wouldn't leave your side. He roared, fought, and growled at anyone who came near you when you were unconscious. Anwyll is your protector. He is already in love with you, but he thinks what he is doing is saving you. Master Monreaux, my brother, he'll give you more answers, so after you shower, come downstairs. We fixed breakfast for dinner."

The thought of food almost has me not showering at all, but the ripe smell coming from my armpit says I can't wait another second. I don't want to smell in front of my mate, and while I don't understand everything that entails, I want to understand it.

So if he is meant for me, he'd better get used to this little thing I like to call communication.

"Sure. I'll be right down," I say to her, my voice nearly muted and defeated to my own ears, and she frowns.

"I promise, he isn't rejecting you."

"I'll need to hear that from him." I keep my head down and disappear into the bathroom, closing the door before I turn on the light.

I'm okay with being in darkness for a few seconds if it means gaining control of the ache in my heart. Taking a deep breath, I slide my hand against the wall, slapping it as I try to find the light switch. It's so odd how alike our planets are, almost like mirror images.

Right as I flip it, a howl resonates in my distant mind, and my heart tugs, wanting me to turn to the door, fling it open, and go in search of my werewolf.

Only he doesn't want me to find him, does he?

"Well, that's just too fucking bad, wolfy." I glance in the

mirror, and my hair is a mess of knots, the odd-colored blonde pieces a nest from nearly drowning. My skin is pale, and I have dark circles under my eyes, but I've looked worse, especially on my twenty-first birthday. I had way too many Irish Trashcans.

Just the thought has my stomach turning.

I just had to meet my mate while I looked like a train wreck.

Any amount of luck would be pretty great right about now.

And what if I don't find it in time? What if Anwyll and I fall in love and have a life I've always wanted for myself, only for me to be cast away to the Unwanted Lands?

Maybe it's me who needs to protect him from future heartbreak.

Sliding the curtain across the rod, I grip the silver knob and twist, hot water immediately pouring from the showerhead.

"What the—" the water is clear.

My water from home is a pale pink.

With a nervous hand, I touch the water and pull my hand away, checking my skin to make sure I didn't burn.

All safe.

Risking it all—because fuck it—I step inside the stall, letting the waterfall of heat and steam drown me.

A sigh escapes me as I tilt my head back. The spot where the stitches are hurts, but not enough for me to pull away. My hair slicks against my skull, and my muscles release the tension they have been holding for a few days, but the growing tear in my heart doesn't fade.

A tear Anwyll unintentionally created.

I want him with me right now, logic and reasoning be damned. I just want him near me. What would his hands feel like on me? Would he bathe me? Wash my hair? Slip his fingers between my thighs and play with my clit?

Wet lashes flutter open at the thought, and I stare at the white wall, twisting the length of my hair to make sure it's all wet. I bet he is a fierce lover, maybe not rough at first, but he would be after some time getting to know my body.

His big cock can slide right— "Nope, don't go there, Ru. Do not go there because once you do, there's no turning back, even though you have never seen a fucking cock like that."

And I went there.

"I'm so screwed." I lean my forehead against the wall and take a moment to myself as water slides down my body. Water drips from my bottom lip, and a pressure in my chest begins to build, tears sting my eyes, and my best friend's face comes to mind.

What am I doing here? I need to go home. I can't be here. I don't even know where *here* is. The thought of leaving Anwyll hurts more than the want yelling at me in the back of my mind to go home.

How does that make sense?

The bottle in the corner of the stall has me moving my languid, tired limbs. I don't know how I'm so exhausted, but I am.

"Three-in-one?" I yelp from the horror in front of me. Seems our language barrier won't be an issue. Everything is written the same on my home planet.

Body wash, shampoo, and conditioner? I can feel my hair becoming dry and brittle as I read the label. The bottle makes a squirting sound when I squeeze the bright orange gel in my hand. "Well, Mr. Werewolf, I hate to break it to you, but this shit is not going to fly. Three-in-one," I grumble as I wash my hair.

It's horrible.

There isn't even a loofah.

Does he seriously wash with his hands?

"Men." I can't help but shake my head again and rub my palms down my body, a flash of need beading my nipples when I picture him in the shower with me.

When I'm done, I turn the water off and grab a towel. Nice and dry, I get dressed in Anwyll's shirt and briefs. His shirt is a dress on me, falling to my knees, and I feel comforted like I'm wrapped in a huge blanket of him. I bury my nose inside the collar and inhale, his scent easing the turmoil in my body.

Is this what it is like to have a mate? The need to always be with them? Smell them? Touch them? And not even know them?

This world is weird.

But I don't dislike it, it's just new to me.

New isn't bad. New is undiscovered territory.

And then when I've learned and explored, this won't be new, but familiar, like home.

Not home being a place, but a feeling, a warmth, a person.

Lost in thought, I towel dry my hair and cringe when I see the rat's nest it has become because of the stupid eight-thousand-in-one soap.

A knock at the door sounds. "I thought maybe you'd want a hairbrush?" Rarity's voice is muffled by the door between us.

I clutch the sink. Holy clovers...can they read minds too?

"I can read your mind, but only because you're being really loud about it," she giggles.

Leaping at the door, I swing it open and lift my chin.

"That's cool, weird, and not sure if it's an invasion of privacy."

"You'll get used to it around here." She holds out a few hair ties and a hairbrush. "I heard about the shampoo. Werewolves are low-maintenance. You're going to have to show him a new world."

"He's showing me one." I take the goodies from her and give her a smile. "I'll be down in a minute. Thank you."

"No problem. I promise you're safe here."

I tilt my head and wait for the rush of fear to hit me, but it doesn't. "I know, it's overwhelming though."

"I understand. When you're ready, come downstairs and I'll have tea ready for you, then we can talk." Rarity leaves, walking so smoothly that she always seems like she's floating.

Brushing my hair takes a bit longer than usual, and then I put it into two low piggytail braids.

"Time to go see the creatures that really go bump in the night," I say to my reflection in the mirror, then turn off the light, and walk out the door.

I bet if these people went to Àdh, they would be a little shell-shocked to see different beings too, but they wouldn't be too weirded out by it. Maybe that's why I'm taking all this so well. Is it really that far of a stretch to know we have unicorns with wings and this planet has vampires and werewolves?

No.

What trips me up more is that I'm *on* another planet. I'm very far away from home, and that is what is most unsettling.

I'm not paying attention as I walk down the stairs, and my foot slips on the polished wood.

Boom. Boom. Boom.

The stairs and my body thud every time I make impact, first my ass, then my side, then eventually, I land on the floor, groaning as I hold my hand.

I swear to chauns, if I don't find my luck soon...

"Ow." I sit up and push my back against the wall, needing a minute before I scream from all the frustration of not finding my luck and being somewhere I don't know while wanting a really hot werewolf who I also don't know.

"Oh my god, are you okay?" A pretty redhead with a round stomach rushes to me.

"I'm fine. I just need a minute. I have really bad luck, so this is nothing new." I really need a scratch-off right now. I'm dying to scratch. Why did I give Mannix my tickets? I'm so stupid. Now, my chance of winning is on another planet. Somewhere.

In the fucking galaxy.

A bone-shaking roar vibrates the house, nearly making my body thump in place.

"Oh no," the man in charge, the one with fangs and red eyes sighs as he pinches his nose. He helps the pregnant redhead to her feet by taking her hand. "Get away from the guest, My Beloved."

"But she's hurt, Lex. I need to—"

She's cut off when something breaks in the house, perhaps a door? It sounds like wood splintering.

In tandem with my heart, a giant's footsteps bang on the floor.

"Son of a bitch, Anwyll! Stop ruining our house. I'm sick of repairing it constantly. Control yourself," Lex—Anwyll's Alpha commands with irritation.

Anwyll's monstrous head turns, and his possessive stare finds me sitting on the floor, cradling my arm. Another ear-piercing roar sounds, and he rushes to me, every step vibrating the floors until I can feel the echoes between my legs—arousing me.

"I'm okay. I'm just clumsy," I tell him, and with the gentle care of a creature small and soft, he lifts me into his arms, burying me in his chest. He has blood dripping around his neck and scratches down his arms. "You're bleeding! Anwyll, what did you do? What happened?"

"He broke free from his silver chains when he heard you fall," Rarity explains from the entryway of the kitchen.

"I should have known he'd break free."

"Alexander, how could you know that?" Rarity asks, taking a step into the living room, and I find myself sinking into Anwyll's beast. I'm so delicate and tiny in his arms. He could break me, but I know he won't. The way he holds me tells me he will always touch me with ease.

"Nothing can keep a beast from his mate. Nothing. Aziel can't get free because the chains are charmed; Anwyll's were only silver. He must have really put himself through pain to get to you. Silver burns us like flames eat wood," Alexander states.

I place my palm on his chest, and he nuzzles my cheek. Tilting my head back, I look up at Anwyll, his fangs peeking out from under his lip. His eyes swirl green. "Don't ever hurt yourself for me again."

"Oh, sweetheart. If there is one thing you can count on, he will always hurt himself for you." Alexander wraps an arm around his wife—mate? No, I heard him say beloved. "Anwyll, if you could shift back. We have something we'd like to discuss with you. About your brother."

Anwyll exhales, his large chest expanding before deflating with a low-pitched whine.

"What's wrong with his brother?" I don't ask anyone in particular. I just want someone to answer.

"Sickness has taken him, which you need to know about too, so you know exactly what you're getting into with a werewolf. Let's all talk in the sitting room, somewhere more comfortable than the conference room." Alexander strolls with confidence right by us, his suit tailored to his every muscle.

"I'll get my books." Maven gives me a tight smile with a nod before walking to another room. When she opens the door, a flash of shelves filled from the floor to the ceiling catches my eye. Maven flips on the light and closes herself in the room.

The shift of Anwyll's body morphing from tough leather skin to soft and human, shrinking a few feet in height which brings me closer to the ground.

"I'm so sorry, Ru. I don't expect you to be with me, but let me hold you, please. Please, let me hold you," Anwyll whispers, the softness of his lips moving against my neck as he speaks.

I want him to hold me.

Chapter Eight

ANWYLL

After she finds out everything about me, there's no fucking way she's going to want to stick around. I wouldn't blame her. Who would want to be with a monster who will rip out their heart?

Everyone comes into the sitting room; a place Alexander and Maven dedicated for people to come and unwind. There is a liquor bar to the side near the fireplace and a pool table at the other end of the room. Chairs and sofas of black and purple velvet are strategically placed near each other, spaced out so everyone is close enough yet has enough room to stretch their legs.

"Here." Greyson hands me a blanket, and in order to cover myself up, I have to set down my mate.

I place her gently on the couch and take the blanket from Greyson, wrapping it around my hips. Not that it will cover my erection. The scent of my mate is driving me insane. She smells so fucking good.

Not wanting anyone else to take my spot next to her, I plop down and tug her against my side, which causes her to chuckle.

"Okay, before we dive into it, anyone want a drink? I'm making a bloody Manhattan."

"I'll take one," Luca raises his hand.

"Me too," Greyson echoes.

"Now I'm a fucking bartender."

"Lex, don't be mean. You asked."

"I didn't expect them to say yes," he grumbles, which makes a smile twitch my lips.

In a blur, Alpha shakes and pours three drinks, plopping blood-soaked cherries on top of the concoction.

"Whoa." Ru's eyes are wide, shocked by how quickly Alexander moved.

"And in the bedroom?" Maven whispers out of the corner of her mouth, but the vampires hear, which causes all of them to laugh.

"Beloved," Alpha tsks. "Don't go sharing my secrets to make you come."

"Lex!" Maven blushes.

A scent sweeter than chocolate permeates the air, and my eyes roll to the back of my head while my talons extend. I sniff, following it to my mate's shoulder, and inhale so deep, I growl viciously. Her body shivers, and goosebumps pucker all over her body.

Her desire is intoxicating.

If anything is bound to make me go crazy, it's that.

"We are getting off-topic. Ru, we can smell..." Luca taps his nose. "Want."

Embarrassment fills the room next, and I bare my teeth at Luca for causing her to be uncomfortable.

Whiskey comes at the perfect moment, plopping right by Ru's feet, letting out a slow grunt from lying on the floor. She bends down and scratches his ear, and his tongue falls out from the side of his mouth as he pants happily.

Lucky, dog.

"Enough. God, we will never get anywhere." Alexander sips his drink and sits down on a chair that's more like a throne. It's tall, wide, and black, with wings framing the back. As he sits, he drags Maven to his lap, a hand cupping her belly. His thumb strokes back and forth, and Maven sags against him.

"Ru, I don't think we have all been properly introduced without mayhem. I'm Alexander, the Master of this coven and the Alpha to Anwyll and his brother Aziel. This is my beloved, the reason for my eternity, Maven Wildes, who is our coven witch. A position of royalty for the witches. She's a descendant of Sarah Wildes, a witch from the Salem Witch Trials."

"No way!" Ru gasps, sitting up straighter, which has her moving away from me. "I thought the trials were a myth!"

I almost snap at everyone.

Almost.

"That's Reuel. He is an elf," Alexander says, moving around the room. "You've met Luna. She's fae. She is able to heal. You've met my sister, Rarity. Dottie, Maven's best friend and familiar, Severide, my father, Luca, my uncle—"

"Howdy," Luca salutes.

Alexander continues, "That is Greyson, head of security. The Viking is Drayce, vampire as well along with"—he points to each person—"Amory, Finnick— he's a grouch—Gullivere, Amberella, Zaffre, Alastair, Alaric, Tala, and Aziel is downstairs along with my brother, Atreyu. You won't be meeting them anytime soon, I'm afraid. My brother is in a coma from a werewolf bite, and Aziel is in a state of sickness."

Ru holds a hand over her mouth, a gasp escaping her. "A werewolf bite?"

"My bite is only poisonous to vampires, but no vampire here," I rush to say. "They are immune because Alpha was awakened by Maven, her blood woke him, and any vampire who pledges to him to be a part of the coven, is also protected."

"And your brother?" She turns to me, her questions of my bite a thing of the past.

"My brother, along with all werewolves, is susceptible to something we call sickness. It's where we want our mates so badly, we become infected until we kill everything in front of us until we find our fated. We can be so far gone, when we do find her, we kill her, then kill ourselves. He is in the beginning stages of his sickness, so he is chained to the wall. He can't get free."

"Oh my chauns, Anwyll. I'm so sorry." She covers my hand over hers, then laces our fingers together. "There isn't anything that can be done?"

"No."

"Well..." Maven speaks at the same time as me.

"Maven, nothing can be done," I repeat.

"I was doing some research—" she hops off Alexander's lap and kneels by the coffee table, flipping a brown leather book open "—and I think there might be something to slow it down, but it's risky, and it will take you on an adventure. Literally. And you don't have that kind of time."

"Why?" Ru asks the question I've been dreading. My stomach turns to knots, and I scoot over, putting space between us before she can.

"Just tell me," Ru says. "Listen, this world is different, but if you went to mine, our ways would shock you too. I'm not easily put off."

"We have two weeks until the full moon," I begin, my

voice deepening at the thought of mating her. "You'll go into heat, and I'll go into a rut. Basically, nothing else will matter until I knot you—" I blush, not even wanting to get into how I've never had sex before. "And the mating is complete. If you deny me, I become unforgivingly savage. I'll hunt you down, rape you, rip your heart out, then rip out my own." Shame fills me when I lift my eyes from the spot I was staring at on the floor to look at her. "And I've already made a deal with the Alpha," I jut my chin. "He's to kill me before it ever gets to that. I'm a monster, Ru. Plain and simple." My past is proof of what I'm capable of.

"And we can't mate before then? I mean, why worry about something that won't happen?"

I blink at her, confused. "You need time. I won't force you. I won't pressure you."

She rolls her eyes. "I know. I'm also capable of making my own decisions. I know I have plenty to learn, and I'm not saying I'm jumping into bed right now, but I'm not saying I don't want you."

"I should terrify you. If you only knew the things I've done, you'd run."

"And by the sound of it, you'd find me anyway." She straightens her spine and thrusts her shoulders back. "Like I said, does it have to be two weeks?"

"Yes. It has to take place under a full moon," Maven answers, flicking her finger in the air to flip the page by using magic.

"Really? Why?"

"I don't know. I don't know a lot of things about my kind. Maven has been teaching me."

"Why don't you know?" she asks gently, scooting closer until our legs our touching.

"I'd rather not..." I swallow. "I'd rather not talk about it."

"He was put under a spell by an evil warlock for fifteen years that made him take a backseat to his beast, and the warlock controlled his werewolf. When the spell broke, I'm afraid Anwyll had spent from the time he was fifteen up until recently, under the control of someone else. So he has a lot to learn."

"Oh my chauns!"

I have no idea what that means, but Ru is crawling onto my lap, the warmth between her legs warming my cock, and it feels so fucking good. I leave my hands on the couch, my talons digging into the cushion, and she cups my face, staring directly into my eyes.

"Do I need to kill him? I know people back on my planet who could do it. Leprechauns are violent when we need to be, especially if we don't have our luck. We could find this warlock and send him to the Unwanted Lands on my planet." She bites her lip and nods her head with excitement. "Horrible things happen there. His screams will live forever."

"That's so fucking dark," Luca points out the obvious.

"And what happened to Anwyll was even darker." Ru comes to my defense, her touch bringing me solace in ways I never thought I could experience.

"While that would be amazing, the warlock has been taken care of. It's why Anwyll is with us today. The spell is broken," Alpha explains further.

"As long as he is no longer a threat." Ru turns her head, placing her cheek against my chest so she can see Maven.

I'm frozen.

I'm afraid to move.

If I do, something is going to happen. I'm going to

explode. I feel it in my cock. I squeeze my eyes shut and take deep breaths.

"Relax," she croons, but even her using that tone, sultry and sweet, makes matters worse for me.

A growl forms in my throat, and my werewolf is at the surface.

"Anwyll. Rest." My Alpha's order releases the knot in my chest, and I can breathe again, sweat dripping down my temple.

I'm not used to a woman's touch, and it couldn't be more embarrassing.

"Okay, back to the remedy for a werewolf's sickness."

I don't believe it. Nothing can cure madness, but I'm willing to try anything.

"I don't have the book that has the proper ingredients. You'll have to get that from the Veiled Library. I have what goes in the potion, but not the amounts or where you can find them. I honestly have never heard of most of these." Her finger runs in a horizontal line across the page. "You'll need wolfsbane, but there are two kinds. One is poisonous and purple." She squeezes her hand and throws it in the air, and a large purple flower hangs above us.

"Whoa."

"Cool, right?" I whisper my own awe into Ru's ear, finding that I want to suck the lobe into my mouth.

"Purple wolfsbane is very deadly to werewolves, but to counter it, there is another wolfsbane." She makes a fist again before another flower appears above us. "This is called---"

"—heartsnow...wolfsbane," Ru whispers, standing to her feet. She reaches for the flower. "It is so rare. We learned about this flower in school. It's medicinal and can nearly cure anything. It is said to grow in one place."

"A land where fire is met by ice," Maven reads off the page. "I don't know what that means. We can talk about it later, next we need a six-leaf clover, the tears of a vampire, the blood of the maddened werewolf, and hair from a— oh, come on." Maven slams her fist on the table. "This list is insane. It is asking for unicorn hair."

"That's interesting." Ru's brows pinch together. "I'm from Àdh. Most of what you want is back home. Unicorns are protected there. I mean, if anyone gets near them, it is a death sentence. Clover isn't hard to find. It's everywhere since it is a planet of leprechauns. As for the heartsnow, I've only heard rumors of where it is at." She sits and rubs her temples. "The unlucky leprechauns spend their entire lives looking for it because heartsnow is said to give permanent luck to my kind."

"Tell us more about leprechauns, Ru. I'm intrigued. I didn't know you existed." Alpha sips his bloody Manhattan, a red line over his top lip before he licks it away.

Ru sighs and flops back on the couch. I find myself captivated by her puffs of breath, the way she slings her arm over her eyes, and when I follow the curves of her body, I lock onto the swell of her breasts.

"Anwyll!" Alpha snaps his fingers, and I'm forced out of my trance.

"You were growling," Ru worries her bottom lip.

"I'm sorry." I look away, and her fingers press against my cheek, forcing me to come face-to-face with her fear.

"I like it when you growl."

"Wha-what?" I sputter as she leans closer, and I do the opposite; I press my back against the arm of the couch.

I feel like the hunted.

I feel like the prey.

"I. Like it. When..." she drags her finger up my chest "...

You. Growl. I expect it more. Understood, Anwyll?" Her green eyes suck the freedom of my making my own choices away, and I find myself loving it.

"Yes, Ru."

"Jesus Christ. Open a fucking window before I'm suffocated with lust or die from needing to fuck, right now." Finnick, the grouchy vampire, slides a window open and gasps in a dramatic breath.

"Grow up, Finnick. It's lust. Breathe it in because it tastes so fucking good," Drayce groans, his eyes fluttering shut, and Dottie's mysterious creature pulses from red to orange, growing larger around her.

"Back on topic, please," Reuel, the elf asks this time, a man usually quiet and never speaks. "Leprechauns were said to be extinct where I grew up, so I'm very interested in learning about Ru."

Tala and Amory play pool, listening to us while minding their own business.

"Right." Ru's spell is broken, and I miss her attention on me immediately. "I'm twenty-three and I have until I'm twenty-five to find my luck. I know the myths, but we aren't born with luck. Finding it is like a leprechaun finding his or her worth, and we become addicted to things very easily that we think will give us luck. For example, my best friend Mannix found his luck really young, and he can charm happiness into seashells, giving people moments of pure joy. I don't have my luck yet, but I'm addicted to scratch-off tickets. Anyway, let's not talk about that. I'm dying to scratch." She rubs her palms against her legs, and that's when I notice she's wearing my fucking clothes.

Oh god, she looks so damn good.

I never want her in anything else but my t-shirts.

"If we don't find our luck, we get cast into the

Unwanted Lands. Basically, nothing good lives there. Everything is unlucky, creatures that will kill you in an instant, tricks are played, and it can be a mirage and a maze all at once. The heartsnow that you need, I hear you have to go through the Unwanted Lands, and if you make it, there's a cave."

"And on the other side of the cave?" I ask.

"I don't know. I'm assuming the flower is on the other end."

"Maybe the Veiled Library will have more information. Maybe we can buy some books to add to my collection."

"And how do we get there, Beloved?"

"We go to the portal, hold hands, and I think of the library. I have to be with you though. Only a witch's magic can enter the library. It's how the books remain protected from outsiders."

"We'll go first thing tomorrow. Everyone get a good night's rest. This journey ahead of us seems to be life and death. Meeting over."

"Thank god. I need food," Finnick blurs out the window.

"Me too. And a good fuck," Greyson says.

"Me three." Alastair leaves next with a few others.

"Me four." Alpha Monreaux snags Maven and vanishes, Maven's giggle the only sound left behind.

"Well, I better get to bed too."

"Not until you eat." Rarity holds out a plate of food, and Ru grabs it, shoving a piece of bacon into her mouth.

I stand at the same time as Ru, and I nod. "Sure. Ya. Have a great night, Ru."

She cocks her head, then shakes it ever so slightly before gripping my chin. "Is that how you say goodnight to your mate, Anwyll? Kiss me goodnight so I have sweet dreams."

"I—" I want to kiss her, more than anything, but I've never kissed anyone before.

What if I'm really bad at it?

She stands on her tiptoes and her fingers brush over my mouth. "So soft, Anwyll."

"Ru—" My chest begins to heave as she leans in closer. Every part of my body is alert, over-sensitive, and hot.

I tremble. My cock straining against the blanket. Her arm wraps around my waist, her touch a searing tattoo on my skin while her hand skims up my torso, her fingers rubbing over my nipple as she travels my body.

"There it is," she whispers. "There's that growl I love so much."

I step away, breaking the moment before my animal instincts take over. "I can't. I can't..." I run away from her, like a coward, afraid to kiss her, afraid of everything because I don't know what I'm doing, and I don't trust myself.

"Anwyll!" she calls out to me, and as much as it hurts, I don't stop.

I take four steps at a time, dash to my room, then slam the door. My teeth grind together in frustration, at the annoyance of how fucking pathetic I am, and I grab the lamp on the nightstand and throw it against the wall.

The growl that leaves my chest isn't of want, but of pain.

I shift, letting my beast take over to comfort my weak human side. Tilting my head back, I howl in the agony of not being able to taste my mate.

And the tickle of sickness laughs in the back of my head.

Ru deserves more, not some broken monster whose time is limited.

She should run and stay the hell away from me. It's what is best for the both of us.

Ru will keep her heart, and I'll die knowing my heart belonged to her, the only bright side to a dark future that lies ahead.

"You'll have to be patient with him," Rarity declares, making herself the same drink her brother had. "He has had a very rough, traumatic life."

"What happened?"

"That's not for me to say. That's his story."

We listen as a howl fills the house with mourning and sorrow, my heart breaking for the man who is supposed to be my everything.

"I accept him for who he is, not what he has done."

The ice dings against the crystal as she lifts the rim to her lips, her violet eyes assessing me. "Why? You don't know him."

"I want to," I sneer, not that she deserves a reason. Have I ever felt this way? No, but if I'm his fated mate like he says, then I should feel like this.

Protective.

Possessive.

And slightly obsessed with his touch.

Okay, a lot obsessed.

I know in order to sleep tonight, I'm going to have to get that kiss, but I don't want to force him either.

Communication is key. We won't get anywhere in this relationship, besides dead, if we don't talk.

And I'd rather keep my heart inside my chest.

"Just making sure. Easy," she chuckles and walks away, but before she leaves me, she pauses, turning to look over her shoulder. "Anwyll might need a firm hand. He is an alpha werewolf, but his dominance is suppressed by fifteen years of trauma."

The thought of healing him has warmth blooming in my chest. Is this a task I want to take on? Hell yes. It might be hard, but I know whatever lies ahead, Anwyll is worth it.

I feel it.

"Thank you." Not wanting to waste another second, I run by her, Rarity's laugh teasing as I stretch my legs over as many steps as I can. I use the rail to help lift my body up. Whiskey is at the top of the steps now, drool pooling on the hardwood as he sleeps, snoring up a storm.

When I get to the top of the stairs, there's a window in the middle of the wall that gives a view of the sunflower fields. I bet stargazing would be gorgeous out there.

Another loud snort from Whiskey pulls me out of my daydream, and I run my hand along the railing, the floor creaking under each step as I head to Anwyll's room. I expect the door to be closed, but it's cracked open, and when I take the handle, slowly peering into the room, the first thing that catches my attention is a broken lamp on the floor.

Thinking he hurt himself, I burst into the room, only to find it empty. I spin in a circle, looking for any clue that he is here, when I notice the window open, the curtains floating from the soft breeze trickling in.

I tilt my head out to see him sitting on the roof in his werewolf form, perched right at the edge as if he is about to jump off.

"Anwyll?" I say his name as softly as I can, stretching my arm out for him to take my hand.

He stares at it, then lifts his beautiful, monstrous, beastly head to look at me. I'd know that expression from anywhere.

He's ashamed.

"Don't leave me to sleep alone. Come inside. Let's talk, my sweet werewolf. Come on," I urge.

Anwyll's giant hand falls across mine, his long, deadly claws tickling my forearm, and his fur soft across my skin. His palm is rough and scratchy, but I find myself loving how different he is.

He has to bend at an odd angle to fit through the window and to come back into the room, but when he does, and he straightens, I'm at eye level with an impressive chest.

"I love this form, but please shift back so we can talk." I don't break eye contact as I back away and close the door, not locking it, so he doesn't feel trapped.

Anwyll flexes his hands, shakes his head, then shuts his eyes, struggling with if he wants to shift or not.

Impatience causes me to tap my foot. "Shift if you want this mating to work."

Snagging a blanket, he covers up his very sexy, very nude, and very large werewolf cock before his human body shrinks his beasts.

Focus.

He doesn't even want to kiss me. Why would he want more?

He tucks the corners of the blanket around his hip, my eyes glued to the valley carved on either side of his torso.

My mouth waters because I know what the path leads to, and I almost whine and throw a tantrum just so I can explore.

Anwyll runs his fingers through his long hair, a tormented cloud hanging over him. "You shouldn't be here, Ru."

"Don't tell me where I can and can't be, Anwyll." I cross my arms, and he jerks his head up, his Adam's apple bobbing as he swallows. "Why did you deny me my kiss?" I saunter to him, putting an extra sway in my hips, and I don't miss his eyes wandering down my body.

His hands clutch the blanket, his body frozen. He licks his lips, the bottom fuller than the top, and there is an ache inside me that needs to know how they feel against my own.

"I can't."

"Why?" I stop in front of him, peering up at his statuesque form.

"Please, don't make me say it," he begs, the desperate plea almost making me forget what I want.

"I need to hear it in order to make this work between us. Be honest. I won't ever judge you." I place a hand over his racing heart. "You're safe with me. You're secrets and your fears are safe with me."

He wraps a hand around my wrist, his fingers circling my arm so long they overlap one another. This strong, gentle giant presses my hand harder against his chest as he hangs his head. The ash-colored pieces of his hair fall across his forehead. With the ragged, unsteady rasps of his breath, I know he is nervous.

"Take your time," I tell him. "There's no rush. I'll stand here forever, for as long as I need, until you're comfortable."

"I'm ashamed. I'm afraid of losing you when I haven't even had you." His brows dip, and his voice strangles with an edge of pain someone has when they have lost something they care about.

"And I won't go anywhere. Let me prove it to you. Take a chance on me." I brush my knuckles over his cheek, and the amber gems of his irises flash green as they meet mine, and that's when I see it.

Through the agony, the fear, the trauma, the uncertainty, I'm able to see it swimming in the windows to his soul.

Innocence.

Naivety.

"I can't kiss you."

"Because you're afraid to poison me? I don't think that will happen."

"No." His hair fans around as he shakes his head. "I mean, I *can't* kiss you. I can't. I... I don't know how. I've never kissed anyone before."

I rein in my shock and school my features fast. This gorgeous man has no experience? Is he a virgin?

"Have you ever had sex?" I go ahead and ask because people have sex and don't kiss all the time.

"No." There's the sound of shame again. "And I know how it sounds, okay? I'm a grown man—"

"—Who has not been in control of his own body. When will you stop being so hard on yourself?" I slide my arm around his waist and pull him against me. "Does this mean I'm your first?"

He stares at the ceiling, nodding. "You'd be my first everything."

A moan leaves me before I can catch it.

"You… like that?" hope flares in his shaken words.

"Look at me." I grip his chin and force it down. "I love it. I love that I get to be your first. I love knowing no other woman has touched you. I'm obsessed with the fact that in every way, you're mine. No other will ever have you; no other will kiss you," I rub my thumb over his lips. "And no other will have your cock." I slide my hand down his abdomen, the hard ridges of muscle flexing. "You could say I've become easily addicted to the idea of that."

He relaxes, his entire body sagging with relief, and he wraps his arms around me now. Being wrapped in his embrace while he is human feels different, yet I love it just as much.

"I still want some time to get to know you before we have sex," I inform him, not wanting to just hop into bed immediately, but that doesn't mean we can't explore one another until then. "But until then, I really want that kiss, Anwyll. I'm dying for it."

Anwyll's lips part, his pink tongue flicking out, and he skims his fingers up my arm until his wide palm cups my face. "We can't have that."

"No, we can't." I step on my tiptoes and still can't reach him. Tilting my head, he cocks his to the other side.

"Be easy with me."

My heart melts. "You'll never know difficulty again. I swear," I whisper, my lips ghosting over his.

Ever so slowly, he bends down to meet me, and finally, the give of his lips touches mine. We gasp in unison, an electric current buzzing through my veins from the feel of him. His lips are perfect, fitting against mine like a puzzle piece. There's a roughness too from the shadow of his stubble, and it brushes against the top of my lip.

His broken breaths are warm as his resolve begins to crumble, his body trembling.

"Let me in, My Gentle Giant," I whisper, parting my lips to show him what I want, and he picks up on it quickly, his lips separating for me to slide my tongue against his.

That fucking growl I love so much vibrates down my throat, and a whimper leaves me. Chauns, I love that sound. My pussy wets the boxers I'm wearing, my clit throbbing from the monstrous ability.

His tongue mimics mine, dancing and wrapping around my own, until the kiss turns from curious and unsure, to demanding and needy. Anwyll cups the back of my head and presses, so our kiss is harder.

A constant rumble fills the room and it's coming from him. He lifts me up, wrapping my legs around his waist, then slams me against the wall, the force causing the blanket covering him to fall to the floor.

My nails scrape down his back until I'm gripping his ass with both hands, loving how thick and firm each cheek is. He nips at my lips before diving back in.

"You feel so fucking good, My Lucky Charm." His voice is a mixture of human and animal. When I lean back, breaking the kiss, I'm staring into the eyes of his werewolf. And that makes me feel good, knowing I'm making him lose so much control, his beast threatens to surface.

Not sure I'd even mind that.

It's still Anwyll.

Maybe that's something that can happen later.

His fangs prick his lips, and he dives to my neck, kissing, licking, and nipping before sliding his tongue along my jaw until he owns my lips once more.

Gripping the back of my thighs, he carries me and

tosses me on the bed. I bounce, getting a full frontal view of him.

"You're stunning," I say, admiring every defined line, but my attention is grabbed by the giant appendage between his legs. "And huge."

He grits his teeth. "Fuck, I burn. I don't know what to do, but it feels so good yet hurts so bad." Anwyll stares down at his cock, a pearly drop beading at the slit.

It hits me that he truly knows nothing of pleasure, and if everything I've been told is true, my Gentle Giant has only known pain.

"I want to tear you apart," he warns. "But Maven said that didn't mean I wanted to hurt you. It means desire."

"Come here." I shove down his boxers I'm wearing, and he stares at my pussy, nostrils flaring as he inhales. "Do you smell my desire?"

"And it smells so fucking good."

"It's all for you." I strip off his shirt next, and he kneels on the bed, slowly sliding up to me. "What do you want to do, Anwyll?"

His beast's talon drags down the middle of my chest, then he glides the sharp point to the left, over my nipple. I inhale a sudden breath from how good it feels, and my pussy becomes wetter.

"You like my claws?" his beast-ridden voice asks.

"I love them." I toss my head back while he explores the other, then his warm mouth wraps around my left nipple while he pinches the right between his fingers. "Yes," I hiss.

He sucks and flicks his tongue, trying to gather as much of my breast as possible in his mouth, devouring me like a starved man.

I reach between us, gripping his cock. I don't have time to explore how I can't fit my hand around the width or how there are ridges along the side that I imagine would feel exquisite inside me.

He rips his mouth off me and moans, his eyes closing as his orgasm explodes through him. The thick, flared head is coated with white come, the slit hidden by the fertile clouds of his seed. Never-ending streams land across my stomach and drip down my hand while I get to experience the feel of his cock flexing in my grasp.

I moan too, his come warming and tingling my hand. Does he know it did that? My clit throbs thinking about it filling me, heating my depths.

It's so much, I don't think he's ever going to stop.

"Fuck," he grunts. "Oh, fuck, fuck, fuck," he chants, slanting a kiss across my lips while one last jerk spasms his body. He's quaking, his cock still hard in my grasp, and our breaths are mixing together in the same ragged rhythm, as if I came too, but I'm high off what I've just made him feel.

His cheeks heat, and he scrambles off me, my hand slipping from his gargantuan length, and I miss the weight of it already. "I'm sorry. I...I'm sorry. I didn't...I wasn't...I didn't know...I didn't mean to...I...it felt so good to have your hands on me. I've never...no one has ever...I haven't ever..." he tries to explain and to shut his cute, rambling self up, I crawl across the bed, his come dripping down my stomach and onto my legs.

I grab his stalk and lick up the side; another small burst of come escapes his slit. I drink him down, my throat slightly numbing from the tingly sensation his come gives. "I'll suck you another day. I plan on worshiping this beauty." I kiss the tip, dipping my tongue in the slit, and his body shakes again, a smirk forming on my lips.

I fucking love how inexperienced he is because it means all of his experiences of pleasure are from me and are mine.

"You're beautiful when you come for me, Anwyll."

His eyes become hazed, riding the endorphins of his orgasm.

"Now…" I lean back and spread my legs, running my fingers through my wet lips between my thighs. "Be a good boy for your mate and make me come."

Anwyll's eyes zero in on my pussy, and his fangs glint in the light as he stares between my thighs like it's prey he's about to catch and devour.

But I see the hesitation. He wraps a hand around his cock and gives it a lazy stroke. "I don't know how to make you come," he admits, his shoulders sagging in defeat.

"I'll teach you everything you need to know unless you don't want to. We never will do anything you don't want." Now I'm wondering if I pushed him too far. We are jumping into this fast, but it's like I can't help it, or I have no control over how much I want him.

I want to fuck him right now, but there's another feeling in my chest, one telling me to wait until it's time to mate in two weeks.

He falls to his knees, grips me by my ass, and yanks me to the edge of the bed. "I want to more than anything, Ru. Tell me what to do."

Running my hands through his hair, I guide him between my legs. "Sheath your talons."

He does what I say, following my directions effortlessly. "That's my good boy." He leans against my palm and hums, liking my praise for him. Taking his hand, I curl all but one finger and glide it through my pussy's lips, the wetness an erotic song as he discovers his mate's body for the first time.

I guide his hand to my clit, and he watches intently as I press his finger against my clit. "Yes," I groan, arching my back from how good it feels to finally have relief. "That's my clit. Think of it as a pleasure button that, if pressed enough, will make me come."

His eyes flash between man and beast again, and he circles the bundle of nerves next, causing my thighs to shake.

"Mate," he growls as a gush of fluid escapes me, and he inhales.

"Yes, your mate. You're making me feel so good." I glide his finger down and slip it inside. I'm so wet for him, there's no give, no force, and I take him until he is at the knuckle.

His chest heaves, his shoulders rising and falling with how dangerously hard he is breathing.

"Slide your finger in and out," I instruct.

Testing my logic, he does as I say, in and out slowly, and he watches as his finger disappears, then comes out glossy with my need.

"Harder. Faster."

"Want to taste," he snarls, his finger picking up speed, and I whimper, clawing at the bed.

"Yes, yes, taste."

His lips pull my clit into his mouth, and his free hand whips around my neck, squeezing it as he eats away at me. I notice his body is bigger, his hand wider, his hair longer, and when he peers up from between my legs, feasting, I notice he's half shifted.

The tether of control is broken.

I'm only here for him to use now.

That fucking growl creates tremors inside me, my clit's nerves bursting from overstimulation.

"Anwyll!" I cry, tugging the mane of his hair. "Don't stop. Oh, chauns. Don't stop. That's it." I sit up, needing to watch as he eats his first and only pussy he'll ever fucking taste. My mouth drops open, and I yank his head back by the thick of his hair. His lips are shining from my nectar, and he sneers at me, pushing against me to dive back in. "Do you like that? Do you like my pussy, good boy? It's all yours."

His hand dips below, and by the jerk of his arm, I know he is touching himself. "I want you to do what feels natural. You know what to do now." I pull him to my weeping cunt. "Make. Me. Come."

With a curl of his lip, he wraps his mouth around the sweet piece of candy and slides another finger in, stretching me with his strong digits, fucking me with his hand so hard, I move up the bed.

"Yes, like that. Oh, yes, yes," I moan, tossing my head back as I ride his face. His arm holds me down by lying across my hips now. His tongue circles my clit before sliding down the slit, pushing it inside to accompany his fingers before he groans. Anwyll laps at the middle, giving me long, hard strokes with his coarse tongue before nibbling my clit.

Huffs of attempted words come out as strangled breaths. My belly flexes, my hands clutch the covers, and I toss my head to the left. "Anwyll! Yes, don't stop. More. More. Give me more."

He slips in another finger, kneeling on the bed while hoisting me closer to his mouth.

I'm surrounded by him.

I end and begin with him.

I peek down at his cock, bigger in his half-shifted form, leaking and smearing precome along his thigh. A bulbous knot is at the base, and while I don't know what it's for, my pussy flutters with wanting to feel it.

Game over.

I cry out, pulsating around his fingers, wishing it was

his cock inside me instead, milking him of every drop he has to give.

He hums in appreciation as he drinks me down, his eyes shutting as his own body tenses. Anwyll slips his fingers free of me and sits up, wrapping his hand around himself as he points his shaft between my legs and comes for the second time tonight.

I'm painted like a picture, his scorching seed covering my pussy, then redirects to my thighs and stomach, until I'm covered in him.

Sweat shines off his chest as he stares down at me, the angular edges to his jaw and cheekbones more pronounced, and he begins to rub his come into my skin, that damn growl sounding again, but it's one of content.

"Are you...marking me?" I giggle, drunk off the amazing orgasm he gave me.

"Mine," he snaps at me. "All mine. Need to smell of us."

Us?

Oh.

I'm talking to his beast.

"Need to bite. Need to claim. Need to—" the green eyes fade and Anwyll returns, his brown eyes staring back at me.

I saw a glimpse of the alpha hiding within.

And I can't wait until the day I get him to truly come out and play.

Chapter Ten

ANWYLL

I don't know where I am, but I'm looking through the eyes of my spellbound beast. Everything is hazy, even to him. The surroundings before us are swaying, and everything is dark with blues, blacks, and greys. There's no vibrance. No color. Even the grass has lost its green, and I know it's because of the spell we're under.

It reminds me of a sweltering day when I could see the humidity and heat rolling in the air, causing a mirage of sorts.

"Attack," our Controller commands, pointing at the village underneath a blue moon.

Without question, my beast roars, running toward the village.

"No, stop! Please, no more. Don't listen to him. We aren't like this. This isn't who we are." I beg my other half, the animal bound to my soul, but he can't hear me. I'm a million miles away, locked inside the deepest parts of him.

I'll remain unheard.

"Please," I sob, pushing against the barrier between us, not wanting to see another death or hear another scream. "Please!" I bang against the wall, the spell not even vibrating from my

attempt. "Don't. We aren't murderers," I whisper, wincing when I hear the first scream of death.

The other werewolves, previous friends and family members from the pack, smash through the walls of homes, snarling as we destroy just to destroy.

A woman holding the hand of her daughter runs away from me, her nightgown flowing behind her. Her child trips, unable to keep up, and the mother bends down, swinging her into her protective arms. She runs again, her tears soaking her face.

My beast falls on all fours, sprinting to catch them. Our claws dig into the dirt, the blood from innocent people already pooling under our feet.

And it won't stop us.

Nothing stops us.

I watch in horror as we lift a hand, our sharp talons twinkling under the gorgeous star-filled night, and slash.

The woman trips, shouting from the pain as five long marks appear on her back. Blood seeps from her skin. Her gown ruined.

And it only makes my beast thirstier.

I've learned that's what makes this spell so bad. The more we kill, the more we crave the kill.

The more we want it.

I grip the young girl by her neck and lift her into the air.

"No! No, please, take me. Kill me. Don't take my daughter. Take me," the mother cries, her love for her child giving her strength to crawl to me, pushing through the pain we've caused.

"I'm so sorry," I tell her, knowing she can't hear me. "I can't stop. We can't stop." A tear rolls down my cheek, and my breath hitches when my wolf slaps his paw against her face, slinging her hundreds of feet.

The little girl screams in terror, her high-pitched cries a sound I'll never forget. "Mo-mmy!" The word breaks in two, struggling to speak through the fear and sobs.

I stare at her just as my beast does.

I take note of every feature, every tear, every cry for her mother, while my beast has one thing in mind.

Digging down deep, I shout at him, roaring my own agony, hoping this once he can hear me before we do something we'll never forgive ourselves for.

"Anwyll!" An angelic voice pierces my nightmare. "Anwyll! Wake up. It's a nightmare. You're okay. You're here with me. Come back to me, Good Boy."

The little girl fades in my grip, and we spin around, watching our surroundings morph.

"Anwyll." A warm touch hits my cheek.

I wake on a snarl, my wolf still so close to the surface, and I grip the hand that touched me, rolling us until they are under me.

"It's me, Anwyll. It's Ru. Your mate." This woman doesn't panic. She stares up at me with glowing green eyes and bravery. "It's okay," she chokes, my hand squeezing her throat. Her hand gently cups my cheek, but I can barely register it. My wolf growls, not trusting her, not noticing her because we are still so lost in our nightmare.

"Anwyll," she inhales. "I can't breathe."

Her hand fumbles with the nightstand and slaps a book off it, knocking it to the floor.

The door bursts open, and I'm slung off her so hard, the breath leaves my lungs as the thunderous meat of Alexander's shoulder meets mine.

The woman gasps for breath, coughing while I hold her throat. It's the woman from my dream.

We have to kill her.

"Anwyll! What the fuck are you thinking? That is your mate!" Alexander charges at me, his vampire challenging me, daring me to go against my nature.

"Stop! No, don't hurt him." The woman crawls from the bed, wrapping the sheet around her gorgeous naked body, and something familiar stabs my mind. I know this body.

I think.

She stops in front of a very powerful vampire, who is quickly surrounded by many others. "I know it looked bad, but he's in a nightmare. He was having a horrible dream, and I tried to wake him up. I didn't know how bad his nightmares were. I don't know...I don't know why I know this, but he'd never hurt me if he were in the right state of mind."

I can barely see her through the haze. The more I stand here, waiting, the further into myself I retreat.

"His nightmares are from the time he was spelled by the Warlock," Rarity speaks.

Alexander's anger fades, and he stares at me with so much sorrow, but I can also see he has no idea how to help me.

My werewolf and I pause, standing at attention as we wait for our orders to kill.

"Let me try again," the woman whispers, wondering where this confidence is coming from for her to confront me. She's as good as dead once I receive the command to kill. But there is a voice in the back of my mind telling me this woman is different; this home is different.

I don't have to kill to prove myself.

"We're here if things go wrong," Master Monreaux states, his talons and fangs at the ready.

The unique light blonde hair with a pink tint splays around her when she turns, her face calls out to me, and I want to move, but I remain locked against the wall. She has a pale face, pink lips, lips that warm a memory, dare an emotion other than anger to whirl inside me.

"Anwyll," those lips form my name, but I have to remain strong. Nothing can make me deter from my position, my goal, the ultimate win. I don't even blink. With tentative steps, she comes forward, and a welcome surge of protection rushes through me to make sure she doesn't get hurt.

She shouldn't come closer. I'm not good for her. What is she thinking? I'm going to kill her the moment I get the chance.

No, you're not. She's different. She's special.

My beast tries to speak to me. After all the years I begged him to listen, to not kill, and now he talks to me? Over a woman we don't know.

We know her. She's delicious. She's our first. She's our mate. Don't kill. We can't. Sickness. Must remember sickness.

I'm not like this because it's who I am. I was turned into this. I was made into... this unlovable monster. I barely remember who I am. I don't even want to fall asleep because I know what lives in the dark.

And it's me.

I'm the dark. I'm the thing this woman needs to be afraid of, yet she stands in front of me with her chin held high and eyes that weep.

For me.

It isn't easy containing myself. To not whisk her away—out the window—and steal her for myself, but I must remain in control.

And for some reason, she's wrecking every ounce of control I have.

"Anwyll." Her delicate voice finds a way to penetrate my soul again. Her hand touches my arm, but I don't move, even if my body is dying to wrap her in my arms. "Hey, come back to me." She stands on her tiptoes, running her palms over my chest. Tears fill my eyes, wishing I could fix the broken pieces of my mind.

She's breaking me.

"You're not there." She climbs up my body, wraps her legs around my hips, and locks her arms around my neck, continuing to whisper into my ear. "You aren't under the spell of that warlock, you're here with me, your Lucky Charm." She kisses my cheek, rubbing those soft lips back and forth over my stone-frozen flesh.

"You're my Good Boy, Anwyll." She tries to remain as quiet as possible, so no others can hear.

Why do I like that nickname so much? It isn't manly. I shouldn't like that, but I do. *I really fucking do.*

"You aren't that man. You aren't that werewolf. Whatever that warlock made you do, it wasn't you. It isn't who you are." This woman takes a killer's face in her hands, staring into my vacant soul, she's somehow sparking to life.

Is she a love I've barely known and is lost in wayward seas?

How will I reach it? How can I break free?

She leans forward, pressing a kiss against my lips.

And the feel of her softness, the taste of her tongue, the first-time experience of having her rushes back to me.

Her kiss is enough to subdue a killer.

There can't be anything more powerful than that.

"Mate," I mumble the word against her lips, and I barely hear it. "My mate," I repeat, wrapping an arm around her as she breathes life back into me and deepens the kiss. My tongue seeks hers, and I eagerly let them dance.

"Anwyll." Master Monreaux interrupts the breakthrough session with dread hitched to my name. "Do you remember anything?"

"Just my mate kissing me," I say, shaking my head of

the fogginess. "I didn't know a kiss could be so powerful." I press my forehead against hers. "Nothing has ever been able to bring me back from such a dark place."

"She almost didn't," Alexander states. "She tried to wake you, but her attempt backfired. I felt your confusion through the bond and ran up here." By the way he sighs, I can tell he doesn't want to admit the rest. "You were choking her, Anwyll. And by the looks of it, you weren't going to let her go."

I stumble to the side and gently set my mate on her feet, my eyes locking onto the redness around her neck from my hands. I touch the mark, it's warm, and might bruise.

Lifting my hands in front of me, I stare at them, flashes of blood and flesh clinging to my nails from the carnage I've created.

What have I done?

"You should be afraid of me." I've never felt so disgusted with myself. With every ounce of who I am, I never wanted to hurt her. Ever.

"I should be. Someone with so much trauma can be unpredictable. I should run away, but my heart is saying this is when my mate needs me most. He hasn't had anyone be by his side to help him through the horrors he had to live through," she answers, sliding her fingers across my palms, folding them together to hold. "I'm thinking that's why mates exist, to help them through the darkest times, and hopefully bring them a little light. I have a lot to learn, but I'm willing. I'm so fucking willing to save you, to save us, even if it means losing myself."

"I'm not. I never want you to lose yourself for me, believe me, being lost is something you don't want." I brush my fingers across her cheek, my eyes never leaving the mark I've put around her neck.

I should be sentenced to death.

Ru shakes her head and laughs, a genuine smile tilting her lips. "This mate bond is strong. I had to rethink everything the moment I felt it because I typically wouldn't feel so intensely. I think I'm already lost to you, Anwyll. You have to give this a chance. It won't be perfect right away, but maybe one day it can be."

I push her away and bury my face in my treacherous hands. "I knew I would hurt you. I knew it!" I scream, letting out a painful sound full of regret that's mixed with the voice of my untrusting beast. I point to Alexander and Maven, angry at them. Angry at myself. "You said I wouldn't hurt her! You said I wanted her. I said I wanted to tear her apart, and no one listened to me. No one listened!"

"Anwyll, you didn't tear me apart. I'm fine. You weren't you," she attempts to excuse my unforgivable behavior, but I shake my head, stepping out of reach so I can't feel her touch.

Because her touch ruins all reason and logic. I'm two seconds away from falling to my knees if she told me to. She takes the horrible ability of making decisions away from me, and it brings me peace.

Something I don't deserve.

And with every piece of me I've lost, she's the peace I've dreamed of.

Ru should remain just that—a dream.

"Next time, I could kill you. I would kill myself if I did that. I'd rip my own heart out because while it's nearly impossible to live with what I've done. I couldn't live knowing I took your life. You need to stay away from me."

"You'll fall sick." She's in disbelief, staring at me with parted lips like I've lost my mind. "You don't want me?"

I scoff at the idiotic question. "Want you? I love you." I

slam my fist against the wall. "I love you enough to let you go. I'll risk the illness if it means you're free." Loving her happened the moment I breathed in her scent. There's no going back. "If it means you'll live."

"And what of my sickness?" The hushed words are spoken through an ache, and she wipes tears from her cheek.

"You don't experience it. You wouldn't have to worry about it." I'm confused why she thinks she'd fall sick.

"Not experience it? I might not have the ability to rip my heart out, but sickness comes in different forms, and I have no doubt that this intense, overwhelming possession I feel toward you would send me spiraling. I'd fall ill, Anwyll. I'd be on the brink of death with missing you, needing you, wanting to hear your voice. I'll get depression. Isn't that what happens? Mates can't be without each other. Sickness doesn't always end in death. Sometimes, it's a process of torture. You'd do that to me?"

"No. I never want to hurt you, but I did…" I stare at her neck again, and my werewolf is at the surface, buzzing my flesh with the need to shift and run away. A pathetic whine leaves us when I allow our forms to melt together into a half-shift. Our extra-large hand floats to where we choked her, and we rub our scarred knuckles down the injury. "We're so sorry. It isn't enough. We can't promise it won't happen again," we say, hating the truth while knowing it needs to be said.

"I think the sooner we plan to visit the library, and we can make preparations for the journey, the better. We're under a time constraint. If we can get the potion, and you don't want to mate, your sickness could be held off, Anwyll."

"Why would you even offer that?" She spins around and snaps at the leader of the coven—my Alpha.

"Not for him. For you. So you have options, and you aren't rushed or put into any more danger. I'm sorry, but Anwyll is unstable. I can't promise what will happen to you."

I growl at my Alpha's words because I don't fucking like them.

He's right.

"It's too late for that. I'm rushed. I'm in this, damn it. And I'm too stubborn for my own good to ever not see something through. I am in this because while it's insane that this is my life right now, I know in my heart that this is what I want. Anwyll is what I want."

"For now," I grit painfully in what I'm about to say. "For now, we should stay away from each other. Until you're safe from me." I run out of the room, trying not to imagine the broken devastation across her face from my rejection of us.

It's time to go on this journey to create this potion. The sooner the better. There has to be hope.

Not just for my brother, but for me.

Chapter Eleven

RU

Luca was a saint and brought me scratch-off tickets. I'm sitting at the kitchen table, angrily peeling the coating off to see if I've won, and the leprechaun inside me has settled from the stress of the last few hours.

I've scratched ten Lucky Number 7's and haven't won a damn thing. "This planet is rigged." I toss the last one in the trash pile. "I sometimes will win a few chauns."

"Haven't you thought that maybe you're just addicted to these and your luck is something else entirely?" Dottie asks with a smug grin.

"No." I sink into my chair and cross my arms over my chest because yes, yes I have.

She sips her coffee, but her eyes follow Drayce when he enters the kitchen, shirtless. He has scars all over his body, some old and faded, some new and pink. He's a warrior through and through, and I see why she's interested in him. He's very handsome in an old-world way. His long hair, the shaved side, the braid, and beard, then there are the muscles.

So many muscles.

When he turns around, I watch as Dottie stares at his chest, also covered in scars and blonde hair.

The pulsating red cloud around Dottie gets bigger, almost as if it's reaching out to Drayce. The vampire stares at her with just as much heat, his eyes flashing red and not hiding how much he wants her.

She isn't hiding it either, but their hypnotized state is cut off when Maven and Alexander enter the kitchen next.

"Okay, who is ready to go on an adventure?" Maven is so happy, holding the grimoire she's constantly carrying around the house. "We have to go today. We can't waste any more time. The two weeks are slowly closing in. Where is Anwyll?" she asks. "Is he not coming?"

I lift a shoulder casually, trying to show that his absence ever since last night hasn't bothered me. My throat isn't even bruised. He didn't have that firm of a grasp. Sure, it was hard to breathe, but that might have been from my panicking. I realize his issues are serious, but this bond has the ability to grow into something amazing.

I can feel it.

I've never been the one to back away when life gets hard, and Anwyll's life has been nothing but difficult. While running away from pain, after everything that has happened to him is normal, he can't back away from me now.

"Let me see if I can see where he is at," Drayce says, closing his eyes for a moment and when he opens them, the red is flickering like an old movie playing on film. "He's downstairs with his brother."

"You can see the future?" I've never met anyone who can do that. "Do all of you have gifts?" Now I really feel like I'm lacking. I have nothing but clumsy feet and a potty mouth.

"Some of us," Alexander states, leaning against the kitchen island. "I can dig deep into people's memories, most vampires can, but I can go further, I can feel what is felt in that exact moment."

"I can only see pictures of what someone is doing in that instance," Drayce explains. "As long as I have a scent or a bond, I can help locate them by seeing their surroundings."

I wonder if he used his ability to stay alive. By the looks of his scars, I'm assuming he's been in battle too many times to count.

"I'm a healer," Luna's voice calms the riot I have going on inside my mind. "It's a fae's natural gift." I love her long, pointy ears.

Mine are slightly pointed, but not like hers. Hers are long, slicing through her hair and almost past the back of her head.

"I can go wherever I want." Reuel snaps his fingers, vanishing into thin air, and pops up right beside me. "And I can make you feel things you wouldn't normally feel, and times it by a million. I usually work from what you're already feeling." He touches my wrist, causing the strife and pain from missing Anwyll to burst from my chest, and I scream, falling onto the floor in a childlike pose with a sob.

"Oh my god, leave her be, Reuel. You know right now is hard on her." Luna helps me up and wipes my tears.

"You're about to have company," Drayce warns the elf. The introductions to everyone's gifts are cut off when a loud, shattering howl has my body trembling.

"I know," Reuel knowingly states. "Werewolves are most stubborn creatures, Ru. They need to be pushed."

"I have the door," Greyson zooms to the basement door and swings it open.

"Thank you. I'm so sick of replacing it," Lex sighs, checking the time on his expensive watch. "We really need to get going."

Thumps from the distance have the pots and pans bumping into one another.

"See you later." Reuel waves his fingers just as a large paw swipes through the air at him. He pops away and reappears on the other side of the kitchen.

Anwyll flashes his teeth at Luna.

"Don't you dare growl at me."

"It's okay," I tell him, hating how sick I feel right now after that rollercoaster of emotions.

Anwyll shifts into his human form and picks me up. "Who is causing my mate so much pain?"

"You are," Reuel states without so much as a flinch of showing fear to the werewolf. "I only made her feel what she was keeping inside. Maybe if she's your mate, you should begin to treat her as such."

"Watch it, elf." Anwyll holds me tighter, and immediately the chaos thrumming through my veins and into my soul vanishes when his skin is on mine.

Does this need get worse? How will I survive two weeks? Or worse, how will I survive if he denies us?

"I'm only stating the truth. If you want to blame anyone for her overwhelming agony, blame yourself. You are the root cause. You can't stay away from her during these next two weeks. It's vital that you strengthen your bond until the full moon."

"You sound like you know a lot about my kind," he spits, running his claws through my hair. It feels nice. I like it.

"I was raised by werewolves. I know many things,"

Reuel says, stirring his cup of tea by waving his hand over it.

"Okay, let's go to the cove. Hey, Reuel, can you transport more than one? Who all is coming?" Maven asks, heading straight to the door.

"I'm staying," Finnick says, lifting his hand. "I don't want to travel by portal. I hope you understand, Maven."

"Of course I do," Maven replies, sorrow frowning her eyes.

"Us too." Amory stands beside Finnick with Amberella, Amory, Gullivere, and Zaffre. "Besides, someone needs to be here to make sure Aziel and Atreyu are okay."

"My son isn't going anywhere." The ache in Severide's tone has me clutching my stomach. "But nevertheless, thank you for watching over him." Severide's hand grips Alexander's shoulder, holding onto the one son he can see and touch. "I'll be going with Alexander and Maven."

"I'm curious about this Veiled Library." Alastair's smile curves, and there's something about it that seems different. His teeth are sharper than a regular vampire's, and his eyes are black.

"I'm staying. I don't want to travel either." Alaric removes himself from the kitchen and strolls into the living room.

"Sorry, I don't want to go either," Tala, a gorgeous vampire with a seductress tone, follows Alaric.

"So me, Lex, Greyson, Luca—"

"Not me, sorry. Someone who can heal needs to stay just in case."

"Makes sense. All of us don't need to go anyway," Alexander nods with his agreement.

"Rarity?" Maven asks the young vampire, and Rarity's

white hair seems to glimmer like frost when the lights hit it as she looks up from her hands.

"Couldn't stop me."

"Great. Now that's taken care of, let's go." Maven grabs Reuel's wrist and tugs him outside.

Everyone else follows in a line, awaiting orders from Maven.

"I'm sorry I'm hurting you," Anwyll whispers, his chin right against the side of my temple as he carries me outside. "It's the last thing I ever want."

"I know, let's just do what comes naturally, okay?" I tell him. "Don't fight anything anymore. Let's just be."

He wants to protest, I can see how his mouth tightens, but eventually, he relents. When we form a circle on the porch, Reuel holds out his hand and Maven takes it. Everyone else follows the coven witch's lead. Drayce holds Dottie's hand, and the aura of her beast engulfs them both. Drayce's eyes widen, but then he looks down at Dottie, the tender, lovesick expression is impossible to miss.

If they were beloveds, wouldn't they know by now?

Luna, Reuel, Greyson, Drayce, Dottie, Alastair, Severide, me, Anwyll, Maven, and Alexander stand in a circle, holding the hand of the person next to us. All while I'm in Anwyll's arms.

A place I'm finding brings me more comfort than the thought of my luck.

"Maven, imagine the cove, and I'll be able to take us there," Reuel says. "Once I get a connection with you, we will be there in a blink—" his words are cut off as our surroundings change.

We're in the middle of the woods next, and immediately I notice how much cooler it is; there's a bite in the air, a hum causing the hair on my arms to stand up.

My ear is pressed against Anwyll's chest, and with every exhale, a low, hushed growl tickles my cheek.

"—of an eye," Reuel finishes, wiping the imaginary dust off his shoulder.

Maven squeals and bounces in place. "That was awesome! How did I live such a boring life before when this existed?"

"I'm glad you're happy, Beloved." Alexander smiles, watching his woman as if she's the only one in existence.

"I don't like it here. It's where I found Ru, dead," Anwyll states, which makes the sound in his chest make sense.

"I'm okay thanks to you." I press a kiss to the middle of his chest.

Such a strong, wide, sexy, muscular—

"Mate, your scent is distracting," Anwyll rumbles, the gravel of the baritone slithering down my spine. "You must stop."

Shit. I forgot he can smell me.

"Well, I'm hoping I can create something that makes traveling between portals easier. Right now, according to my book, I have to prick my finger, and the water will part."

"Do we know if it's safe for the babies?" Alexander asks. "What if we land on a new planet and you hit too hard? I can't risk it."

"We have to. For Aziel. I have a feeling we will be okay." Maven holds up a finger to Lex's mouth. "I'm in need of your services, Beloved."

His eyes morph red, and he snags her wrist. "You know I love it when you tempt me." Alexander opens his mouth, and his fangs descend slowly. Without a flinch, he stabs the tip of her finger, and he licks his lips. "Better hurry before I lose all sense of control."

Maybe we need to give them some time alone. I could

use another night learning Anwyll's body. My heartbeat pulses in my clit as I watch the heated stares between Maven and Alexander. I need Anwyll right now. Squirming, pressing my thighs together, turning my head into his chest, I inhale, my tongue flicking out to taste his nipple.

The wind gusts, my lust drifting away on the breeze. I painstakingly look away from the broad chest I want to lick all over to see Maven has placed her finger in the water, chanting words I can't make out or understand.

An extraterrestrial beat drops, the water morphing from black to red until eventually, it swirls, a violent tunnel whipping leaves and dirt into the air. The cove grows bigger, wider, and longer, the water parting to show nothing but darkness.

"Think of the Veiled Library!" she shouts as the winds become harsher, the sky becomes darker, and thunder crashes above us.

Dottie's eyes flicker gold with every roll from the sky, her veins starting to shimmer.

Alexander holds Maven as they fall into the pit of the unknown. One by one, without reservation, the coven follows until it's just Anwyll and I left.

I barely remember what happened last time I was in the portal, but Anwyll hasn't. His talons curl around my arm, and he holds me with protective strength before leaping into the air and dropping into the cove.

There's no water.

No struggle to breathe.

The air whips around us in pure darkness, my eyes unable to adjust to our surroundings.

I'm blind. Nothing can be seen.

But I can feel.

And Anwyll is there, tucking me so hard against his body, if it were possible, I'd meld to his bones.

Chapter Twelve

ANWYLL

Instead of a hard landing, we float, easing our way out of the darkness, only to find that what I'm looking at can only exist in dreams. We're on an aureate bridge floating amongst the clouds. That isn't even the most shocking detail. The bridge itself leads to a building so tall, when I tilt my head back, I can't see where it ends.

"Excuse me," someone says from behind me.

"Oh, sorry." I stand to the side with Ru in my arms to watch a creature with red skin, a long, leathery tail, and horns on his head walk by.

"Oh my chauns!" Ru rolls out of my arms and stands, spinning around and around. "That guy had a tail. A tail!" She grins.

"Look at that one." Luna points.

"It isn't nice to point." Reuel slaps her hand down, but Ru and I look at where she was gesturing.

A group of large men with glowing tattoos all over their bodies and wings that vary from black, red, white, and purple walk towards us, a bunch of books in their hands.

"Damn," Ru breathes... a little too breathlessly in my opinion.

I tug her to my chest and growl. "Mine."

Maybe I need to shift and show everyone what I am, so they can't fuck with me or what's mine.

"Are you okay, Beloved?" Alpha lies his hand across Maven's stomach, and pure joy and relief wipe away the concern. "I can feel their heartbeats."

"Everything is fine. I'm okay." She kisses the tip of his nose before turning to the library. "This is amazing. I never could have imagined this existed."

Her question is overheard by a stranger. "You must be new," a masculine voice has us all spinning around.

"Holy mother of—" Greyson slaps a hand across Rarity's mouth to keep her quiet.

The creature chuckles. "It's fine. I like seeing the reactions of people who have never seen creatures before. Granted, it's been a long time since the portals were open, so traffic here has been slow until recently."

"That's because of my mate," Alexander states, tugging Maven behind him.

"You must be Maven Wildes." He falls to his knee and bows his head. "Thank you. I'm now able to see my family again. I never thought it could happen. I thought the Wildes' line was dead and only a Wildes can keep the portals alive."

"Wait, what?" Maven peeks around from Alexander. "I thought it was any witch?"

"No. A Wildes Witch is the most powerful. The original descendant of the first witch. Did you not know?" The unknown beast tilts his head, his yellow eyes confused.

"There's a lot we are learning. It's why we are here," Alexander informs, holding out his hand to introduce himself. "Alexander Monreaux. Master of the Monreaux Coven and Alpha to a few werewolves. This is my beloved, Maven Wildes, our coven witch."

"A coven witch!" The creature bows, refusing Alpha's hand and taking Maven's instead. "If I can serve you in any way, I'd be honored."

"She serves only me!" Alexander's thunderous voice has the clouds shooting lightning between one another.

He gains the attention of a few other creatures, and they head over to us.

"Oh man, this is not good," Alastair mumbles the obvious.

"Apologies, that is not what I meant. I mean to thank her for setting us free. This is all because of her. We creatures are able to live again."

Maven scoffs. "You're sleeping on the couch because I do not *serve* you."

Alexander opens his mouth to say something, but the kind stranger stops him.

"Let's start over. I'm Roola, Orc Captain of the Ritcha Clan."

"An orc." Rarity steps in front of all of us and holds out her hand. "You're really cool to look at. I like your tusks. I'm Rarity."

"Roola." When their hands meet, Rarity gasps, and Roola has a blissed-out look on his face.

"Oh, the pain you carry," Rarity whispers, and her magic seeps into the orc's veins, turning them blue. He begins to shiver from the cold, and Rarity lets go of his arm as if it bit her.

"Your power is strong, Rarity, the vampire. You almost froze all of my bad memories."

Rarity seems confused. "I don't know why that happened. I'm sorry."

"Don't be. It was nice to meet you all." The orc disappears into thin air, leaving us wondering if that encounter just happened.

"That was amazing," Greyson laughs. "Rarity, your power gets stronger every day."

"Freezing someone isn't necessarily fun." Rarity glanced at her hands. "Why am I so different?"

"It's your differences that will matter to our kind, Rarity. I know it." Severide takes her hand, and he exhales, the air a frozen cloud.

I take Ru's hand as we start walking to the library, passing a few people who are human from the waist up but have hooves for feet pass and I can't help but stare. Ru tugs on my hand, nodding her head in another direction towards a man with tentacles, throwing us for a loop. He holds a book in each one as he walks.

Seeing all these different creatures makes me realize just how much I don't know about the universe.

"Whoa." Maven stretches her head back, and there are a countless number of floors.

It's chaos, and yet it's quiet. Small, little things with opal-colored wings fly above us, inserting books in the right spots on the correct floors. While they are rushing, magic itself is tossing books from left to right.

"Do you have a membership?" A harmonic, smooth question has us all spinning, and a man with expansive leather wings is sitting behind the counter, legs crossed, reading a book. Never once does he look up. "You can only enter if you have a membership."

"And how do we get one of those?" I ask, annoyed that

we need a membership to get books. Books are to be read, not to hold hostage.

The winged menace sighs, licking his finger before flipping the page. "You must prick your finger on the needle, but it must be the one that holds the most power. If you are late with your returns, the library shall absorb that magic you sacrificed to borrow the book and will not return it."

Maven takes a step forward and presses her finger against the long, sharp needle. Blood swirls and trickles around it until it bursts into flames, her and Alpha's crescent sealing on the desk. An M and a W intertwine with roses and vines.

The winged man behind the desk finally removes his eyes from the book when the small explosion happens. His glowing orange irises are as round as a full moon. "I never thought I'd live the day to meet a Wildes in person. Forgive me for my rudeness." He stares at Maven as if she's royalty. "Can I help you with anything? Anything? Anything at all?"

"I'm Maven," she holds out her hand. "I'm the coven witch for the Monreaux's and we've got a ragtag coven. One of our werewolves has fallen ill."

My heart purges when I see the pity on his face. "I'm so sorry to hear that. I've seen what happens when a werewolf is sick... It's awful." He walks around the desk and takes her hand, giving it a small shake. "I'm Tyslen. It's a pleasure to meet you."

"This speak of pleasure and service is starting to piss me off," Alexander grumbles. "She is with my children. My beloved." Alexander bares his fangs, and Tyslen lifts a brow.

"Oh, that is not what he meant. Stop it." Maven elbows her beloved in the gut. "Don't mind him. In my grimoire, it says there is a book that lists all the ingredients necessary to help treat the illness in a werewolf. I also would like a book on all the creatures, rare ones too."

"Maybe we can figure out what I am."

"That's the goal, Dottie." Maven gives her a small smile.

"Sure. I know exactly what book you're talking about. It's been ages since someone has retrieved it. It's in the mythical section."

"I'm sorry, what?" I blurt. "Why?"

"Well," Tyslen bounces from foot to foot. "The book has never proved the potions work. They are fairytales."

"That's a joke, right? You see what you're surrounded by," Dottie points to a stone that shatters, and a winged, fanged beast takes its place.

"Those are gargoyles. They help protect the magic within the library. A lot is held here. In the wrong hands, it could cause devastation. And I know it seems hard to believe that in our world we would have fiction too, but we do. And that book is considered fiction."

"Well, I'll take it. How long am I allowed to have it?" Maven asks.

"For you, Ms. Wildes? As long as you like." Tyslen's wings expand, and he flaps them, lifting into the air. "I'll bring it myself." He flies high, a tail whipping around him as he soars to the ceilings of the library.

"What is he?" Alastair watches Tyslen fly in awe.

"No idea, but hopefully the books will let us know what we need to. And then you and Ru can be on your way," Maven explains.

"No one else is coming?" I'm surprised. I figured everyone would jump at the chance.

Alexander has a moment of guilt cross his face. "I'm sorry, but it's too dangerous to send anyone with you. With you in your two-week bonding period, you will become more unstable, Anwyll. I can't risk the other members."

All this is because werewolves are a poison to everything and everyone around them. "I understand."

"I'll be packing you a ton of potions and easy spells to help defend yourself with. As for Ru, I'll make sure she's protected from you too."

"How?" Nothing can protect her from me, not when I'm dying of insanity.

"I'll be giving her a vial of wolfsbane. Not enough to kill you, but enough to subdue you."

I scrub my hands down my face. "Awesome." This adventure is sounding more like a death sentence.

Not just my death sentence, but Ru's too.

Chapter Thirteen
RU

Anwyll has been quiet ever since we left the library, and when we sit down in the conference room with all of the other coven members, he doesn't sit next to me. He sits across, close enough, but far enough away that I can't touch him. Even if I were to stretch my arms out along the table, I'd only reach halfway.

I know he is worried about hurting me. I see it every time we are caught in each other's eyes, but I know he won't.

He's afraid of his beast, but what he doesn't know is, there isn't anything I don't want him to do to me.

"Okay." Maven stands, flipping through her new books, smiling from ear to ear as she soaks in their magic and information. "Wow, so many different creatures. Those were fairies in the library flying above us. How exciting is that? Oh my gosh, so much to teach everyone and not enough time because we have to get Anwyll and Ru on the road." She closes one book with the flick of her wrist, sliding the potions book across the table. "Show me the potion to help werewolf sickness," she whispers, holding one hand over the book. The pages flip fast, stopping almost at the end of the book. "Okay, I'll need an entire vial of vampire tears, three heartsnow petals, three wolfsbane petals, three unicorn hairs, and one six-leaf clover. I didn't even know those existed. And then a drop of powerful blood. That must mean a witch's blood. So mine. Then we need an entire vial of blood from a werewolf overcome with sickness."

"Can you guys get that from Aziel while we are gone?" Anwyll asks, not taking his eyes off the table.

"We should be able to. Don't worry about that. Only focus on the unicorn hair, the clover, the wolfsbane, and the heartsnow."

"Okay, Alpha," he says, refusing to take one look at me.

"I don't want any potions or spells to protect me from Anwyll," I decide, speaking my truth.

Ha. That grabs his attention.

His talons scrape the conference table. "What do you mean? You have to have them. Tell her, Alpha. Maven, tell her she has to have them. She needs to be protected from me." Anwyll is frantic, his wolf pulsing at the surface to be set free.

"I can't, Anwyll. When it comes to protection potions between mates, it will only work if she wants it to. If she's refusing, it's like pouring gasoline on a fire. It won't work."

"Bullshit!" he roars, the word deepened by the anger of his beast. "You are fucking taking those potions with us, Ru. So help me, you're taking them."

I stand next, slamming my palms on the table. "I'm not taking shit, and you can't force me."

"I will kill you," he seethes.

"No you won't." I shake my head.

"Then you're a fool. I've killed children, Ru. I've killed women. I've killed hundreds. I'll kill you too."

"You won't," I whisper, my heart breaking at his admission. "You aren't that man. You were controlled—"

He picks up the chair and throws it across the room. The wood smashes on the wall and splinters fly. He growls, incisors lengthened, eyes glowing the same green as mine. I finally know why.

We're mates.

He's half-shifted, his breaths rough and ragged, a dangerous sound drilling in his throat.

"You don't scare me." I lift my chin and stare at my mate. "Stop trying to because you want to push me away."

He leaps onto the table, and Master Monreaux takes a step towards me, but I hold out my hand and shake my head.

"What are you going to do, Anwyll? You aren't sick. You aren't your brother. You won't kill me."

"I'm falling ill slowly." He hits his head with his fist. Anwyll falls to all fours, his body more beast than man as he walks over to me until we are nose to nose. "You have no idea what I'm capable of."

"And you have no idea how capable I am." I press my hand against his cheek. "My sweet wolf, My Gentle Giant, stop thinking you have to fight because it's all you've known."

His eyes blink, his lashes longer in this form, and his green eyes fade to normal. Anwyll slumps. "I don't know what's happening. I feel messy inside. I don't know if I can wait two weeks, Ru. I want you too much. And the longer we wait, the more violent I feel."

"You haven't had sex yet?" Reuel, the elf, has everyone looking his way.

"No." Anwyll blushes. "We have to wait for two weeks."

"No, that's when your souls will bind and your knot will lock inside her, but you need to be having sex. She needs your…" his eyes flicker around the room. "Does no one know this yet? I thought you went over werewolf sex 101 with him?"

"I did, but the book only says so much."

"This is about to get awkward." The beads of Reuel's hair clink together as he turns his head. "You've done other things?" He coughs.

Anwyll growls, placing his body in front of mine.

I rub his back. "Yes, we have."

"You didn't notice anything special about, you know." His eyes flicker down Anwyll, then back up at me.

"His size? I mean, he is fucking huge. I don't know how we will have sex."

"I don't like people knowing our private business," he hisses.

"It's okay. I don't mind. You were saying, Reuel?" I question the elf so we can get back on track.

"His come. It tingles, yes?"

"How do you know that?" I press a hand against my heated cheek, and a few of the vampires are smiling, some impressed, some curious.

"I was raised in a werewolf family. I know things books don't. You need his come. Other werewolves sometimes get more time than two weeks. In those two weeks, you need as much of his…you know…as possible. The tingling, that's to relax your muscles, to prepare you, to adapt your body so when the time comes, no pun intended"—he snickers at his own joke—"it won't hurt because when that full moon comes, he will be more beast than animal. You'll need to run because werewolves love the chase, and it won't be sweet. It will be rough—"

"—Animalistic?" I finish for him, my clit throbbing, wanting these two weeks to hurry up.

"Definitely."

Anwyll's wolf nearly purrs learning this, and when his brown eyes meet mine, they turn clover green, the fangs dripping with saliva.

"He'll bite you."

Flashes of him tearing out my neck come to mind, and the idea turns me on.

"You'll run."

I imagine the lick of the leaves stinging my arms as I try to outrun a predator.

"He'll catch you. They always do."

His humanoid hands toss me on the forest floor.

"He'll pin you down."

Anwyll will force my face into the floor and drive into me, causing me to cry out into the night.

"And he will ravage you for days, for nights, until his beast knows his seed has taken."

"Seed? Taken?" I ask, trying to focus, but Anwyll is right in front of me, hungry.

"You won't be able to get pregnant until you mate," Reuel says in a 'duh' tone. "The mating always results in pregnancy. That's what the knot is for. Every three months, you'll go into heat, and you'll trigger his rut."

"And he can tell when...its taken?"

"They can smell it. You'll be pregnant for three months. And you'll need his come during the pregnancy to prepare for the birth. Werewolf babies are big."

"Jesus, this place reeks of lust." Finnick opens a window, pressing a hand against his erection.

"You're lame, Finnick. This sounds fucking hot." Luca holds up his thumbs. "Anyway, can you give us more details? This is crazy." The smile on his face makes me giggle.

Maven is waving her hand across her face, her hair billowing from the small breeze she's creating.

"You want to be hunted, My Beloved?" Master places a hand on her stomach. "I'll hunt you. I'll fucking devour you, Maven. You know it."

"Didn't mean to cause everyone to get hot and bothered, but you need to know everything. Every day that passes, your need for each other will grow to extremes. He will kill for you, and don't take his warnings lightly; if he isn't in his right mind, he will kill you too. I've seen a werewolf rip out his heart. It's... devastating to see a powerful, beautiful creature succumb to heartache like that because that's what it is—heartache."

"I still don't want the spells or potions. Give us weapons to protect ourselves, a way for us to have fire—"

"Yeah, my fire-making abilities are on the fritz ever since I got pregnant. I can't even light a candle, so you guys are on your own with fire. I'm sorry."

"It's okay, Maven. I don't expect you to be able to do everything for us."

She pouts. "I do."

Dottie stands and closes her eyes, a charge of electricity surrounds her, and her beast comes to life, exorcising out of her. In unison, they lift their arms and swirl them around themselves, yellow, gold, and orange sparking. Thunder rolls next, lightning cracks, but there is no flash, only Dottie becomes brighter, then the color is gone, and Dottie returns back to normal with her animal cocooned around her.

"What was that?" I ask her.

"I thought I could do something, make something for your travels, I think, but I'm not strong enough. It's like my creature only wants to come out sometimes." She exhales, stressed. "I don't know."

"It's okay. Like I said, we don't need anyone making anything for us or going out of their way or getting upset with their creature, but thank you for trying."

"What are you?" Drayce asks, taking Dottie's hand in his, and the creature doesn't flinch, but forms around Drayce, bringing him into her bubble. "You're amazing." His eyes flash like lightning just before the creature vanishes.

"I wish I knew. I don't feel amazing. I'm something really annoying right now," she mumbles in frustration.

"You're something else." Drayce is in awe, unable to take his eyes off her. "Not annoying, but wondrous." The Viking vampire sounds like he's spellbound.

"Something..." she echoes, a crooked frown curling her lips. "Maybe the books say something?"

"I'll read up on it, Dottie. I promise you, I'm going to do everything I can to give you answers."

"You're perfect how you are." Drayce rubs a hand on her shoulder, and Dottie shuts her eyes, enjoying his touch.

"But what if I'm a bomb waiting to go off? We need to know what I am. For the coven."

"Let's tackle one issue at a time. Anwyll. Ru. You'll leave first thing tomorrow," Master Monreaux announces— his red-tinted eyes commanding. Maven is glued to his side, and he rubs his chest where their mating mark is.

Oh, I suppose it is feeding time?

Everyone leaves, and Anwyll kisses my forehead. "I'm going to see my brother before we leave. Don't come down to look for me, okay? I can't risk your life near him."

"I promise. I'll meet you in the bedroom."

His eyes heat and those damn irises swirl with green; that naughty wolf is itching to mate me.

Rarity takes my hand with her cold one, but it doesn't take my breath away this time. "They aren't done, but I'll slip them in your bag in the morning. Just teas. Something for you to enjoy out there."

"Thank you, Rarity." I wrap my arms around her cold frame and squeeze.

"He'll come around. You'll see." She touches my cheek slightly, my worry frozen all of a sudden. "Sorry. I can't seem to control whatever the hell is wrong with me."

"Nothing is wrong with you."

She doesn't seem too sure. "Be careful, okay? And take care of him. Dottie is right. He's a hurricane. A lightning storm. He was born an alpha, Ru. He's dying to break free."

"I know. I get glimpses. Healing is a process, though, not a race. He'll get there."

"And you are the process, Ru. Don't doubt how strong you are when it comes to him." She rubs my shoulder and leaves me alone in the room, leaving me with thoughts that do not make sense.

I'm dependent on Anwyll's come, and I could die on this journey.

How do those two things make sense together?

They don't.

Chapter Fourteen

ANWYLL

Too much has happened in the last twenty-four hours. I can't seem to keep up. I'm tired. My eyes can barely stay open, but out of everything I just learned in that room, the only thing my wolf is latching onto is giving our mate our come, preparing her for the full moon.

Stumbling from the image, I slam my shoulder against the wall, plagued with dreams of drenching her in what she needs to take me.

To take us.

I growl low in my throat, wanting to march up the steps and take her.

What would I know about pleasing her?

The fucking doubt is driving me insane. My growl echoes through the tunnel, and I throw my fist into the wall. The rock crumbles as I sag against it, my shoulders rising and falling, my nails digging into the cement.

I need leverage.

Something to stop me from going upstairs.

"I smell her on you."

My brother's voice has me turning my head to the left in the dark, the flame of the torch down the hall.

"She smells good, brother. She smells of another world. Is there magic in her veins? Ah, yes, she's a leprechaun, right? Do you get lucky, brother?" He laughs, the twisted and sardonic kind that leaves traces wherever it is heard.

Marching down the dark tunnel, my claws unsheathe, growing longer than usual from my brother talking about my mate in such a crude manner.

Only I can talk about my mate like that.

To my mate.

In bed.

With my tongue or cock buried inside her.

Before I can think, I'm sprinting, turning the corner, and launching myself at Aziel, slamming him against the wall. The charmed silver bracelet touches my skin, and the smell of burning flesh should cause me to yank my arm away, but I don't, I'm too irate.

"You dare speak of her that way?" My arm is choking his throat, lying straight across it. His Adam's apple bobs, and his black eyes are pits of nothing.

The sickness is stronger than it was yesterday.

"You haven't even mated her yet." He snaps his fangs together. "Can't fuck a woman the right way if you never have." He pushes me off him, his skin a sickly gray color. "I'm going to break her just like I should have broken you." The tips of his fingers started turning black the other day, and the color has only gotten worse. The color has seeped into his veins and traveled up his fingers.

"Too late for that." I cock my fist back and slam it into him, knocking him out cold. He slumps against the wall, head sagging to the side, but his chest is rising and falling evenly—his breathing is normal.

There's that.

"I'll be leaving with my mate in the morning to travel the dimensions for you, for your madness. My mate is risking her life, *for you*. I am risking my life *for you*." I squat down, my elbows on my knees, and stare at my brother. I remember when he was strong and happy.

The man before me... I don't know him.

My brother is gone.

"I love you. I'll be back. It will work, Aziel. I swear it will work." If it doesn't, I have no idea what I will do.

Ru and I have until tomorrow morning before our lives change forever. I inhale as I walk down the tunnel, and I freeze, the scent of Ru invading my lungs. The bond she and I share is new but strong, and even from the catacombs, I scent her sadness.

I only want her to smell of happiness, a field of dandelions, but in doing that, it means giving in.

Giving her the one thing, I don't know how to give.

How the hell can I trap a good woman to me?

A monster.

That kind of life isn't fair to her, but she deserves to live. She's trapped either way.

Either she lives with me, or she dies by my hand.

I stumble against the wall, my shoulder scraping the ancient cement, when I hear her cry. My wolf snarls at me, swiping his claws beneath my chest to try and punish me for my actions.

It's my fault she's crying.

Pressing my forehead against the wall, the harsh rock slightly scratches my skin, and I listen to her soft tears become sobs. I focus in, following the sound to my bedroom. The bond between us allows me to see images of her, and she's burying her face in my pillow. Rarity and

Maven are there, trying to console her, and I cringe when I feel their anger.

And it's directed at me.

"It's okay, Ru. He'll come around."

"He won't," she says through the haze. *"I should just go home. Back to my planet. He doesn't need me. He doesn't want me."*

My werewolf whines, and a tear escapes, sliding down the curve of my cheek. The thought of her leaving is like a double-barreled shotgun right to my heart, creating a gaping hole in my chest.

Maybe I can try happiness. I can learn to deserve it, right? Even if I believe I don't, I can try. For Ru.

Because she deserves happiness.

My bones crack as I bring the half-shift forward, my claws growing black and sharp. I fall to my hands and sprint, using my strength to jump from wall to wall, my nails leaving grooves behind as I rush to my mate.

The tunnels are dark, the only light is the pulsing gold coming from the black roses lining the wall. My vision sharpens, and everything is enhanced in a green glow, the same green as my mate's eyes.

One of the many ways I will change for my soul to become one with Ru's.

When I make it to the basement door, not only is Rarity standing there, but Maven, Dottie, Luna, Amberella, and Tala are flanking her.

Arms crossed.

Amberella and Tala have their fangs out.

Dottie's creature is large and tall, surrounding her as if she's ready to pounce.

Maven's fingers wiggle, and vines wrap around me, no

roses, just thick thorned vines that pierce the surface of my skin.

I don't bother fighting it. Maven will overpower me. I'll take their anger and welcome it because it's deserved.

"You'll fix this, Anwyll." A vine wraps around my throat. "You'll fix it because you deserve her." It's Rarity that's speaking while Maven is threatening to tighten the vines. "She deserves more from you too, and you deserve more from yourself. For yourself. Do you know how amazing Ru is? She is here from another planet. She crossed dimensions for you. She heard you, Anwyll."

"What are you talking about?" I struggle to speak through the vines.

"She heard you. Your howl. You know that. From the portal. She risked her life for you because she heard your pain. Her heart knew the sound of her mate, and she came here to find you. She has done nothing but help and show her strength but don't take that as she isn't a damn mess inside, Anwyll because she is, and only you can fix that."

"She's a beautiful soul," Amberella states, her voice soothing with an edge of another time, sophisticated and lethal. "That's my gift, Anwyll. I can see souls, their intentions, their pain, their goodness, and she's pure through and through." Amberella places her hand on my chest, a pinkish glow pulsing from where we connect. "And you are too, no matter how much you've convinced yourself you aren't."

The vines loosen from my neck and start to unwind from the rest of my body. I focus on Ru. She sniffles into the pillow, the blankets swishing and bunching as she curls her legs. Her fingers curl and Ru presses her fist against her heart as if applying pressure will help it hurt less.

As if the open wound I've caused will stop bleeding.

"I need to talk to Reuel," I say to the angry, protective, and scary— I'd be an idiot if I didn't think a fae, a witch, whatever Dottie is, and two vampires weren't— women standing in front of me. "Rarity, will you come with me?"

She takes my hand and squeezes, the cold touch stealing my breath. "Of course."

"I'm going to see Ru. I'll make it right," I vow to them. "I need her too." I need to be a better man, a stronger man for Ru. Hiding behind fear is so easy when the terrors of this world is all I know.

The screen door opens with a creak, and I follow Rarity outside, where Reuel is clipping orange flowers that are randomly growing where Maven's grandpa died.

"Isn't this amazing? I haven't seen sunset magnolias since I was a teenager. These are amazing to create instant travel powder for someone who can't pop in and out as I can." He's smiling as he only trims the ones pulsing a glowing orange. "Smell one," he offers, lifting a flower from his sitting position.

What's the harm?

I gently take it from him, marveling at this flower that I have never seen before. It's gorgeous. The petals are wide and in the middle, an orange dust permeates like clouds. In my thirty years, I don't think I've ever seen a flower quite like this.

Inhaling, I open my lungs, taking in as much of the sweet scent as possible. The magnolia smells of Ru— rain and salt, like the ocean on a stormy day.

"Whatever scent you smell is the scent that gives you the best memories and feelings. This magnolia brings out hidden loves and interests people forget about until they are reminded of a scent that made them the happiest they have ever been. Interesting for a flower, isn't it? Such a small thing but it holds so much power."

"But why are they growing here where her grandpa died?" Rarity asks.

"Where magic dies, magic grows," Reuel states, holding the flower to the sun. "These can also be used for a protective barrier. For instance, Maven has a barrier casted to the city limits of Salem. Anyone who crosses that barrier will forget they met us, and they will forget anything about paranormal creatures. They might be superstitious, but the locals don't know we actually exist. We want to remain in the dark. Humans have a tendency to destroy what they don't know. But I have a feeling you didn't come to me to talk about this flower, which, by the way, if you put this in tea, can be used to make werewolves drunk."

"We can't get drunk," I snort, liking I know so much more about werewolves than Reuel does. "Our bodies burn off the alcohol. We run too hot."

"But your bodies can't digest this flower. You become dizzy and disoriented. If you are ever in a place where you have enemies, I'd watch whatever they give you. Anyway —" he wipes the dirt on his pants and stands "—How can I help you, Anwyll?"

I blush and stare at the ground. "When you said Ru and I could have sex—"

"Yes?" He tilts his head, pinching his lips to the side to hide a grin.

"It won't mate us? Do I bite her? I don't know…" I rub my hand over my face, stressed with wanting to make sure I know what to do or what to expect from my beast.

"No, it won't mate you. You need to have sex within this two-week window. I explained why before. You won't bite her until the full moon. Then, after the full moon, you can mate her whenever you want. Her body will be yours, then. Prepared and used to you. Think of this two-week window as a safety net for her. Your werewolf knows she isn't ready. So it's his way of protecting her."

A sarcastic chuckle escapes me. "Well, I guess there is a first for everything."

Reuel stands in front of me, his white eyes circled in black rings, staring into my soul. "Do not be ashamed of your wolf. You don't want him to turn against you."

I rub the back of my neck, kneading the muscle. "Rarity, can you freeze my bad memories?"

"I haven't done it before. The orc let go of my hand before it could happen. I don't even know what to do."

"Please," I beg her. "They stop me every time. To move forward with Ru, I need this."

"I don't know how long it will last," she warns, offering me her hand. "I can't promise anything."

"I know." Without hesitation, I grip her slender hand and hold my breath as I watch ice travel up my arm, freezing my veins. I shiver.

My teeth clink together, and my breath comes out in frozen puffs. The chill sweeps across my chest, and I stretch my neck back, trying to get away from the migrating ice, but it's too late.

It reaches my mind and dives in, freezing the memories that have plagued me my entire life.

I have to do this.

For Ru.

For me.

I won't go on this trip and be the reason I've put her in more danger.

I feel the moment the most painful memory freezes. There's a weight lifted from me.

"There," Rarity says, her tone curious and unsure. She's watching me, waiting for something bad to happen. "How do you feel?"

The ice recedes from my veins, taking the cold with it.

"I haven't felt this good in fifteen years," I croak, the relief stinging my eyes as I try to control the peace I feel. Not that it's deserved, but Ru deserves the best of me, and I can't give her that without help. "Thank you." I hug Rarity tight. "Thank you so much."

"Be careful. I don't know what happens."

I lift my head when I hear Ru move. The curtain to the upstairs bedroom is swaying back and forth, but no one is standing there.

Shit.

I let go of Rarity and run, taking three steps at a time. When I get to the bedroom, she's sitting on the edge of the bed.

Calm.

Collected.

But I sense it, the hurt, the pain, the rage.

"Do you have feelings for Rarity? Is that why you don't want me?" She lifts her neon green irises, water pooling in the corners. "Am I so bad?"

My werewolf growls at me, then whines, finding the deepest part of me he can, and leaving me alone to clean up the mess I've made.

"No. No, Ru. Never. Rarity is my friend, that's it. I swear." I kneel on the floor and tilt her chin up. "I had her freeze my bad memories because I wanted to have a good night with you."

"You *are* like a hurricane. I don't know what to do with you, Anwyll. You confuse me." She buries her face in her hands and shakes her head slowly, back and forth.

The night just took a turn for the worse, I'm afraid.

Standing, I slam my hand on my chest, the burning twisting and churning around my heart, and the tears sting my eyes. "And you think I know what to do with you? You make me mad, but you make me mad in all the ways that revive me."

"What are you talking about?" Her voice is a timid whisper in the room, her big, clover eyes round with the innocence that only not knowing love brings.

I'd know.

I shut my eyes and exhale a deep, haunted breath. "You say I am a hurricane, why?"

Her chest heaves, the attempt to find her words exerting. Ru's eyes dart up and down my body before landing on my face, and her hand mimics mine, only her fingers curl into her palm as she rests it against her heart.

"You are a hurricane because of the emotions you bring out inside me. They are swirling and causing havoc in my mind, in my heart, things I'm meant to believe are real while going my entire life not knowing it was true."

"And what is this 'it' you talk about?" I push, taking a step forward, needing to be in her space, needing the air she has breathed so I can say I've experienced her.

"Love, the kind written in books and people wish for on stars. Love that is supposed to last forever. Love that declares me your mate and you mine. I didn't know love like that existed so easily. Why is it so easy?"

And that's where I have to correct her. This time, I let the tears fall, the warm drops heating my cold cheeks as I dare to invade her space more. "Easy? Finding love, no matter your species, is not easy. Finding a mate is one in a million, one that I never thought would happen for me. Love is not easy for us, it is born, it is made. What makes love possible is that our souls are tethered, allowing love to bloom— effortlessly, but that doesn't mean it doesn't take effort."

I take her hand in mine and blow out a breath, placing her delicate, feminine hand against my chest. My heart thumps loudly, and my beast purrs from the simple touch. "You say I'm a hurricane, but do you know what you are to me?" I close my eyes, another round of tears gathering along my lashes. "You are the gentle waves after the destruction of the tsunamis that plague me every night, that destroys me every night, monsoons that reap reminders of my true nature, and then there is you— the gust of wind that changes the direction of the storms inside me."

"Anwyll—"

"It would make sense that I was your hurricane because all I've ever done is bring destruction." I drop her hand and step away. "I would be a bad mate if I didn't spare you of that."

She sinks her nails into my arm as I turn away, gripping me with such force, my skin breaks. "You think you're a hurricane because you are destroying me?" She invades my space this time, pressing her body against mine while cupping my jaw with her hands, her fingers skimming my cheekbones. "You are a force, yes, ripping everything I thought I knew to shreds, but you're bringing change. You make me feel... alive. You—" She chuckles slightly with a shake of her head. "You are rebuilding my soul on a fresh foundation, and while it is scary and unknown, and maybe I won't construct how I feel about you right all the time, I do know I love you. Even the tsunamis that stain your beautiful..." Her brow furrows, sadness bringing a frown to her smile "...innocent, sweet, and tender heart. A part of you is cursed, but I'll give up my chance at luck every day to find a way to break it."

She wipes a tear away, and I nestle my palm in her hand, wanting to bury myself in the comfort she brings my werewolf. "You'd do that? Your luck is everything."

"I'm starting to realize that maybe there are more things in life than luck."

Chapter Fifteen
RU

After an unexpected burst of emotion, Anwyll and I are left staring at one another, and I feel progress between us. He's in this. No more running away from me. No more hiding. If we are going to face fear, we are going to do it together.

I glance at the clock, noticing it's just past midnight.

"Twelve more days until the full moon. What do you think will happen?" I ask him as he kneels between my legs while I sit on the edge of the bed. His eyes are shut, and there's a small, relieved smile playing on his lips as if he's having a good dream while leaning into my touch. I'm stroking his cheek, and a purr fills the room.

I roll my lips to keep my giggle inside. I didn't think werewolves could purr, but I do not want to ruin the moment. He's so content. Whatever Rarity did, truly worked.

"I don't know, but the thought has my beast wanting to break free." The words deepen as he speaks, and he clears his throat with a shake of his head. "God, the thought—" his nails lengthen to steel and his fingers dig into my thighs, tearing the material from my thighs to my ankle "—makes me want you."

I glide my fingers from his cheek to the defined edge of his jaw, then press it under his chin to lift his head. "Undress me, then."

His shoulders rise and fall, and I watch in wonderment when he begins to half shift, his features becoming bigger, sharper, and his shirt tears from the muscles bulging.

"With your talons," I add, leaning back on my hands to watch his eyes dilate.

"I don't want to hurt you."

"With. Your. Talons. Anwyll," I repeat, clipped and stern.

With a sneer, he slashes his hands through the air, the long fingers dancing furiously over his shirt I'm wearing. I moan, the material tearing and showing more of my skin.

He growls when he watches my breasts appear as the shirt falls to pieces on the bed. His eyes glow the familiar shade of green, and he licks his lips when I'm left naked in front of him.

"Are you going to fill me with your come, or are you just going to stare at me all day?" I ask daringly, rubbing my hands over his rock-solid shoulders. I spread my legs, and his eyes drop to my pussy. "Remember, Anwyll, I need it," I tease him, keeping my voice level and filled with seduction.

He stands, towering over me, and I drag my eyes slowly up his body, memorizing every line and defined muscle. Anwyll's thighs are thick like tree trunks, and his arms are branches I want wrapped around me. He yanks off the tattered clothes torn from his shift and tosses them on the floor, standing in all his fucking glory in front of me.

"I always want to give you what you need."

I wrap my hand around his cock, and he hisses, flexing

his hips, which causes the skin to pull back in my fist, revealing a wide, light pink crown.

"Don't come until I tell you to. Control yourself, My Gentle Giant." The words are whispers, gusts of a warm breeze over his slit. A bead of precome gathers, and I flatten my tongue, licking it clean and hum when the tingle dances over my taste buds. "I can't wait to know how you taste."

"You can't say things like that! You can't say—" he pulls out of my grasp and squeezes his cock so hard the head nearly turns purple "—So embarrassed."

"I love that my touch does that to you." I hold out my hand and bend my fingers in a come-hither motion. "Now come here and put your fat cock in my hand again. I want you to come, but you will wait until I say. Understood, Anwyll?"

He nods, walking over to me again, and places the heavy weight in my palm. So fucking big and long. I have no idea how I'll take him, but I'll trust Fate to know what she's doing.

"Good Boy, Anwyll. I love it when you listen to me," I praise him, and the stress melts away from his body. His cock is leaking all over my forearm, and I drag my fingers up the vein before circling them around the base.

They can't touch.

"Fuck," he growls. I lift my eyes to see him watching me, those neon greens showing me his werewolf.

I love it.

"Fuck what, good boy?" I ask, wanting to hear his words. "Tell me." I trace the crown of his cock with my tongue, the glands sensitive from never feeling attention like I'm giving him.

That's so fucking hot to me. I love that I'm his first. In every single way. My pussy weeps from how turned on I am, and all I want to do is throw him on the bed, straddle him, and fuck him into the sunset, but he deserves better than that.

He deserves someone to show him care and attention. He deserves to feel good.

"Your hands on me, your fingers can't touch, and it looks so fucking good. Your tongue, I've never felt anything like it. I'm already so close. You make me feel things I've never felt," he barely manages to say between breaths.

"It looks so good because you're so big." I stroke him up and down, wrapping my lips around the flared head and moan, giving him a good tug at the base while I try to suck him down.

"Don't say things like that—" he moans, flexing his hips, and his cock slides further. "Fuck, don't say things like that."

I pull away, dragging my lips across the sensitive, hard shaft. "Oh, but you are. So big. The biggest I've ever seen." I dip down to lick up the impressive length again, using one hand to cradle his sack. He whimpers, his body trembling from me.

"Ru," he warns, his hands fisting my hair, and the sharp nails of his talons pinch my scalp.

I would chuckle, but I decide to suck him down a few more inches until he gags me. I can't even take half of him, so I use my other hand to stroke him from the base, and squeeze the knot, wishing it was full and inflated.

But it won't be for another twelve days.

I can't wait to experience it.

Spit drips down my chin as I look up through my lashes, and his fangs surpass his bottom lip, his fur bursts over his body, and his eyes narrow at me, his control hanging on by a thread.

"That's it, my mate, take my cock." His werewolf makes himself known. "You take it so well. I want to fuck your face and pour my come down your little fucking throat," he snarls.

I moan, and Anwyll shakes his head, the fur receding from his body and his eyes changing to golden cinnamon again.

He won't let his wolf have control.

We'll have to change that.

I continue my efforts, sucking his cock by hollowing my cheeks.

"Ru, I'm close. I'm so close. Please, don't stop. Don't stop. Please, let me come," he begs, and it hits me then that it isn't the entire being of Anwyll that is submissive.

His wolf is alpha and wants to come out, but his human form is submissive.

And to have two different emotions swirling inside you at all times must feel like a rollercoaster ride.

I don't want to torture him too much tonight. I drag my teeth gently down the width of his stalk. "Come," I order him. "Fill my mouth, Anwyll. Let me taste you."

"Ru. Ru. Ru! Damn it." His hands grip my face, his nails daring to pierce my skin, and he thrusts his hips, planting his cock as far as he can. I have to watch him. The muscles in his neck protrude, the tendons tense, and he tosses his head back; the magnitude of his roar causes my ears to ring.

His come hits my tongue. It's hot and thick, but sweet as sugar with a slight saltiness to it. It tingles, and my throat relaxes, opening wide as I easily drink him down. I can feel the effects of his come when I swallow, then it settles in my stomach, a warmth spreading all over my body.

Slipping his cock free from my mouth, I lick my lips.

"Look at you. You're still so hard, my sweet wolf." I praise him, wanting him to know how impressed I am with his stamina. "You listened to me. You controlled yourself. You're such a good boy." I kiss down his shaft and give his full sack a good squeeze.

His knees buckle, and there's a part of me that's a little shocked at our dynamic and how easily it comes to me. I've never been like this with anyone before. It comes so naturally with Anwyll, like my soul knows I'm giving him what he needs.

I scoot up the bed and spread my legs. "Come here, Anwyll. Unless you don't want to, then we won't."

His Adam's apple bobs, and he lazily strokes himself as he stares at me, his eyes sliding up and down my body. The way he looks at me makes me feel like a masterpiece, a canvas, a precious piece of art he has never seen. I love the way he looks at me.

"I don't want to disappoint you," he whispers, a shifted hand grasping my ankle, and his talons bite into my skin. "I never want to disappoint you."

"You could never," I gasp at his admission and sit up, pressing a hand to his chest. He holds so much power, so much strength, but so much kindness. "Everything we do in this room could never disappoint me." I wrap a hand around his cock and squeeze. "We are experiencing new things. Your firsts. That's special to me." I tighten my grip until the head turns a deep shade of red. I pull away and slap his cock, not easy, but hard, and he gasps, then groans. "Tell me you won't disappoint me, Anwyll." I give him another slap, his cock bobbing and leaving a trail of milky precome on his thigh.

"Ru," he whines.

I slap his balls next. "Does that hurt?"

"Yes."

"Do you want more?"

"Yes." He nods eagerly.

I slap him again.

And again.

His sack now red from the abuse, and his cock leaking profusely.

"I told you what I wanted," I tsk, bringing my hand down hard once more, and he grunts.

"I won't disappoint you, My Lucky Charm," he says.

"And why?" *Slap.* A stream of come jets from his slit and hits me in the chest, but then his fists clench together and he growls, controlling himself. "Oh, good boy," I praise him for not coming again.

"Want to save it. I want to come inside you," he struggles to say through broken breaths.

I lean back and he crawls over me, his entire body covered in a sheen of sweat. As he drapes over me, his werewolf peers at me from behind his eyes, the green a faint hue in Anwyll's iris.

My mate captures my lips in a hot, slow kiss, one that has his palms gently cupping my jaw, his tongue wrapping around mine before thrusting harder. His control slips, and he moans, pressing his weight against me, his cock at my entrance. I wrap my legs around his hips, and his elbows drop to either side of my head.

He presses forward so slowly, the thick crown stretching me. That growl I love so much vibrates between us, and I moan when he fills me inch by inch.

I'm soaked for him, needy, my pussy aching for his cock. My nails dig into his shoulders, the skin breaking the further he gets.

"You feel so fucking good. So wet. So fucking tight. Fuck, can't believe you're mine."

His praising me has my body on fire, and I whimper, biting my lip into my mouth, and when he is pressed to the hilt, both of us groan.

Nothing. No one has ever felt this good. I already feel like I'm flying, and he hasn't even moved.

"Ru?" He kisses down my neck, wrapping his massive arms around my back to hug me to his chest. "What do you like? What do you want? Tell me what you want from me." He bites along my collarbone with his blunt teeth.

"Anything you do. Just move, My Gentle Giant. Move," I beg him, licking up his neck and moaning when he slides out.

"Oh fuck." The words sound like a sob as if he can't believe how good it feels. "Oh fuck, Ru. Oh, damn it. I'm not going to last. You feel so good. I never thought—I never thought it would feel like this."

"It doesn't. This feeling is just between mates." I arch my back when he thrusts in, his pace growing faster the more confident he becomes.

This time, his eyes aren't faint, but bright, a neon clover that could light up the sky. His incisors lengthen, and I raise my hand, my fingers brushing down the weapons. He shudders, his talons digging into my thigh before yanking them apart, his eyes riveted to where we are connected.

The V sculpted in his hips deepens as he slides in and out. "Look at my mate," he growls, his half-shifted form growing larger as his werewolf comes out to play. "Taking my cock so well. You should see it, Ru. You should see how you take us. My cock is so big, stretching your perfect pink pussy."

I tweak my nipples, whimpering when he drives in so hard the bed moves across the floor.

His hair becomes thicker, muscles wider, cheeks sharper, and when he looks at me, he sneers. "Fucking perfect. My perfect mate. I'm going to fill you up with so much come, you'll drip of me."

"Not yet you won't." I snap at the wolf.

He chuckles and bends down, biting the air, and his fangs clink together. "Not a chance." They gather my legs and place them on those wide shoulders, slamming into me so hard, I can't help the loud erotic sounds escaping me.

He sneers, dragging his talons over my breasts, and one digs in a little deeper. "Mine," the werewolf appreciates his work, and I cry out when the claw slices into me. "All mine." His hot tongue lashes across the skin, sealing the wound. When I look down, Anwyll's name is written in scratchy letters above my heart. "All fucking mine!" he roars, pulling out of me and gripping me by my hips. "You'll fucking take anything I give you. You're a fucking slut for my cock, aren't you?"

I'm shocked when I hear him. By the sound of his voice, the deep gravel, I know I'm getting fucked by a beast.

"Aren't you?" he nearly howls. His talons scrape my scalp as he yanks me to my knees. "Aren't. You?" A tremor vibrates my ear in warning.

"For you. I love your big werewolf cock, Anwyll."

"Mmmm," he moans, satisfied with my answer. He slams his cock back into my weeping hole.

Our skin slaps together, the claps between us coming faster as he picks up speed. He tosses me down on the bed again, straightening my legs, and fucks into me again. I hold onto the edge of the mattress for dear life, my orgasm building to a dangerous level.

This isn't easy or gentle like I thought it would be.

When he grips me, it's hard and punishing with all his strength. When he slides his cock into me, it's with purpose and drive. And when his teeth ghost on the flesh of my shoulder, I know nothing about fucking a beast is delicate.

His growls, sneers, and snarls, all fill the room.

The bed breaks. Half on the floor, half on the frame, forcing Anwyll to slide out of me again. He grips my ankle and drags me off the bed. His other hand grips my hair and slams me against the wall. Then his long claws dig into my ass, lifting me until my legs wrap around him.

He plunges into me again, his knot unable to form, but I hold on tight while he ruins me for anyone else.

"Anwyll! Oh, don't stop. I'm so close."

"You'll come on my cock, My Lucky Charm." Our eyes meet, and the green fades to a rich brown. My sweet, innocent man is fucking me now.

In the blink of an eye, it's like getting fucked by two different beings.

My eyes roll to the back of my head, my mouth falling open, my fingers gripping at the muscles flexing in his back.

"Anwyll, Anwyll..." tears brim my eyes when my orgasm washes over me, from the tips of my toes to my fingers, I feel the buzz, the way my body is owned now. "Yes! Oh, chauns, yes. Just like that. So good, your cock is so good. Yes, more." I rock my hips, like a real slut, just like he said, wanting every single inch of him inside me, and that's when I wish his knot would inflate.

Is this what it is like? To be starved for him, to wish he could lock himself inside me forever?

With one last thrust, he wraps his arms around me again, twists us, and falls onto the broken bed. His beast makes one last appearance, something between a mixture of a growl and a howl, but it's deadly, primitive, a sound that shakes the house and my body, creating another orgasm to hit me.

I clutch his cock, milking the long length with my muscles as they spasm.

"Fuck, take my cock. Your pussy is ruined now, isn't it? Ruined for anyone else. You're my mate." He grips my chin and stares, his golden amber eyes penetrating mine. He plants his feet on the ground, every thrust trying to get deeper, and he groans, filling me with his come.

"Oh my chauns." I slap my hands on the bed when the tingling heats and spreads through my womb, my clit, everything feels it. "I'm going to come again. Oh my chauns!" I whimper, gripping his arm with all my strength and toss my head back, crying out at how good it feels.

With every spasm, his come swims further, relaxing every muscle in my body.

He continues to rock into me, every jet leaving him, he thrusts, syncing his momentum with his come, wanting it as deep as possible.

If our first time is like this, I can't imagine how it will be under the full moon.

"Ru..." he drops his forehead to the middle of my chest, and his lips press against my sternum. He continues to kiss down my body as he pulls out of me. He is so long, it takes longer than the ordinary man, and I feel him drip out of me.

His eyes flash green and he gathers his come from my thigh, pushing it back in. "Mmm, all mine. Under the moon, I'll be stuffing you every second, not letting a drop go to waste. You'll be pregnant by the end of the night. I wish it could happen now. I want to see you round with our child."

With a shake of his head, the beast is gone, and Anwyll is back, rubbing his come into my skin.

"Need you to smell like you're mine."

"I am yours, Anwyll. I'm all yours."

His lashes are sticking together from sweat, and his chest heaves with exertion. His cock lies half-hard against his thigh.

He smiles as if something switches inside him, then he sees his name on my chest, scarred over by his saliva.

I wait for him to freak out, but I stroke his name lovingly, showing him I like what he did.

"You are mine, aren't you?"

"For all the moons, Anwyll."

Chapter Sixteen

ANWYLL

Last night was the best experience of my life. I realize how cliché that sounds. Every teenage boy probably says that after their first time, but I finally got to experience *that* night, and I get to say that I had the best fucking night in my entire life.

And that means more than any other person's experience.

For fifteen years, I had my choices taken from me, and last night was a passage I should have had before I reached this age.

As I stare at Ru sleeping, her peaceful face and plump lips, her lashes shadowing the tops of her cheeks, I realize I'm glad it didn't happen before her.

All those bad times, those horrible memories I have, dying for peace year after year, I finally have it.

I got to experience peace last night.

Ru is my peace.

My long-awaited salvation, I begged for in the corners of my mind, in the darkness of my soul, I was trapped in, and she's my light.

After all those years without hope, I know what hope feels like again.

"Damn. You made a mess in here. Looks like you're going to need a steel bedframe to keep up with all of your... enthusiasm," Luca teases, leaning against the doorframe.

"Luca! What the fuck—" I make sure Ru is covered. I'm not. My ass is hanging out.

"Just checking to see if you're alive. So much growling and howling, moaning and screaming last night, I had to make sure." He whistles when he sees the marks on my back. "Good for you, Anwyll. I tease, but I'm happy for you. Today is the day. Your Alpha wanted me to wake you up so you can get started on your journey. While you're gone, I'll prep your bedroom for werewolf sex." He winks at me, and I smother a shy smile in Ru's shoulder.

I know my werewolf came out to play last night, as if I could hold him back, from Ru, but I like that he took control.

Luca leaves, and I kiss Ru's cheek. "Wake up, Ru. We have to get ready to leave." I shuck the blanket off her body, and my eyes round when I see all the marks covering her flawless skin.

Scratches.

Bruises.

My name is carved above her heart. Is that normal?

"Don't panic. Don't freak out." Ru sits up and touches every spot. "I love it. I love every single mark because you let go with me last night, and it was... it was perfect. Don't ruin it, Anwyll. I'm perfect. I feel amazing." She touches my name my werewolf carved into her chest, and she smiles. "And I'm happy to have something marking me as yours."

I hope when we mate, she heals; if not, I'm truly afraid I'll kill her when the moon is at its highest.

She looks around the room, and her eyes widen. "Oh, wow. We broke the bed."

I stand and stretch, my back popping as I twist and turn. "And the wall." I help her to her feet, and her tits bounce, causing my cock to stir. "We don't have time," I groan, wanting nothing more than to slide into her again.

And again.

And again.

I have so many years to make up for.

"Come on, let's shower, but don't get any ideas." She shakes her fingers at me. "We have responsibilities."

With reluctance and a very hard cock I'm trying to control, we shower. It's so hard to focus when her sleek body is wet and her nipples are hard, but I manage to control myself, though not without my wolf huffing and puffing, which makes Ru giggle.

We get dressed and pack, slinging two bags over our shoulders. Then we head down the steps and into the kitchen.

Ru steps over Whiskey as he sleeps in the middle of the entrance to the kitchen. An owl hoots, and she looks out the window to see him perched on a branch, staring straight at us. "Look at that," she says in wonderment.

"That owl is always hanging around," Alpha states.

"Here." Maven thrusts another bag at us, and she wipes her eyes of tears. "Don't mind me. I haven't been able to stop crying since the sun rose. I charmed the bag. It has a ton of stuff in it. Food, water, supplies, potions for enemies, books on creatures, everything," she begins to sob. "The sword Dottie left is in there."

"It's in there?" I open the bag, and Ru peeks in.

Looks like a normal bag to me.

"The potions I used are in there. Ingredients list for the

one you need for Aziel. Spells won't work for you because you aren't a witch. Rarity tossed in some teas. I—"

"—Beloved. Relax." Alpha soothes his mate, wrapping her in his arms as she weeps. "They will be okay. We will see them soon."

She nods, giving us a watery smile.

"I've made travel powder. It can't take you into another dimension, but if you're in a bad position, use it," Reuel informs.

"I don't want to say goodbye," Ru says. "No hugs. I just want to wave and say see you later because I won't be able to handle anything else."

I wrap my arm around my mate, almost telling her she didn't have to go, but nearly everything we need is on her home planet, and we have to be together. Our bond depends on it. I already feel closer to her than I did yesterday after last night. Reuel was right.

Bonding for my werewolf is important. He is calmer today, even... happy.

"Go to the portal and Ru, touch the water with your fingertips, it will open and take you where you want to go," Maven explains, clinging to my Alpha's side.

I look around and bow my head. "I am forever grateful to be a part of this coven. You are my pack. Thank you for taking care of me and my brother."

"He'll be safe with us. I promise," Alexander says. "Now go before you lose daylight." He clears his throat and coughs.

I hide a smile, not wanting him to notice I see him getting emotional. I hear when a Master loses a coven member, he can feel it. I just hope if anything happens to me, it's different for him, and he doesn't.

I open the side door, the one connecting the kitchen and the porch, allowing Ru to go through first. Giving one last wave, I walk out, but Rarity stops me, her cold touch pausing me mid-step.

"How do you feel?" She keeps her voice lowered.

"Like a new man. Thank you." I pull her in for a hug, not wanting to leave her. She's become my best friend. "I'll see you soon." I let her go, backing away. Ru is standing in front of the sunflower fields, the green stalks towering over her, and the large yellow petals cast shadows.

She looks beautiful.

My own sunflower in a field that's been dead for far too long.

"Remember, I don't know how long it will last, so be careful, and take care of one another. And promise me you'll come home."

"I promise. I have luck on my side." I glance at Ru. Her hands are gripping her backpack, and she is trying to reach a sunflower that's five feet taller than she is. I have no idea what will happen to us, but I'll give my life to protect hers.

"You can always come home if things get too difficult."

I narrow my eyes and take a step away, rolling my lips together. "That's not an option. My brother needs this. I don't care what it takes."

"Even if it takes your life?"

I raise my voice. "Especially if it takes my life!" My yell echoes across the acres, and the owl hoots again, flying over my head. "Rarity— I'm sorry. I didn't mean to yell." I pinch the bridge of my nose and exhale. "My brother risked his life for me. He protected me. He is sick because of me. I'm doing this. If it means Ru comes back alone, then that is what it means."

An opal-hued tear falls down her cheek, the life-saving drop quickly wiped away.

"Don't waste your tears on me." I wipe one away. "They are too precious."

"You better not die. I'll kill you if you do. Your soul would have to exist somewhere. I'd find it and torture you."

I grin and chuckle as I back away to head toward my mate. "I wouldn't expect anything less." Spinning on my heel, I clear my throat of all emotion, and Ru reaches a hand out.

Eagerly, I take it.

"Ready?" she asks on a deep breath.

"With you? Always." We walk by the sunflower field, the air chilly, stalks and leaves rubbing together as the breeze blows by.

I take lead, knowing these woods like the back of my hand since I've patrolled them so much. The coven will be at risk now during the day. I hope everyone remains safe. My heart aches at the thought of anything happening to them. I won't be able to live with knowing they got injured because I wasn't here.

"How long do you think we will be gone?" Ru asks, a twig snapping under her borrowed boot.

"I want to say not long, but neither of us has ever done this before. We don't know where to go, so we might be gone longer than we want to be."

"If I had my luck, we'd be better off."

We stop in the middle of the woods, the air damper the closer we get to the cove. I grab her shoulders and dip my head as I look her in the eyes. "I don't care if you never get your luck, Ru. Ever. You're mine. With or without it."

"I want to help." She takes a step forward, telling me

silently she doesn't want to stand around and talk, so I follow her.

I'd follow her anywhere.

"I want to do more. I want to be useful like Maven is, like Rarity is, like they all are. Here I am with the ability to have luck. I'm useless."

"You aren't useless. Not to me. Don't ever talk about yourself like that again. You're everything. Do you realize that? Do you know how much power you hold when it comes to me?" I invade her space, my heart thumping in anger that for one second she thought she was useless. "I'm a werewolf, Ru. I'm strong, fast, and deadly." I close my eyes and inhale, her scent stronger than the wet leaves and dirt. She's so sweet. "But without you, I'd be like my brother right now, barely hanging on to reality. Without you, I'd die. If anything happened to you, I'd die. Do you get it? Do you understand how strong you are? I wouldn't exist without you, Ru. You do that, luck or not." I bend down and kiss her lips, a soft purr in my chest as our mouths meet. "Don't let me hear you talk like that again."

"Okay," she agrees, the word soft and sweet.

We begin walking again, and every time I look at her, she looks away, cheeks pinking from being caught, and I can't help but smile.

I think...we're flirting.

Now I blush.

I rub a hand over my face. I need to get it together.

But then she glances those big, glowing green eyes at me and those barely pointy ears, and I lose it all over again. She's so fucking gorgeous.

Moving skinny branches out of the way with my arm, Ru dips her head and pauses at the edge of the cove.

"Fuck," I curse when I let go of the damn twigs and they slap me across the face. I rub my cheek, grumbling as I stomp through the brush.

Ru giggles. "We might run into a monster, and you're already bitching about a tiny little branch?"

"That branch has thorns."

"And the next one could have claws," she teases.

I unsheathe mine with a quick flick. "Like this?"

She slaps my hand away. "Show off." Ru looks around, readjusting her backpack. "It's nice here. It's relaxing."

"I hate it." I'll always hate it. No one will ever know what it was like to find their mate floating.

Dead.

"This cove nearly took you from me. I'll never forgive it for that."

"That's where you're wrong." She crouches down and dips her finger in the water, the still blackness rippling until a swirling vortex twirls in the middle. "This cove brought me to you."

I growl under my breath. "Semantics." Staring into the abyss, I wrap an arm around her waist and pull her to me. "And now we have to go down there again. You won't be alone this time. I won't let you go."

She turns to me, wrapping her slender arms around my waist, tight, almost taking my breath, and she swallows. Ru's nervous.

Sliding my arms around her, I lock them behind her back, holding her to me as tight as possible. There's no space between us. Shoulder to shoulder, chest to chest, thigh to thigh.

No way am I letting her slip through my fingers.

"On the count of three," I say. "And remember, you need to think of your home planet."

She squeezes her eyes shut to the point her nose wrinkles. "Okay. Yeah, I'm thinking of it."

I kiss her forehead and take a deep breath. "One."

"Two," she says next.

"Three."

Chapter Seventeen
RU

I groan from landing with such a hard thud. It knocked the breath right out of me. That experience was not like floating to the library.

This was like a rollercoaster, and when we hit, we hit hard.

Anwyll landed first, holding me tight and never letting go, not even when we hit the beach.

I push off his chest, placing my hand on the side of my head when my vision swims, the moons blinding me in the eyes.

"Are you okay?" Anwyll plucks something off my face.

A seashell.

I rub the indentations in my skin the shell left. "Are you?" I question him, rubbing his chest and arms to make sure nothing is broken. "You hit first."

"I'm a werewolf. I heal." He pops his neck and groans. "Why didn't we float?" The cut on his arm begins to stitch together, and I gasp, rubbing the faded pink scar with my fingers.

He's amazing.

"I don't know." I wince when I try to turn my head. "But I wish we did. Maybe it's because Maven was with us last time."

"My god, if it feels like that every time, dimensional hopping is off my 'things to do' list." He helps me stand as the small waves crashing against our shoes.

I inhale the air, the sweet taste of sugar on the back of my tongue. I forgot how much I missed it here. It's such a beautiful place to be. So different than Salem. Don't get me wrong, it was gorgeous there, but nothing beats the colors here.

"The ocean is pink." Anwyll dips his hand into the sea. "And it smells... sweet?"

The look of wonderment in his eyes makes me giddy for some reason. I can't wait to show him my home. He's excited. While the mission is important, it doesn't mean we can't enjoy things along the way, right?

He lifts his fingers to his mouth and tastes the water dripping down. "It tastes like cotton candy. What is this place?"

I don't know what cotton candy is, but it must be sweet. "Welcome to my home planet, My Gentle Giant. This is Àdh." I spread out my arms with a smile, leaning my head back to feel the light of the three moons on my face. Unlike Earth, where they have the sun, and it's hot and bright, the moons here provide light and warmth during the day, but at night, keep the sea at bay.

Anwyll stands, staring up at the sky, and his jaw drops when he sees the moons. "There are three, and the sky is green! It's green, Ru! What? Oh my god, this is so fucking cool." He whips his head back and forth, smiling from ear to ear. "Yeah, this is so much cooler than my planet."

"We can explore later. The first person we need to see is Mannix. He must be worried sick about me."

"Who is Mannix?" The primal element of his tone tells me it's his beast coming forward.

I turn to look at him, his glowing green eyes matching mine as he half shifts.

"Who is he?" he snarls, taking a large step towards me, the seashells crunching under his feet. His hand snakes around my neck, and he yanks me to his body. He tilts and turns his head as he glares at me; the moonlight catches the sharp edges of his cheekbones. "You. Are. Ours. Mine." He bites the air, and his fangs clink together.

Anwyll presses his lips against mine until I can feel the bumps of his fangs behind his mouth as he kisses me. His wide tongue pushes forward and owns my mouth, snarling and growling every time he deepens the kiss, controlling the movements.

"Mine," he snaps, then drags me to the nearest tree coverage.

"Anwyll? What... what are you doing? We have places to go!" The breath is knocked out of my lungs when he slams me against a tree. I can hear the waves of the sea crashing just behind us where the cove is. In between the spaces of the leaves, I see civilization.

If someone focuses enough, they could see us.

Maybe.

Anwyll yanks the backpack off my shoulders and tosses it on the ground.

"Anwyll? What is your—" He tugs my pants down next, unbuttons his jeans, and gives himself enough space so he can free his massive cock.

"Be quiet, mate. Unless you want to get us in trouble."

His clawed hand covers my mouth, and the other dives between my legs.

What the hell is happening?

"You think you can introduce me to another male?" He rubs his deadly talon along my seam and pulls it away, humming when he sees I'm wet for him.

I'm always wet for him.

"You think you can get away from us?" he speaks of him and Anwyll as if they are two different beings, but one at the same time. It confuses me, but I understand too.

He pushes his body against mine until I'm tight against the tree, and the bark scratches the sensitive flesh of my ass.

"You'll never be free of me. Of us." This must be the side of Anwyll that is buried. The possession, the dominance. I know it won't last long. Anwyll doesn't allow it to, but that's okay.

I can play the role of a submitting mate, or I can take control when he needs me to.

Whatever he wants.

I'm his for the taking.

I shake my head in disagreement, wanting to tell him that there isn't anyone else, but he takes that as me not wanting him.

Anwyll turns me around, and his hand cups the back of my head, shoving me against the tree as he forces my thighs apart.

Fuck yes, I love this.

He slams his long, big cock inside me in one full stroke, and I keen, my sounds muted by his hand.

"You're ours. You'll smell of us. No other male will touch you. They will know you're our mate. We waited so long. Never going to give you up." His voice becomes deeper, lost in his werewolf until gray fur sprouts along his arms, but then vanishes the next second. "Will kill anyone who threatens to take you from us."

I scream again, my orgasm approaching quick and fast. He hits that spot inside me every time he surges forward.

"Forever, you are ours. Not even death can or will take you away from us. You'll take our knot. Won't you? You'll take it and swell with our come." He moves quicker, our skin slapping faster as he picks up speed. He pulls my head back by my hair and looks down at me with shifted eyes. "You'll be a whore for our knot. Won't you? No other male will ever have you."

I nod the best way I can in this position, and his lips pull back, showing those long fangs, and he stares at my neck.

I know he wants to bite me, but he won't. Not until the full moon.

His name is a muffled shout under his palm as my orgasm explodes through my body. I clench around him, milking his humanoid cock with every spasm.

I love it when he loses control.

He growls, his teeth at my neck as he comes, his come splashing inside me, warm and tingly. My entire body relaxes, and my muscles become loose, and he takes advantage of it, shoving himself as far as he can, knowing it won't hurt me.

"Such a good mate," he praises, and I moan again, loving how the endearment makes me feel. He pulls out and his come follows, but not for long. Anwyll dips his fingers and pushes his come back inside me, the slick sounds erotic and forbidden in the small space of the woods. "Love how you look with our come dripping from you, but every drop needs to be inside you. Need you to smell of us, mate."

I moan when he pulls them free and forces the two fingers into my mouth. I choke and gag but lick him clean eagerly.

"Now, when you speak, they can smell your mate on your breath."

My eyes widen at the barbaric, caveman thought, but I love it. I want more of it.

But just as quickly as the alpha personality came, it disappears.

Anwyll tugs my pants up and buttons his, pushing his mouth down on mine in a slow kiss. Those brown eyes have a tint of shame, but he doesn't say a word.

"I liked it," I reassure him. "Oh, I liked it a lot, Anwyll. I would never fight you on a repeat. Ever."

He grins and tosses his head back to laugh. "Good, because I have a feeling it will happen again. "We don't like hearing about other males." His eyes flash green again, but his browns win control.

"Well, if you would have let me answer, you would have heard me say Mannix is gay, but he is my best friend, so I need to let him know I'm okay."

A bright red blush of embarrassment takes over his cheeks. "Oh."

I pick up the backpack and giggle, pausing at his cock, and give it a kiss over the jeans. "I really don't mind."

"You make us crazy, you know," Anwyll says, following me out of the wooded area and back onto the beach.

I march off the sand dune, the grains a pale green. "Why do you say 'us?' Why not just say 'me' when you're talking about the two of you?"

"I don't know. Not every werewolf is like that. I have a

disconnect with my wolf. So we are one in a sense but separate in another. Like we share the same body but can't connect our minds."

"Why? Is it because of what happened when you were spelled?"

He nods and stays quiet for a moment. I can't imagine how hard it is to live with all the horrible things he was forced to do. "Yeah, and honestly, it's more on me. He wants us to be one. I feel it, but I keep him at arm's length. I'm nervous about what will happen, I guess. No, I'm not nervous." He pauses in the middle of the sidewalk and sighs. "I'm terrified. I'm terrified if we became one again that I'd be a murderer again. I can't risk it."

I take his hand in mine and begin walking, crossing the street and passing the gas station I bought the scratch-off tickets from. O'Molly's smells amazing. I can smell the fresh bread even after we pass the front door.

"Well, maybe you weren't one when that warlock spelled you. You said you were separate. Like you could see everything, but you couldn't communicate, so maybe you don't want to be one because you can't remember what it's like? You're used to being separate."

"Maybe."

"What happened? When you were spelled?"

"I killed. That's the easiest way to put it, Ru. I don't want to talk about it, okay?"

"Maybe you blame him. Your wolf. That's why you have a disconnect."

"I don't blame him. I blame myself. I should have been able to stop it."

I grip his wrist and pull him to a stop. "You can't put that pressure on yourself. Magic is strong, Anwyll. You can't be mad at yourself for not being able to break a spell. Just imagine how your werewolf feels." I start walking again, but his hold on me stops me from taking two steps.

"What are you talking about?"

"Well, it was your wolf that killed, Anwyll. It can't be good for you guys to be separated like this. I bet he lives with guilt too. Imagine the life you could live if you stopped fighting with the other half of your soul." I place my hand on his heart, and he wraps his fingers around my forearm.

"I never thought of it like that, but make no mistake, he and I agree on one thing."

"And what's that?" I bite my lip, batting my eyelashes at my mate.

"You're ours." He tugs me close and slides his fingers up my neck until he runs them through my hair.

When we break apart, we are breathless, and his eyes are a dim green, his werewolf peeking through to be in the action too.

"Well, that's a step in the right direction, isn't it?" I fold my hands together behind his back and tilt my chin up so I can look at him.

He brushes his calloused fingers across my cheek. "I have a feeling you'll be helping me take many steps in the right direction, My Lucky Charm."

I love him a stupid amount that makes no sense for how quickly all this is happening.

"Watch it!"

Anwyll growls at the tone, and we stumble to the side to make room for the rude Luricawne Leprechaun.

Ugh, it's that asshole from the gas station.

"Oh, it's you. How are you doing, pretty? Ya know, I'm surprised to see you here. We had a funeral, thinking you died."

Anwyll lunges forward, but I keep a hand on his chest. "Don't," I warn. "They are real bastards."

My mate stares down at the leprechaun and curls a lip, showing a fang. The disgusting man takes a step back. "Well, if ya be needing any more of ya scratch-offs, you know where to find me. Good day," he says, taking off his black tattered top hat.

"See, when I picture a leprechaun, I picture someone like him."

"Yeah, there are different kinds." I push against his back to get him to start walking. "We need to get to Mannix. He thinks I'm dead. Oh my chauns, I can't believe I didn't come to him sooner. I feel terrible." I put my fingers in my mouth and blow, a high-pitched whistle echoing through the air.

A honk grabs my attention, and I look up to see a yellow taxi shooting down from the sky, a rainbow in its wake from the exhaust.

"Please don't tell me that's how rainbows are made," Anwyll says in horror when the taxi stops in front of us.

"Uh, is there another way?" I slide into the taxi and smile at the Northern Leprechaun driver. I'm glad. They are so nice. "I like your hat." It's pointed and high, but the only issue with Northern Leprechauns is they like to be upside down.

"On Earth, rainbows are a reflection of light and water."

I snort when I buckle my seatbelt. "Sounds nice, but it could just be from us. Rainbow Taxi service."

"I'll keep my delusions, thanks," Anwyll grumbles.

"Wher'to Miss?" The driver smiles, and a gold tooth shimmers in the rearview mirror.

"I need to go to 1001 Buckham South, please," I say, reaching over to buckle Anwyll in his seat. "You're going to want to hold on," I whisper, wrapping a hand around the gray handle above the door. "I suggest you do the same."

"Why?" he asks, keeping his hands in his lap.

"Here we go! Weee-heee!" the driver shouts, slamming his foot on the gas.

"Fuck!" Anwyll shouts as we soar into the sky. "You've got to be kidding me."

"Keep your hands up! We'goin' for a wee ride!" The driver jerks the wheel to the right and flips us until we are upside down.

Anwyll is yelling at the top of his lungs, and his claws are out, digging into the ceiling, and I can't help but laugh.

Chapter Eighteen

ANWYLL

I roll onto the ground, literally dropping from the car, and groan while holding my stomach.

"Thank you!" Ru scans her finger on a pad, and a ca-ching sound chimes.

"Thanks for the extra chauns, Miss!" And just like that, he shoots into the sky, leaving us in his rainbow wake.

"Are you okay?" Ru asks so sweetly, helping me onto my feet.

I sway. I'm a little dizzy. "How did you pay?

A lot dizzy.

Werewolves aren't made for leprechaun taxies.

Ya, my beast agrees. I feel him nodding in the back of my mind.

"It's kind of... like... magic? Our bank accounts are linked to our DNA. Anwyll, are you okay?"

I snort. I'm invincible. Doesn't she know that? "I'm fine. I'm good. I'm a werewolf. Nothing bothers me."

"I know. I didn't even think to warn you about Northern Leprechauns. They tend to be a little wild."

I wave her off and scoff. "No." I stumble and slam my shoulder against a beam. "I'm fine," I slur. "I'm good."

I'm not good. I'm five seconds away from throwing up, but I won't do that, not in front of my mate.

Who the fuck drives upside down? Who?

"What the hell is going on out here—" Someone shouts from the porch I just smashed against. "Ru? Oh my chauns —Ru? Is that…" their feet pound down the steps, and the sound makes my head hurt. "Is it you?"

"Hey, Mannix," Ru answers, staring at her friend with watery eyes. "I'm sorry. I'm so sorry."

Mannix runs and gives her a giant hug, holding her tight as he cries. Ru begins to cry too, but I can't really focus on them. The more I try, the more my vision sways. Stumbling again, I find a step and sit down, holding my head in my hands to wait for the dizziness to pass.

"You're alive. I can't believe you're alive. I went back for you. I went every day. I searched. No one believed me. They all said you got cast into the Unwanted Lands like your father, but I knew. I knew you didn't. I knew it." Her friend holds onto her tight, and I wait for my werewolf to do something out of rage and jealousy, but he doesn't move.

Hell, I think he might be dizzy too.

"I have so much to tell you, but can we do it inside?" Ru asks, then points to me. "This is my mate, Anwyll. And we took the Rainbow Taxi Service."

I hold out my hand to the Mannix on the left. "Hi."

"Aw, he's adorable. I'm over here, buddy." He takes my hand and shakes it. "What were you thinking having him take that taxi? No wonder his marbles are lost."

"So many of you, Mannix," I poke the space in front of me, thinking it's him, but it's just air.

"I guess werewolves don't travel upside down very well," she mumbles under her breath.

"A werewolf!" Mannix shouts, all three of him taking a step away from me.

"I'm tired." I manage to say just before my eyes roll to the back of my head and darkness sucks me under.

I groan when I wake up, noticing I'm lying on a couch in a house I don't recognize. Staring at the fan, I watch the blades for a moment as they rotate. Cool air relieves the sheen of sweat on my forehead, and I take a much needed breath until I can't fill my lungs anymore. In the distance, harsh whispers are spoken, but I can't decipher what is being said. Sitting up, I grunt and shake my head. What the hell happened?

The last thing I remember is that damn car ride.

My werewolf backs away in my mind and shakes his head. Is that big bastard afraid of a little taxi?

My hand holds my stomach when it rolls from the memory.

Yeah, I am afraid. Fuck that taxi.

"Don't worry, we are in agreement to never ride in those again," I talk to my werewolf and sound like a crazy person.

"You're awake." Ru skips into the room. I notice there are bags under her eyes from the lack of sleep. "I was getting worried."

"I'm fine." I bend down and press a quick kiss to her

lips. "I'm sorry. I've never felt that way before. Are you okay? You look tired, My Lucky Charm."

"I'm okay. I was just worried about you." She wraps her arms around me and sighs. "I should have warned you. I didn't even think it would affect your werewolf."

"Let's just not ever take that ride again, okay?"

She snickers, tilting her head back to look me in the eye. "You got it." She bends and presses a kiss in the middle of my chest, and my beast rumbles with delight.

I kiss the tip of her nose. "My beast really likes you," I blurt out of nowhere.

"Well, I like him too." Her hands drop lower and grip my ass. "A lot." The sexual meaning draws my wolf to the surface. I want to claim her right now. Right here.

"Did we make it to Mannix's?" Her scent surrounds me like a love spell, sucking me in and pulling me under. "Maybe we can sneak—"

But I'm interrupted. "—You did." The man in question walks into the room and hands me a bottle of pink water. "She caught me up on your plan. I'm sorry to hear about your brother. It's hard to believe any of this is real."

"Tell me about it. I just went on a leprechaun roller-coaster."

Mannix grins. "It doesn't bother us. Must be a werewolf thing." He chuckles, scratching the back of his head. "I can't believe you exist. She heard howling. I told her she was crazy, but she jumped in after you anyway. And now look, she's got a fated mate. That's... amazing."

"It is. It's rare." I pull her to my side, and my werewolf is content. He doesn't find Mannix threatening at all.

"Mannix said he would take us to the border of the Unwanted Lands, but we will be on our own after that."

"You're insane for going, but I understand. I just hope you understand the risks."

"We know them," I reply, rubbing small circles on Ru's back, then guide us to sit down. "I have to for my brother. I'm glad to do this on my own, but Ru and I have to be together—"

"So she says," Mannix wiggles his eyebrows. "11 days, well, 10 days now."

"10?" I question.

Ru exhales a large breath. "You were passed out for an entire day. We have 10 days until the full moon."

I slump against the couch and run my hand down my face. "I'm sorry."

"Don't be. It gave me time to catch up with Mannix and tell him our plan."

"Ya, so you're going to need valuables." Mannix stands and disappears into his room. He comes out a moment later with a tan bag in his hands. "You will need to make deals and trades with whatever lives on those lands. Just know I can't promise they won't take this and then try to kill you."

I open the bag to see silver and gold rings, necklaces, and earrings. "How did you get this?"

He blinks at me with a tilt of his head. "Every leprechaun has a goody bag." He pulls open a drawer and grabs a fistful of shells, emptying them into the tan bag too. "These are charmed with happiness. Maybe it will buy you some time with a grumpy creature."

Ru takes the bag from me and ties it, dropping it into the bag Maven gave us.

"I wish you didn't have to go," Mannix says. "I can't be here without you again, Ru. It's too hard. I hate it. When I had to bury you..."

"Mannix," Ru whispers, scooting to the edge of the couch.

Her best friend jumps to his feet and points his finger in her face, big tears cascading down his cheeks. "I had a funeral. A funeral! I buried you. Me." He slaps his chest. "My best friend. There wasn't even a body. No one came. No one but me, because I knew you weren't cast away to the Unwanted Lands. I thought you had drowned. I needed closure. I mourned you."

"It's only been a few days."

"You know how they are when a leprechaun goes missing. It's assumed you're in the Unwanted Lands. I had to bury you," he whispers sadly, slumping in his chair. "I can't lose you again. You aren't staying here, are you? You're going back?"

Ru takes his hand and rubs her fingers across his knuckles, and nods. "I am. That's my home now. You'd really like it there."

"In a coven of vampires?" He shivers, which makes me chuckle. "I don't know, but I'd like to go back with you. If I can." His eyes slide to mine, and I can see the permission he is asking me for without him actually asking for it.

"I don't think Alpha would mind," I say. "He likes that the coven is growing."

"Then I'll come with you on your adventure." Mannix begins the statement as if it's a great idea.

"No, Mannix—"

"No, hear me out. I can go with you. I can help. Maybe we can find everything faster, and then we can leave together."

"But your family—"

"—They hate me because I'm gay. You know you're the only family I have Ru. Just like I was yours."

I don't like how that sounds. Not because I'm jealous, but because he sounds so alone. "You're still her family. And if you're her family, then you're mine. I can't say it's a good idea for you to come. My werewolf...he's dangerous, and Ru and I need to have sex during the trip to make sure she's ready—"

He sticks out his neck, waiting for me to say the most important thing, and rolls his lips together, crossing his legs. "Ready for what, please, don't leave anything out."

"Uh—it's just not safe for anyone else to be around. It's best if it's just her and I."

"His come is magical and tingles and relaxes my muscles, so when we can mate in ten days, I can take his knot."

I give Mannix a tight and embarrassed smile. "That... that covers it." I look away from him as fast as I can. My cheeks hot.

"A knot." He glances between my legs. "Oh...*oh!*" he realizes what it is. "I see. That's amazing. Do you have any other brothers by any chance? The one with madness, is he gay?"

My laugh booms across the house. "No, sorry. He's straight."

"Well, I want a werewolf. Where do I find one?" Mannix pouts, crossing his arms in a huff.

I frown because the more I think about it, the more definite it becomes. "I don't know."

"Oh. That's right. I'm sorry. Ru told me. I should have known. I'm so sorry, Anwyll."

"Don't worry about it. I suggest you stay here though, okay? It isn't safe for you out there. We will come back for you, Mannix. I promise." I stand and pat his shoulder. I like him. He's brave, eager, and he cares for Ru.

But I can't have him on the journey.

When the moon is at its highest, if anyone or anything gets in my way, I'll kill them.

And I am already finding it hard to forgive myself for what happened when I was spelled, but if I killed Ru's best friend?

I'd stay in the Unwanted Lands and become the monster I've been trained to be.

"What if it isn't up to you? I want to come." Mannix stands in front of me, and I look down at him because he's so damn short. He lifts his chin and clears his throat. "I am useful. I can fool people into thinking they are happy. I can be a weapon. And I can give wishes, let's not forget that handy little trick."

An annoyed growl builds in my throat, and I bend down, letting my werewolf come to the surface. "You really want to know why?"

He gulps audibly.

"Anwyll," Ru clips my name, warning me not to say anything else.

"No, he needs to know." I grip his shirt, my nails shifting and tearing through the material, yet I don't smell any fear coming from Mannix. I lift him off his feet until he is eye level with me. "Because when the full moon comes and I have no control, anyone who gets in the way of me fucking Ru like the beast I am, will die. I will shred you to pieces. If I scent another male around, I'll go on a murder spree. I will have my claws drenched in your blood, and I won't fucking care. The night of the full moon is too important not just for me, but for Ru. She'll need me, and if you're there, your life will be meaningless. To me. To her."

I wish it wasn't like that because he could help me not lose control if my werewolf allowed it. The thought of having him around doesn't bother me, but I can't risk it on the full moon.

"I'd bathe in your blood, chew on your bones, and pick you from my fucking teeth all while filling Ru with my knot. Is that what you want to know? Is that what you needed? I'm a monster and monsters do monstrous things."

"Anwyll!" Ru scolds me, pulling at the hold that I have on Mannix.

"He asked. He wanted to know why he can't come. You think I like that? You think I like how I am? That I have to warn your friend away from me? I don't." I drop him onto the seat, and he is a bit pale, but not trembling, which makes me wonder what horrible things Mannix has had to deal with if he doesn't tremble in a werewolf's hold. "Nice house, by the way," I add out of nowhere as I head down the hall and enter the first spare bedroom I see, then slam the door.

The house *is* nice. It has high ceilings and big windows. I don't feel too big.

I slam my fist on the mattress and suffocate my face in it, screaming at the top of my lungs.

Her friend should come on the trip. Maybe then Ru would have a chance at surviving me.

That's all I want. With all my heart. With all my soul.

I want her to survive me.

Chapter Nineteen
RU

"Mannix, I can't—I don't even know what to say. I can't believe he did that to you." I'm furious. I understand why Anwyll said what he said, but it doesn't make it right. "I apologize. We will be gone first thing in the morning."

He frowns and rubs his eyes. "Don't worry about it. He must be really scared, Ru. I want you to be careful, okay? I'm going to be worried sick about you."

"I'll be okay." I give him a tight hug, almost crushing him. I can't think about the ifs of this journey. Something horrible can happen. I could die. Anwyll can die. I could never see Mannix again. I swallow the lump forming in my throat. "I missed you so much when I was on another planet, and I'm going to miss you even more than that while we are in the Unwanted Lands."

He squeezes me in return. "I missed you too, but I'm so glad you're alive." We stay like that for a few more seconds before he pulls away and wipes his eyes. "Okay, enough of that. Go." He juts his chin to the room Anwyll disappeared into. "Go. And I'll make my famous coffee in the morning."

I love his coffee. No one has been able to compare. Something about mixing happiness into every cup. It really works. I always feel happier after the first sip. "Goodnight, Mannix."

"Night, you lucky bitch." He snaps his fingers in the air as he walks away. "You'd better find me a damn werewolf. I want all filthy things for my charms."

"Ugh, gross. Go away!" I shout after him, giggling as I crack open the bedroom door. Anwyll is on his knees by the bed, elbows on the mattress, and he is holding his head in his hand as if he is living with regret.

His shirt is off, and his gorgeous back is on display, the muscles causing defined grooves, and the dip of his spine is pronounced in that position.

I happen to enjoy seeing him on his knees.

I want him to beg.

But I don't want him to beg for forgiveness.

Not tonight.

He's beautiful. A dark, misunderstood beauty who doesn't understand he is more than a violent shadow, but a sensitive, loving man.

Leaning against the door, I close it behind me, then lock it for good measure, and I stare at his kneeling form.

He rocks his head back and forth. "I'd never hurt him, not intentionally. It's why I warned him away."

I take my shirt off too, followed by my shoes, and pants until I'm left in my bra and underwear. "Come here," I whisper, gesturing with my fingers that he can't see.

He lifts his head and turns around, but goes to stand, and I stop him. With my palm out, I tsk. "On your knees, My Gentle Giant."

The fight in his eyes, the one that has his human side so

tired, disappears. An eerie glow fills his irises, his lovely wolf simmering at the surface, allowing me to play with them.

Maybe Anwyll's werewolf knows what he needs. Maybe he is closer to Anwyll than my mate thinks. It's only Anwyll causing the disconnection. Not his wolf.

He slides across the floor, the button of his jeans open. I can see the trimmed pubic hair settled above his cock, and my mouth waters.

"Don't come any closer. Put your arms behind your back, Anwyll."

He does as he is told and hangs his head. His shoulders are tight, his entire body tense, and every muscle is on display. Taking a step, I brush my fingers across his chest, trailing them around to his back as I circle him— and he relaxes.

His entire body goes pliant.

Taking my time, I slide my fingers down his impressive arm, the muscle cut and large.

By the time I'm standing in front of him, his cock is hard and has lengthened down his thigh, trapped in the fabric prison of his jeans.

"You were very rude to my friend." I slip off the straps of my bra, then reach behind my back to unclasp it. My breasts are freed, and the air circles my nipples, tightening them to small peaks. I toss the bra on the floor, right in front of Anwyll, and he raises those colorful irises. When he looks at me, he knee-walks closer, but I stop him again, a pained expression etched across his face.

"You don't get to enjoy me yet," I say, playing with the hem of my panties. "I want you to sit there, your cock aching as you watch me. Consider this punishment."

"Ru, please. I need to touch you."

"No." His entire body trembles from my refusal.

There's something very powerful about a werewolf kneeling at my feet.

I slip my panties down my thighs, never taking my eyes off Anwyll. His eyes go from a dull green to a neon clover, his fangs lengthen past his lips, and his body grows bigger.

Swaying my hips back and forth for a few steps, I twist my panties, then shove them against Anwyll's face. "Smell what you can't have, Gentle Giant. Scent what is yours, what you aren't allowed to taste due to your behavior."

A growl shakes the entire room, and Anwyll inhales. The material sticks to his face as he breathes in.

And then I yank them away, tossing them to the other side of the room.

He roars, a sound similar to a lion about to battle.

"You like the scent of what is yours, Anwyll?" My fingers trickle down the middle of my chest, down my stomach, and pause before dipping between my legs.

Anwyll licks his lips, his hands still behind his back. "We love how you smell, mate. It makes us crazy." His cheeks chisel to sharp edges and fur spreads down his jaw, those fangs pointed and ready to attack.

The rough, animalistic tone of his voice makes me drop my hand to my clit. I gasp at the initial touch. His hands fall to his sides, the nails digging into the wood, and his top lip curls as a continuous growl resonates in the room.

I feel it in the bones of my body, and I groan again, sliding my other hand between my legs. Making a show of it, I spread my thighs to give him a good look, and his fist hits the ground, chest heaving with ragged breaths.

Dipping two fingers inside me, I keen, stretching my body against the door when pleasure begins to curl my toes. One finger pays attention to the sensitive bundle of nerves while I fuck the others, thrusting faster and harder.

Anwyll's claws shred his jeans, cutting them into pieces until they are nothing but scraps on the floor. He's naked. His cock long and thick, the light pink tip glistening with precome. His palm reaches for the massive muscle, but I yank my fingers from my pussy, and slap his hand.

"Don't even think about it, Anwyll. Your cock is mine, and I'll do what I want with it. You are not to feel good right now. Not after you treated Mannix so badly."

"Mate, it hurts. Hurts not to touch you. We need relief," they beg, my man and my beast dying for more.

I gather his hair in my fist and yank his head back. "You'll get it, Gentle Giant. You'll get it when I say you get it. You're so tense today, aren't you? And stressed," I croon, slipping my pussy-slicked fingers between his lips so far he chokes.

He gags, but those gorgeous eyes, the irises that changed to match mine forever, burn brighter, and he moans, sucking and licking the juices from my skin. His incisors nick my fingertips, and I hiss, yanking it away from his mouth.

A constant, dark, menacing sound fills the room.

And it's coming from Anwyll.

"Look what you did," I tsk, watching the bead of blood gather before slipping down the length of my index finger. I grip his jaw and pry his mouth open, his fangs on the top and bottom shining from his spit, then I rub my finger across his tongue, his teeth, and his gums, and he moans.

Warmth hits me around my ankles, and when I look down, I watch his cock flex and creamy ropes of come leave his wide-flared cock.

He blinks at me, cocky and arrogant, but his hands are still behind his back.

I bend over, never taking my eyes from him, and wipe his come from my leg. It's already tingling my flesh. "I didn't say you could come, Anwyll."

The huff he exhales sounds shredded. "You taste so good, Our Lucky Charm. We felt you binding to us. Your blood merging with ours. We couldn't hold back."

I spread my legs again and bury my fingers to the knuckle, gasping, then whimpering when the tingling spreads. "Now you'll get to watch me fuck myself with your come inside me, and you won't get to join in."

He falls to his hands and knees, dragging those nails across the wooden floor, five grooves left forever. He tilts his chin up, nostrils flared, barely holding his control together as he watches, powerless, while I fuck myself with his come.

"I can't wait until the full moon. I can't wait until you really fill me up and knot me, locking your delicious come inside me." My entire body heats at the thought, a fever rushing through my soul, my veins pumping with desire, and with every second that passes, I become wetter, needier, but my fingers aren't enough.

I need more.

"Mate," he bites with a warning. "When I knot you, you're going to fucking feel me for days. I'll have to carry you everywhere. You won't be able to walk." He hangs his head, and his shoulder hunches. "Mate, please!" he yells savagely. "I want to tear you to pieces."

Taking what I need, I grip him by his hair, giving him a harsh tug when I shove his face between my legs. "Make me come, Anwyll. Be my good boy," I say. "But keep your hands behind your back. Let me use your tongue."

A soft whine escapes him, one of love and relief.

His wide tongue licks me from front to back, and he sneers when he tastes me, that control snapping at last. His fangs threaten to harm me, each scrape against my pussy causing me to inhale a sharp breath, wondering how it would feel if he bit me down there.

His tongue flicks and twists, gathering the honey he creates from me. I lift my leg onto his shoulder to give him better access, tossing my head back, his growl vibrates against my clit, and I choke from the lack of air.

"Anwyll, yes!" I shove his face against me harder, rocking my hips, diving his tongue deeper inside me. "Look at you." My fingers comb through his hair, and his lust-filled eyes lock onto mine, his mouth soaked. "You look so handsome feasting on me. You like the taste of my pussy? You like licking my depths?" He pulls his tongue free of me and licks the seam, latching onto my clit to suck the bud between his razor-sharp teeth.

"Fuck!" I scream, curling over him and scratching my nails down his back. My orgasm is right there, boiling beneath the surface of my skin. "You eat me so good, Anwyll. Don't stop. Don't. Stop." My entire body begins to tremble, and as I urge myself to tumble into the high only an orgasm can bring, my attention is stolen. I see his claws digging into his palms, and blood drips down his fingers, creating a small reflective puddle on the floor.

Yanking back to scold him, he bites me, not hard, but enough that I feel the pain. He licks the sting away, and that's all it takes for me. I burst, an aurora light-filled sky dancing above me, a hallucination only I can see. Greens, blues, pinks, a gorgeous painting only an orgasm with Anwyll can paint.

His chin becomes drenched, reflecting the light from the lamp in the corner of the room.

My body jerks from being oversensitive as he continues to lick, so I pull away, falling to my knees when the kaleidoscope of colors finally fades from my sight. Then I grab his arms and gently untangle his hands.

"Anwyll…" I gasp when I see marks from his nails. The wounds are deep and wide, blood tainting each nail. "Why? My Gentle Giant, I'm so sorry. I never want to bring you pain."

He's still breathing hard, lust swirling in his green eyes, and his cheeks covered in fur. "Pain reminds me to remain as human as possible," he says. "Pain keeps my beast at bay."

Right before my eyes, the blood reverts into his wound, and the skin closes, leaving no trace of his self-inflicted marks. With a feather-soft caress, I trace the lines on his palms, then move to the veins bulging in his arms, down his defined, lightly fur-covered chest, then circle each finger, one-by-one, around his cock.

"What of this beast?" I whisper, scooting closer to him. "How do you tame him?" I tease him, my lips ghosting over his, but I back away before he can kiss me.

The floor creaks as he shifts his weight. He wraps an arm around me and tugs me to his chest. My skin is sensitive from the orgasm—every part of me is—and the gray fur coating certain areas of his body teases me, a delicate tickle leaving me confused.

I don't know if I want to giggle or moan.

He looks so unique in this form. While half-shifted, he carries certain aspects of his human form and beast. The fangs are long, the eyes glow, the fur is soft, his muscles are bigger and firmer, and his skin holds a very light tint of grey.

It's almost hard to see, but it's there.

He's beautiful.

I touch his face, tracing the sculpted lines of the supernatural, and his eyes close, taking in my touch. He gasps when I give his beastly cock a squeeze at the base.

"Tell me"—I settle myself on his lap, the crown of his cock pushing against my entrance—"how do you tame this beast, Anwyll?? I slowly sink down, the thickness of him stealing my breath.

He circles a hand around my shoulder, pressing me to the hilt, and growls low, the submission gone.

I'm at his mercy.

"We fuck you."

He doesn't bother taking me to the bed. He fucks me right here on the hard, unforgiving floor, thrusting his hips using his wild, never-ending source of power. My tits bounce from every possessed stroke he gives.

Placing his hands on my hips, his claws bite into my skin, bouncing me on his cock. I hold my tits as they bounce from the force, teasing my nipples between my fingers. His attention stays entranced on his cock sawing in and out. That fucking growl that nearly makes me come every time I hear it is a constant in his chest, rattling his ribs as if it's wanting to be free from a cage.

In a way, it is.

And I want to free it.

I want to know what it's like when the beast finally gets his freedom.

"We hear your heart pounding. It's racing, mate." He licks up my chest, gathering the sweat shimmering on my body.

"You hear it?" I gasp, gripping his shoulders as I ride him, and he thrusts into me.

"We hear it, feel it, and we smell your lust." He rams himself to the hilt, and I cry out, the massive girth of him robbing me of my ability to breathe yet again.

"You...smell...me?" I stutter, leaning back as I relish in the ache he brings my cunt that I'll feel for days.

"Oh, mate," he grumbles low, his tone wicked and sinful. "We always smell you." His talons rake down my hips, almost breaking the skin. "Drives us crazy. We always want you. You're so sweet and delicious."

Our thighs slap together, and when I moan, he picks me up and races across the room, slamming me against the wall next to the window. He opens it, which I find odd when the cool air sheets my body as he manhandles my legs over his hips.

"You smell of honey, clover, and candy." He rams into me, and I slam the back of my head against the wall, but I want the pain. Each stroke, each grip of his talons, I'm reminded that I'm his.

And he mine.

"Scream for us. I want the entire planet to know you're mine."

That's why he opened the window?

The animal...

"No," I pant, holding onto him as he takes me on the ride of my life.

His hand circles my throat, the points of his nails sinking into my skin, a deadly grip that can easily kill me. "Yes," he growls, staring down at me as if I'm prey.

I lean forward. "Make me," I dare.

Snarling, he pulls out of me and flips me onto my stomach, pushing half my body out the window while keeping half my body inside, my feet on the ground. He slams into me again.

I do. I cry out. I scream. My voice echoes across the green sky. Gripping the windowsill, I press against him to match his pace.

"Anwyll!"

His teeth threaten my shoulder, and with one last thrust, he buries himself until I feel his heavy sack pressed against me, and there, at the base of his cock, the bump of his knot hitting against me.

It isn't swollen, but the promise that it will be one day soon sends me spiraling down into the emotions of my orgasm. My throat hurts, calling out his name into the night just like he wanted.

He roars, a deep guttural primal sound that has the hairs on my body standing up as it rolls across the entire planet.

His come warms me from the inside, tingling like it always does, only this time, I feel something open wider inside me. I groan, slumping against the window.

Let me hang here.

I'll be fine.

He drags me into the house again, lying us on the bed, and he kisses my shoulder. Anwyll pulls out of me, the long drag of his length rubbing all the right spots, and I moan, watching as his come spills from me.

Anwyll turns me around so I'm facing him and gently slides back in from the front. "I want to sleep with my cock inside you," he says.

I blush. That's another level of intimacy I've never experienced before. I brush a finger down his fangs, and his eyes flutter shut, a purr singing from his wolf.

When he opens those gorgeous eyes, the green retreats,

and his golden chocolates are staring back at me. Then, in something that should be considered a tale, I watch his beast vanish from his features, replaced with his human body.

"You're beautiful," I tell him, cupping his jaw with my hand. "A beautiful beast."

"Your beast," he says.

Aren't I lucky?

Chapter Twenty

ANWYLL

My body has only ever hurt after going on a killing spree, but waking up with my mate in my arms, my body aching from fucking her with everything I have to give, is a different kind of pain I want more of.

I turn my head and stare at Ru, pushing her hair out of her face so I can see her long lashes. She sighs, nestling her head against my shoulder while wrapping her arm around me.

So delicate, so fragile, yet her will is stronger than mine has ever been.

I want us to stay in this bed, wrapped up in blankets, losing count of the days and nights, until we don't know what month it is. We are safe here. We don't know what will happen when we get to the Unwanted Lands, as she calls them.

When will we have another night like this?

"Why are you thinking so loud?" Her words are groggy, but her eyes are still closed. She stretches, raising her arms above her head, and the covers drop below her breasts, her nipples bead, and I can't help the growl that escapes. She opens one eye and giggles when she catches me staring.

There's a bite mark on the underside where her tits curve deliciously and I can't wait until I can mark her permanently.

"You're going to have to wait." She swings her legs over the side of the bed, the marks from my nails on her shoulders where I clutched onto her as I rammed into her last night are red and irritated.

My beast is pleased.

Too pleased.

I yank her back by her hair and press her against the bed. My wolf takes her words as a challenge, and I keep her pinned. "Before we walk out these doors, you're going to suck my cock until you choke, My Lucky Charm."

Her lips form an 'O' and I let my fangs drop as I straddle her face, angling my cock toward her lips. "Suck me down your throat and fucking choke on it." I snarl, then clear my throat.

I'm not sure where that came from, but Ru listens. She sucks on the sensitive flesh of my sack first, licking one orb before moving to the other. My entire body bows, and I groan, falling onto my hands while she laps at me.

Her pussy is right in front of me, the lips pouty and swollen from the previous night. I bury my face between her legs and inhale, causing a rumble to shake my chest. She smells of my come, the lust still lingering from last night. Spreading her thighs, my tongue stretches out, circling around her clit, and her moan is muffled from being so full of me.

"What a way to wake up," I add before kissing her lips and diving my tongue into her sweet pot, groaning when I taste her.

This is going to be fast. I'm already on edge. I can feel the full moon already and it isn't for another nine days. I nip her clit, and she screams for me, the vibrations tickling the head of my cock.

I thrust into her mouth, every other stroke she gags and chokes, her hands gripping my ass.

Taking my fingers, I spread her pussy, wanting more access, learning every crevice her cunt has. I want to know every single thing about her body, so I always know how to please her.

"I want to make you come. Every fucking day. I want to taste it. I want to smell it. I want to fuck an orgasm out of you all day, every day." I slide a finger inside her sheath, and a groan, something mixed between pleasure and need fills the room. I can't tell if it's coming from her or me.

She's addicting and I dread when the nine days are up and the moon is full because the addiction will turn deadly. I'll hunt her. I'll chase her.

I won't stop until she's full of me.

If she says no, if she begs me to stop, it will be too late.

I can't be saved on a full moon.

And neither can she.

Her palms fondle my sack, rolling and squeezing my orbs that are full and aching.

Ru coughs around my cock when I thrust too far, hitting a spot inside her throat that causes her to gag.

Anyone else would find it disgusting how much I love hearing her struggle. I push my hips forward again, and a gathering of spit ruffles in the back of her throat as she chokes all over again.

Something about that...it's like she's reached inside and has shaken loose a volcano.

"That's it, Ru," I encourage her, needing her to know

how good she's making me feel. "Your mouth feels so good." Sliding another finger inside her, I pump in and out, precious little whimpers sound from her that the moon will be dying to hear when the mating night comes.

She chokes again, the muscles constricting my cock. Moving my hips, I shallowly thrust into her stretched mouth, her struggle burning my fucking blood. "That's it, Ru, fucking choke on my big cock, ruining your mouth for anyone else," my voice deepens with my wolf, my eyes shifting, and hair begins to sprout along my arms.

Unable to wait a second longer, I inhale a long breath and dive between her legs. I suck her clit into my mouth, rolling the sweet piece of candy between my lips while finger fucking her without forgiveness.

She shouts around my cock, her pussy clamping down on my fingers, wetness soaking me to my wrist as she comes. I hum in delight, loving how sweet she tastes, and I lap her up like a dog who needs water right out of the bowl.

My entire body ignites, and a growl vibrates the entire room as I flex my hips one more time, planting my cock so far into the back of her throat, she slaps my ass because she can't breathe. I fill her, coming in quick jets, and she has no choice but to swallow.

When I'm done, I carefully lift off her and spin around so I can get a good look at her face. Her cheeks are red, her lips are swollen and irritated, and there are tears streaming down her face. Spit and come dribble from the corners of her mouth and down her chin. Her breaths come in fast and heavy, and she whimpers, a smile playing on her lips.

My beast wants to clean her up. Combing my fingers through her hair, I grip the strands by the roots and lift her from the bed. My eyes roam her face in appreciation, my wolf too happy with the mess he's created on her face, and I bend down, licking my come and her spit, loving how good they taste together.

"Your wolf is close," she whispers when I pull away, her fingers gently rubbing down my temple, but it isn't horror she's staring at me with, it's love.

"You make us wild, Ru. You make me want to free him from the chains I've given him and let him take over. You make us unpredictable."

"I trust you, and I trust him. You're one and the same. You would never hurt me, Anwyll. I know that."

I stare at her with a mixture of disbelief and happiness, lifting her into my arms while wrapping myself around her, I kiss her passionately. I pour my love into her, hoping it fills every molecule of her being, so she never goes a day without knowing— without feeling— how much I love her.

I bring our kiss to an end and reply, "I wish I had the same faith."

"One day," she whispers as she pets my face. "You just wait and see."

I want to stay in this bed forever. I want to be wrapped up in her comfort, in her love, in the safety she brings to my scarred and wounded heart, but that would mean ignoring reality.

"Let's get going. We have a long road ahead of us," I say, not voicing how worried I am about what waits for us in the Unwanted Lands.

A knock on the door sounds. "Hey, you whores. I have coffee. It's strong because I was kept up all night by howling and moaning. You animals," Mannix chuckles. "Seriously, I need me one of those." The words drift off as he walks away.

"Oh chauns." Ru covers her face and laughs, which

causes her breasts to jiggle. "He will never let me live this down."

"I don't want him to. It makes me happy another male heard me claim you. It helps calm my wolf."

"Even if he is gay? Because Mannix is gay. Very gay."

"My wolf doesn't see that. He doesn't recognize that. He only cares that a male heard us."

"The window was open, you made sure of that. I'm sure the entire planet heard us."

A satisfied purr rumbles in my chest. "I hope so."

"Werewolves." She rolls her eyes and gets out of bed. "Such beasts."

I circle my arms around her and throw her back down, climbing on top of her until I am staring into her neon green eyes, so unique, so different. "You have no idea, My Lucky Charm." I kiss her cheek and finally let her go, watching as she disappears into the bathroom.

We both shower, separately, because I'm too on edge, and if I see her again, I'll take her. Over and over until she's sore and begging me to stop. If I feel like this now, I can only imagine how the full moon will feel.

With teasing glances, Ru giggles as she slips on her jeans, jumping into them because her ass barely fits inside them. "Stop looking at me like that," she giggles, tugging on a comfortable t-shirt that is nothing special. It's old, tattered, a faded red from being washed too many times, but it looks soft and reliable. I wonder if it holds any meaning.

She catches me staring, and she stares down at her shirt. "It was my dad's," she answers, tying the extra mate-rial in a knot by her hip since the shirt is a few sizes too big. "It's all I have of his, and I might not have seen him for years, and he might have been an ass most of the time, but I have good memories too before—" She swallows, swinging the bag Maven gave her over her shoulder. It still blows my mind all of the things we need for this trip are contained in that bag, along with the potions from Maven and the powder from Reuel. If anything happens to that bag, we'd be fucked.

"—You don't have to explain." I take her hand in mine and finally open the door, the scent of coffee slamming me in the face.

"Yes," Ru groans. "You haven't had good coffee until you've had Mannix's." This time, it's her pulling me to the kitchen, and Mannix is sitting at the kitchen table, looking like he didn't sleep at all while reading the newspaper.

He peeks over the top of the paper. "Well, look who decided to get out of bed. I don't blame you. If I had the big bad wolf rolling me around like a piece of meat, I wouldn't get out of bed either. Bitch," he grumbles at Ru when she walks by, and she chuckles, bending down to kiss him on the cheek.

"Aw, don't be mad." She sits down and grabs a piece of toast from the plate in the middle of the table.

"Not mad. Just stupid jealous." He places the newspaper down on the table. "Oh, look." He points to a section of the newspaper, and I rear back when the article comes to life in front of us.

"What is that?" I reach out and touch it; the image is made of an array of blue sparks.

"It's leprechaun magic, stud," Mannix says. "Makes reading so much more fun. Especially romance novels." He wiggles his brows, and I steer my gaze to Ru.

"Looks like you'll be reading to me at night before we go to sleep," I say, taking a seat at the table and piling the breakfast Mannix made onto a plate. Eggs, bacon, biscuits, grits, and it smells fantastic.

"We would never get to sleep." She sips on her coffee next, washing down the toast she ate.

"I would never get sleep. Think of me," Mannix says. "Anyway, look. A unicorn was killed at the border of the Unwanted Lands. Its blood drained. They have never left a unicorn so close before, Ru. Please, rethink this. It isn't easy to kill a unicorn, you know that."

"I know, but we have to. His brother needs—" Ru's eyes widen. "Oh my chauns." She tosses her toast on the plate. "We need to go. We need to hurry."

"Why?" Mannix asks.

But I'm scooping the rest of my breakfast down my throat because I'd be a cranky werewolf if I went about my day without it. I see the urgency in her eyes, and I get up to follow without question.

"Because six-leaf clovers grow in spilled unicorn blood, and we need those clovers. Remember in biology class, we learned about clovers and how they grow? It's significant because of how important the unicorns are to the ecosystem."

"I don't remember that." Her friend's brows bunch as he tries to remember.

"Probably because you were making moon eyes at Lox."

"He was hot." Mannix is unapologetic and grins. "That I do remember."

This time, I laugh, slapping Mannix on the shoulder, and it knocks the breath out of him. "You've been a great host, Mannix. Thank you for housing us for the night to allow us to rest before we go on this... adventure. When we come back, I promise, we will take you home with us to Salem."

He stands and stares at us, fear evident, but he doesn't voice his concerns again. We all know the danger. We all know what could await us in the Unwanted Lands. "Promise me you'll keep her safe," he says to me, desperation watering his eyes. "She's the most important person in my life."

I hold out my hand and he shakes it. "She is mine as well. She's my mate, Mannix. I know you don't understand just how important that is to a werewolf, but we live and breathe for our mates. I'll give my life to protect hers, I swear."

He walks us to the door, and Mannix tugs Ru into a hug. It's tight and long. He's holding onto her as if he never wants to let go. "I love you, Ru. Please, come back. We don't know the monsters that live in the Unwanted Lands. We only know of stories."

"I have my own monster to protect me. You don't need to worry," she says, kissing him on the cheek.

With a final goodbye, we step outside and begin our journey.

We don't take the taxi again because we can't afford the time it would take for Anwyll to recover, so we walk. Anwyll has his talons out the entire time, standing on the left side of me, so I'm not near the threat of traffic. He surveys our entire surroundings, ready to attack.

At dusk, we pass the old Wicker Farm, an abandoned property. It's a shame. It's a huge farmhouse with hills of green land, but it's too close to the border. No one wants to risk living in it, but the unicorns love it there. They have made the hills their home.

"Look," I point, stopping at the broken wooden fence. I lean against it, propping my foot on one of the rails. "A baby unicorn."

Anwyll wraps his arms around me, and we watch them graze. The baby is frolicking and kicking with happiness, a silver sheen to its young coat, and its horn is small, nothing but a knot on his head.

"He's so cute," I say with adoration. "How anyone would want to kill them is something I'll never understand."

"You said their blood gives luck, right? If the Unwanted Lands are anything like you say, then no one knows the difference between right and wrong. They are desperate. People do desperate things when they feel like they have no other options. It isn't okay. These creatures are beautiful. It's no wonder they are protected. Will they find the person who killed the unicorn?"

I take his hand in mine and begin walking down the unused dirt road. The weeds have overgrown the sides, creeping into the middle of the road from being so unused. "No, they won't. No one dares to cross into the Unwanted Lands territory. If it happens over there, it stays over there. It basically has its own set of laws."

"So no laws," he says, and a growl escapes him, filtering into the night, and the bushes jostle from animals being spooked.

"No laws," I repeat. "You fight to live, or you die."

Fur sprouts over his body, and his face contorts with his wolf before he gains control again, a vicious snarl curling his lip. He doesn't say anything, but the rage is evident. He walks quicker, staring down the empty path in front of us.

The further we walk, the thicker the trees become, the quieter our surroundings get, and the darker the skies become.

We stop at an old wooden bridge, and on the other side are the Unwanted Lands. So simple, so plain, but beyond that bridge holds a world of pain and suffering. The wood of the bridge creaks from the rushing water beneath it, and a heavy fog drifts on the other side.

A loud, blood-curdling screech echoes from somewhere in the Unwanted Lands, and it carries over to us.

A spine-tingling, constant growl comes from my right. When I look over, Anwyll has half-shifted. His skin is a light grey, and his eyes glow the brilliant shade of green that matches my own. He grows a few inches, and his muscles are bulging, but not enough for his shirt to rip. The long fangs peek from his lips, and he stares at the bridge, waiting for a threat to come.

I touch his arm, and he is snapped out of his trance.

"You won't walk in front of me. You will stay by my side. Do you understand?"

I gulp from the deep timbers of his wolf, edging his vocal cords. "I understand. I promise, Anwyll." Something catches my attention from the corner of my eye, and I do something I just said I wouldn't do and walk in front of him.

I guess listening will take some getting used to.

"Ru." He grips my arm as I crouch.

"Look." I point to the small cluster of clovers growing by the edge of the post that makes the bridge. The dirt is darkened from the blood, but the clovers are tall, sprouting six leaves as if they were flowers in bloom.

Anwyll bends down and plucks one from the ground, analyzing it by bringing it close to his face. He smells the plant and hands it to me. "I hate that a unicorn had to die to give us this, but I'll forever be grateful for his or her sacrifice. Do you have a container? We're taking all of it."

I open the bag and reach in, my arm disappearing as I fumble around. "I have no idea what I'm looking for. There is so much in here." With no luck, I poke my head in. "I only need a container or a jar." I straighten, and a small glass jar floats from the bag. "Wow," I say, tapping the jar lightly and it spins, catching the small amount of moonlight peeking through the clouds.

"I'll never get tired of seeing magic." Anwyll wraps his hand around the jar, careful as his talons clink against the glass. Opening the lid, he places the clover he plucked inside the jar, being extremely careful not to harm it. With his claws, he digs around the clover in the ground and tugs them free, revealing their roots. "Think they will grow if we plant them at home?"

"I don't know. I've never heard of it being done before."

Anwyll closes the six-leaf clovers in a jar, and the moment it's sealed, a gold glow lights the jar, and we both are shocked. For a split second, I think we did something wrong, but when the brightness fades, a barrier is locked in place around the clover.

"She casted a protective spell," Anwyll says with so much emotion, my eyes begin to sting. "She wants to make sure it lasts for the journey. For my brother." He hangs his head and pulls the jar to his heart. The way he is crouched, the way he hangs his head, the way his talons seep into the dirt, he looks every bit defeated in his primal stance.

"We will get everything we need." I ease the jar from his hand and slip it into the mysterious bag of goodies. "The next item on the list won't be as easy to get."

"What's next?" he asks, staring off into the misted side of the Unwanted Lands.

"Either Unicorn hair, heartsnow, or wolfsbane petals. We need all three. I have no idea how to get any of them, Anwyll. I have no idea where we go from here."

"It's not about knowing where to go, Ru. It only matters if we get there," he says, his grey-tinted hand cupping my cheek. His talons tickle my hairline, but the tender touch has me leaning into his palm. Anwyll makes everything seem like it will be okay.

"I'm scared, Anwyll. I've never been over the bridge. What if this is it? What if we don't get the rest of our lives together?" The enormity of the situation weighs down on me, hitting me full force, and I dig my fingers into his hand, the one that's pressing against my cheek. "What if I never get more time than what I've had with you? I can't live without more—" A sob bubbles free, and he glides his hold on me, moving it to the back of my neck and holding it tight, pressing his forehead against mine.

"—Listen to me. Listen." He squeezes my nape harder. "Look at me, Ru."

I stare into the irises that morphed to match mine. His brow bone is raised from being in his half-shifted form, his cheekbones are more pronounced, and there's a dusting of fur along his jaw that trails down his neck. His lips are a darker slate color, and his fangs shine with stories that need to be told.

He's beautifully dangerous. And he's all mine.

"I will do everything in my power to keep us safe because a future with you is what I've lived for, what I have fought for, what I have killed for, what I endured for. All the times I wanted to kill myself to keep the night-mares at bay, the guilt that ate me alive—that still eats me alive—it all led me to you, and you're the only fucking peace I know, so I won't be giving us up easily. I'll kill again. I'll rip anything that touches you to shreds. I'll fight. And I'll endure it all over again because I do not care about becoming the monster that warlock made me be, for you. We will live because I refuse to not have mornings where I wake up to your smile, your light, or not to have nights where we make love until we fall asleep. You're my heart, Ru. I live to fight for you. Do you understand that?"

"Yes. Yes, I understand. You're my heart too, Anwyll."

He bends his head down to kiss me, and the moment our lips touch, a grumble leaves his wolf and vibrates the back of my throat. I love how I affect him. He never hides what he feels for me, and I'll always love that.

His tongue slides between my lips until I sink into him, grabbing his cheek as we get lost in one another. I run my tongue down a fang, and he nips at my lip, silently telling me to behave.

"I love you," he whispers. "And I won't let anyone take that from me." He stands, holding out his hand for me to take. Without question, I slide mine into his, and he helps me up.

Another screech from the Unwanted Lands echoes from the distance.

"What is that?" I ask under my breath, staring down the tunnel created by the bridge. I'm unable to see through the fog awaiting us.

"Only one way to find out," he says, and I take a step forward only for him to pull me back. "That's twice now you've started to walk in front of me. Do not make me angry, mate," his wolf bites with impatience.

"I'm sorry," I reply, a bit breathless as heat buzzes between my thighs.

He inhales and slams me against the beam of the bridge. "We will fuck you right here, Ru. I don't give a damn where we are. Do not tempt me with the scent of your honey because I will not be gentle, and Anwyll is fighting me. He doesn't want me to fuck you so close to danger." My werewolf is fighting his full-shift, and Anwyll is being suppressed by his beastly nature. "But I think you'd like it, wouldn't you? You'd love to be full of my dick while wondering if any minute you'll die?"

"Yes," I answer honestly, forgetting where we are for a moment when another scream pierces the air.

His eyes lift away from mine, and I know the moment

Anwyll has returned because he is pushing me behind him instead of threatening to fuck me.

I want to giggle at the difference. His wolf is very primal and loves to give in to his animalistic sex drive. Not saying he wouldn't protect me, he would, but with the full moon being nine days away, sex is starting to be the only thing I think about too.

Anwyll rolls his head over his muscular shoulders, his hair shaggy and reaching his shoulders. The dark contrast of his hair against his gray skin is majestic. He grabs my hand, and we step onto the bridge, the wood creaking under our feet and threatening to give.

Something pounds under our feet.

Once.

Twice.

And then a sounding board of bangs loosens the wood on the bridge. Anwyll lifts me into his arms and runs, sprinting over the wood before we crash into the river. I watch behind us, the planks falling into the water below, and that's when I see hands. They are covered in water, grabbing at the air as they reach for us.

One grabs onto the bridge, lifting itself up, and fear turns my bones to stone. Water makes the creature's body. It's slender, small, has no eyes, and sharp teeth, but then it's pulled into the water again, splashing its way to try to get to us again.

When we finally get to the other side, the bridge is destroyed, but I hear the chattering of the water creatures as if they are talking about us and wanting to rip our flesh to pieces. Anwyll places me on the ground, keeping one arm tight around me as we stare at the fallen bridge. The creatures crawl up the riverbank halfway, keeping their bodies in the water, but they hiss at us, and Anwyll bares his teeth and growls, taking their threat as a challenge.

Most of them skitter away, but one stays, eyeing my beast before slowly sinking into the water.

The river turns still. It's calm, returning to the natural flowing state it was in before we walked onto the bridge.

"Well, there's no turning back now." I grip his hand and turn to the Unwanted Lands, waiting for every nightmare I've ever heard to come to life.

Chapter Twenty-Two

ANWYLL

Already the journey starts with a threat. The only good thing is the clover so far. I'm happy to have that off the list, but who knows what else will be waiting for us if those water creatures are just the beginning of what these lands have to offer.

"You know, we probably could have gotten unicorn hair from the ones in the field," I curse myself, remembering how they were in reach.

"No. Never confront a unicorn with a baby. They will kill you in a heartbeat, and some of the unicorns have wings. They will spear you through the heart," Ru explains quickly, digging her nails into my arm. "Please tell me you won't go near a unicorn with a baby."

"I promise. I didn't know. I won't approach one, I swear."

"We have to find one alone. If they are in a herd, they will protect one another and attack."

"And here I thought unicorns were peaceful creatures."

Ru lifts a shoulder as we begin walking through the fog. "All creatures are peaceful until they feel like they have to defend themselves. They don't like to be bothered. They like to be left alone."

The heavy clouds drifting close to the ground finally part, and I stare at the vast, dead land before me. It's nothing like the other side. There are no bright colors. Everything is in shades of black and grey. The trees are sticks in the ground with no leaves. The sky is a smoker's lung, and the Unwanted Lands are the end of a cigarette, covered in ash and left to be forgotten.

"Holy shit." Ru wasn't exaggerating when she said it was a wasteland.

"I know," she says sadly, taking my hand in hers. "We can do this. Your brother needs us."

My brother, the man who sacrificed himself for me. He deserves this effort. He deserves me trying to get him the help he needs. How lucky am I to have found a mate willing to be here with me? I kiss the top of her hand and take the first step. The grass crunches under our feet from being so dry, as if each step is a cry for water from the planet's ground.

"Tell me about your time under the spell of a warlock while we walk into the unknown," she says after a few minutes of silence between us.

My hackles rise, but she deserves the truth, and there isn't anything else to do. "You know most of it. I killed. A lot. I have a ton of blood on my hands. I killed children"—I choke the emotion back and blink away the tears—"I don't want to talk about that. Please. It's a demon I fight every day."

"I don't care what I have to do to find that warlock and kill him, I will," she threatens, the words deepening with her murderous promise.

"He's in a coma somewhere," I explain. "Alpha turned

him at the last moment, used a werewolf bite to curse him to a coma, and now the only way he can wake up is from the blood of his beloved."

"But Lex woke up from the coma and all his vampires are immune, right? Wouldn't that make the warlock immune?"

"Loophole. You have to want the change in order for the immunity to work, so since Lex forced it..." I trail off to leave her to fill in the rest.

"So no one knows where he is? We should find him and rip his heart out."

"We should," I agree, liking the idea of going on an adventure with her again to hunt down something else. "He has something very important too. Since Lex was bit by a werewolf, he nor any of the vampires who pledge to him can be in the sun, and that fucking warlock has the page of the sun spell for them to be in the light again. I'd love to find him. I'd love to tear him to pieces and watch him choke on his own blood." My werewolf begins to rip from my body, my feet elongating, my arms widening, and my spine lengthening as rage causes me to shift fully.

Ru has to tilt her head back to look up at me, and her tiny hand takes my paw. Her fingers can't even wrap around one of my fingers. "I'm sorry. I shouldn't have said anything. I won't bring it up again."

I whine, not wanting her to feel bad. She only wanted to get to know me, but there's not much to know. Everything she's learning about me, I'm learning about myself. When she kisses my palm, I morph into my half-shifted form again, my wolf insisting on being present while we are in the Unwanted Lands.

"Never say sorry for wanting to get to know me," I speak quietly, afraid if I make too much noise, something will hear us. "I wish I had more to give you, but I don't. What you know of me is all there is to me. As you learn, I learn. I want to give you so much more, but what I am, it's all I have."

"Don't think for a second that you aren't enough for me. Who you are, what you are, the heart you have, that's all I need. You're all I need."

I'm about to lift her into my arms and kiss her when the hairs trailing down my spine stand. I tug her against my chest and survey the wasted land, waiting to see what the threat is.

"What is it—"

I place my finger against my lips, telling her to not make a sound because we are not alone. Something is out here with us. We need to get to the woods. Being out in the open only makes us a target.

All I can see are the tendrils of fog breaking as it's creeping across the ground, but my werewolf is never wrong. Something is here with us. I spin around when a breeze hits my back. Laughter follows next, and Ru stays completely still, but she can't stop the shakes that rack her body.

Why can't I see this thing?

Ru's eyes widen, and I tilt my head, wondering what the issue is. She slowly looks down, and I follow, not seeing anything of concern.

Her arms tighten around me, and everything after that happens on the high-pitch cry of her scream. She's yanked from my arms, and she slams against the ground, her chin catching the majority of the hit. Ru is dragged away from me, something gripping her by the ankles, and she's clawing at the ground, blood dripping from her lip.

My werewolf bursts free of me as I drop to all fours, roaring my threat as I run to her.

"Anwyll!" she yells for me, leaving marks in the dirt as her fingers try to grip the soil.

Laughter chatters again, but I still can't see the creature dragging my mate. It's headed for the woods, and I can't let it get that far with Ru. Snarling, I lunge, flying through the air, passing Ru, and land on something solid.

I let out the most deadly roar I have in my chest. I slash my talons at the invisible figure, slashing its body, and that's when I see it. Blood covers what I can't see, giving me a view of its true form.

"Run, Ru! Run!" I shout, my human voice breaking free from my wolf's throat, and I don't take my eyes away from the monster. The blood is thick, sticking to him like glue, and his fingers have long claws. They slash across my chest, but I don't feel the pain. The more I attack, the more reality around me fades, and the grotesque beast the warlock created comes forward again.

Its eyes are small for its head, black, and its long tongue lashes out to wrap around my neck, but with one slice of my talons, I cut it in half. A shriek escapes him, the same one we heard before we got on the bridge. To end this, I punch through its chest and rip out its heart, holding the vile organ in my hand.

The heart pumps still.

A slow beat struggling to stay alive. Blood drips down my hand, my wrist, and my arm, coating me in victory. The chattering from the creature dies even as its heart still beats in my palm. Thinking of how it ripped my mate from my arms and dragged her, I sink my talons into the muscle. Like butter, my nails puncture the useless organ, onyx coating me, and the stench of death is quick as it hits my nose.

The heart stops beating, and I toss it to the side, adrenaline coursing through my veins. I'm ready to keep killing, to keep protecting my mate.

"Anwyll?"

My shoulders tense when I hear Ru's small, frightened voice.

I don't want her to see me like this. I have blood on my hands. I'm a mess. I can't have her see me like this. Crawling off the dead creature, I give Ru my back and wipe my hands on the grass. My mate just saw me kill for the first time. This isn't good. What did I do?

"Anwyll." My mate is gentle as her hand touches my back.

I hunch over, exhaling in harsh breaths. She stands at my side and turns me to face her, her fingers against my cheek.

So small, yet she has the power of the world to bring me to my knees.

Her eyes dance over my face before she leans in and kisses me, a long peck that has my wolf receding into a half-shifted form. I don't move. I'm stunned.

"You saved my life."

"I'll always save you. I don't care what I have to risk," I answer truthfully. "Even if it means risking myself." I examine her, noticing her torn jeans at the ankle. I sniff the air and drop to the ground, growling in discontent when I smell her blood. "He hurt you."

"You killed him for it."

"And I always will." I grab each ankle and lick the scratch marks, watching her flesh stitch together. She sighs in relief as the pain fades. "We need to find safety. I know there are more of those things, and I don't want to risk being seen in the open. Are you okay to walk?"

"Yes. I'm okay." She dusts off the dirt from her shirt and lifts the bag onto her shoulder. I can't believe she held onto that. "Let's go." She begins walking, and I huff, a snarl leaving my lips. She freezes, then takes a few steps back to be at my side. Her wary smile is cute. "I forgot."

"Forget again and see what happens, mate," my werewolf answers for me. "No walking in front of me."

She intertwines our hands and agrees.

We head toward the forest— not knowing what it holds —but I know what's hiding in there can't be good.

Five minutes in the Unwanted Lands and I've already had to kill. Whatever lies ahead of us won't be good.

We stop at the edge of the tree line, knowing if we take a step forward, there's no going back. The silence is consuming. There's no sign of life. Some trees have no leaves, leaving their branches to look like bony tendrils trying to reach out and grab you.

Others have black leaves while the bark is ashen. The bushes are twigs of what used to be a desert of death.

With another step forward, we don't look back.

Chapter Twenty-Three
RU

I'm not sure how long we have walked, but my feet are aching and I'm exhausted. I can barely keep my eyes open. We've been traveling without interruptions, and I'm not sure if that's good or bad. What if someone is following us? The naive part of me hopes attacks only happen in the open, but that's a best-case scenario.

"We should pause for the night," he says, stopping at a nearby tree. "You're exhausted." He tugs me close and kisses my forehead. "I can't promise we will be safe, but I don't think we will be safe anywhere."

"Me either." I drop the bag and groan, rolling my head over my shoulders as I stretch out the kinks. "Let's see what Maven packed us for the night. I'm so hungry," I complain, sagging against Anwyll, my own tree.

"I would say I could go hunting for us, but I don't think there is anything here."

"I don't think we would want to eat what is here anyway. We'd probably die."

"I'm sorry," he apologizes after a few minutes of silence.

"That you have to be here with me because you're my mate."

"Don't apologize. I wouldn't want to be anywhere else. I'm happy to be here with you. I'm not happy about the circumstances."

He wraps an arm around me, and I lean my head against his shoulder. My eyes droop, and I fight the urge to fall asleep, but I can't help it. Exhaustion pulls me under as I'm nestled against Anwyll's side.

I gasp awake.

A crackling sound of wood pops, and an orange glow catches my attention. I rub my eyes, bolting up when I notice I'm in a tent with blankets. The orange light is coming from outside. Wrapping the blanket around my shoulders, I step out into the night to see Anwyll by the fire. He's rotating something over the fire that smells delicious. He's in his half-shifted form, the gray skin illuminated by the firelight.

"You're awake," he smiles, truly happy to see me.

"How long was I out?"

"A few hours. I told the bag we were hungry, and of course, Maven prepared for that. So, I'm cooking a turkey."

"A whole turkey?" My eyes round. "How did it fit in the bag?"

"Magic. Plus, it will barely be enough for me. I could eat three of these." Just as he speaks, two other turkeys appear on the spear, cradling the original one. "Huh. Did she spell everything to do what we need?"

"I think she tried to give us everything she could." I take a seat next to him. "I can't believe there's a tent and blankets. She thought of everything." I yawn, wanting to go back to sleep, but my stomach won't allow it. I'm too hungry. "Smells so good. Thank you for preparing all this."

"I made some tea too," he says, picking up the silver pot in the flames and pouring it into a cup for me. "I figured you'd want something when you woke up."

The cup warms my palms as I take a sip, the steam dampening the tip of my nose, and the floral warmth spreads down my throat as I swallow. "It's delicious. Thank you for taking care of me during a time like this."

"Ru, I could be on my deathbed, and I'd still find a way to take care of you." He pours himself a cup of tea and leans back, one knee bent and the other straight, his arm propped on his leg. He's never looked so casual, but I know he is anything but relaxed.

"I know," I sip the tea, relaxing almost instantly. "It's one of the many reasons I love you."

He grins, showing his pointed cuspids, and a swirling of heat boils in my blood. Hiding my face in the teacup, I know he can smell me, but this is different. There's almost a bite of pain to my lust.

"Ru," he groans, taking a large swallow of his drink. "Do not make me come over there. This is not the place. I can't be distracted. I have to be able to protect you." He cuts the turkey with his talon, giving me a plate that Maven also packed. I mean, what else can fit in this damn magical bag? And why doesn't it weigh a ton? And how did the turkey not go bad?

I need to remember these questions when we get back home.

I pop a piece of turkey in my mouth and moan when the

juices burst across my tongue. There are no seasonings. It's plain, but it's good, and it's food. I am not going to be picky. "This is so good, Anwyll. I don't know if it's because I feel like it's my last meal"— I chuckle—"but it is delicious." I lick my fingers, and a carnal thunder comes from Anwyll.

Sliding my eyes to him, the turkey falls from my hand when I see the animalism across his face. He's holding the turkey leg in one hand while crouched on the ground, and he is staring at me as if I'm going to be his last meal.

He tears into the meat with his fangs, a constant snarl emanating from him while he eats.

"Mate," he warns again, the snap of bone making me jump as he bites into it.

He eats the bone too, and I shouldn't like it. It's so...wild.

But I do. I do like it. I love knowing how powerful he is. Knowing he could snap me in half, but he won't. He'd never do that.

I set the plate down, chewing the turkey, and take another sip of my tea. I press my thighs together when another roll of pleasure shoots through me, and I wince when it bites me again. I don't understand what is happening.

"You're already feeling it," Anwyll states, sighing with regret.

"Feeling what? I'm fine." I pour myself more tea and blink away the fuzzy edges creeping along the sides of my vision.

"You are for now, but the bite of pain you're feeling, it's the heat."

"The heat..." I trail off, the memory of him telling me I'd experience this. "But it isn't the full moon."

"I know, but it's already starting. It is faint." He inhales and moans, pressing his hand to his groin. "God, you already smell so fucking good. We can't. Not here. Not until we are somewhere safer, Ru."

"I'm fine. The pain is gone. It only lasts for a second." My head sways, and a glowing butterfly flies in front of me, flapping its wings. I reach out to touch it and another one appears.

"Let me know if it gets worse," he says, the heat of his body next to me. "What are you doing?"

"You don't see those?" I ask, watching the butterflies float around us. One lands on my nose, and my eyes cross to look at it. I giggle. "They are so pretty and blue."

"I don't see anything, Lucky Charm." He drifts his talon down my cheek, and it scares the butterfly away.

"Aw, you made it fly away." I pout, watching the butterflies flutter above me. I lean back on my elbows and watch them.

He leaps over me and lands on all fours. "Got it." He lifts his hands and huffs. "Where did it go?"

"What?" I say, never taking my eyes off the butterflies. "Whoa." A huge dragonfly zips around the trees. I've never seen a dragonfly so big.

"Rabbits. My werewolf loves rabbits." He snaps his head to the left and growls again, launching himself into the air and lands on nothing but empty space.

"Don't eat the cute bunnies." My head spins, and my body feels light as if I'm floating.

"But I love bunnies." This time, it's his turn to pout. "They are so yummy." He stares up at the sky and stands, spinning in circles. "The stars are out." He ducks, and his green eyes widen as he covers his head. "The bunnies have wings."

I roll to the left and hold my stomach, laughing so hard

I can barely breathe, then screech when a vine bursts from the ground.

Anwyll wraps me in his arms and carries me away. "I have you. I'll protect you, mate."

"It had teeth. Vines don't have teeth."

He squeezes his eyes shut and shakes his head. "I think... I think we're high, Ru."

"From what? The turkey?" I hold up my hand when fireflies float around each finger.

"The tea," he growls.

"Rarity did pack a few different kinds." I twist my hand left and right, the fireflies lighting up the dark forest—at least to me.

He dodges to the left and snaps his teeth together. "Fucking rabbits," he grumbles. He tilts his head back and watches whatever he sees. "I see stars and planets. They are swirling around us, creating a tunnel as if we are in the middle of a tornado."

"I see butterflies, dragonflies, and birds. Colorful birds with large beaks and wide wings."

He takes me in his arms and spins me around before tugging me to his chest. "It's not often you get to see life in such a dead place. Let's take advantage of the beauty."

None of what we see is real, but we are. Anwyll is. His touch is.

And as his hand with black werewolf talons drifts down my arms, my nerve-endings react as if every stroke is a match striking to ignite a flame.

That bite of pain returns, and he inhales, burying his nose against my neck. His coarse tongue flattens and licks my flesh, tasting me. "I can smell it on you. It's barely there. I have to focus, but I can almost taste the heat in your sweat. Fuck, it's good. So good. It's driving me insane. I can't imagine what you'll smell like on the full moon." He sucks the same spot he tasted, and I tilt my head back, fireworks—actual fireworks—are exploding in the sky. An array of colors consisting of reds, greens, blues, and yellows burst in front of me.

"Do you know how bad I want to knot you?" He jerks my head back by my hair and nips my lips. "Do you know how bad"—he groans with impatience—"I want to be stuck inside you, filling you full of my come until you're dripping of me? Until you think you can't take anymore?" He grips the hem of my shirt and pulls it up over my head.

"I thought you said—"

"—Fuck, what I said. I'm seeing flying bunnies right now. I don't think I could recognize the enemy right now, not if they show up looking like rabbits." He lowers my pants, and I step out of them; the ground vanishes beneath our feet, and I hold onto him, afraid to fall. "I see it too," he calms me. "I have you, Lucky Charm. I have you." His lips meet mine, and a kaleidoscope of emotions becomes an image of diamonds, spinning in different directions every time his lips move against my throat.

I'm lost in the sensation.

"Can you imagine, mate? Can you imagine us fucking you all night?" his wolf rumbles. "I can't wait until Anwyll fully accepts me. His fear of hurting you will no longer be a problem. I think you'll like getting hurt. I think you'll like the chase of me hunting you on the full moon. You'll be in so much need, you'll be begging for my knot."

"Anwyll," I breathe, wrapping my hands around his neck.

"Ru." He's back, his tongue tangling with mine. "You smell so fucking good. I need you. I fucking need you." Anwyll deepens the kiss and forces me onto my back.

I forget the ground is there and I close my eyes waiting to fall, but I'm reminded the tricks my mind is playing on me aren't real.

He's real.

And he forces my legs apart, thrusting inside in one stroke. "Fuck, so wet. So tight. You feel so good. You smell so fucking good. Fuck!" He tosses his head back and roars, the guttural sound echoing through the dead forest, and the butterflies I see scatter from the threat of a predator. With a snarl, he pounds into me, relentless, hard, punishing, and his fangs scrape down my neck. "I want to sink my teeth into you, fill you with my knot until you're trying to escape me because it's going to hurt so fucking good. You'll want more, you'll beg for less, but you'll take it, won't you? You'll take me because your pussy is greedy for my cock."

"Yes! Chauns, Anwyll, don't stop." My mind plays another trick on me, and we float into the air as he rails into me. The bite of pain returns, and he growls, his skin a molten metal against mine.

"I feel it. The beginning of your heat. I feel it at the tip of my cock. Your body is getting ready, and I fucking feel your womb wanting to open for me, heating just for me."

"Anwyll."

His muscles strain, and his talons sink into my back, fur sprouting over his chest as he fights the shift. He stays human, but his control is slipping.

He curls over me, his lips against my ear, and he says through broken breaths, "In the darkest night, even in the vilest of places, you are the beauty. You are the stars and the planets I see. You are my universe."

I cry out, sinking my teeth into his shoulder, and he bellows, howling as he plants himself deep inside me, filling me with his come. The bite of pain in my belly fades the moment the heat of his seed seeps into me, and I sigh in relief.

The butterflies fade.

The high leaves.

And we float back down to the ground we never really left.

Chapter Twenty-Four

ANWYLL

I gasp awake, my senses telling me we need to get the hell out of here. Ru is fast asleep. The tea knocked us out. I barely remember anything that happened last night. I know we fucked, that I remember— like I could ever forget how wet and tight my mate is— but everything else is a blur. I don't even remember falling asleep. We crashed into oblivion.

Ru's still naked, pressed against my side, and I inhale, the sliver of heat coursing through her causing my cock to harden.

Fuck.

I rub a hand down my face and think about the full moon. We're only eight days away from it now, and I can't imagine how intense, dangerous, and life-altering it is going to be. The way I want her now, there's no way I can want her more. If I do, I might end up killing her. I want to inflict my need for her on her skin.

I want to imprint myself on her. I want to scar her, mar her, ruin her, make her undesirable for anyone else.

That's the wolf talking. Not you. You'd never hurt Ru like that.

My wolf laughs in the back of my mind, mocking me. He knows better. He knows that I've been hiding my darkest desires because giving into them means fully giving into him. I'm tired of being separated from him. I'm tired of talking about us as if we are two different beings. We are the same. He is me. I am him.

The moment I tear down the barrier between us, what will happen to Ru? What if I kill her?

I'd never hurt our mate. She's ours. Mine. She's mine. We protect her. She's perfect for us. Trust me. I am not the same werewolf as I was when the warlock controlled us. I am sorry. I am sorry I wasn't strong enough to fight his spell on us, on me. I tried. He was too powerful.

I gasp, holding a hand over my racing heart as a throbbing in my head hits me full force. When was the last time I had a conversation with my wolf? Why didn't I ever think about how he felt after the nightmare the warlock put us through?

What if he's just as damaged?

What if he needs me like I'm finding I need him? There's a spot in my mind, my soul, and my heart where my werewolf side used to fill, but after all the things we did, accepting him became my own nightmare.

I am lonely.

He whispers to me, and a lump of remorse fills my throat. I unzip the tent and stumble out, digging for my sweatpants from the bag and tugging them on.

"You know what this means? If I accept you?" I ask, sounding like a crazy person talking to myself.

We will be stronger. Faster. We will be able to protect her.

"It won't be good for us in the long run if I keep denying

you," I say, remembering the warning my brother gave me before the warlock found us. Being separated at the soul from your werewolf will kill a man in time. Slowly, I'll slip into insanity, and eventually, my wolf will take over.

And I'll be trapped in that form forever; feral and self-destructive.

I stare at Ru through the open flap of the tent and know the best thing for her is for me to be at my best. She's lying on her back, peace etched across her face, and the blanket is tugged down past her breasts. Her nipples are hard, and there are a few red marks from where I got carried away last night.

She's so fucking perfect.

My head tilts back as I inhale, the sweet scent of her honey, warm and heating up just for me, has a growl forming in my chest. My nails shift, and I take a step forward while she sleeps so soundly.

One mark.

One across her shoulder. To imprint. It will only hurt for a moment.

She stretches, stretching her arms over her head, and turns, her piercing green eyes staring right at me. She smiles. "Good morning," she mumbles through a yawn.

My talons vanish, and I'm a fucking bastard for having those thoughts of hurting her. Why would I ever do that? What's wrong with me?'

It needs to be known she's claimed. Any other paranormal creatures need to be warned away. She's ours. We have to mark, claim, own.

"Anwyll? Are you okay?" She turns to her side, the curve of her waist dipping as she props herself up on her elbows, her hand holding her head.

"I'm fine, Ru. We need to get up and get moving, okay?

Something about this area is making my instincts go haywire."

She quickly gets dressed and tosses her hair in a messy bun. Ru decides to wear a tank top, the thin straps delicately placed on her shoulders, showing her flawless, smooth skin, and my wolf pushes into my mind.

The temptation to scar it is strong—too strong. I'm not sure how I'll fight it. I'll be able to resist more if I accept my wolf again.

"Okay," I whisper to him internally. "Join me again. Let's be complete."

With a roar that rumbles my bones, his soul stitches with mine again. I expect pain, agony, and torment, but all the ache I've felt since the spell was broken vanishes. My bones no longer hurt. I fall to my knees in relief, holding my hands out in front of me, and watch our skins morph, the fur spreading. Our bones form, our hearts mend, and the emptiness inside me becomes full.

"Anwyll? Anwyll!" Ru jumps over the smoking wood that was once a fire and skids to a stop, falling to her knees. "What's wrong? What is it?" She grabs my face, her hands cupping my jaw, and watches the bones in my cheeks move; everything contorts. My human form is bigger now. I'll be taller, my bones harder to break, and I'll be stronger.

"What's happening?" she asks with astonishment. "Is it your wolf? Are you fighting him again? Anwyll, let him out. Let him be free."

Even my teeth move and my jaw hurts for a split second, my eye teeth becoming permanent miniature points.

I spit out a wad of blood, then fall backward, exhausted from the change. No longer do I hear him in the back of my mind. It's different now. We are one. We are the same.

"You're scaring me," Ru climbs over my body, straddling my waist as she holds my face. "What's happening? You look different, but the same?"

I wrap my arms around her, feeling more like myself than I ever have, and bury my face into her neck, scenting my mate. She smells of me.

"I accepted him, my wolf. He's one with me now. It's why I look a little different."

"You were supposed to look like this?"

"You... don't like it?"

"Does it smell like I don't like it?" she purrs, tracing the edge of my jaw.

I flip her over until she's on her back, settling between her legs, and smile, showing my new teeth.

"Wow. You're the same, just everything is bigger." I rock my hips forward, and she gasps. "Definitely bigger. How will it fit?"

"I'll make it fit," I growl, dipping down to capture her lips in a heated kiss. The new energy I have makes me feel like I can climb a mountain. Like I could fuck her all day and night and barely break a sweat.

"Anwyll," she gasps, running her nails down my back just as a shadow passes out of my peripheral.

With a snarl, I curl over her, signaling my half-shift, and stare out into the forest, watching.

Waiting.

The hairs on the back of my neck stand up.

We aren't alone.

"We need to get out of here. Now." I wrap my arms around her and pick her up, setting her on her feet.

She grabs the bag Maven got us and opens it. The moment she does, the tent folds in on itself and flies into the opening, disappearing completely.

I spin around, trying to scent our surroundings when Ru screams. My wolf bursts free without question, and I turn around to see tree roots wrapping around her body. I lunge forward, but the roots drag her away from me. As she fights, the roots multiply, and one wraps around her throat.

Dropping to all fours, I sprint, eating the distance the roots are putting between me and my mate. Her screams become muffled because she can't breathe, and then she's slammed against a tree trunk, the roots pressing her against the bark.

Her legs begin to change, from beautifully long and lean, to the ash tone of the bark.

With a savage roar, fangs bared, I throw my entire body into the tree, snapping it in half. The roots are tentacles, whipping through the air and lashing at me. One stabs my shoulder and I howl in pain, gripping the wood and snapping it in half as if I broke its arm.

But when one breaks, three more roots grow from it. They begin to wrap around me, and I cross my arms, curl over, bending my knees. I jump, breaking free by spreading my arms out and arching my back to widen my chest. The roots crumble into a thousand pieces, and I'm on the tree again. The bark has climbed up Ru's legs to her knees.

With my talons, I desperately claw at the tree, tearing it to pieces. The roots feel like bones, hardening, making it difficult for me to break, but nothing will stop me from saving my mate.

Nothing.

Something wraps around my ankle and slings me through the air. I land on all fours, snarling as the woods begin to move. The trees change their positions, trying to confuse me, but I have Ru's scent. I have the mate-bond.

I'll be able to track her no matter where I am. No one will ever be able to hide her from me.

My claws dig into the dirt, and as I run, I kick up the soil with my elongated feet. I follow her scent, dodging in and ducking as the trees try to grab me. With every hit of my paws, my breath leaves me in heavy huffs.

When I reach her, her arms have soaked into the wood, and her eyes are shut. She's pale, and I can't tell if she's breathing. I dive headfirst into the cage the roots have created around her, punching through the tree trunk to wrap my arms around her and pull.

One of the wayward tendrils from the tree tries to pry my mouth open, and I bite down, snarling.

Every muscle in my body trembles as I fight the power of the possessed tree. I yank and pull, I fight and take every lashing the roots give my back. I roar to the skies in pain, but I'll die before I give up.

"I won't let you have her," I sneer through my were-form, pulling her free from the bark. "She's mine!" With a final tug, I fall back and hit the ground, Ru safely in my arms and unconscious.

The trees try to grab her again, but they stop, frozen in mid-air. That's when I feel the ground rumble, the same beat as weighted footsteps. I hold Ru close, watching as a creature wraps the roots around the tree itself.

"You will no longer be able to grow," the creature states to the possessed tree. "And any other tree who dares to take a life, I will burn." When he turns around to show me his face, I get to all fours, keeping Ru under my body so she's protected.

I growl, letting the saliva drip from my fangs.

"I will not hurt your mate, wolf," the creature says, standing on his legs that are tree roots themselves. He has the body and face of a man. His fingers are long, like branches, and spots of his body are covered in bark and moss. He crouches down to seem less threatening. "To bring a leprechaun into these woods is very foolish. The Unwanted Lands is not a place for you to be. These trees, they eat lives which makes them grow stronger."

"What are you?" I ask, keeping my position over Ru.

"I am a Drutayla, a tree god," he explains, unclenching his fingers. A green leaf grows, and he plucks it, handing it to me. "She needs to eat this, or she will be hardened to wood in only a few hours."

"How can I trust you? You could be one of these trees for all I know."

"I saved your life. Why would I take it after giving you hope to survive?"

"Because cruelty lives in these woods."

"But good does as well; it only remains hidden because of the bad, but I do my best to keep the peace. It isn't often we get fresh blood in the woods. The trees will want her. You will need to get out of here as quickly as possible." He holds the leaf out, bringing it closer to my face. "If you don't want your mate to be stuck in these woods forever, please, she needs to eat this."

"Why? What is it?"

"A leaf from a tree god contains the magic needed to combat the venom of the tree ghouls. Please, her bones are turning to wood as we speak." His large eyes have no whites. They are round with a blend of coffee and gold, showing nothing but earnestness.

I take it from him and press it against her mouth.

He stops me, wrapping his branch-like fingers around my wrist. "You must chew it first and then place it in her mouth. She cannot chew it on her own."

Morphing into my half-shifted form so I have my human teeth, I chew the leaf. It doesn't taste special. It tastes like fucking grass, and I hate it, but I chew until it's nearly liquid, lift Ru into my arms, then pry her lips apart.

Her teeth are wooden now.

"The venom is working fast. You have to do it now," he says, urging me to heal her. The other tree roots begin to creep forward again. With one lash of his hand, the roots are bent back, and the trees fall to the ground, turning into piles of ash. "I can only kill them for so long. They are like a phoenix. When they die, they are reborn from the ashes."

I press my lips against her and pour the green liquid into her mouth. When I'm done, I massage her throat, making sure the cure slides down.

She inhales a deep, sharp breath, one that has her clawing at my chest, wide-eyed in panic.

"It's okay. You're okay. I have you." I push her hair out of her face and almost cry with relief. "I have you." She cries into my shoulder, and I hold her close. The hole in my shoulder from where I was stabbed with the root finally stitches itself back together.

"Thank you," I tell him, never in my life expecting to talk to a tree god. I didn't even know they existed, but it makes sense. If I'm possible, if Ru is possible, if vampires are real, then anything is.

"It is my pleasure, wolf," his deep voice grumbles low, and his legs snap as if the wood is popping as he stands.

Ru turns to face whom I am talking to and presses into me further. Her shoulders rise and fall with every fast breath.

"Calm, young leprechaun. I am not here to harm you."

"He saved your life, Ru. He's good."

"You remind me of someone," his voice echoes through

the forest as his branch-like fingers brush under her chin. "Someone I haven't seen in a very long time."

"Who?" she asks.

"I cannot remember him, but he is not good. Not like you."

"My father," Ru whispers. "He is here? He's alive?"

"If you call what he is living, then yes, he is alive."

"What's your name?" I question. "How can we find you again?"

"I am called Qauloch. I am everywhere. I must go. You need to leave this area of the forest at once. Head west." He points. "You will find what you are looking for there." And he begins to walk away, his long legs carrying him further than I thought was possible. "The forest holds mysteries. I suggest not becoming one of them," he says in the distance, fading until the rumbles from his steps vanish.

I wrap my arms around my mate tighter, doubting if we will make it out of the Unwanted Lands alive.

Chapter Twenty-Five

RU

Anwyll hasn't put me down in hours. He's been in his shifted form ever since the possessed tree roots nearly killed me. I'm wrapped up in his arms, feeling small, fragile, yet protected and warm. So warm. He's like a furnace. I blink away the sleep and look up at him, the strong, angular line of his jaw. From here, I can see his fangs peeking out between his gray lips. His fur is soft, but it doesn't cover his entire body. Just his arms, a bit of his chest, and his legs—it isn't thick. His body is still very human, considering how much larger he is in this form.

"You're staring at me," he says, peering down at me.

"Your ears are cute." I reach up to touch them, but I can't quite reach high enough.

They flicker as he huffs, amusement playing on his lips. He bends down and leans his head against my palm. "My ears are not cute," he says, and now that I think about it, I've never heard him speak in this form. I didn't think it was possible.

"They are." I scratch behind them, and he growls. They

are kind of fluffy, but the hair tapers into sharp points at the very top. I giggle, "You like that. Don't you?"

"No," he mumbles, nearly purring as he leans his head into my hand again. He stops walking, and one of his hands cups my face. "Are you okay? I've never been so scared in my life, Ru."

"I'm okay." My hand moves to his chest, so I can feel his heart pump against my palm. "I'm okay because of you. I always am."

"I can't lose you." He leans down and nuzzles his snout against my neck. "I can't."

"You won't." I kiss his cheek, and he holds me tighter, his paw covering my entire back.

He curls his talons into my skin, gripping me tightly as if I'm about to slip free from his arms and be taken away forever.

"Why don't we stop? You've been traveling since yesterday without a break, Anwyll. You need to rest, and you won't put me down. You have to be tired. Let's rest."

"We can't." He begins walking again, staring straight ahead. "When we stop, something bad will happen. I can't do that. I can't risk falling asleep and something happening to you."

"We won't be able to do anything if we can't go to sleep. We need to eat, Anwyll. We need to sleep. You need a break."

He sighs, stopping again, and studies the area. The trees are more spread out, and I can't tell if that's natural or if they are leaving us alone ever since the tree-man creature found us.

"Qauloch said we had to get out of the forest. It isn't safe for us here. I'll stop as soon as I see a place where I think we won't be attacked by invisible creatures or tree roots."

"Promise?"

"I swear, Ru. You're right; we need to stop. I've been traveling all night."

His steps break the silence of the forest. The twigs and dead grass snapping under his elongated feet. Even in his werewolf form, he is attractive. Broad shoulders, a wide, defined chest, abs that are harder than rock, and still very human-like. I peek around his arm and smile when I see his tail. It's long and fluffy.

And it's wagging, swaying back and forth.

I giggle.

"What?" he huffs, looking down at me with a human expression. One brow lifts in amusement.

"You're wagging your tail," I point out and watch as it stops, then wraps around his leg. "Aw, no. Anwyll, don't be embarrassed. I think it's so cute."

"I'm a werewolf. I'm not cute," he grunts and, if I'm not mistaken, pouts.

"But I think so," I argue, nestling my head against his chest. "And always so warm."

"Werewolves naturally run hot," he explains. "My body temperature will always be around one hundred."

I notice his tail still hasn't moved, and I pinch his nipple.

He hisses, then growls, "Ow. What was that for?"

"Move your tail, Anwyll."

"No," he says bashfully, his cheeks darkening even in his wolf form.

"Why not?" I ask, keeping my voice soft.

"It's embarrassing."

"You can tell me anything." I pet his chest, trying to be

as reassuring as I can. I don't like that I made him self-conscious.

He curls his arms up, and my body falls against him as he tightens his hold. "Holding you makes me happy. Even given the circumstance…"

I grin against his chest while all the warm fuzzies flutter in my stomach. "You know what would make me happy?"

"Hmm?" he asks without looking down at me.

"You wagging your tail."

He sighs, but as I look around him, his tail begins to wag, and I can't help but squeal in delight when I see it. I reach for it, wanting to feel how soft his fur is, but he growls when I wrap my hand around it.

"Oh, I'm sorry. I didn't know you didn't like that." I release it, sticking out my bottom lip as if I'm a child who has had their favorite toy taken away.

"That isn't the problem," he grumbles.

He lowers me, his long arms still holding me, but I brush against his cock that's tenting his sweatpants.

"Oh."

"Yeah, oh," he grumbles, the vibrations from his chest tickling my cheek. "I didn't know I like it touched."

"Maybe… I can take care of that for you when we stop," I suggest, running my finger seductively down his chest, and it makes him do that rumble sound I love so much.

"You make it impossible for me to be aware of my surroundings."

I giggle, and he laughs, then moves me to his back. "Wrap your legs around me and your arms around my neck," he says, pushing me toward his back.

Climbing him like a tree, I grip his shoulders and swing my legs around his waist, then circle my arms around his neck. "Whoa, is this what it's like up here? You're so tall. Everything is so different."

"Ready?"

"Ready? Ready for what?"

"Just hold on," he warns before falling to all fours on the ground.

"No, no, no! No, Anwyll. What are you—" I scream when he takes off, digging his paws into the ground and flinging dirt back.

I can barely see the trees blur by us as he sprints, zooming around any obstacle. The longer he runs, the faster he becomes. I hide the majority of my face in his shoulder to protect myself from the air whipping against my cheeks.

I didn't know he could run so fast.

With a primal roar, he jumps through the air and pushes off a tree, only to leap to another.

I scream again, but it ends on a laugh, the adrenaline rushing through me as he jumps from tree trunk to tree trunk before landing on the ground again.

Why haven't we been traveling like this the entire time? We could have saved half a day.

He leaps over puddles of water, and I hold onto him tighter when he lands, and my body moves. I don't want to fall.

The trees become more spread out and become more difficult to see until we are in an open field, running free. Anwyll picks up the pace, a speed only a paranormal creature can get to, and I wonder if there could be a race between him and the vampires back home.

I hold on to him tighter, squeezing my legs around his waist and my arms around his neck. Not because I'm afraid, but because I want to be closer. He is warm, a constant sun flaming under the leather-like hide of skin. The dusting of fur over his slate gray body is the perfect soft contrast from his skin.

He slows, turning his head to look over his shoulder, and he must feel what I feel because his eyes soften, and a whine escapes him. I reach and scratch his ear again, kissing his shoulder to show my love.

I look up just in time, and my eyes widen, my fingers curling into his shoulders. "Anwyll! Stop!" I shout, pointing ahead of us. His head whips around to look ahead, and he immediately tries to stop. He presses his feet into the ground, plowing through the dead grass and leaving twin trails of disturbed dirt behind us.

I fly over his shoulder from the force, and he catches me in midair, bringing me to his chest as we stand at the edge of a lake.

Anwyll morphs into his half-shifted form and sets me down on the beach. The sand is the color of ash and smoke.

"How are we going to get over to the other side? It looks like this lake goes on for miles," I say, checking every direction to see if there is another way.

"We swim," he says, stepping closer to the water.

I grip his arm and tug him back, giving him an incredulous stare. "I just got attacked by tree roots, and you want to go for a swim? In an unknown lake? That we can't see through? I want to make something very clear. I do not swim in water I can't see the bottom of. If the water isn't crystal clear and a pretty pink—"

"—Blue."

"—Pink," I correct him.

"On Earth it is blue."

"Where I'm from, it's pink." I roll my eyes. "Agree to disagree. Anyway," I point my finger to the water that's so dark, it reminds me of black ink. "And you want me to go in there? There are probably monsters in there, Anwyll. Creatures we didn't know existed. Nope. I'm not doing it." I huff and cross my arms. I'm going to stand my ground. "If a tree god exists and some invisible thing dragged me away, there are definitely awful creatures under that water."

"I know," he says gently. "But I don't know another way. We are trapped by water, and we need to get across."

"It's probably made of acid. We take one step in there and poof, we are gone, nothing but bones will remain."

He kicks a few rocks into the water and cackles. "Your mind is something else, Ru."

"She's right. Not about the acid, but there are creatures lurking in there, waiting to take you to their depths," an unfamiliar voice says from behind us.

With a growl, Anwyll's werewolf burst free and shoves me behind him. I peek over his shoulder to see the person who spoke to us, and I forget how to breathe.

It's a creature I've never seen before.

He takes a step forward, and Anwyll snarls in warning. "Don't even think about taking another step, or I'll tear you limb from limb."

"And you could," the creature agrees, arms spread out in surrender. "I don't mean you harm, Lycan—"

Anwyll straightens to his full height. "It's been ages since I've heard that term."

"Well, I'm ages old, so that makes sense," the creature states.

The creature has gills on either side of his throat, webbed fingers, and fins on the back of his arms. Seaweed covers the private bits of his body, but I'm able to see everything else. His body is a pale green, his abdomen ivory, like the belly of a fish, and he has a few blue spots on his sides.

His face is human-ish, with long, fin-like ears, and his nostrils consist of two slits. From here, I can see his large, reptilian eyes, but everything else about him seems normal.

His hair is wrapped on top of his head by a piece of seaweed, and he takes a seat on the beach, proving he does only want to talk. "I remember when these lands were beautiful, and my home used to be a place I wanted to be."

"These weren't always the Unwanted Lands?" I ask, my curiosity beating my fear.

He leans back on his elbows and shakes his head. "No, it used to be a place where the more unique creatures could live. Your kind gave the name to the Unwanted Lands, but before that, it was called Gleminor. We might be attached to your planet, but the moment you stepped over the territory line, you entered another world."

"That's impossible," I scoff at him, not believing a word. "I would have known that."

"Would you? It's been called the Unwanted Lands for years, decades, perhaps even centuries, and only the creatures that live long enough can tell the tales of what used to be. Your fallen leprechauns, your luckless beings, killed Gleminor. And they have made it into a place of nightmares."

The way he says it makes my heart hurt for him. He sounds so sad.

"I'm sorry. I didn't know."

"Not many do because anyone who comes here does not make it this far and back out again." He stands and wipes the sand from his butt. "I recommend you do not go swimming. At least not here. Walk about a mile that way and you'll find stones you can cross, but it won't be easy. I am one of the few friendly creatures of this lake. There are sirens, nymphs, and so much more. Some are not happy to be here for as long as we have without taking their revenge. You risked your life, Leprechaun. I hope whatever you seek is worth it."

"We are here gathering ingredients for my brother. We seek unicorn hair, wolfsbane, and heartsnow."

The creature's brow ridges move upward in surprise. "You are brave going on this journey for that. If you make it across the water, you'll be where you'll need to be for unicorn hair but gaining it won't be easy. You have to prove yourself to a unicorn for them to sacrifice their magic like that."

"My name is Ru and this is Anwyll." I point to my mate, who is practically frothing at the mouth to attack. "Thank you for this information."

"Sure," he says indifferently, lifting a shoulder as he walks toward the shore. "I am called Irving."

"Irving," I repeat. "How can we repay you for your kindness?"

He stares off into the distance, eyes roaming over the desolate plains, probably seeing what used to be. "If you know of a home that is safe and beautiful with water, perhaps I could save some of my kind and leave this place. If you could let me know..."

"You'd leave your home?"

He frowns, then takes a step into the water, the color so endless his feet disappear. "This is no longer my home." And with that, he dives into the water, only to pop his head back above the surface. "Just call my name and I'll hear you. Please, come back."

"—Wait!" I stop him before he vanishes, and he swims closer to the shore so I don't have to shout.

"We are from Salem, a place on a planet called Earth. We are with the Monreaux Coven, and the Coven Witch is

Maven Wildes. I'm sure if you came with us, she could find a home for you."

"Maven Wildes? The witch who opened the portals?"

"Her name has traveled far, then," I state.

He swims closer. "When you are done with your journey, please let me know. I'll gather my people. And you should know, a man has a scent similar to yours here with a girl. I've seen her.

"Her? What are you talking about?" Anwyll argues with Irving, clearly confused.

His ears flap with disagreement. "A man and a girl are here. I've overheard him talking, trying to find a way out of this place. He and the girl were fishing in the lake. Good luck on your journey, new friends. I wish you to survive." Without needing to take a breath, he dives underwater again, leaving nothing but bubbles popping on the surface.

"What do you think that means? Maybe it's my dad. He's here. Irving must be talking about him."

"No, that can't be right. Your dad still alive after all this time? I don't know, Ru."

"Yeah, you're right. Someone who has survived all this time in the Unwanted Lands wouldn't have any humanity, right?"

"As much as I would love to figure out that mystery with you, we already have too many tasks on our hands. If we are successful, then we will worry about what Irving said."

"He was kind, right?"

"Kind enough. We still don't know anything about him." Anwyll takes my hand, and we begin to walk in the direction Irving told us to.

"We know he's sad and lonely," I say, a solemn air in my voice. "That's enough to help him."

"I love that your kindness exists in every world we are in. It's everlasting." He tugs me against his chest, shifts into his humanoid form, and kisses me, his fangs nipping at my lip. "No matter the time, no matter the place, your kindness lives through it all."

"It's the only thing that matters at the end of the day." Thunder breaks the moment between us, and lightning cracks across the sky.

Anwyll moves me to his side, and we watch the bolts dance across the sky before crashing into the water.

"Fuck." Anwyll picks me up and stumbles backward to get away from the electrified current. Electricity dances over the water, pulsing through it like a live wire. "Well, this has complicated things," he says.

This journey becomes more complicated with every step we take.

"If we die, we died trying."

"Death helps no one. We will not die. We will wait for the storm to pass, and then we will walk the stones Irving spoke about. Until then, we rest. Let's set up the tent here, eat, and get some rest."

I nod, dragging the bag from my shoulder, unable to take my eyes off the ominous lake. Kindness won't help us survive in the end because death is so much stronger.

ANWYLL

We set the tent up in the woods on the edge where the trees meet the shoreline. It's raining, the storm swirling wind and sharp cracks of lightning. The tent's material rustles from the force, but we stay dry inside, the howl of the storm's rage reminding me of my kind when we are seeking each other.

A pang hits my heart. It's been so long since I've heard a dozen howls calling out for one another. I know I'm not alone. I have Ru. It's a different kind of loneliness. I feel like I'm the only werewolf left in existence. I haven't seen any others besides my brother since the spell was broken.

"You're deep in thought." Ru straddles my lap and places her arms on my shoulders. I can't bear to look at her right now, not when I'm like this.

Ever since I accepted my wolf, I've felt better. There are more moments I feel Alpha and in control, more powerful and destructive.

Yet I still have this side of me that's different, that's needing more right now. I don't want to be in control. Maybe it makes me weak, but it feels good to let go. Even my werewolf is feeling the effects of being an alpha. He's tired.

And we both want to be taken care of.

"What's wrong, Anwyll?" Her fingers drift through my hair, petting me gently.

In my half form, her fingers trace along my neck, then slide to my ears, where the tips are pointed with hair. She touches me like that for a while. Nothing special or sexual, just soft, barely there touches showing appreciation. They skim down my jaw and over my lip, then my fangs.

"I'm so curious about this form. How so many things are the same, but different." She continues to touch me, exploring and discovering, with my hands gripping her hips.

The rain pellets against the tent, a constant white noise.

We're sitting on piles of blankets and pillows, cozy and warm because of my body radiating heat.

If I had to describe her touch, it would be like a feather swaying through the air, and you hold out your hand to catch it, then it falls into your palm, the silkiness kissing your skin.

That's her touch.

Pure fucking silk, light and airy, and enough to settle the raging ocean crashing inside me.

"I'm glad you find my forms so appealing," I say, humming while she continues her exploration down my neck and chest.

"You're so unique. I love how your skin remains the same color as your wolf in this form, a gorgeous slate." She slides across my lap, my erection pressing between her legs, and I hold in a moan. "Will you tell me what's on your mind?"

"I want us to shower," I blurt out of nowhere. I don't

want to get into my feelings. "Probably best to do that now while it's raining." I shuffle her off my lap, strip my sweatpants, ignore my cock, and grab a bar of soap from the bag.

Stepping outside, the rain is cold and does wonders for the heat searing my system. We haven't bathed in days, and I don't know if we are ever going to be able to with not being near fresh water.

I let the rain soak me, standing outside completely bare, readying myself for lightning and thunder. Fog rolls over the lake, lightning still dancing over the surface, daring someone to touch it.

Why did I run away from Ru just now? I have so many conflicting emotions inside me. I want to throw her on the ground and fucking mount Ru from behind, fucking her in the most primal animalistic way, and roar to the sky as I fill her with my come.

Then there's the other side of me, the one that wants her to make me kneel, to make me beg, to put me on the edge. I want to be at her mercy, but now this new alpha power I've found doesn't like the idea of kneeling for anyone.

My breaths are growls as they leave me, my chest expanding faster with every gulp of air. I tilt my head up to the sky, and the rain soaks me. The heat inside me doesn't diminish, but the alpha inside takes a seat, realizing there is a part of me that needs more than it can give.

I don't want to be the last of my kind. My eyes burn at the thought, and I scrub my body with soap, the wind mocking me by howling again. Memories surface from when I was a child, going on pack runs under the full moon. I remember my mother trying to teach me how to howl. I was horrible at it at first. I couldn't seem to get enough air and have enough force to do it correctly, but eventually, I learned because howling comes naturally after a while.

"Anwyll."

I turn away from Ru, not wanting her to see how weak I am.

"Damn it, Anwyll. Look at me right now."

The command in her voice has me turning instantly. I have to listen to her, and already I feel better.

"Tell me what's going on with you," she demands, no longer asking nicely.

Her hair becomes darker as the rain soaks it. The strands stick to her bare shoulders, and my eyes roam down her perfect body.

She snaps her fingers in front of me. "No, you don't get to look at me. You don't get the privilege of admiring what you love. Not when you won't tell me the truth, and Anwyll, if you look down from my eyes, I will make sure you don't come for hours. I will bring you to the edge over and over again until you beg me."

I whine at the horrible thought, but my cock jumps at the idea.

I want to be denied.

"Now, tell me what's going on."

I hang my head, the soap washing from my body, and Ru takes the bar of soap from my hands and begins to wash my hair. A purr builds, and my eyes close as she bathes me. My bones become weightless.

"I feel alone," I finally admit. "Not in this sense of being with you. I love you with every fucking beat my heart gives; you are my existence. I miss being with my kind, other werewolves. I miss going on pack runs and howling. I miss going on a full moon hunt. The wind in the storm." I point out just as it howls again, sending the rain sideways. "It reminded me of them. What if my brother and I are the last of the werewolves, Ru? What if the only memories I have are from when I was a pup? I can't stand the thought. It hurts so much. The coven is my pack, yes. Lex is my Alpha, but it doesn't change the fact that there are no other wolves. I have no one to run with. I have no one to hunt with or howl for." The ache runs deeper than I thought, and the more the wind blows, the more I'm reminded of what I'll never have.

"I know it isn't the same, but I'll be happy to do those things with you. If you want to hunt, I'll hunt with you, if you want to run under the moon, I'll run with you. I'm not a wolf, but you're my wolf, and that means anything you want to do, I'm going to do it with you." She washes herself next, the suds of soap drifting down her body, slowly, teasing me, taunting me. A few bubbles stop in the strawberry blonde thatch of hair between her legs.

I want to bury my nose there and inhale deeply until I'm high from the scent of her.

"You can look. You've been such a good boy, telling me the truth."

A pathetic whine slips from me, and I fall to my knees, the alpha inside me wanting to bow at her feet, to worship her, but first, I need her to take care of me.

Her hand cups my cheek, her thumb rubbing the fur along my jaw. "Is this what you need, Anwyll?"

I nod against her palm, my entire body relaxing until my weight is resting on my knees, and I sink into the mud. The rain pours, a constant sheet hiding us so no one can see, but maybe they can, I can't be sure.

The thought doesn't bother me. I don't want to know if anyone sees, but the thought of it...it causes my cock to pulsate. The heartbeat throbs inside my shaft, and the rain washes away the evidence of the come dripping from my slit.

"Stand up," she orders, gesturing with her finger, and I begrudgingly get to my feet. Ru takes my hand, sliding her fingers along the gray skin and fur, and then presses the tip of her finger against my talon. "So monstrous," her admission a white noise in the static of rain.

"In a bad way?" I ask, needing to be hopeful because only a special woman could love the murderer living inside me.

"In the best way, My Gentle Giant."

She wraps her fingers around my wrist and lifts my arm, pressing the sharp point against the middle of her chest. "Would you hurt me if I asked you to?"

I shake my head, not even wanting to entertain the thought.

"Why? What if that's what I want?"

My eyes shift at her request, calling on my most primal instincts. "Because in a week, you'll be praying to whatever fucking god you believe in to make me stop fucking you, to stop hurting you, to stop feasting on you, and no one, not even your god, will be able to stop me, Ru." A guttural growl, mixed with possessiveness, eagerness, and primal instinct, echoes louder than the rain beating against the ground.

"What if the only being I worship, that I pray to, is you?" She wraps her small hand around my throat and bends over, curling her lip at me. "Bathe me. And then, I want you to eat my pussy, Anwyll. Don't you dare touch yourself either. If you come, I'll punish you."

"What will you do?" I question, my body becoming lighter as the alpha inside me practically rolls to his back and surrenders.

"I'll edge you for hours. I'll bring you to the brink over and over again until your sack hurts, until you're whimpering, crying, and begging me to let you come. I'll tie your hands to make sure you can't come, but I'll come. I'll ride your cock over and over again until my body falls limp, and only then will I consider letting you come. Maybe I won't. Maybe I'll wait days until I touch your fat cock again."

"Ru," I gasp her name, the cruelness of her promise only turning me on more. "Please, don't do that to me."

"Then I guess you'd better make me come on your tongue and don't touch yourself." She lifts her leg and wraps it around my neck, using her foot against my back to pull me between her legs. She shoves the bar of soap in my palm. "Clean me."

"Whatever you want, My Lucky Charm." I lather the soap between my palms, then drop the bar on the ground, dirtying it with mud. I slip my fingers through her, the silky glide of her lips parting from my talons. I'm careful not to cut her, but the beast inside me wants to.

I want to see her bleed.

I want to see her flesh stained in red, and then I want to lick her clean. I want her blood infused with my DNA, molding to me, becoming one with me.

And I'll finally be able to do that on the full moon.

She moans, tilting her head back until her face is pointed to the sky. The rain drips from her skin, her hair soaked to the scalp, and her tits are on full display, her nipples tight and dark red, beaded from the cool kiss of rain.

The suds from the soap build while I rub my fingers through her cunt until bubbles drip down her inner thighs. I tilt my chin to my chest, staring at my throbbing cock, the ridge of my knot at the base, wishing it could inflate.

Soon.

Soon, I'll be able to knot her every fucking night, filling her until she's so full of me, my come leaks from her greedy little cunt.

"Behave, Anwyll," she says, tightening her grip around my neck.

I didn't realize I was growling. "I'm sorry. Touching you ignites my most animalistic instincts." I press my palm against her clit, creating small circles that cause her thighs to tremble.

"Don't apologize, but the next time you growl, I'd better feel it inside me."

I close my eyes and take a deep breath, trying to calm myself because I need to come. I need to earn it. All I have to do is listen to her.

Checking in with my werewolf, I notice the alpha is quiet, lurking in the shadows of my soul. Ready to take control, but only when she says so.

Bending one knee, I wrap an arm around her waist and bend her over my leg, spreading her legs so the rain can wash the soap away. I watch as her pretty pink clit comes into view, and I lick my tongue across my fangs, dying for a taste.

When she's clean, I stand her up and kneel at her feet again. My shoulders rise and fall, my talons dig into the ground, and my werewolf threatens to burst free but stays just under my skin.

With a grip of my fur, she yanks my head between her legs as she widens her stance. "I'm ready to come, Anwyll. Don't disappoint me."

Goosebumps travel over my skin, and I get between her legs, diving in without hesitation. I shift my tongue to lengthen it, plunging into her tight cunt that I can't believe I get to fuck whenever I want. She's all mine.

There will never be another.

A growl escapes me, filling her just like she wanted, and her nails scrape across my neck.

"Anwyll," she moans my name just as thunder rolls.

My eyes roll to the back of my head as I quench my thirst. The taste of her settles in my bones, and the rain pouring into my mouth hydrates me best when flowing from her cunt. I do as she wants. I eat her, growling and snarling, nipping her lips. I wish I could devour her in the worst of ways.

The killer inside me wants to tear her to shreds just so I can be as close as possible to her. I literally want to burrow myself under her skin until we are one. It's sickening and grotesque, but it's true.

"Yes, Anwyll. Just like that. You're so good at eating my pussy. Such a good boy doing what he's told." She combs her fingers over the top of my head, scratching behind my ear.

I suck her clit into my mouth, and she screams, the sound meshing with the lightning veining across the darkened sky.

"More. More, Anwyll."

Flipping my tongue out of her tight hole, I flatten it along the slit, gathering the nectar and rain. My talons dig into her ass and yank her closer to me until I feel like I can't breathe.

Fuck yes.

I want to be suffocated. If the last breath I ever took was filled with the scent of her, I'd die a happy werewolf.

My knees slide through the mud, and I latch my claws

onto the thick of her ass to keep me in place, sucking her clit harder, then rolling the sweet candy between my teeth.

Her nails rake down my neck and shoulders. "Just like that. Yes," she rolls her hips. "Yes." Ru's voice becomes higher the closer she gets to having an orgasm. "Yes! Anwyll. Fuck!" She tosses her head back and holds my face between her legs as her orgasm trembles through her body. I drink her down, practically purring from her taste.

She pushes me back, and my knees slip in the mud as I fall onto my back. She climbs onto my lap and slides herself down onto my cock, taking every inch just like she was meant to. "You aren't allowed to come yet, Anwyll." Her mouth parts as she rocks against me. The strands of her wet hair fall over her breasts. "Do you like being used?"

"Ru..." I gasp when she reaches behind herself and squeezes my aching sack.

She leans down, wrapping her other hand around my throat, and squeezes. "Answer me. Do you like being used like my little fuck toy, Anwyll? Do you like being used for your big cock and like you're no good for anything else?"

"Yes," I moan, my talons scraping down her thighs. "Fuck!" I growl, snapping forward as my wolf takes over for a split second, but she slams me back against the ground, then sucks my bottom lip into her mouth. Ru bites it while she rides me.

"I'm in control. Not you. Do that again, and I won't let you come."

"I have to... Ru, please." I beg her, needing to roll her onto her stomach and fuck her from the back. I want to knot her.

I smell her. The promise of her heat. It's coating my cock. I need to own her.

"I don't care what you want." She rolls her hips again and straightens, cupping her tits while she fucks me. Lightning strikes above the lake, igniting a flash of light in the sky above Ru. Rain pours harder, slicking our skin, making it easier to gain speed. "Your cock is so good, My Gentle Giant. It's the best I've ever had. So big. So thick. It almost hurts."

I whine, her dirty words causing my cock to tingle, threatening my orgasm.

"You touch the deepest parts of me. You stretch me so wide. I can hardly take it, but I want so much more. I want your come inside me, Anwyll. I want you to fill me up. I want to feel you dripping from me. I want your bite. Your mark. I want you to hunt me down."

I squeeze her hips, trying to control myself, and shake my head. "Ru..." I gasp as she rides me faster. "Get off. Get off. I can't..."

She slides off, my cock slapping against my stomach, and then she grips it so hard my orgasm fades. "What did I say about coming?"

"I didn't. I didn't come. I warned you." I can barely think. A burning blaze sears my veins as my orgasm subsides. My sack becomes heavy, a steady throb killing me.

She lets me go, and I inhale a sharp breath, letting the rain cool the fever in my cheeks. "Crawl to me," she orders, walking backward until she's a few yards away. "I want to see your cock swing."

My eyes hood as a new wave of lust hits me. I'll do whatever she wants. I get on my hands and knees, my fingers slipping through the mud. My wolf growls in excitement, knowing we are making our mate happy.

But we're happy too.

"Look at you. You're so beautiful coming to me like this. I love your body."

I stop in front of her, staying on all fours as I wait for her to tell me what to do. Her hand rubs down my back until her fingers trace my crease. I shudder as her finger rubs against my hole. I don't jump away, but I'm not sure how I feel about it. No one has ever touched me there. I haven't even explored that part of myself.

"Would you let me have this, Anwyll? Would you let me own that round, fuckable ass?" She slaps my right cheek, and a moan escapes me. "Oh, my werewolf likes that." She yanks my head back by my fur, forcing me to look at her. "Don't you?"

I nod, the rain filling my mouth as my lips part. I lick my tongue over my fangs.

She spanks me again, and my cock jerks, my entire body buzzing for more. I want my mind to shut off. I want the nightmares to be at ease. I want to forget everything and be in the moment, and I want to give my past up for Ru. I want her to take my pain away.

She spanks me again, and my body flinches, the water causing a sting. I wrap my hand around her leg, holding on for dear life and hoping I don't come from her assault.

Thunder shakes the ground, vibrating my knees, and she spanks me harder and harder. My cheeks burn, and I whimper, then groan. My cock flexes, and my orgasm is threatening me again.

My claws break her skin, and the scent of blood fills the air. She doesn't flinch. Ru keeps spanking me in the same way I want to spank her. I love this dynamic. I love that I can give myself over to her, to take the weight off my mind, and when she wants, I'll always do the same for her.

It isn't just her spanking me. I don't feel like less of a

man or a werewolf. I feel empowered, because finally, in all my life, I can trust someone to take care of me.

Her voice is far away when she stops, and my vision blurs as I drift off into space. She rubs the burning skin, crooning sweet nothings at me.

"What a good boy. You look so good with your skin red from my hand." She kneels in front of me and slams her lips against mine. I moan when I taste the iron of her blood coming from where my fangs nip her lip. Our tongues slip and slide against one another, and I growl down her throat. "Fuck me, Anwyll. Take me."

Ripping my lips from hers, I slam her onto her back and ram myself inside her tight cunt. I roar to the sky, a savage howl sounding more like a beast than a wolf. The pleasure burns through my chest, and I have to stop the full shift from taking over.

"Harder. Harder, give me more," she begs, surrendering herself to me.

It's my turn.

With every hard thrust, we move through the mud. I lift her hips from the ground and pummel my cock into her tight hole. I watch the slate gray shaft spearing her, stretching her pussy wide, and the sight makes me fuck her faster, deeper, harder. My sack slaps against her ass, and her cries to the sky are left unheard by the rain.

My hands shift into my werewolf, my palms tripling in size, and I snarl, barely holding onto my humanity. At the tip of my cock, I feel it, the simmering warmth of the heat preparing her womb for me, and saliva drips from my fangs at the thought.

I ram into her with every ounce of strength I have, my ass still burning from her assault. Then her pussy clamps around me, and she tosses her head back as she comes.

I fuck her through it.

I want more.

"Anwyll! Oh, chauns. Yes. More. Like that. Just like that. Come inside me, I need it. I need to feel it."

I wrap both hands around her throat as I slide in and out at a punishing rate.

And she orgasms again, tightening her muscles around me to milk me dry.

I toss my head back, letting every creature know around us that I'm owning my fated mate, roaring for all to hear. The sound is louder than the thunder, shaking the bones inside my skin, and I come voraciously, my come jetting from me at a rapid pace.

The moment she feels my warmth, her cunt sucks my seed to her womb, and I bet she wishes it would stick.

In a week.

Seven days, if I don't kill her, she'll be pregnant with my child.

She'll be mine.

And all I'll need to do is remind myself not to rip her heart out.

No pressure.

Chapter Twenty-Seven

RU

I'm sore in all the right places and aching for more in all the wrong.

I turn to my side, watching Anwyll in his sleep, and scream when I see Irving staring at us through the tent entrance. Anwyll shifts, roaring so loud I have to cover my ears. Fur sprouts along his arms, and his werewolf form is so big he tears the tent to pieces, bursting out from the flimsy material as I hold the blankets to my chest to make sure I'm covered.

We went to sleep naked because we may or may not have had sex two, three, or four times. I lost count.

With a sardonic snarl, he wraps his giant paw around Irving's neck and lifts him off the ground. "Why are you watching my mate?" Anwyll's voice is the darkest I've ever heard it, dripping with the vow to murder.

I watch him tighten his fingers, and Irving claws at Anwyll's paws.

"Anwyll. Let him go. He can't answer you if you're killing him." I grab my mate's shoulder, and he turns his head to look at me. Anwyll's features soften, but when he looks back at Irving, he snarls, letting him go while he is lifted in the air.

Irving lands on the ground, sand covering his feet, and he coughs, touching his throat with his webbed fingers. "Apologies," he says, his voice hoarse. "I didn't mean to intrude. I was about to wake you because now is a good time to head to the stones to get to the other side of the island for your unicorn hair. I saw you sleeping, and I debated whether I wanted to wake you. I wasn't staring at your mate, Lycan. I promise."

Anwyll growls, taking a step forward, but I stop him by wrapping a hand around his arm.

"I believe him. He's been nothing but helpful," I remind my werewolf, and he nods, shifting into his half-form that I've become obsessed with.

"You need to get going before another storm comes through. They come in cycles of three. So you don't have much time."

"Thank you for the warning, Irving. We will pack up and go."

"And I suggest not getting too vocal on the other side of the island," he clears his throat, a bluish color deepening his cheeks. I think he is blushing. "There are centaurs over there that love a good show. Just to warn you."

"You heard us?" Anwyll grumbles.

"The entire lake heard you," Irving replies. "Nothing to be ashamed about."

"I'm not ashamed. I want everyone to hear me claiming my mate, so they know she's taken."

"Message received, Lycan."

I open the bag and everything we have used drifts inside. The blankets fold together; the pillows settle somewhere deep in this magic bag that I'll never understand.

The tent is useless. It's scattered in pieces along the beach since Anwyll couldn't contain himself.

Now where are we going to sleep?

"Thank you for your help, Irving. You've been very kind. We will come back, okay? If that's what you truly want."

"It is," he says quickly, taking a step forward. "I'd love to leave this place."

"Come with us, then," Anwyll offers. "It will be easier."

"I have to convince my kind first. I'm hoping they will be on board by the time you're ready to go home. Be safe. I'm afraid your journey is only going to get harder from here." He holds a webbed hand out to Anwyll. "Good luck, Lycan."

Anwyll and Irving shake hands, but I give Irving a big hug. "Thank you for everything. I promise we won't leave you behind."

"You are kind. I'll be hoping for your return. Farewell… friends." He sounds like he's unsure how to feel about the last word but settles on it with a smile. The gills on either side of his neck move with every inhale and exhale. "And remember, don't fall into the water." Irving walks into the water, giving us a final nod before he dives under, never coming up to the surface.

"Ready?" Anwyll says, holding out his hand.

I slap mine against his and lock my fingers through his. "As I'll ever be."

We walk down the beach, and the view of the sky is forgettable. It's nothing special. An overcast of gray with slightly darker clouds filling it. The trees to the left of us sway, the branches reaching for us but flinching away when they reach the beach.

I expect to see shells in the sand, but I don't.

There are bones instead. I bend down to pick one up.

It's small and thin, reminding me of a tiny animal, and it's polished with an opal finish. "It's like a pearl," I whisper, finding it beautiful even though it is a reminder of death.

He half shifts again, the showoff. "Let's take it with us. Maybe Maven can use it."

"I don't know. It feels wrong to take it." I set it down in the sand again and stand. "And for all I know, if you take a bone, you'll probably be cursed for life. I'm not willing to risk it."

Anwyll laughs, his cuspids showing from the grin stretching across his face. "That's true. I didn't think of that."

He holds out his hand, and I watch as his fingers morph, yet again. Long talons take the place of his nails, and his fur sprouts halfway up his arm. When I lie mine across his palm, I stare at our differences for a second. His dwarves mine, and when his talons curl over the top of my hand, I peer up at him.

I stand, and his talon drifts down my face, the sharp point threatening to break my skin. "Are you ready for this?" he asks, the water drifting gently against our feet. "I swear, I'll protect you. Even if it costs me my own life."

"Never if it costs you your own life." I kiss the inside of his palm and blink up at him, his features stark and unique, his shoulder-length hair swaying across his shoulders. Typically, it's a dark shade, but when he's half-shifted, it's gray to match his skin. "Promise me," I tell him.

"Never will I promise such a thing." He grips the back of my neck and tugs me forward, his lips falling to mine.

His fangs tickle my lips, and the slight tease of them has me sighing into him. I fall against his chest, and he pulls away, pressing his warm lips against my forehead. "I love you. Let's get to that side of the island." He takes a step back and changes into his werewolf, growing a few more feet, his frame widening with muscle. "You'll get on my back. It's the only way we can jump between rocks. Your tiny legs wouldn't make it."

"I should take offense to that. You didn't seem to mind my weak, puny legs last night when they were wrapped around you."

He growls as he grips my legs and hoists me onto his back. "I love your legs. I want to make sure they don't get injured. Let me do all the work here. I won't risk you."

I wrap my arms around his neck just as he steps onto the first stone. "And I love you for it." I kiss his cheek, and his tail brushes against me as it wags. I smile against his shoulder, loving the little things I can't get enough of when it comes to Anwyll.

"This isn't so bad," he says.

The rock is sturdy and bigger than I expected. The edges are submerged underwater, and there's the island in the distance.

I won't admit it out loud, but the spaces between each stepping stone are huge. I wouldn't make it with my 'tiny' legs. Anwyll crouches, then leaps into the air, landing on the next one. He jumps on the next one, then the next, the island getting closer, and I enjoy the breeze in my hair with every leap he takes.

"You okay?"

I tighten my hold around his neck and shut my eyes when we go through the air again. "I'm fine," I shout, letting out a breath when we land.

He squats again, and I bury my face against his back, preparing to leap through the air again when we fly forward. Anwyll hits the stone with a hard thud, and we are dragged across the rock.

I look back to see a tentacle wrapped around his ankle.

Anwyll roars, reaching back to slice his talons through it, and it spews black blood. A scream can be heard from underwater. Tentacles wrap around the stone and lift it from its spot. I scream, clutching his neck so hard, I know he can't breathe.

Without warning, Anwyll gets to his feet and runs, leaping into the air, and lands on the next stone. Only this time, he doesn't stop the momentum. He gains speed, jumping again.

And again.

I make the mistake of looking back only to see a dark purple kraken with long tentacles following us. It's tossing the stones from left to right, its eyes locked on us like we are prey.

Anwyll stumbles and his claws scrape against the stone, stopping us right at the edge before we fall in.

"Are you okay?" he shouts, gasping for breath.

"I'm fine. I'm scared, but I'm fine."

Anwyll stands again, taking another leap when a tentacle wraps around us both.

"Anwyll!" I shout as pressure begins to crush my lungs. "Can't. Breathe."

My mate roars as we are wretched through the air. The water is below us, and other creatures bob their heads as they watch the show. Anwyll latches onto the tentacle wrapped around us, sinking his fangs into the meaty flesh. Black blood fills his mouth, and a high-pitched scream leaves the kraken just as it unravels its thick tentacle.

We free-fall through the air and land on one of the stones. The air gets knocked out of me, and my head spins, but Anwyll gets right back up.

"Ru? Talk to me."

"Hmm, fine," I mumble, barely able to keep my arms wrapped around his neck. He reaches around and lifts me from his back, carrying me in his arms. He leaps onto another stone, missing the swipe of another angry tentacle.

Another sweep of a tentacle and we fly to the right this time, and I'm separated from Anwyll. I fall into the water. It's ice cold and tastes of burnt wood. I close my eyes and move my arms, kicking my legs to get to the surface. When I break free, I gasp for breath, water stinging my eyes.

But it doesn't just sting.

It burns.

And the pain is unlike anything I've ever felt. "Anwyll! Anwyll!" My voice breaks from how loud I scream, and my vision blurs.

Something tugs at my leg. I bring my other foot up, then kick whatever it is in the face.

I swim. I can't see where I'm going, but I swim, moving my arms and kicking my legs as hard and as fast as I can.

"Ru!" Anwyll calls for me, and I stop moving.

"Anwyll?" I swim in a circle, trying to figure out which direction I heard him. I'm terrified. His roar calls to me, and all I want to do is go to him.

Something grabs my foot again, and this time pulls me under. I can't see what I'm fighting, but I feel myself being pulled deeper.

It's colder too. My bones are numb, and my muscles begin to weaken. I hear gorgeous songs of harmonic beauty I've never heard of before, and then I feel myself begin to float.

I'm dragged, I think. It feels like I'm being pulled through the water, and it's to the point where I need to breathe.

And I do.

Water fills my lungs until my head feels like it's about to explode.

The feeling of being pulled through the water stops, and I feel sand beneath me, air chilling my frozen skin.

"Ms. Ru? Can you hear me?" Something wet and smooth hits my cheek. "Ru? Oh, dear. This isn't good."

"What happened to her!" Anwyll roars, but he must be okay because he sounds like he is right next to me.

"One of the creatures I warned you about snagged her. The sirens distracted the water dragon with a song, so I could grab her and bring her to shore."

It's Irving.

"I told you it was dangerous."

"You could have given more warning," Anwyll sneers, and then my back is lifted from the ground. "Don't do this to me again, mate. Please." He presses against my chest, once, twice, and I cough, gasping and choking for air as I spew water from my throat. "That's it. Oh, good girl. Good. I'm so fucking proud of you. Thank you for not leaving me." He lies me down again, moving the hair out of my face.

I open my eyes, and I hear both of them gasp. "I can't see," I admit, reaching for Anwyll, and his giant paw takes it. "I can't see anything!" I panic and begin to cry.

"It's okay. It's the lake's defense mechanism. It blinds its...prey, but it isn't permanent if you live. You'll see again in just a few hours," Irving informs, hope bright in his voice. "I promise. You'll be okay, but you need to keep moving. You can't stop here. The krakens don't like land, but if they see you on the shore, they will try and get you again."

"How can I travel if I can't see?" I ask, still clutching onto Anwyll's arm, shivering.

I'm lifted into the air and shoved against a hot, werewolf chest, and I sigh, my body soaking in the warmth. "You feel so good."

"I'll always take care of you, Mate." He runs his talons through my hair, untangling the knots.

"You'll have to carry her, Anwyll. Get away from the shore. If you want, rest, but don't you dare stop until you can't see the water. Understand?"

"Yes. Thank you. I'm forever in your debt, Irving," Anwyll says.

"We will consider us even when you get me out of here. Now, go." Irving taps my leg, and I can tell it's his hand because it's colder than Anwyll's, and a bit smaller too.

Everything is smaller compared to Anwyll.

"How did you get away from the kraken?"

"I ripped out its heart," he rumbles. "And I'd do it again and serve it to you on a platter."

It should gross me out, but I feel taken care of, and thought of, and it brings me happiness. Something about him hunting for me makes me feel important.

I know I am important to him, but that is another level.

"Rest, My Little Lucky Charm. I'll wake you when we stop."

"Okay," I whisper, wishing I could see him, but it's all a blur. A blank blob. I rub my cheek against his chest, feeling his fur, and I sigh, wishing I could get closer.

He is my armor, the reason I'm always protected.

Chapter Twenty-Eight

ANWYLL

I didn't have it in me to wake her up. I wanted her to rest, so when I couldn't see the lake, I stopped and put together a small hut for us. I destroyed our tent, so the least I could do was make one for her. It can only fit Ru, but I'm okay with that. I'm happy if Ru is safe, warm, dry, and at peace.

She sighs, and I bolt onto my feet, crawling into the shelter to check on her.

Ru is lying on her back, head turned to the side. I watch as her chest rises and falls. She's okay. Her stomach growls, and it gives me the idea to hunt for her. The feeling to hunt has been getting stronger as the moon becomes closer. My wolf wants to take care of her, and I plan on doing that, but I don't want to leave her alone for too long.

I back away from her, staring into the trees, and let my instincts take over. My vision is sharper, my smell enhances, and I survey everything around me.

Unlike the land across the lake, the trees here are green and healthy. I'm wondering if it's because of the unicorns. They hold a certain type of magic; if most of them are here on this island, it would explain why the environment is more alive.

I inhale, trying to scent any prey, and I close my eyes, letting my enhanced senses take the lead on this. We can't depend on that fucking magic bag forever.

My head snaps to the right when I hear rustling in the bushes. I inhale through my nose, trying to catch a scent. I fall to all fours and prowl toward the sound. I'm careful where I land each paw. My talons dent the dirt, and I see some chips in the soil I dig every time I lift my arm or leg. I crouch, creeping forward, the bushes brushing against my abdomen.

Remaining as quiet as possible, I pause when I hear shuffling. Through the tall grass, I see it, and I tilt my head in confusion when I try to figure out what kind of creature it is. It's the size of a small hog but has the legs of a rabbit and the face of a cow. It's grazing lazily, its mouth chewing the long, straw grass. It has a bored expression while it eats, and its eyes are big, wide, and open as if it is surprised. Shaggy walnut-colored hair hangs in its face, but the rest of its body is bare, with just a tuft for a tail.

An odd-looking creature, but it looks edible, and that's all I care about right now. I could scare it paralyzed, but that takes the fun out of the chase, and now that we are less than a week from the full moon, the urge to hunt is beginning to simmer in my blood.

I leap through the air, and the damn thing leaps away quicker than I've ever seen any other prey animal.

Now I'm just pissed off.

I run after it, dodging between the trees, and swipe my paw, my claws grazing its sides. I'm glad Ru isn't here to see this. She'd be upset I killed it, but it's the way of my kind.

This is how I used to eat growing up. We lived wild. We didn't live in a big house like Maven and Lex do.

The prey groans, slowing until it's whining. No creature deserves to suffer. I crack its neck, putting it out of its misery fast.

"Thank you. I'm sorry it had to end this way for you," I say, picking it up with my mouth, then sprint back to Ru to make sure she's okay.

I shouldn't have been gone so long, but I really wanted to hunt for her.

I hope she likes it.

When I'm at the hut I made her, I drop the creature next to it and peer in to make sure she's okay. She's still asleep, her hands tucked under her cheek, and her knees curled to her chest.

Leaving her be, I gather some broken branches and long grass to build a fire. Once I have that started, I begin to skin and clean my kill before placing it over the flames.

I lean back, watching the blaze blacken the underbelly before giving the stick a turn so it cooks evenly. I twist my neck when an urge of raw power rushes through me, but it's gone just as quickly as it presented itself.

Eventually, that power will stay for a full night.

And Ru will be at the receiving end.

"Anwyll?"

Her sleepy voice has me pushing onto my feet, morphing into my half form when she stumbles out of the shelter. She rubs her eyes, and I tilt her chin up so I can look at her.

"Can you see me?" I ask the question that's been plaguing my thoughts since she lost her sight.

If worst comes to worst, I'll be her sight. If she can never see again, I'll lead her to safety, and I'll be her guide.

"I can," she smiles, blinking those gorgeous green eyes at me. "I can see you." She touches my cheek, and I lean into her palm. "It would have been a catastrophe to never have been able to see your face again."

"This old mug?" I tease, glancing away as she stares at me intensely. I'm not used to compliments. "It's nothing special."

"It's everything I look forward to seeing every day." She presses her fingers against my cheek to turn my head. "Your face is the beauty of Àdh but holds the fierceness of the Unwanted Lands. If I only could choose to see one thing, Anwyll, one thing in this entire world, it would be you."

The wood crackles as it burns, the silence of the forest both calming and concerning.

"Do you think we will make it out of here alive?" she asks, her breath ghosting over my chest while she leans against it.

I sit down on a fallen log covered in moss and take Ru's hand, bringing her down to sit on my lap. "I don't care what I have to do to make sure you make it back, I'll do it."

Her pupils widen, and tears fill her eyes. "You make it sound like you won't be coming with me, and if you aren't coming with me, then I won't be going home."

I set my chin on her shoulder and stare into the fire, holding her tighter than usual. There won't be a day when I can't be without her. I can't live without her, but Ru is a leprechaun. She might be able to go on and live a happy life without me, and I can't deny that I don't want to be the reason why she can't live a happy life.

But the thought of her with anyone but me makes me manic. A low growl escapes with every breath I take, and Ru sinks even further against me as if she knows what I'm thinking.

"Promise me we either go back together or not at all. Promise me," she says, twisting in my lap and wrapping her legs around my waist.

I drift my hands up her back, relishing in the warmth of her body and the fire in front of us. Inhaling the succulent scent of the fresh meat roasting, I relax and let the truth wash over me.

There's no living for me if anything happens to Ru.

And there's no living for her either.

"Either life or death, but together," I state, hating the thought of a world where Ru doesn't exist.

"Together," she agrees. "Always together." She slips her hand in mine and we sit there in silence, letting the weight of the situation fall over us.

It's exhausting carrying around tons of the unknown because if I decide to set it down, it means I've given up. And I can't give up. My brother depends on me too much, and if I fail at this task, I fail him, and I can't allow that.

"What are you cooking?" she changes the subject.

I blow out a breath and tap my fingers against her thigh. "I don't know."

"You don't know?"

"I went hunting for you, and it was unlike anything I've ever seen. I don't know what to call it. It had rabbit legs." I show her how a rabbit bounces with my hands. "And then a cow face. I knew you had to eat, and the urge to provide for you the closer we get to the full moon, is becoming stronger." I look away and lift a shoulder. "It's okay if you don't want to eat it." I won't tell her, but I'll be sad. Now that my werewolf and I are one, our feelings are meshed together, and the thought of her not eating what we hunted for her is a form of rejection.

If she rejects it, I'll have to keep hunting until I find something she accepts.

"You hunted for me?" Her voice changes into something soft and sweet. Ru angles herself so she can look at me, and an appreciative smile crosses her face.

"Yes. I'll always provide for you," I say with earnest, lifting my partially shifted hand to her cheek. "You really don't mind?"

"Mind? I'm starving. You hunting for me is kind of hot. Will I ever be able to watch you?"

The thought of her watching me maim and kill causes my dick to rise.

"I think you like the sound of that."

"If it means having your eyes on me, I like the sound of anything you want to do."

She reaches down to grab my cock just as her stomach rumbles so loud, I'm sure the entire island can hear it.

I take her wrist to stop her. "As much as I enjoy your touch, you need to eat. If you eat, I'll be more than happy to devour you right here."

"Promise?"

"On my life," I let my werewolf speak for me, the words rough as gravel, and her lust permeates the air.

"Fine." She scoots off my lap and sits on the ground, crossing her legs.

She's cute when she pouts.

Smirking to myself, I stand and check the meat. It's done. I grab the stick and carry it over to her. "Be careful. It's hot."

"You aren't going to eat?"

"I'll eat when you're done. When we hunt, our mates eat first. If not, we get pretty antsy."

"We wouldn't want that." She plucks one of the legs off

and rips a large chunk of meat off. She moans, closing her eyes as she chews. "This is so good." Before she's done chewing, she's tearing more meat from the bone.

I can't help it, my werewolf emerges from me, and I fall to all fours, pacing by the fire as I watch her eat. I love it.

She's mine.

She's eating what I killed for her.

She likes it.

Ru licks her fingers, and there's a bit of juice trickling down her chin. Before I know it, I'm in front of her, grabbing her neck, and licking her chin clean.

"Is it good, my Little Lucky Charm?"

"Delicious. I'm full," she states, holding the stick out to me.

Half of the creature is gone, nothing but bone left.

"I want you to have the other half."

"If you're still hungry—"

"—I'm not. I'm full, Anwyll. Please," she begs, a hint of worry in her tone.

Not wanting to hide my true nature, I bare my teeth. Bone and all, I bite into it, chewing without looking away from Ru.

I know she can hear the crunch of bone. It must be sickening to her, but the longer we stare at one another, the more I notice her heavy breathing.

She smells like desire.

Pressing my left paw against her hip, I lean forward, sinking my teeth into the belly of my kill. Juice flings against her face, and I lick her clean again, not wanting to miss a drop.

"Anwyll," she gasps, her nipples hard and pressing against her shirt.

"Do you like it when I'm a savage? Do you like knowing

I could do this to you?" I hold up the stripped skeleton of our meal and throw it against the tree behind her. "I could skin you alive and you'd let me, wouldn't you? Because it would be what I wanted." My thoughts become darker, the instinct to overpower her riding me hard and fast.

"Ye—s," she whimpers, breaking the small word into two beats from her chaotic intake of air.

"You need more of my come, don't you?" I push forward until she's lying down under me. "You want to be ready for me on the full moon. Your body is craving me, isn't it?" I press my monstrous hand against her lower belly and exhale through my nose. "And soon, you'll be so full of me, you'll carry my child." I shift into my half form, my hand pressing against her throat to keep her still. "Answer me."

"Yes. Yes, I want it all. I'm craving your come."

She isn't lying. She needs it. Her body is dependent on it, so when I knot her on the full moon, she'll be able to handle me.

God, I can't wait to be able to knot her whenever the hell I want.

"Only I can give you the relief you need."

I slip her pants off and push her panties to the side, not giving a damn about foreplay. Not right now. I need to be inside her. There's a deep ache in my cock that only her cunt will be able to ease.

In my middle form, between half man and half werewolf, my appearance is humanoid, but there are features of me that remain large. Between the slate-colored skin and pointed fangs, my cock remains the size it would be in my shifted form.

And my favorite part about it is Ru's expression.

I love the way she gasps every time she sees me.

Her heat engulfs the tip, and she's already soaked for me. I don't ease in. I don't tease. I take.

I drive my hips forward, slamming into her without remorse, and she shouts for the entire island to hear. My knees dig into the ground, and the violent urges to consume her plague my body. Ru drips with desire, drenching my cock, and my hips stutter when I scent her heat.

It's stronger today. I slam my fists against the ground, curling my talons into the dirt, and roar to stop myself from shifting fully.

"Yes, Anwyll. More. I want more," she begs, turning her neck to the side.

She doesn't know what that means. She's surrendering herself to me, unknowingly asking me to bite and claim her.

Has her heat already started? I won't be able to satisfy her urges until the full moon. I won't be able to properly take care of her. That thought enrages me. It's up to me to make sure she's taken care of. She can't start her heat yet. She can't.

I slam into her, over and over, with all the strength I have, fucking her as if she were nothing but my fuck toy to fill with come.

"Yes! Anwyll. Oh my chauns, you feel so good. Give it all to me. Come inside me, please. Oh my fucking chauns, come inside me. I need it. I need it!" she screams, clutching at the ground.

I pull out of her and growl when I see how wet she is. Her honey drips from my flared tip, proof that her heat is close. I spread her legs and see her desire shining on her inner thighs, cream leaking from her tight cunt.

"Your eyes," she gasps, another wave of intense heat filling the air and hitting me in the face.

"What about them?" My voice is different, uncontrolled, unsteady, and dark.

With a sneer, I flip her onto her stomach and place her on all fours, wanting to mount her from the back.

"They are black."

I thrust into her, shoving her face into the ground, and use her, my cock hugged by her tight walls.

"Your heat is affecting me." I watch as my cock slides in and out, her ass shaking from every thrust, every inch disappearing to fill her womb. "Fuck!" I growl. "You're going to take every drop. You won't let it go to waste. You're going to be so full of me. I'm going to tear you from the inside out when I knot you. You'll be a fucking mess. My want for you might kill you." I rake my talons down her back, leaving red lines across her skin.

She claws at the ground to get away from me, and her whimpers are borderline sobs.

"Where the fuck do you think you're going?" I grip her ass and drag her against my cock, groaning from being submerged in heaven.

"It's so much," she whines.

"You'll deal with it." I ram into her harder, the faster my cock pummels her cunt, the louder she screams. "Trying to get away from me will get you killed." I slice my talons across her ass, and she cries, blood pouring from the slash marks.

"Anwyll!"

"You think you can get away from me!" I yell at her so loud my voice breaks. I curl my hips, needing my cock to lodge inside her.

I'm frustrated.

I want my knot to swell and lock. I want her to have no choice but for her womb to soak in every drop of my come.

Only then will I be satisfied.

I have to breed my mate. If I don't, I'll go insane.

Digging my fingers in her hair, I yank her head back by clutching the luscious strands. I want to ruin these too. I want to have her on her knees while I fuck her face, and just when I'm about to come, I'll pull out, coming on her face, hair, neck, and tits. She'll be covered in me.

"You can never get away from me. Ever. I'll fucking find you, do you understand? I'll hunt you down, and I'll make you pay for leaving me." I wrap my hand around her throat from behind, digging my claws into her windpipe.

There's a small part of me that wants to rip it out— it's the animalistic part— the part that has no sorrow for killing. It's more than that with Ru. I want to bathe in her blood while I fuck her and make her scream.

I want her to wish she were dead because death would be so much easier than me.

"Fuck!" she screams, her pussy clutching my cock in a tight grip. Each spasm of her orgasm ripples down every inch I'm giving her. "Anwyll. Oh chauns, yes, so good. So good," she slurs, drunk from the bliss I'm giving her.

I shove her face into the dirt and toss my head back, a primal roar ripping from my chest as I come, thrusting deeper to push every drop into her womb. Fur sprouts along my body, and my face contorts as I fight the full shift.

Burying my beast deep into my bones, I control myself enough to keep my middle form and fall against Ru's back. I kiss her neck, her sweat tingling on my lips.

She moans again, exhausted, and the trace of heat in her body vanishes.

If this is only a taste of her heat and I react like this, I can't imagine how dangerous I'll be on the full moon.

"Mmm, wow," she chuckles, exhausted. "That was…"

"I was too rough with you." I pull away, gasping when my cock slips free, and I curl my lip with hatred when I see my come spill free. The slash marks on her ass aren't as bad as I thought. The blood has already dried in the shallow marks.

I lean down and lick each mark, watching as the wounds heal.

Her arms shake as she lifts herself up, dirt and grime sticking to her. She dusts her cheek off. "Don't do that. Don't diminish what just happened."

"What just happened? Do you even know?" I'm so fucking disappointed with myself. "I hurt you. I cut you with my talons, Ru. I stopped you from getting away from me." I tug on my hair and snarl at her. "I'm not good for you. The closer you get to your heat, the more I can't control myself. I feel it. I smell it. And god," I groan. "You smell so fucking good."

"I don't care. I loved what just happened. I want it to happen again. And again. I want you to stop me. I want to fight you, and I want you to dominate me. I love that your eyes turn black because you lose all control. I want more of that. I don't want you to hold back."

"I need to be perfectly clear. On the night of the full moon, I won't be coherent. What you say will not matter. You are okay with that? If you say stop, I won't. If you fight me, I'll fight you back. Nothing will stop me from claiming you. Not even you."

"Good."

"Ru. You don't understand—"

"—You need my consent for non-consent," she sums up my worry. I turn away from her, ashamed and disappointed. Her hand touches my shoulder, and I tense up. "You have it. You have my consent, Anwyll. I want this with you. I loved what you just did. I loved how you overpowered me and gave me no choice. You have my consent," she repeats. "And I look forward to being hunted by you."

"You're sure?"

"And if I wasn't, what would happen?"

My werewolf bursts free, and I open my mouth, fangs threatening her, and a guttural bellow causes my own ears to ring.

"Don't you dare take that tone with me." She shakes her finger at me, and I morph into my middle form.

"I'm sorry. I'm unstable right now. The thought of you denying me made me lose it."

"It's a good thing I'm not denying you then," she reminds me. "I want what you want, what your instincts want. If I didn't, I wouldn't be your mate, Anwyll. Now, be a good boy and come kiss me."

Her lips tilt in a salacious smirk, and I hook an arm around her waist. "Yes, ma'am." I slant my head to lower my lips to hers. My thumb brushes off dirt stuck to her cheek, and I sigh, laying my forehead against hers. "I'm the luckiest man alive."

She's about to say something, probably full of sass, but a spine-tingling cry in the distance causes her to jump, then look over her shoulder.

"What the hell was that?" Her voice is a low whisper, just as an eerie breeze causes the leaves to dance around our feet.

"I don't know." The sound pulls at my chest. I bend down to grab the bag and give it to Ru. "Something is telling me to go to it."

"And that is why we will die. People don't rush to weird sounds; you know that, right? That's how people die in scary movies."

"I wouldn't know. I've never watched one."

"Well, if we make it out of this alive, we are having a marathon, and you're getting me a bunch of scratch-off tickets. I need them. I'm feeling antsy without scratching for luck. I should have done that before we left. Think about it. How much easier would it be if I had my luck? I bet this journey would be easier."

"If it's easy, it's too good to be true." Whatever my mate wants, she'll get, but for now, my beast is telling me another creature needs help. It's just a feeling, a twist in my gut.

And I hate it.

It's the exact feeling I had when I was trapped under the spell, but I have something different now that I didn't have before.

My humanity.

Chapter Twenty-Nine
RU

A deep bellow echoes through the surprising foliage on this island. Unlike the branches from the trees on the other side, these don't reach out like they want to snag you and force you under the soil. These branches sway and dance. The leaves rustle together from the wind, and there's a sweet scent hanging in the air. It reminds me of the wild clover field I used to play in as a kid. The smell is relaxing, freeing, and I stop dead in my tracks.

Inhaling, the memory plays in my mind like a vintage film, skipping and flickering as my mind tries to piece together what actually happened.

The moons were warm on my cheeks. I remember the sky being an odd color, a lighter green than usual. The solas bugs flashed blue and fluttered around me. I remember laughing, trying to catch them with my hands.

The small amount of moonlight that gave the clouds over this island a gray hue, disappears and we're left in complete darkness, which pulls me out of my daydream.

"Whoa," Anwyll says, confused as he looks around the forest.

The leaves transform from a beautiful emerald green to an eerie black as another cry echoes in the distance.

I look up, gasping when I see stars decorating a purple, pink, and blue sky. It's so similar to the sky on the planet Anwyll's from. "What do you think is causing this? This isn't the same sky as Àdh."

"Remember, it isn't Àdh. We don't know what Gleminor used to be like. It probably has a ton of magic we know nothing about." Anwyll's beast rips from his middle skin, and his fur thickens between his thighs, covering his impressive, massive cock.

He grumbles when he catches me looking, and I blush. He smirks as best as he can in this form, flashing those long teeth I want him to eat me with. He falls to all fours and lowers his front half to the ground.

Gripping his mane, I hurl myself over his expansive back and sit. I look up to the stars again, hoping the one thing that will be beautiful when we mate is the sky. I'd love to be under the beauty of the stars while under the brutal force of Anwyll.

Another soul-tugging cry ricochets through the forest, and Anwyll begins walking, his heavy paws leaving large prints behind.

The leaves brush against my shoulder, and I notice water dripping from the tips. Just as another heart-shattering sob makes its way into my bones, another drop of water flows down my skin.

"The leaves are crying," I awe, holding out my palm as we pass each low-hanging branch to catch the tears. "That's so sad."

"Something must be happening. Something bad." Anwyll picks up his pace, and I lean forward so I'm stable and don't fall off. His fur brushes against my cheek, and a small fire shoots across my skin and to my stomach. Burying my face in his neck, I try to take a deep breath, wanting the small cramp of want to go away.

He tilts his head to the side, looking up at me with eyes that match my own, and growls, his nostrils flaring as if he can scent my need.

Taking a few deep breaths, the ache goes away, but it reminds me how bad the full moon night will be. If one minute of want is this bad, I can't imagine the pain I'll be in soon. As the creature in trouble weeps, the leaves begin to rain, matching the pain, but the sky is clear.

The trees begin to sway, and faces appear on the trunks, frowns replacing the plain bark. Anwyll whines as if he can sense their pain. The green grass withers and dies, and the blooming flowers on the vines swirling around the trunks of the trees wilt.

Roots break free of the ground in front of us, and Anwyll slides to a stop. Qauloch emerges from the ground, his legs long and thick with grooves and moss, his abs and pecs similar to a man's, and long leaves make his ears pointed like an elf's. He is oddly good-looking for a tree god.

"I didn't think we would see you so soon," Anwyll begins, and his entire body tightens when the bellow happens again.

"I told you, I'm everywhere. As long as there are trees, I can be wherever I please. I'm here to warn you."

I run my fingers through Anwyll's mane, more to comfort me than him, but I see his ears flicker. He likes it.

"The sound you hear," Qauloch begins, his body creaking as he moves. The sound of his feet pounding against the earth shakes everything around us as he inches closer. His voice is deeper than any baritone I've heard; it's almost unrecognizable.

His face is full of expression, his moss eyebrows moving as he speaks. He reaches inside a hole in his chest, pulls out a bird, and sets it on a nearby branch.

"You let a bird live inside you?"

"I am nature. I am their home," Qauloch explains, smiling as the bird chirps and ruffles its metallic purple feathers. He bends down, and I notice even his leaves, once stark with life, are just as dark as the ones surrounding us. Water drips from them too, but it's the bark under his eyes I notice the most.

It's darker than the rest of him, wet, and I notice the tears swimming in his eyes as another scream reverberates through the forest.

"This side of the island is so much better than the other, but nature has balance. With the good, there has to be bad, just like there are predators and prey. The sound you hear is a baby unicorn being pulled under by Quicksand. It's crying for its mother."

"Oh my chauns." My hand falls to my chest as my heart breaks. Now that I know what the sound is, when I hear it again, I catch a sob in my throat. "That's terrible."

"I'm here to give you advice. You help the unicorn, you can get the hair. They are thankful creatures, but it won't be easy. Quicksand is a fickle predator. He will want something in return. Every creature needs to eat."

"You act like quicksand is a being," Anwyll states, but I know it's more of a curious question.

"He is. And he is not kind."

"That's why the leaves are crying, isn't it?"

"The unicorns magic on this island is different. While they travel everywhere from here to Àdh, they are from *here*, so their magic is strongest here, which causes everything around them to be affected by their moods. A unicorn is in pain, and so is everything else they keep alive and well with their magic."

"What if we don't have anything to give Quicksand?"

"Hmmm," he hums, and as he rubs his mouth with his branch-like fingers, bark falls from his face from the friction. "Then I'm afraid you're in for the fight of your life. Do you want to know a secret about unicorns that a lot of people don't know about? If you save the baby, the centaurs will be forever in your debt."

My mouth falls open in shock. "There are centaurs?"

"Every story, every myth, they come from somewhere. The centaurs are special. They have a mutation in their DNA that doesn't take form. Every so often, one gives birth, and their child will have that mutation. That mutation is how unicorns exist."

"But we just saw an adult unicorn with her baby."

He shakes his head, leaves shaking water from them. "Once a unicorn is born from a centaur, an adult unicorn senses it. They come to take the baby away and raise it as their own."

"So the centaurs are without their child? That's so sad." I frown at the thought.

"Certain magics belong with certain magics. Unicorns are very powerful. They have to remain together. It isn't often a unicorn is born. Most of the time, they have baby centaurs."

Another cry rips through the air, and shivers run down my spine. "We can't wait much longer. They sound so weak."

"I will leave you. Be careful." Qauloch straightens, his roots seeping into the ground, and in the next blink of an eye, Qauloch is gone.

"Hold on," Anwyll warns before leaping into the air. His

front paws hit the ground first, and I lower my head to dodge the pieces of the earth being thrown in the air from his talons as he runs.

We follow the haunting cries, dodging the sad, drooping branches. I'm not sure how long Anwyll runs for, but I'm starting to doubt we heard anything at all. We aren't getting any closer to the wails coming from the unicorn. At this rate, we won't get to the baby in time.

A chill rushes down my spine, the kind that tells your soul that something is watching you. Anwyll growls as if he can feel it too, and he slows to a stop. We stare into the darkness, our breaths coming out in heavy pants as we try to calm down. Anwyll's ears flicker as he listens and waits. The wind yowls, and the facial expressions on the trees turn from a frown to nothing at all. They vanish.

A twig snaps to our left, and both Anywll and I turn our heads.

"Do you see anything?" I ask him, clutching his mane tighter.

"No, but that doesn't mean anything," the beast caustically grouses.

He takes a step, his shoulders rolling forward with every step, and it causes me to rise on his back. A black shadow dissipates in front of us, an apparatus of evil fog.

"Anwyll." I duck my head down and hide my face in his fur.

Breath ghosts over the back of my neck, and I whimper, a cold shiver freezing the length of my spine.

"Leprechaun," a wispy, hushed tone licks my ear.

I scream, rubbing my ear on my shoulder.

"You need to turn around," the voice warns, taking form in front of us.

Anwyll growls and begins to back up away from the shadow.

He holds out his arm, a charcoal color, and his silver veins decorate his arm. The shadow cloak sways and drifts around him, his eyes swirling with the shimmer of a cloud-covered sky.

"I don't mean you any harm."

"You smell of evil intent," Anwyll snaps, circling the void of what I think used to be a man.

"Because I am cut from the cloth of hell and sin," the shadow explains.

"What are you?" I ask him, unable to hide the quake as I speak.

"I am nothing. A shadow people seek. I am a Void. A darkness. The spot in your heart that can never be filled. The thing that eats away at you, day after day, haunting your mind, reminding you of all your regrets. That is what I am."

"Then why are you telling us to turn around?" Another scream from the baby unicorn calls to us, then a deeper bellow wraps itself around me.

"I might be a void, but you need to understand these woods. If you die, I take the place of the space inside some-one's heart that cares about you. I'll become their void, and while it feeds me," he hums in satisfaction, his eyes closing as he slides his tongue across his sharp teeth, he shakes his head. "It does not mean I do not want to warn people of their fate." He looks behind me, and I turn to see another shadow—void—creature. "This is one of my abyss—"

"Abyss?" I don't know what that means, but it doesn't sound like something I want to be a part of.

"What you people call family, a pack, a coven. He is part of my abyss."

"Oh." I swallow, not knowing what else to say.

"Anyway, we have been following you since you arrived on the island. If you save the unicorn, you also take from us. There will be no empty space for us to fill."

"What do you want?" Anwyll hesitantly asks.

"I'll find you when I want the favor returned."

Anwyll shifts his weight. "How is this a favor?"

"I'm letting you pass instead of sucking the soul out of your lungs and leaving your mate alone to feel how useless her life would be. This is a favor," he hisses, and the swirls of his shadow spin like a tornado before he vanishes, the dark fog nothing but a confusing memory.

Another bleat sounds, and with my heart pounding with adrenaline from the oddest conversation I've ever had, Anwyll takes off. I yelp, fisting his mane at the last second so I don't fall off.

As he runs, I look to the left, noticing the vexed fog following us. The ground beneath us breaks, cracks vein across the earth, and roots shoot into the air. They roll across the surface of the forest, like waves chasing the shore.

Qauloch.

The devastating screams for help finally sound closer. Qauloch's roots beam into the air, pushing the trees to the side to give us room, and his roots multiply, barricading the trees in a makeshift cage.

Anwyll slides to a stop, and I propel over his head. I hear Anwyll roar, but all I see in the sandpit below is the small, helpless unicorn kicking and fighting to stay alive. Qauloch catches me, wrapping his roots around my midsection.

I hover over the sandpit, gasping for breath, my back aching from the whiplash.

"Ru!" Anwyll paces back and forth, unable to reach to me. "Are you okay?" The words are a savage gravel in his throat since he wasn't able to catch me.

"I'm fine! I'm okay." I lift my hand for him to stop pacing and worrying.

"That was a close call," Qauloch announces from somewhere around me.

"Thank you, Qauloch. Whoa!" The branch dips, bringing me closer to the sandpit.

"Damn it, Qauloch. If you drop my mate in that pit, I will rip you into kindling and use you to make a fire," Anwyll snarls, tiptoeing at the very edge before the ground dips into the sandpit.

"Stop! Anwyll. Please, stop moving closer. The bank is giving away." I watch as the dirt falls apart under his clawed toes, barely able to sustain his weight.

"I don't like this."

"Me either," I agree, stretching my arms to try to get the baby unicorn.

Arms of sand stretch above, trying to wrap themselves around the baby. The unicorn's mane changes from a frosty white to rageful red, which cuts the sand and doesn't allow the arms to wrap around it.

"That only keeps the sand at bay. Eventually, the baby's magic will run out. She is too new to the world and only has a small amount," Qauloch informs.

I begin to panic, watching the poor creature suffer. It bellows again, and a neigh nearby has me turning my head.

A unicorn stomps its hoof, flinging its head in anger and worry.

"What if...." I lick my lips as I map a plan together. "What if you lower me, Qauloch? Lower me enough so I can pick up the unicorn."

"If you do, there's a chance you'll be sucked under," a new voice responds.

"Who the fuck are you? I'm getting real sick of these surprise visits from everyone. Who the hell are you?" Anwyll charges at the new guest, only to find himself surrounded...

By centaurs.

"Told you," Qauloch states.

"Just lower me." I'm losing my patience. This baby is going to die if we don't get it out of the sand. I give one last look to the centaurs surrounding my mate, and it's hard not to lose focus when I see how unique they are. Half their bodies are human, male, some have long hair, some short, but the other half of their bodies match those of a horse. Brown, white, black, and paint fur, and their size reminds me of a Friesian horse that protects the sea. Rumor has it, you can see them galloping across the ocean, fighting Poseidon's battles.

If I remember what I learned in school, the Greek Gods are the one thing that remains constant throughout all planets and realms. There has to be truth to that, right?

"If I do, you'll probably die," Qauloch reinforces, lifting me away from the quicksand.

"And if she doesn't, we'll forever be in her debt," one of the centaurs says. "By law, we can't save it. That child belongs with the unicorns now, but it doesn't mean we ever stop trying." He walks closer, his hooves thudding against the ground. "See?" He lifts his hand, and a barrier stops him from coming forward just as the grown unicorn charges, head down, horn straight.

He steps away, showing signs of peace, and the unicorn accepts his surrender.

"Just fucking lower me already. I'm sick of waiting around."

"We need a plan, Ru. You can't just dip your hands in and hope for the best."

"Well, Anwyll. That's the only option. Hopefully, Qauloch can pull me out. We need this, right? For your brother?"

Anwyll runs to the edge again. "Not if it means losing you."

"That's the risk we take," I say to him as our eyes meet. "I love you, but I'm already here, and this hasn't gone according to plan. I have the strength of a tree god wrapped around me, so hopefully, that works in our favor."

"If anything happens..."

"You'll continue on and get the ingredients to the potion for your brother," I tell him, not wanting to hear him argue.

"You know I can't. I'll rip my heart out if anything happens to you."

I tap the tree root. "We will have to make sure that doesn't happen. I happen to like your heart right where it is." I look to my right and nod to Qauloch. "Lower me. Let's get this over with."

A low grumble of disagreement echoes around us, the deep bellow coming from Qauloch. The root around me creaks as he lowers me slowly, and I hold out my arms, only for the sand to shoot from the pit and wrap around my forearms. With a hard yank, my arms feel like they are about to pop out of their sockets. Qauloch lifts me higher, and the sand finally lets me go.

I hiss as my arms sting, and I notice a red rash forming on my skin.

"What the hell?"

"It's the sand's defense. It burns you," one of the centaurs yells out. "It will stop at nothing to feed."

"Lower me fast, Qauloch. So fast, he doesn't have time to think."

Qauloch nods, and I swoosh down, my stomach dropping as if I'm falling through the air. I reach out my arms, and Qauloch doubles the branches around me, then they spread out, giving me additional limbs.

I hold my breath and hit the quicksand, wrapping my arms around the unicorn.

And the sand attacks.

I can't hear anything. I can barely breathe. The sand compresses me, pushing against my back and ribcage at the same time.

I'm being crushed. I squeeze the baby unicorn to my body, doing my best not to let go. I'm being whipped back and forth, slushed through the grains of sharp sand. I can already feel the microscopic scratches on all of my exposed flesh.

While the roots are wrapped around me, the arms of quicksand embrace me too, tugging us deeper, pulling us further into the unknown. It's like I'm swimming through mud. Qauloch finally pulls up hard enough that we slice through the sand, but the quicksand doesn't forgive easily.

It continues to fight.

My head becomes fuzzy, and I don't feel the unicorn kicking anymore. Maybe my attempts killed the poor thing. Maybe it would have gotten free without my help. The last thing I ever wanted to do was be the cause of anyone's pain. It's a feeling no one gets over. It's heavy, a weight from guilt and regret, and a lot of the time, those negative emotions end up there because all you do is try to help.

Sometimes help isn't needed, but it's difficult to try to figure that out in the heat of the moment.

Sometimes... helping someone means not helping at all.

Maybe death is better than torture.

Finally, I have to inhale after holding my breath for so long, and sand fills my mouth, traveling down my throat like an onslaught of knives.

Back and forth, Qauloch, holding the power of a tree god, fights with Quicksand. My stomach begins to turn from being pulled in different directions. The stress my body is taking, the way my spine is being stretched, I just know my body is about to rip in two.

But then, suddenly, I'm yanked into the air, free of Quicksand, but I'm not put down. I'm flying, barely conscious, the rumble of hooves, the howl of my mate, and the ground breaking from Qauloch tells me we are on the move.

I can't see anything.

There's sand in my eyes, my mouth, throat, and every other inch of me. I keep a tight hold on the baby unicorn and wait until we land.

When we do, I'm laid on the ground gently, and then water is splashed on my face and poured down my throat. I cough, spewing more mud than sand, and try to open my eyes, but I can't. I reach out for someone until I feel fur and a broad chest, and I cry.

Anwyll.

He's here.

"Ru. Oh my god, that took so long. Qauloch fought with that sand for ages. I knew you were dead. I thought... I thought there was no way anyone could survive being held under like that. What do you need from me? How can I help?" He clutches my chin, and the sharp points of his claws press into my skin.

"My eyes. There's so much sand." As soon as the words are out of my mouth, I'm swaying through the air again, screaming. "Put me down!" I yell, kicking and smacking Qauloch's arm.

I'm ducked underwater, then pulled back up by Qauloch, wrapping a root around my wrist. He dunks me again.

And again.

I use the opportunity to open my eyes and gently try to rub the sand free. I'm brought to the surface, and I inhale enough air before I'm shoved under the water again, and then swished around. The water feels good. It's cold and refreshing. I open my eyes and I'm able to see how blue the pond is. There are shades of green that seem to glow, and unlike normal ponds, this one has stone around it, and it goes down like a tunnel.

Or a cave.

I'm finally pulled to the surface again, and I gasp, wiping the water from my face. "Will you stop! Shit, you're going to drown me if you keep going."

"I am sorry. I thought I was helping get the sand off you," Qauloch explains, his roots sinking back into his form.

He looks ashamed.

"No, it's okay. It worked. You were right. I just need to breathe." I swim to the edge and see the baby unicorn with its adoptive mom. "She's okay?"

"She is, thanks to you." Anwyll helps me out of the water, and he looks me over, cursing when he notices all the scratches along my arm. "I wish I could kill that damn Quicksand for what he did to you."

"It's why I made sure to get far away. That's his territory. He won't leave it," Qauloch explains. "But it's best if we stay clear of that side of the forest. Forever. He won't forget."

"I won't either," Anwyll rumbles, his giant paw cupping my cheek. "I can't wait to get the hell out of this dimension. It's given me enough scares for a lifetime, and that's saying something."

I grip his wrist to hold his palm against my cheek and sigh, hating that I know the truth to his words.

While he is free from the spell that trapped him for so many years, the torture, the guilt, and the pain of everything he has done will consume him forever.

His pain is not temporary.

It's permanent.

And all I can do is try to make the rest of his days better.

A neigh comes from my left, and I turn to see the unicorns step forward. They are beautiful. The adult one spreads its wings, and its horn perfectly swirls, shining a gorgeous opal color.

"They want to repay you for what you've done," the centaur explains, looking down on me since he's so tall. "What is it that you would like?" he asks.

"We need unicorn hair."

The centaur grimaces but speaks in clicks and pops to the unicorn. "Unicorns do not freely give their hair away. It is a part of their magic. It can protect them like it did the little one in the sand pit." He strokes his hand down the elegant neck of the mother unicorn. She turns her head and bows. "But it seems she wants to make an exception since you saved her child."

Anwyll elongates his talons. "May I?"

"You may," the centaur says, lifting a few strands of hair.

I grip Anwyll's arm as he steps closer to the majestic animal. He gently swipes one claw near where the hair grows, catching more than one strand in his palm. Anwyll has the bag that I dropped when I went flying over his head.

I open the bag and reach my hand inside, annoyed with this bottomless pit now. "I need an empty vial. Come on," I groan with impatience and a little exhaustion. I'm hungry too. The bottle floats up from the bag, and Anwyll snags it, popping the top off as if it were a bottle of champagne, and places the hairs inside.

"Thank you for your help. All of you. And you." He drops to all fours and bows to the unicorn who gave us something so sacred and meaningful.

"This is where you are on your own," Qauloch states, his roots planting into the ground once more. "I'll see you around, Anwyll. Ru," his voice grumbles before sinking below the earth's surface.

The two unicorns run into the forest, and the leaves on the saddened trees turn upward, changing from the color of mourning to the fresh green after a rainstorm.

I look around, gasping as I watch the forest come to life again. Birds sing, and a splash has me turning my head to see bright purple frogs leaping across the pond onto large lily pads.

The grass under my feet turns from a dull brown, and each blade straightens from its wilting stance.

"No emptiness to fill today. Pity," the void grumbles from the shadows of the branches before dispersing into thin air.

The centaur next to me chuckles. "The void's are better

than you think. Don't let his darkness fool you. He has soft spots."

"I'd rather not take my chances," I answer, wringing out my hair of water.

His hooves shuffle, and he steps in front of me, his large body rippling with muscle, and his tail flickers behind him. "I know what you're looking for. Not many people want unicorn hair. You're wanting wolfsbane and heartsnow next, aren't you?"

"You know what we are looking for?" Anwyll steps forward.

The centaur nods, placing his hands on his waist. "I do because no one has survived the journey. I have to warn you not to go further."

Anwyll shakes his head. "That's not an option. My brother needs it, or he will die."

"You will too if you go try. If you think your journey has been difficult now, you have no idea what lies ahead."

"So why don't you tell us?" Anwyll's tone borders on a threat as he cocks his head and narrows his glowing eyes.

"I'm not to talk about what lies ahead. They would hear, and my entire herd would be in trouble. I'm sorry, but I can't help you. Prepare for the fight of your life, that's all I have to say." He turns and begins to walk away.

"Fuck," Anwyll curses.

"Wait! Wait." I run after the centaur and make the mistake of touching his back when he rears on his hind legs. The unexpected move has me tumbling backward, and Anwyll is in front of me instantly, roaring his warning for the centaur not to hurt me. "Anwyll, it's fine! I'm okay. It's my fault. I'm sorry. I shouldn't have touched you..." I search for his name, remembering he never gave it.

"Altian," he says for me. "I am called Altian. Only my mate can touch me. It's the way of the centaurs."

"Oh my chauns. I'm so sorry. I didn't know. I was only trying to stop you. Please, that wasn't my intention."

"It was an accident. It's okay." He takes a few steps away from me, a hard line on his lips with anger. That rule must be very important to him. "What can I help you with?"

"What kind of fight? Please, any help would be welcome."

"The kind of fight you won't win. I hope different for you both. You two seem loyal and brave. Those are great qualities. Good luck, my friends." This time, he gallops away, his friends flanking his sides, and one turns his head to look at me, giving me a dirty look.

"You really pissed them off." Anwyll laughs, holding his hand to his chest as he tosses his head back. "Only you would piss off centaurs. What are the chances of that?"

"First off, I didn't know I wasn't allowed to touch them."

"You don't just touch people without their consent, Ru." He wipes his eyes because he is laughing so hard.

I wrap my arms around his waist and tilt my head back to stare my werewolf in the face. "Hey."

He tilts his chin down, the tips of his fangs pointing over his lip.

"You know that right there is what makes you different from your past, right? The spell you were under didn't care about consent, but the soul in you does. Just hold onto that for me, okay?" I lean in and kiss his chest, sighing in contentment when he holds me in return.

"I'll do my best, but you might need to remind me every now and then."

"I'll remind you every day."
All we have to do is make it through this alive.

Chapter Thirty

ANWYLL

We're resting for the night. This part of the forest seems safe. It's quiet, peaceful, and beautiful. The sky above us is dark with hues of blue and purple, with a million stars shining above the canopies of the trees.

"Come swimming with me." Ru's hands grab the bottom of her shirt, stripping it over her head. She unhooks her bra, and her perfect tits bounce free. I fall to all fours, tilting my chin down as I inhale her scent.

I growl, inhaling her intentions.

And they aren't to swim.

She wiggles out of her pants, kicking them to the side, and I'm left staring at her gorgeous body. I shift into my middle form, the one caught between human and were-wolf, because my instincts still won't accept me in my weakest body. Being only human isn't in question, and it won't be for a while.

She saunters by me, dragging her finger across my chest as if she didn't almost die in quicksand an hour ago.

I don't know where to look. Even in the dark, I can see

the freckles on her shoulders, and I want to kiss every single one of them.

My eyes fall to her ass as she stands on the edge of the pond. The colorful plants around her turn as if she awakens them with her seduction. The flowers are an array of colors, with an ombre effect of blue to purple. The petals spread wide, opening to show the glowing middle where the pollen shimmers like dust being caught in the sun's light.

From their hiding spots, butterflies randomly appear, spreading their unique wings to show intricate designs that are one of a kind. All are bioluminescent. Some are neon blue, and some pink, yellow, and purple. They dance around Ru, twirling around her body. One lands on top of her head, and when my mate holds out her hand, another butterfly lands on her fingers.

She looks like a goddess, a woman in control of nature and every being that comes into contact with her.

She holds the power of divine femininity, an effortless strength that exudes from her.

In rain, she's thunder.

In heat, she's the flame.

And in my darkness, she's a beacon.

Ru watches as the butterflies fly away, climbing higher into the air until they disappear over the tree's branches and fade into the starry night sky. She turns until her chin touches her shoulder to look at me before smiling and diving into the pond.

"Aren't you going to join me?" she asks when she breaches the surface. Her hair is slicked back, and she hides her smile under the water. "The water feels so good."

I prowl forward, the grass parting under my feet. Butterflies don't greet me, but that's okay, I'm not the power they are drawn to.

I'm the type they fly away from.

When I get to the edge of the pond, the first thing I notice is how circular it is. The walls are stone, reminding me of an underwater cave. I dive in, swooping under the cool water. I look down to try to see the bottom, but it's endless and gets darker the deeper the hole becomes.

There are no fish. No plant life.

It's only us.

I wrap an arm around her waist and come up for air, pressing her against the edge.

"Hi," she whispers, causing water to drip from her lips.

"Hi." I wrap her legs around my hips, and her arms lie on my shoulders. "How are you doing?" I lean down and kiss the scratches on her arms inflicted on her by the sand.

"I'm good. Tired. So damn tired. My entire body aches. I almost feel sick. Fighting Quicksand really took it out of me. My ribs hurt from Qauloch's roots wrapping around me and being yanked back and forth."

I kiss her shoulders, hating that I had to witness her struggle. I thought I lost her. If Qauloch struggled with the sand, there would have been no chance of me saving Ru. I hated how the sand latched onto Qauloch, twisting his roots, and him deeper into the pit.

And if he was pulled deeper, Ru was further.

"I wouldn't be surprised if some of your issues are because of the heat your body is preparing for. You'll feel more tired over the next few days, sore, achy, and it will only get worse."

"You'll make me feel better though, won't you?" Her fingers play with the hair curling on the back of my nape.

I hum, placing my chin on her shoulder. "Always. I'll always try to make you feel better, mate."

"You know what I mean." She bites the meat of my shoulder, and I hiss, acting as if it hurts.

I swim away from her and float on my back, staring up at the stars. "I can't promise that. I can't promise what that night will bring. The last thing you might feel is pleasure, Ru."

"You want to know what I think?" She floats next to me, turning onto her back, and I can't help but take a peek at her breasts, breaking the surface of the water.

Her nipples are hard, and my mouth waters to steal a taste.

"I think"—she begins without me answering her—"that you're going to be more aware than you think. I don't think you'll do anything to hurt me. Yes, you'll have instincts, but I don't think you're giving yourself enough credit. Whatever happens, Anwyll, I want you to know I look forward to it."

"I have a crazy mate." I flip over and push her against the side of the pond. I roll my neck and growl at the same time, inhaling just as she succumbs to a wave of her heat. Even in the water, I can scent it.

I slam my mouth against hers, wrapping one arm around her waist to bring her body against mine. She's silk against me, the water causing her skin to be slippery, and as we devour one another, our tongues twining, even in her saliva, I can taste the sweetness of the dooming heat about to consume her.

"Anwyll," she sighs my name, her body relaxing in my arms, and I take that as the form of submission I need to do what I want.

I dig my claws into the stone wall, scratching them against the rock how I want to do to her body.

I want to mark it. I want to ruin it for everyone else. I want to imprint on her skin. I want the world to know she's mine, that she belongs to me, that her body is taken and cared for.

Would she forgive me for such a heinous act?

A part of me doesn't care.

She tilts her head back, and the ends of her strawberry-blonde hair dip into the water. Fisting the locks in my hand, I pinch her scalp with my claws, threatening her to obey. She moans in response, and any submittable bone in my body vanishes. I kiss down her neck, paying close attention to where her mating mark will be, and my fangs ache to give in, to bite.

To make her mine.

I can't.

The mark wouldn't scar. It wouldn't stay forever. It has to happen on the full moon.

With one hand gripping her hair and the other digging into the ground, she has nowhere to go; she's trapped.

She's at my will. She's in my prison, and there's no way she can escape. "Fuck, you smell so good," I snarl, lifting her onto the edge and forcing her thighs apart. I don't give her time to ask questions. I bury my face between her thighs and feast on her pussy.

My long tongue slides between her soaking wet petals, then burrow inside her tight hole.

"Anwyll! Fuck. Oh my chauns," she moans to the forest, tossing her head back in pleasure. Her fingers run through my hair and grab, fiercely tugging on the strands. Licking up, I swirl my tongue around her clit, while sliding a finger inside her cunt.

I growl when I feel her clamp down, the aroma of the

heat causing my cock to twitch with a stream of come. I already want to orgasm. I want to fill her and not waste a drop. I sheathe my talons so I don't hurt her. The last thing I want is to pierce or cut her insides. I have to protect them. They have to be ready to carry my children.

Ru falls back onto the flowers, and a puff of golden shimmer falls around her. I lift her hips off the ground by gripping the meat of her ass, my talons pinching into her skin. With her shoulders on the ground, I eat.

The louder she becomes, the more come drips from the slit of my cock. My heart rate begins to pulse in the length, the lust nearly unbearable. My shaft fucking aches to fill her, but I want her to come.

She reaches for my cock, her hand just inches away from wrapping around my girth.

When the delicate pads of her fingertips touch my cock, I groan into her cunt. My orgasm bursts free of me just from her taste.

"I love the taste of your come."

The words have me pausing mid-suck as I pull her clit between my lips. I glance up, watching as she licks my seed from her fingers. Her pink tongue is drenched with me, and her eyes close as if she's licking icing from her favorite dessert.

"My entire body tingles now."

I place my hand in the middle of her chest, every hard breath escaping me has a slight gravel to it, and my fingers curl into her skin. My talons scrape the surface of her flesh, the canvas so bare, flawless, and practically mocking me to ruin it. She mewls, her fists yanking on the green blades of grass, and faint red lines appear down her chest and stomach.

I'm satisfied.

For now.

"You need my come. Your body craves it, doesn't it?" I tilt my head back and show my fangs, taking a deep breath of the heat clinging to her bones.

I might break them on the night of the full moon to get what I want.

She thinks she knows, but she has no idea.

I'm going to drag her body anywhere I please. She'll be sore, drained of her energy, and I'll flip her onto her stomach to take her from behind to take my knot, and she'll still come all over my cock.

"So much," she answers, cupping her own tits. She pinches her nipples, and those bright green eyes, brighter than any shade of green I've ever seen, land on me.

Me.

Her attention isn't divided.

It is conquered.

By. Me.

With a satisfied grumble, I place my mouth on her cunt again, the sweetness of her honey the most natural treat I've ever savored. Every cell firing inside me wants her taste just like her body needs the elements of my come.

She's the peace of the night sky and the calming feather touch of the grass against my legs, but her taste is the equivalent of a man dying of thirst and tasting water for the first time. There's nothing better.

I spear my tongue into her tight cunt, the only body I will ever know, and my cock pulses again at that thought. She becomes wetter as her body heightens in temperature. My palms are warm, and the way she rocks against me, seeking more, tells me she's close.

I suck her clit into my mouth, rolling it between my sharp teeth.

"That's it. I'm close. I'm so fucking close. Ah, chauns," she cries out. Who knows how many hear her pleasure?

It should bother me, but it doesn't. Instead, my chest swells with pride knowing I'm bringing my mate so much pleasure. Everyone knows she's mine.

Let all of nature hear that the most unnatural monster is taking what's his.

Her back arches and her lips part as her thighs shake. Broken moans become higher-pitched as her orgasm builds. But even though she is crying out, she still isn't falling over the edge, and that isn't okay with me.

Shifting my talon to my original state, I slip a finger inside, humming around her clit when I feel how fucking wet she is. The top of my hand slaps against her skin as I drive my finger in and out at a harsh pace. I slip in another, then another, stretching her until she can't catch her breath.

I let go of her clit with a pop, her nectar dripping from my chin, and I smirk when I see her cunt sucking in all three of my fingers.

So I add another.

Then another.

"Look at you," I praise. "Taking all five fingers like a good little mate. Think you can't take my fist? It will give you a taste of what my knot will feel like."

"No."

"No?" I sneer, continuing a forceful thrust of my hand, fucking her like I wish it were my cock. I lay her flat on the ground and curl over her, snarling in her face. My eyes reflect in her pupils, and the neon emeralds that changed to match her own are gone, replaced by ink-filled pools that shine like the water in the nearby pond.

Ru gasps, and a quick hint of fear mixed with arousal fills the air.

"Answer me, mate," I bite, showing my fangs, and she shatters, her pussy clamping around my fingers.

Her fractured cries of pleasure echo through the forest, and that slight, intoxicating scent of her heat vanishes as she tenses while she peaks.

When she comes down from her pinnacle, I slip my hand free of her drenched cunt. Bringing my fingers up to my lips, I suck them clean. "You taste far better than any treat I've ever had." I keep two fingers clean and paint her slick against her lips, adding gloss and shine to the velvet clouds. "Go on," I urge her. "Taste yourself."

She leans forward just as I force her legs apart, and the tip of my cock threatens her entrance.

"I won't let you until you tell me why you didn't want my fist," my voice booms as I shout into her face, my anger whipping around my heart.

But mostly, I'm hurt.

"Does my mate not want my knot? You don't want to know what it will feel like?" I nuzzle her cheek, saddened, the pain crippling my heart. "My Lucky Charm doesn't want to mate me." The rejection is unlike anything I've ever felt. It's as if every bone in my body has broken all at once. A heartbroken whine escapes me, the same kind that a dog makes when they're injured.

It's a sad sound to make when you're a beast my size.

Still, as hurt as I am, I'm not strong enough to pull away from her. My cock sinks in slowly, hugged in the tight space of her cunt.

"Please, want me," I whisper, begging like a dog too.

She cups my face, brushes her thumbs down my fangs,

and shakes her head. "Want you? I need you. Always." She bites my lip and snarls as if she's a werewolf.

Fuck, if she were, the things we could do together...

"I want to experience your knot when I'm meant to. I don't want your fist." She lets go of my lip and kisses my cheek, then whispers into my ear. "Why would I want something that could never compare to the real thing?" She bites my earlobe, and I'm a goner.

I grip her hips and flip her over, pressing her face into the ground until all she can taste is grass. Her flesh gives beneath my fingers while I pin her hips in place. I fuck her like this, hard and animalistic, until her knees dig into the ground and her tits are covered in dirt.

"Fucking take my cock. Every inch of it. It hurts, doesn't it? It isn't easy taking a werewolf's dick, but you do it so well."

"It hurts," she confirms, curling her fingers into the ground. "It hurts, but it feels good. You're just so big."

"You haven't felt anything yet," I warn, pressing her face into the grass. I pick up my pace, our skin slapping against one another, and I take a moment to look down. My slate gray cock sinking into her light pink cunt is an image I want to get framed so I can look at it whenever the hell I want.

In and out, her divinity wraps around me, showing me ways of how salvation exists.

My talons come to a sharper point and staying mid-shift becomes difficult. We don't fuck in our werewolf form until we are mated and only if our mate is also a werewolf, but since Ru is human for the most part, I'll never be crossing that line with her.

Five pinpricks on each ass cheek pebble with blood from my claws digging into her skin as I pummel myself into her. My growls and grunts fill the forest in tune with Ru's moans. I throw my head back, looking up to the sky to see the shadow of the moon is there, and my power—my strength— heightens. Fur bursts across my arms. I hold my shift inside, a howl echoing in my head.

Wrapping my arms around her, I flip onto my back and rock her hips with my half-shifted hands. The long, dark fingers encompass her hips, each paw covering half of her waist. She looks so delicate, so fragile, so breakable, and if I really wanted, I could shatter her.

If I were the beast I was forced to be, I would destroy her.

"You look good riding my cock, My Lucky Charm. Fucking beautiful." I close my eyes and tilt my head to the side, fighting the shift again. I feel my natural form trying to break free, but I hold it down.

Her hands fall to my chest, using me as support as she fucks me harder. I drag my nails down her thighs, then press a tip against her clit. Watching her expression morph with more pleasure has me doubling my efforts. I want her lips parted, brows pinched together, and eyes locked on my face the entire time.

"That's right. Look at me. Look at who is fucking who." I thrust up, burying my cock deeper, and her eyes shut. I spring forward, wrap a paw around her throat, and nip her chin. "I said fucking look at me!"

She snaps her eyes open at the same time as she gasps.

"That's a good girl. A good little mate."

"Anwyll," she groans, rocking her hips harder against me.

Her body rolls, and I bury my face in the middle of her chest, wrapping my arms around her body to hold her close. I can hear the quick beat of her heart. The blood is rushing through her veins, and I can scent how good she feels.

"You're so good at riding my cock. I'll be the last cock you ever fuck. You'll only need me."

"Only you. My mate," she replies, slamming down on me harder. "Oh, my chauns, Anwyll. I'm going to come. I'm going... I'm going to," she stutters as she loses her breath.

"Keep your eyes on me. I want to see you fall apart while you take my come."

She shatters, and her cunt squeezes me as her muscles tense, rippling along my shaft. Without being able to hold in my own ecstasy, I toss my head back, and a guttural roar escapes me, one that would awaken the dead. The vibrations shake my chest. No doubt any prey in the forest has hidden, afraid they'll get eaten by the predator being pleased in the middle of the forest.

"Look at my cock tensing as I fill you with my come, mate." I tilt her chin down so she can see the base of my cock. The outline of my knot is there, and soon it will be swollen and locked inside her, but for now, it jerks and flexes as I spill inside her.

She groans, then sighs in relief as my essence relaxes her muscles.

A grumble of protest escapes me when I watch my come leak from her, dribbling down my cock to my sack.

All I want is for it to stay inside her. Is that too much to ask for?

She sags against me, resting her cheek against my shoulder. I bring us to the ground and change our position, which causes my cock to slip from her.

I lie on my back while she curls against my side, her head resting on my shoulder. We don't say anything while we lie in the grass, staring up at the stars. She shivers as the air cools, and I shift fully into my beast so I can keep her warm. She's so small now but still fits perfectly against my side.

I curl my tail around her, and she snuggles further into my side. Her breaths come out slow and even, telling me she's fallen asleep.

Not me.

I stay awake. She's to be protected at all costs.

I wake to the sound of snarling and growling. Anwyll's body jerks and twists, then his sharp teeth clash together when he tries to bite the air.

Another nightmare.

The last thing I want to do is wake him like I did before. He almost killed me, and getting past that took longer than I wanted. Not for me, but for him. He didn't trust himself around me, and now we are in a good place that I don't want to risk ruining.

A brisk chill wraps itself around me like a sheet of ice, and I tremble, forgetting I went to sleep naked and curled up against his side. I loved cuddling him like that. He's so warm and soft. Not that I'd tell him that because he thinks he is the big bad wolf.

"Anwyll!" His name is harsh, coming from my lips as I try to wake him up. "Anwyll, it's a bad dream. Wake up." But that doesn't work. His talons impale the ground and drag through the soil, tearing the grass.

A guttural roar rips from him, and I scoot back until my

hand slips off an edge and into water. I gasp, looking over my shoulder to see the pond.

An idea travels through my mind, and I slink into the water. "Hol-y shi-t," I stutter from how cold it is. "Don't think about it. Don't think about it." The self-talk does not work. It's too impossible not to focus on how cold the water is.

Pushing my arms through the water, I move them forward and create a small wave. I keep doing that until I gain some momentum. The water flies through the air, splashing onto the ground right beside Anwyll.

"Come on." I push my arms harder and send more water flying over the long blades of grass. The wave splashes on Anywll's face, and he snarls again, roaring so loud, I wouldn't doubt if other realms heard him.

He flips onto all fours, his green glowing eyes locked with mine, and his paw is raised in the air readying to strike. Water drips from his snout. His fur is wet. His fangs shine—the points lengthened past his lip.

"Anwyll?" I say his name gently while treading water to keep myself afloat. "It's me. Ru. You're safe. It's just us. You aren't there anymore. Remember life or death, but we do each together. So if you're going to kill me, you better kill yourself too. You promised me. You promised we'd die together." I remind him of our talk we had the other day, and his eyes come to focus, blinking his way into reality.

"Ru?" he rasps, shifting from the intimidating beast of his werewolf to the fierce form of his hybrid of half man, half beast.

I lift myself from the pond and run over to him. Our chests collide, knocking the breath right out of me. His arms wrap around my being, holding me close, and I sink into his warmth, so it melts the chill away.

"I didn't hurt you this time, did I?"

I shake my head. "No, but you've never hurt me, Anwyll." I take his face in my hands and look into his eyes. I still can't seem to get over the awe of his forms. If someone forced me to pick a favorite, gun to my head, I wouldn't know which to choose.

His human form is hulking and sweet, timid, yet protective. I wouldn't have expected a man like that to be so gentle. Then there is this form, the one where his skin is the color of a storm cloud and his hair matches the tone. His lips are a shade darker, similar to the night sky, and his ears remain a bit pointed. He's stunning, and it's so hard for me to look away.

But then there's his werewolf. Everything about him becomes larger. He becomes so tall and wide, and his face morphs into a ferocious snarl with a long snout. There's the tail too. I love his tail, especially when it wags. It isn't often. His guard has to be down.

He has a form for all my different moods, and I love it.

"We should get ready to go. We have a long journey," he says, opening the bag Maven made us bring on the journey.

I get dressed in comfortable pants and a plain t-shirt where the sleeves reach my elbows, then toss my hair into a messy bun. Anwyll can allow his fur to grow more in some places, and he does that to cover his cock. Still, the damn thing swings and creates a shadow. It's hard to miss.

He can't wear clothes right now, not with how much he shifts.

I brush my teeth and toss the toothbrush in the bag, but I giggle when I see Anwyll. He has his lips curled back, brushing each fang, and he catches me staring.

"What?" he mumbles around the mouthful of toothpaste. The white foam drips down his chin and sticks to his fur.

I wipe it away, smiling. "Nothing. You're perfect."

He snorts. "That's how I know you love me. Even with all my obvious imperfections and flaws, you think somewhere in all that is perfection."

"I don't have to look for it, Anwyll. It's you." I poke his chest. "You're the perfection." A drop of toothpaste drips onto my finger from the fur under his chin, and I sling it away. "At least you have clean fangs."

"Better to eat that pussy with," he growls and slaps my ass playfully as we get started on our journey to find the heartsnow.

"Anwyll," I scold him slightly, blushing because I know there could be creatures lurking around us. Not that it should matter now, considering what we did last night.

"What?" he feigns innocence. "I don't think you'd mind a small show."

I trip over a tree root, and he catches me by the arm, chuckling.

"So easily flustered for a mate who took my cock so well last night."

If it's possible, I blush even harder until I can feel the heat behind my eyes. I stare at the ground, hiding my smile, which causes my cheeks to hurt.

My stomach rumbles, effectively interrupting the flirtation between us.

"Sounds like I need to bring my mate food," he says.

I shake my head. "I'm okay for now. I want to talk about your dream."

The shine falls from his eyes. "I don't want to talk about that. Rarity's magic must have worn off. It lasted a while. Longer than I thought." He exhales a long, weighted breath, the kind filled with regret and exhaustion. "It's the same dream, different night. There's always that little girl. The regret never fades. Hunting for you would take my mind off her."

"How about we keep going for a couple of hours? Maybe we will come across something else while we travel. And maybe when we get home, we ask Rarity to freeze those memories again," I suggest, wanting to make sure he remains happy and healthy.

He nods, sliding his hand through mine, and we continue into the gorgeous forest. The trees hang low, and the leaves are green. I don't get the eerie feeling that someone or something is following us.

It's just us, and for the first time since we started this journey, I feel safe.

He helps me climb over a fallen log, taking my hand in his again, and as soon as my foot hits the path, something bright breaks through the trees. I wince, covering my eyes with my hand.

"What is that?" It warms my skin, something I haven't felt since we started this adventure.

"I think... I think it's the sun," Anwyll explains.

We cross over another fallen log; this time, it's lying across a decent-sized stream. The water trickles over rocks as it flows, and I gasp as I look around. The heavy branches are nearly touching the ground, weighed down with what looks like fruit. Vines curl intricately up the tree trunks, laden with small plants filled with small bright purple berries.

Anwyll picks a bright yellow fruit from the branch and sniffs it. "It smells fine."

I reach for one, but he stops me, pushing my hand away.

"I try it first."

I blink at him and scoff, plucking fruit from the tree. "Together, remember?"

"You're mad, woman," he sighs, taking a step closer to me and holding up the yellow fruit.

"If it means you don't fall into madness, then I'll gladly go insane for you." I hit the sphere-shaped fruit against his. "Cheers," I say.

We bite at the same time, and sweetness bursts in my mouth. It reminds me of a nectarine and a peach dipped in sugar. The inside glows too, similar to the sun above us right now.

I think it's the sun.

"Oh my chauns, these are so good." I take another bite, the juice dripping down my chin, and I lick my lips to try and catch it.

Anwyll finishes his in record-time, then bends down and picks a few berries from the bush, popping them into his mouth. He groans, eyes rolling back to his head. "These are amazing. You have to try them." He pushes a berry between my lips, and the juice shoots across my tongue when I bite down on it.

It's like a strawberry and a blackberry meshed together. It's delicious.

I pluck as many as I can from the bush until my palms are overflowing, and I take a seat on the ground to get comfortable. Anwyll plops down next to me, snagging another yellow fruit from the low-hanging branch. We lean against a tree trunk, enjoying the pleasant snack we stumbled across.

We don't even speak. We keep eating. My palms are stained red from the berries, and when they are gone, I continue to pluck them from the bush, lost in a complete daze of hunger. I look over to Anwyll, and he has changed positions, lying flat on his back, eating a yellow fruit. His entire mouth is stained, and his gray skin and lips are the same color as my palms.

Red like blood from the berries.

Juice drips down his chin, and while he is eating one out of his right hand, he plucks another fruit with his left.

He alternates. Left and right. Left and right.

I watch him, his fangs tearing into the flesh of the fruit, and the way his lips curve onto the fruit with every bite. More juice trickles down. His lips shine. His red tongue darts out, trying to catch the nectar that drips, but witnessing him licking and sucking, gathering every single drop he can, reminds me of how he feasted between my thighs.

My vision tunnels, and everything around me fades until all I see is him. My entire body comes to life, and I crawl to him. His brow lifts when my hand brushes up his thigh. He growls while I straddle his lap. He tries to toss the fruit over his head, but I grab his arm to stop him.

"Don't stop," I slur, feeling a little drunk and high at the same time. "Let me see you eat it," I whisper while grabbing his other hand and bringing the extra fruit he has to my mouth. I moan, my senses only focusing on him. Nothing else matters.

Just him and this fruit.

The hair covering his groin vanishes, and his erect, long werewolf cock settles in the nook between my legs. He brings the fruit to my mouth, rubbing it against my lips, and the sweetness bursts across my tongue, numbing everything in my mind.

Nothing else is important.

I forgot why we are here. Who cares? This is the only thing that matters.

Another deep growl escapes him as he latches onto the fruit, his eyes peer into mine, and nothing can break the connection. He curls his lip, showing his fang buried in the odd peach look-alike. A groan escapes me as he devours the fruit, snarling, and I bend down, to lick his mouth. I need to taste the juice coming from him.

I wrap my hand around his cock, squeezing and stroking. He grunts, biting into the fruit, and it falls from his mouth. I pick it up from his stomach, squeeze the juice from it, and use that hand to fuck his shaft.

"Ru," he growls, his neon green eyes morphing to black. "I smell your heat. It's stronger."

"I want you so much, Anwyll. I hurt. It hurts."

"Let me make you feel better." He leans forward, and I press a hand against his chest, making him stay.

I shake my head, stroking him faster. "I'm already so close. I don't know what it is. Nothing else matters besides touching you." I whimper as wetness dampens my panties, and he inhales, snarling when he scents me.

"I need to."

"I don't want you to." I take his lips in mine, forcing my tongue between his lips, gathering the remains of the peach. "Oh chauns, it tastes even better coming from you," I gasp as I try to inhale a fast breath, quickening the pace with my fist.

"Ru," he moans, tilting his head back.

I kiss down his throat, licking the sticky, dried juice from his skin. I become dizzy. The more I taste, the more I lose control of my inhibitions. When I get to his cock, I can't help but wrap my lips around the crown. He tastes so good, like freshly picked oranges, and I whimper. Ripping my mouth free, I lick the thick stalk, then lift my eyes to him. Half of his arms shift to his werewolf. From his elbow down, he loses control. The talons dig into my scalp, and with every heavy breath he exhales, a deep rumble follows.

"Let me touch you," he begs through tight fangs.

I shake my head, not wanting to stop, but I do because I want his lips again. I want everything. All at once. I need more. I kiss up his chest, and when my face is in front of his, the inky pools blink at me. I tighten my hand around the thick base of his cock, until he growls ferociously. He quickly flips me to my back and straddles my chest, his come hitting me in hot, thick streams across my cheek, chin, and lips.

Opening my mouth, I moan, trying to catch every drop, and even his come tastes like the fruit. The moment I swallow, my entire body tingles, and my orgasm hits me. I cry out, arching my back so high, his heavy sack presses against my chest.

I've never had an orgasm without being touched before. I don't know what's going on, but I never want it to stop.

Anwyll lies down on top of me and licks his come off my face before forcing his tongue in my mouth. I wrap my arms around him, moaning and clawing at his back, wanting more of his taste. It's a mess. I don't know what's gotten into us, but I never want it to stop.

"Let's stay here forever," I whisper between kisses. "Let's never leave. It can be us forever."

"Yes," he agrees. "I don't want anything else but you. Only us. Here. No interruptions. Let's stay." He rolls us again between two of the berry bushes.

"Stop eating the fruit. Stop it, Ru."

I rip my lips from Anwyll's and smile at him, still lost in the waves of pleasure. "What did you say, My Gentle Giant?"

"Nothing, My Lucky Charm. Nothing. I don't ever want to talk again. I only want to kiss and fuck you without stopping."

"Yes," I moan just as he pops a berry into my mouth. "Yes. All yes."

"Ru, you have to stop! Stop it, Ru! It's a trick. Wake up. Wake up!"

I pull away again, pinching my brows. "Stop playing around, Anwyll. I can hear you."

"What?" he asks, kissing down my neck. "I don't know what you're talking about."

"You keep…" I close my eyes and skim my fingers down his back. "You keep trying to talk to me."

He stops, lifting off me so he can look at me. "Ru, I swear, I haven't said anything."

"Ru, you have to stop eating the fruit. It isn't what it seems. It dulls your senses and uses your deepest desires against you. Wake up."

"There it is again." I sit up and look around, the swaying in my head becoming worse.

"What is it?" Anwyll crouches next to me, wrapping an arm around my chest, then tugs me against the broad expanse of his body. His cock presses against my lower back, and he sniffs my hair, humming as the lust still works through us.

It can't be the fruit. It's the heat coming. It has to be it.

"Talk to me," he murmurs, licking the spot where my shoulder and neck meet. "Tell me."

I groan, closing my eyes and tilting my head back. "I

can't focus with your lips on me. You're paying attention to that spot on purpose."

"Fuck yes, I am. I can't wait to sink my fangs into you while I knot you, Ru. I can't wait to fill you, over and over again. Until you're sore. Until you're crying. Until you're begging me to stop."

"You won't, right? You won't stop."

"Nothing could make me," he nibbles the spot, his fangs threatening to puncture the flesh. He can't. Physically. His beast won't let him. With a hand around my throat, he tilts my head back, and his entire eye is black again. "Nothing."

"Wake up, Ru. Please, Wake up. It isn't what it looks like. Wake up!"

I jump when the voice shouts at me, sitting forward. My fingers dig into the grass, and my hair fans over my shoulders as I look from left to right.

"Wake up, Ru. Wake up for me."

I know that voice, but it's impossible. A sharp pain shoots through my head, and the blinders lift for a few seconds as my body fights whatever is wrong with me.

"Ru?" Anwyll sounds concerned, placing a hand in the middle of my back.

I glance around with narrowed eyes. Everything is dark. There's no sunlight.

"Ru. The fruit is a drug for the vexils, small but horrible flesh-eating creatures who love the taste of lust-filled meat. Wake up, damn it!"

A strong backhand across the face snaps me from my amazing mood, and I hear a deafening roar before another slap echoes through the forest, cutting Anwyll's rage short.

I groan, face down in the dirt, but awake. I have a killer headache, and I'm lightheaded.

"I'm so sorry for doing that."

I flip over to see a girl hovering over Anwyll. I try to stand up to stop her from hurting him, but I stumble.

"I have you." Someone catches me just as Anwyll gets to his feet. "These lands are no place for you, Ru. Why are you here?"

I finally look at the person who has me, but I can't answer him because I bend over, throwing up. It's thick, black, and has the consistency of oil.

"That's it. Let it out." The man pats my back. "Get it all out. You'll feel like shit for a few more hours."

I hear Anwyll lose his stomach too, and I want nothing more than to go to him, but I don't have the strength.

A twig snaps in the distance, and I'm suddenly lifted into the air. "We need to go. The vexils are coming. They smell the poison leaving your body, and they aren't happy. Pearl, come on. We have to go. Can he walk?"

"I'm fine."

I notice out of my blurry eyes that Anwyll shifts into his full werewolf form.

"I heal fast. Hand me Ru."

"I don't think so," the man who is holding me says.

"Hand me my mate before I rip your fucking throat out," Anwyll warns with a thundering snarl.

"I see. Okay. I'm sorry. I didn't realize she was your mate."

I'm handed over and I lean my head against my mate's chest, sighing in relief when I feel his warmth. "Anwyll," I whisper.

"I'm here, Lucky Charm."

"We need to go. Follow us," the girl says.

"Why should we trust you?" Anwyll asks.

"You shouldn't, but if you stay, you'll become dinner.

Your funeral." The man and the girl, Pearl, begin to walk away while the manic sneering of an unknown creature comes closer.

Anwyll does the only thing he knows to do.

We follow.

Chapter Thirty-Two

ANWYLL

We're sitting around a fire while Ru rests her head on my lap. We had to cross the small creek to get to safety. Vexils, whatever they are, hate water. Getting away from them was easier than I thought. When we walked across the bridge, I happened to look over my shoulder to see them at the end, making insistent, angry cat-like noises. They were small, something that could fit in the palm of my hand, and furry, with big, round eyes and razor-sharp teeth.

They looked adorable until they opened their mouths.

"Is she okay?" the stranger asks, handing me a cup of water as we sit around the fire he built.

"She's fine." I run my talons through Ru's hair as she rests.

"So you're her mate," he says, trying to make small talk.

I cock my head at him and flash a little bit of fang. "I am. If you try to say otherwise, I'll rip your head from your neck," I warn, curling Ru onto my lap and then wrapping my arms around her until she can't be seen by him because I engulf her.

I'll protect her. This stranger might have saved us, but I trust no one when it comes to Ru. I trust nothing.

Only myself.

I am the only one I know who would risk his life, who would die, who would gladly undergo torture for her.

He lifts his hands as if he means no harm, and the orange glow from the fire tints his palms. "I am no threat to her. Especially her. I won't do anything. I didn't think...I didn't think I'd ever see her again, honestly."

A growl slips from my throat when I realize who is sitting in front of us.

"You're her father." I make sure I sound unhappy and unimpressed. This is the last thing Ru needs right now. She'll leave disappointed again.

He goes to open his mouth, but I stop him with a savage snarl. Both he and his daughter flinch back.

"You won't say another word until I wake her up. She deserves to know, and I'm not going to tell her. You are. And if she wants me to, I'll slice your throat with the tip of my claw and bathe in your blood because your life means nothing to me. It's Ru who matters most. Make no mistake about what I'll do to keep her safe and to keep her from disappointment. I will fucking kill you and what's worse..." I deepen my voice to show threat. "I'll love it."

He swallows, placing his arm around his other daughter's shoulders. "I'm not going to hurt Badru," he calls her by her actual name. "She's my daughter."

I snort, glancing down to see Ru sleeping peacefully. There's a hint of black poison on the corner of her lip, and I bend my finger, wiping it clean from her perfect, pouty mouth. I look at her for a moment, completely lost in her blonde lashes and flushed cheeks. I press my shifted hand

—paw—against her cheek, and her face seems so small and fragile against it. I'm larger than her in every way.

I just hope there is never a day when I actually make her feel small. If it were up to me, she'd be my size— something to match the warrioress of her heart.

I'm afraid for her every day. Her soul, her fire, it doesn't match the body she's been given— don't get me wrong— I love her fucking body. I'm obsessed with it, but I want her to be able to protect herself if, by any chance, I'm not around.

"Lucky Charm," I whisper, brushing my knuckles down her cheek. "Wake up, mate. We need to talk."

She makes a sound of protest and cuddles against me, burying her face in the fur against my stomach.

"Ru." I cradle her head and kiss her cheek. "I need you to wake up."

"You're very gentle with her," her father says.

"Life hasn't been. Someone, something needs to be, and I don't mind being the one chosen to do that. It is not a burden." I kiss her lips, sighing when I feel the moment she wakes, puckering her lips against mine.

Nothing feels better. Nothing can compare.

"Come to bed," she rasps, snuggling her cheek against my chest. "You're so warm. Like my own personal blanky." I don't think she realizes what she's doing, but she rubs her cheeks against my chest. To her, it's probably nothing. The fur is probably soft against her cheek, but to me, she's marking me with her scent, and it's making lust flow down south and my cock harden.

"Ru, you have to stop. You have to." I clear my throat and lift her onto her ass, making her sit on my lap so she covers my growing erection.

It's the heat. It's the tempting moon ahead of us.

We don't have much time before we are out of our minds.

"We have company, sleepy girl." I tap the end of my talon against her nose and her dream-ridden eyes round, big like the moons on her home planet, and the neon irises glow in the deep night.

Goddamn it, she's beautiful.

I don't know what higher being thought to go easy on me instead of killing me, but damn I'm glad they did, or I wouldn't have known Ru.

She's the only type of peace I'll want or need, even if it's the peace I don't deserve.

"Here." I give her a cup of water, and she swishes it around in her mouth before spitting it out to get the nasty taste of the poison from her tongue. After that, she takes a few swallows of water and exhales when she's had enough. "We have company, remember?"

She looks over her shoulder, and all the love that shone in her eyes disappears when she sees the man sitting there.

"Dad," she says, tone flat.

"You knew?" I ask.

"No. I was too out of it before. I'm not surprised. Irving said there was another here with my scent with a girl. I put two and two together." She turns around on my lap and tugs my arm over half her body, which nearly has her vanishing against me. "I wish I could say it's good to see you, Dad, but I wouldn't mean it."

"I deserve that."

"You deserve a lot more than that," Ru spits with disdain and stands from my lap. She looks from her dad to the woman sitting beside him. "And who are you? I suppose I'm related to you? Reddish hair, greenish eyes, but you aren't a witch. What are you?"

"Her name is Pearl," her dad explains.

"Pearl can talk for herself," Ru snaps. "Who are you?"

"Ru." I take my mate's hand and squeeze it. "She isn't at fault here. Okay? She isn't to be blamed."

A tear drips down her cheek, and she bites her lip, giving me a slight nod. "Thanks for saving us back there, but we're going to go. I would say it was good seeing you, but I'd be lying. Let's go, Anwyll."

I stand, not arguing with her at all about what she decides. She's a grown woman. She can make her own decisions.

"Badru, please—" her father tries to stop her, gripping her wrist.

My arm hits his chest with a solid thump, and he flies through the air, smacking into a nearby tree.

I growl in warning, protecting my mate from a man unworthy of Ru's love and care.

"Dad!" Pearl shrieks, running to her father.

The girl can't be older than twenty, maybe twenty-one. She's so...untouched by the real world. No cruelty, no evil, nothing has harmed her. She's oblivious to how it is outside this world her father has forced her to stay in.

"I'm okay. I'm fine." He slowly gets up, and that's when I notice it.

Ru told me stories about leprechauns who have lost their luck. They appear sickly, savage, and hunt anything that will give them luck even if it's for a moment, a minute, even a second of relief to feel the luck pump through their veins.

"You have your luck," I state with realization, stepping in front of Ru so she doesn't have to see this pathetic excuse of a man.

Pearl gives me a confused expression. "He has always had his luck, what does that have to do with anything?"

Ru steps out from behind me and marches her way over to him until she's standing right in front of him. All three of them have neon green eyes, the kind that can glow in the dark, and it's apparent that they are all related.

"You bastard," Ru whispers, choking as her emotions climb up her throat. "You liar!" She slaps him across the face, and he takes it with no complaint. Pearl tries to protect him, but he stops her. With how pissed off my mate is, Pearl wouldn't stand a chance.

I drop to all fours and growl, rumbling my chest for the entire Unwanted Lands to hear as I take the spot beside my mate. Even in this position, I tower over everyone, but Ru is the one in charge. Her anger is so strong, I can taste it, and when rage is that potent, it's bigger than anything in the room.

"Everyone. You had everyone fooled. You know Mom killed herself after you left! She died. I had to bury her. Me." She pounds her chest with her fist.

A whine slips from me, and I nuzzle my snout against her shoulder. I didn't know that about Ru.

"She said she couldn't live with herself knowing she had her luck and you didn't. She said she couldn't live the rest of her life without you. She died. It was one more thing for me to hate you for. And you want to talk?"

"I didn't know..." he cries. "I didn't know she died. I fucked up. I've made a lot of mistakes, Ru. I'm sorry. I'm sorry."

"I don't give a fuck about your apologies!" she screams so loud, her voice breaks, and birds fly from the trees above after being disturbed by her voice. "I don't give a damn about anything you have to say or feel. I don't care if you've imagined this day for years. I couldn't care less what you have to say to me. I was alone. I raised myself. I was an outcast in the village, and the only person who was there for me was Mannix. So we are leaving. You're never going to see me again." She turns to Pearl. "I'm sorry we had to meet like this. Maybe in another world, we could have been sisters. At least, I'm assuming you're my sister?"

"I've heard through the creatures whispering here you're from the Monreaux Coven, where Maven Wildes is… Maven and Pearl both are your half-sisters."

Ru doesn't say a word. She leans against me for support, all of the fight draining her body. "How am I related to Maven?" her voice a delicate whisper, breaking like dried autumn leaves. "You really got around, didn't you?" That's all Ru says, more out of shock than anything else. "I have never said I was a good man, Ru. I was lost. I always wanted you. You know how we get. When we have our luck, we always want more. And I really wanted more. I met your mom, and she was beautiful and amazing. I really did love her the best I could, but my greed was stronger." He twists a gold ring on his finger with an orange stone in the middle. "This ring." He holds up his hand, and the gold band glitters against the fire. "I didn't think anything of it. I found it while walking on the beach of Àdh. I wished I was somewhere else, and that's when I realized I could travel dimensions with this ring. By the time I blinked, I was in Salem."

"That's impossible. Only a Wildes Witch can open a portal," Ru argues.

"I don't travel through a portal, Ru. I don't know what happens. It's more like I teleport. I just think of where I want to go, and it takes me there. I can travel with a guest too if I want."

Ru laughs, but not in a way that is funny. Her hands fall

on her hips as she shakes her head. "You fucked different women in different dimensions? Mom lost her life because you couldn't keep it in your pants? Did she know?"

He looks down, ashamed, and swallows. "No. She thought I never found my luck, and I got banished. I found Maven's mom, and I got lost in her. She was beautiful and strong. Her powers were addicting. You and Maven are close in age, so it all happened around the same time. Pearl is different. I knew I couldn't go to Àdh again. And Maven's mom, Meredith, gave all of her power to Maven, which completely canceled the leprechaun in Maven. It's why you can't tell you're related. We left Salem because someone was after Meredith, some... warlock, if I remember correctly. We left for Maven's safety. We traveled because of the ring, but without her magic..."

Ru covers her hand with her mouth. "She died?"

He nods. "I don't think Maven knows. I haven't gone to check on her since."

"Shocker. Where does Pearl come into the picture?"

"I had traveled to Pyrita. A planet not too far from here. That's where I met Pearl's mother."

Ru slaps him again, then raises her hand to do it again, but I stop her. She looks at me with such heartache, such sadness, and so much pain. Tears plummet down her cheeks, and when she looks away, my own heart breaks for her.

"So you left Maven for her own good with her grandpa, who died, by the way, and then you raised Pearl, but what about me?" she questions, her tears dripping from her face to the ground with every blink of her eyes. "What about me?" she cries, her sob full of pain and hate. "What about me? Did you not care? Was I not good enough? What didn't you love about me? What could I have done to have my father in my life? Do you know how hard it has been? Did you ever think of me?"

"Of course I did." He takes a step forward, and she takes one back. "Ru, I had been gone so long, I didn't think you needed me anymore."

Ru straightens, lifting her chin in the air. "And now I don't."

"Ru. I love you. You're my daughter."

"That..." She tiredly gestures her hand at him in disbelief. "That is not true. I am not your daughter." She turns to me and lifts her hand. "Draw blood, Anwyll."

"What?"

"Just do it," she rushes.

I prick her palm with my fang and blood beads. Ru takes a step forward and takes a deep breath, gathering herself.

"Oh, chauns. Ru, please, don't do this. Please. I have messed up. I know I have, but please. I don't want this. I want another chance. I'll do anything, please."

She looks at him through wet lashes and presses her palm against his chest. "I renounce my blood tie to this man. I renounce any relation, any blood, any bond. We are separate."

"Ru, please! Don't do this. I'm begging you," he cries.

"May this luckline be broken and never be repaired," she finishes.

A dull green light pulses between them, only lasting for a second before it's gone. I expected a boom or something more dramatic.

"Now you really are free of me."

"What did you do? Ru, what did you do!" he screams at her, clawing at his chest as he weeps in agony. "What did you do?"

"I finally did what you should have done forever ago. You don't get to be upset. You don't get to be in pain. You don't get to be angry because you didn't get what you wanted. I'm sure you're a good dad to Pearl. You don't get to beg me for a second chance when you literally"—she lifts his hand in the air to show his ring—" had unlimited opportunity to be my father, to be a good person, and end things with mom, instead of letting her die because of a lie. You're selfish. I don't have room in my life for people like you. Blood or not." She tosses his hand down. "And I choose not. I choose to be free of you."

With that, Ru walks away, leaving Pearl and her dad behind.

"Take care of her," he tells me, cleaning the tears from his face.

I nod, not wanting to say what I really want since the man has lost a daughter tonight. I slide my eyes to Pearl. "I wish things could have been different. Good luck to you both." I follow my mate into the dark, leaving the past behind.

I don't know how this choice will affect my mate, but I know I'll be there every step of the way.

Chapter Thirty-Three

RU

"Ru." Anwyll tries to call after me, but I keep walking even though I have no idea where I'm headed.

I'm fuming. I'm scared. I'm confused. I feel like none of that just happened, but the burning on my palm from slapping my absent father across the cheek is still there. I can't believe I did that. I've never slapped anyone across the face. I've thought about it, especially the leprechaun from the gas station, but to actually hit someone? Never.

And I hit my own dad. Oh chauns, does that mean my soul is damned? Am I going to hell? But he was such an asshole. That fucking man whored his way around the entire galaxy. He managed to get three different women pregnant and forget all about me. He deserved to get slapped.

Maybe unlinking myself from him was impulsive, but I don't regret it. I'm not mad about it, and I'm not having second thoughts. It hurts that I had to come to that decision, but I haven't been linked to my father for nearly my entire life. I've always been without him. It's no different now.

"Ru." Anwyll runs in front of me and stands until he is at his full height.

He is a skyscraper in this form, and I tilt my head all the way back, eyes filled with tears as I stare at his handsome face. Seeing my tears, he shifts into his mid form. His features become smaller, and he loses a few inches in height, but his gorgeous skin maintains that sleek gray I love so much.

He brushes away the tears on my cheek and tilts his head. "That couldn't have been easy."

I glance away, wiping my cheeks, and begin to walk around him. "I'm fine."

"Don't walk away from me, mate." He whips me around and pulls me against his body, his green eyes take on a red hue, and then he shakes his head.

Just like that, the crimson color is gone.

"What was that?"

"I don't know. The moon, I think. My temper is getting harder to control." He rolls his head around his shoulders and tries to relax. "I'm sorry, but please don't walk away from me. I don't know what I'll do. I don't trust myself. This isn't about me. This is about you. Are you okay?"

"It's been a long time coming. I don't regret it. It's sad, knowing I have a sister, and I won't be close with her. That hurt more than losing him because he has been lost to me for years. He's a liar, and he isn't a good man. He isn't a good person. So unlinking my luck with him is the best thing I can do for myself."

"How did you do that?" he asks, his voice taking on a darker tone. I get another glimpse of his eyes turning red. He presses his palms against his eyes, and his chest rises with every breath.

"Anwyll." I touch his arm, and he sighs in relief at the touch, bringing his hands down from his face.

"Your touch helps. Ah, Ru, I'm so sorry. I'm going to need you closer. I'm already needing you."

"I'm right here." I slip my hand into his, and he locks us together.

We start walking again, and his eyes are back to normal as we make our way into the unknown night.

"How did you unlink yourself? Is it magic?"

"No. Kind of? Maybe. I don't know. Unlinking luck from your blood relatives is almost unheard of these days. People don't do it. We are taught it in school, and we are only allowed to use it in the most extreme circumstances. Luck is different for every family. Every bloodline holds a different strand of luck, and we are all intertwined. Removing myself from my father's line, my luck will..." I think of the right word to use. "Reroute itself. I have my luck and my mom's now. If I have children—"

"—You will," he growls. "By the end of this week, you'll be pregnant with my baby."

I blush, forgetting that the heat and knotting won't stop until he breeds me. "—If I have children, their luck will be a new strand of luck now since mine is no longer tied to my dad's, assuming they are leprechaun."

"I see," he says, understanding the confusion of my kind's ways.

"Well, if they aren't leprechauns. They will probably be werewolves," I add. "Which I'm happy with, by the way. As long as they are healthy."

"Who knows, maybe they will be both," he adds.

"You know you can't be both. They will have to be one or the other."

"Guess we will find out, won't we?"

I press the cool top of my hands against my heated cheeks and nod. "I guess we will." And then I yawn, exhausted from crying and yelling. There's still a pit in my stomach from what happened back there with my dad.

I have two half-sisters.

I gasp, stopping in my tracks. "Anwyll, Maven doesn't know her mom is dead. Do I tell her? How do I tell someone that? I can't do that."

He stands in front of me, pressing one hand on my cheek while the other grips the back of my neck. "We will do it together because that is something she deserves to know, but we will worry about that when we are home."

I relax, remembering he will be by my side. "Thank you." I kiss his palm and step away from his reach, then begin to back away from him. His eyes change from green, to black, to red, his body unsure of which to land on. I'm not sure why the red is coming into play, but I don't need to understand it.

All I know is it means he wants me, and that's all I need to know.

I start to walk away, and he growls, his eyes shining bright as a wicked flame sent from hell, and he drops to all fours, shifting into his true self.

"Ru. I told you—"

"—Not to walk away from you." I nod. "I remember." I put more distance between us with every step, and he snarls at me, threatening his fangs.

Something about his facial structure seems different. It's more angular than usual, deviant, lethal.

And then I run, a sliver of fear and instinct wanting him to chase me for some reason. It isn't even the full moon. I don't understand.

A vicious howl sounds from behind me, and I hear the heavy weight of his paws dig into the ground. I slap the branches away from me, and I stumble when the grass turns to stone. I fall to my knees and make the mistake of looking behind me. He pounces, but I roll to the right, missing his attempt to catch me.

And I bolt again.

"Ru! I said not to fucking walk away from me!" The fury in his tone sends shivers up my spine. "I'm going to ruin you," he says under his breath.

I really fucking hope he does.

I see something up ahead, something dark in the wall, and realize it must be a cave. I head for it, dodging in and out through the trees.

And then I feel his warm breath against my neck before I'm tackled to the ground. He embraces me in his arms and rolls so he takes the hard hit against the rocks. I lay still, trying to catch my breath, when he takes my wrist in his mouth, and he drags me to the cave.

"Anwyll," I say his name, confused, wondering what he is doing. He has never done this before. "Anwyll." I try again, but I can't get his attention.

He growls around his hold on my arm. It's light, but the tips of his fangs apply enough pressure for me to know not to move in any way, or the flesh will be shredded.

When we enter the cave, surrounded by darkness, all I hear is his heavy breathing. My heart beats so loud, I know it's one of the things he is focused on. The only thing I can see is the sharp red-orange of his eyes, two searing flames dancing in the void of the cave, but I can tell by the feel of his skin he has shifted to his mid-form.

Without warning, he rips my clothes from my body with one swipe of his talons.

"Anwyll."

"I won't be saving you from myself," he says, forcing my legs apart with a hard swipe of his knee as he settles between them. "I warned you." With another tear to the crotch of my pants, he curls his claws inside and rips my underwear from my body. His hand wraps around my throat, and the tips of his talons threaten to pierce my skin. "I told you not to run."

In one uncaring thrust, he fills me with his massive werewolf cock, and I whimper, my belly beginning a slow burn.

My heat.

He sniffs the side of my neck and licks it, a rumble of pleasure filling his chest. "Your heat is so close. I can feel it under your skin. I smell it. You're going to be such a fucking slut for me, aren't you? You're going to be good and take my cock in any way I want to give it to you. Won't you?"

"Anwyll..."

"Won't you?" he yells, his voice echoing in the cave as he fucks me with no remorse.

It hurts.

The stretch. The burn.

But I want more.

"Your pussy is going to drink every drop of my come. When you try to crawl away from me, after being used like the little fuck toy you'll be for me, you'll be covered in blood, sweat, and come. You'll be ruined for anyone else. Your cunt will only be fit for my cock because I'll be fucking the imprint of it into your goddamn womb, mate."

This doesn't even sound like Anwyll. He's the stranger that he warned me about, and this is only a taste of what is to come.

"My mate is so tight. You can't even take all of my big

dick, can you? It would break you if you did." One singular claw scrapes down my neck to my chest and I whimper when it begins to sting.

He cut me.

Moaning, he licks the blood from me, bringing his lips to my ear. "I can't wait to break you under the moon. You'll take every inch and more. And if you don't," he sounds furious as he says the words. "I'll fucking make you." He rams himself inside me, and I swear, I feel him in my stomach, trying his best to keep his promise.

Tears trickle from my eyes, but only because I feel so good. It's freeing not having any control. It's being taken from me.

Without pulling out, he flips me onto my stomach and takes me from behind.

Like animals do.

I'm soaking his cock. I can hear the wetness with every thundering stroke he gives me. The sharp claws sink into my skin as he holds onto my ass, fucking me with no remorse, no care, using me as if I don't matter to him at all.

But he does, or he wouldn't be fucking me like this.

Werewolves only fuck their mates like he is fucking me, and that makes me feel better than everyone else who has sex with someone who only gives half an effort.

"Anwyll. More. Give me more."

This time, it's him who whines because he can't give me what I want.

"In time, I'll give this hot, desperate cunt what it deserves, and every night after that." He drives into me, my breasts scraping against the stone below us. "And every morning. I'm going to knot you every moment I can and fill you with so much come, I'll be dripping from you for weeks."

He yanks me by the hair until my back can't bend any further. "Beg for my come." His fang nips my ear. "Beg me like I know you want to."

My orgasm is so close, and it's going to wreck me with intensity.

I can't do as he says. I like him too much like this. I don't want it to end.

He lies down on top of me, his cock barreling in and out, the flared tip of his cockhead pressing against every sensitive spot. "Tell me, Ru. Tell me how you can't come without feeling me spill every drop inside you."

Is that why I can't seem to fall over the edge? Every part of my body feels hot and heavy, even my bones ache like if I don't feel him come, I won't be able to function another day.

"Anwyll, please," I cry, clawing at the ground. "Please, come. Please. I want it. I need it. I'm aching. I hurt. I hurt all over. Give it to me. I want all of it. I need more." I press my ass against him, seeking more, wishing his knot would swell.

"I shouldn't give it to you. You ran from me when I told you not to, but there's no way I can pull out and leave you empty. I need to see your cunt weep with my come. Only then will I be satisfied." His teeth dig into my shoulder, and his palm slaps on the ground above my head. The grinding grit of his talons drags, leaving grooves in the stone as he takes, takes, and takes.

His other hand smacks the ground, directly parallel to the other. His fingers curl, and his claws scratch the rock again just as he growls, releasing every drop inside me like he promised.

Everything inside me eases. The aches are gone. My muscles relax, and I even feel the heat recede. My orgasm washes over me, my muscles rippling along his shaft, pulling his seed deeper into my womb.

I want it to stick. I already crave his child.

If this is what I have to look forward to, I'm excited.

The full moon is rising.

And I wish it would tonight.

ANWYLL

I watch Ru sleep for hours. I can't sleep. Every sigh she breathes, every move she makes, every whimper that escapes her, I have to dig my talons into the side of the cave to stop myself from taking her. She smells so fucking good. My cock hasn't stopped leaking since last night. She has to rest, but all I want to do is fuck her.

No, no.

Not even that is enough.

I scratch my head with my talons, inhaling when the scent of heat hits my nose. It's stronger now. Potent. The smell is... delicious. It slides across my tongue, teasing me, toying with my taste buds and my sanity. All I want to do is lose myself in her and drown in it. Her heat is like an energy, pulsating through the air, and every time I inhale, that energy sears its way through my veins, my heart, and my blood.

Lust is formed in ways that are beyond what the human mind and body can comprehend. Her heat will only get stronger, and my lust will surpass healthy levels.

I'll become manic.

I already feel the edge of it tickling in the back of my mind.

The cave echoes the shallow growls, leaving me with every breath I take.

I sag against the wall, closing my eyes to control myself. My fur sticks to my body from the sweat of restraining myself. Taking one last look at Ru, I head to the mouth of the cave and let the cool air wash over my heated face.

The next few days are going to be hell.

"You need to be careful."

I swipe my paw out in front of me and snarl, turning my head left and right to see whose slithering voice that is.

"Calm down." The void appears in his shadowy form, keeping to his truer form. I can see the skeleton-esque face. "I'm not here to harm you or your mate. I shouldn't be here at all, actually, but for some reason, I find myself giving a damn."

I take a step closer, my talons cutting into the dirt. "About?"

His eyes cast over my shoulder to where Ru is, and I growl, flashing my fangs.

"Don't even think about going near her. I'll rip you from limb to limb."

He laughs, dispersing into molecules I can barely see, then forms again next to me. "You think you can kill me? Only one thing can kill me, Spot. You do not hold the power."

"Then, what?"

"You two surviving this journey changes things for a lot of people. You might not think so, but it does. And let's not forget who she is related to. Being related to a Wildes Witch comes with its pros and cons." He breezes in front of me. "Your mate doesn't need to be a witch to be in danger all the time. If it means getting one step closer to the witch, then Ru is a means to an end, along with her sister."

"How do you know that? We just found out ourselves."

"The trees talk, Spot. It won't be long until other planets know, other dimensions, old enemies who want revenge, or people who just want power. If you two complete this journey to cure sickness in wolves, who knows what else it could cure, or who it could help? I'm here to help you because even though half my soul is damned to hell, I still have half of it that seems to give a fucking shit about..." he eyes me up and down then exhales "...things."

"How thoughtful of you," I growl, twitching my nose.

"Listen, Spot. I have orders."

"Stop calling me Spot."

"Why?" He scratches behind my ear. "You look like a Spot. Such a good boy."

With a violent growl, I manage to grab him by the throat before he can disperse. "The only person in the entire world who can call me a good boy is my mate." I bring him closer to my face, my eyes flaming red. His calling me that threatens my mating with Ru. I won't let anything interfere. "Want to see what a werewolf bite will do to a Void?"

"Okay, but I'm not going to stop calling you Spot. I like it."

"I don't."

"I don't care. Take my help or go on with your journey and most likely die."

Growling in annoyance, I set it down, and he rubs his neck. "Thank you. Now, I have orders—"

"From who?"

"My boss. I believe you know him as...Death."

A breath catches in my throat, and I stop breathing as his words sink in. "Death... as in—"

"—The Four Horsemen." He snaps his skeletal fingers. "Ding. Ding. Ding. Winner, winner, chicken dinner for Spot."

I curl my lip to show some fang, but he isn't impressed.

"Put those away. You're going to embarrass yourself."

The last time I saw Death, was at the carnival over Halloween, where Azazel, a rogue demon, kidnapped paranormals and made them a freak show. It took a lot of manpower to take him down and save the creatures he kidnapped. Death and his brothers were able to form a giant demon, sending Azazel to purgatory.

None of us has heard from him, his brothers, or the creatures we saved since.

"Is he okay? The people we saved? Do you know anything about the carnival?"

"I don't know, Spot. I'm not BFFs with Death. He's my boss. We don't pillow talk and braid hair."

"You're a fucking smartass, and it's pissing me off."

"And you get so cute when your ears flicker."

I narrow my eyes, reaching up to touch my ears. "They do not," I argue weakly.

"Anywho, he wanted me to give you this." Out of his cloak, he pulls out a unicorn horn.

"But anything from a unicorn—"

"—That's where there are exceptions to the rule. Naturally shed horns can be the greatest weapon, Spot. If you take a horn from a unicorn, saw it from its head, you'll be cursed. Death will come for you."

I take the horn from him. It's lighter than I expected. The point is sharp too. There is an opal hue to the swirls. It's gorgeous. It's hard to believe it can be used as a weapon.

"Thank you," I tell him.

"It's the only thing that will stop what you're about to be up against. Listen to me." He flows closer until he is right in front of me. "You have to remain quiet. The slightest sound will wake them up, and once they are awake, surviving them will be nearly impossible. They are stronger than you will be. They protect the wolfsbane on the cliff. It's thousands of years old. The older the wolfsbane, the more potent it is. You're wanting wolfsbane, you're about to walk into a field of it, but it won't be easy, especially for you. You'll be walking into toxin, Spot. She'll be left vulnerable."

I sneer, placing the horn right under his chin. "I'll protect her until my dying breath."

"And then what?" He presses his chin against the horn, daring me to stab him. "You leave her alone with stone giants? One flick of their finger and her bones break. She'll be dead too."

Infiltrating his space, I push him against the wall of the cave, hating the words spewing from his lips. "I'll never let that happen to her."

"That's exactly what is going to happen if you go any further."

"Anwyll?" Ru's sleepy voice echoes from the cave.

The Void and I turn our heads at the same time, and Ru's figure comes from the shadows. Fuck, she's gorgeous, and she reeks of heat.

"Get back, Ru," I shout, my eyes rolling to the back of my head, the closer she becomes.

The Void chuckles. "You smell good, Lucky."

I rake the horn across his skeletal face and lift him from the ground by his neck, then slam him onto the ground. Roaring in his face until I know the island can hear me.

"I will fucking spread your shadowy ass all over this fucking dimension if you say one more thing about my mate."

"You can't kill me. Only a reaper can kill another reaper."

My eyes widen. "But you're a void."

"And what do you think we do? We stay in the void until we have to take a soul."

"So Death is actually your boss," Ru says. "That's... kind of cool."

"Thanks, Lucky."

"Don't call her that. I'll make a mental note to talk to Death and make sure you aren't the void I ever do business with."

"Sorry, Spot. Why do you think I'm here all of a sudden? I've been assigned, but to help you avoid death instead of meeting him. Apparently, all souls in the Monreaux Coven are off-limits." He smacks his lips. "I bet all that immortality tastes so good."

"You'll never know. Keep craving, asshole." I throw him through the air, and he dissipates, then regenerates in front of me again.

I step in front of Ru, her scent making me dizzy, but I don't want her in his eyesight.

"I'll go, but don't say I didn't warn you. Oh, and I suggest you go now, while the giants are asleep. Tootles." He waves his bony fingers, blowing a kiss to Ru.

I try to reach him, but he disappears just as my arms wrap around his neck. He turns to dust, drifting through the air.

"Oh, I don't like him at all."

"I don't know. He's kind of charming."

I pin Ru against the wall, forearm across her neck, then

lick my long tongue down the side of her throat where my mark will be. "You won't speak of another man being charming or anything else again, especially while the moon is close, and your heat is reaching its peak."

"Is it?" she sighs seductively. "Is that why I feel so hot?"

"Mmm," I hum, sounding as if I want to eat her right here and now.

She reaches between my legs, and I take a step closer, shifting into my mid-form, and all my hair recedes. Her hand wraps around my cock, and I whimper, already wanting to come. I lift her from the wall, then slam her against it again, a warning for her not to continue.

Her mouth parts as my talons dig into her shoulders, scraping down her arms to stop myself from pushing her panties to the side and sliding into that delicious cunt I love so much.

"Fuck." I push away from her until my back is against the cave. I punch the stone, and bits of rock fall onto the ground. "We can't. We have to go."

"Just real quick, Anwyll. Please." She pulls one strap of her tank top down her arm, her breast popping free, and her nipple beads against the chill in the air. "Anwyll, please," she begs, pushing her panties to the side.

Her fingers rub her cunt, and a burst of sweetness fills the air as if cotton candy melted and is drenched all over my tongue. She's soaked, and by the smell of her arousal, she's already close.

"I'm burning for you, Anwyll. Please. Oh chauns, it all hurts. Every part of me. Please."

I attack her, that's the only way to describe it. My vision flips to red, the feral beast becoming unlocked. I throw her onto the ground, uncaring if it hurts, if she cries, if it ruins her skimpy little clothes.

I push her panties to the side and fuck my cock roughly into her tight, drenched hole. With both hands, I push her into the dirt. Her hands claw the ground, the soil digging under her fingernails, and with every brutal stroke I give, she screams.

"Is this what you wanted?" I ask, noticing my knot is slightly bigger, reacting to her heat. It still isn't enough to lock myself in place, which only irritates me more. It angers me.

Why can't I knot her now? I want to know.

"You like this, don't you? Being my little fucking bitch." I yank her head up by her hair until her neck is bent back. I know it has to hurt, but I don't care. "You love taking my werewolf cock. You can't get enough."

"I can't," she whimpers. "I can't." She turns her head, and her cheeks are wet with tears. "I'm so damn hot. I feel like I'm going to explode."

"You'll feel better in a minute," I grunt, her silky hot walls hugging every inch of me until her pussy can't take the extra few inches where my knot is. "I'll give your greedy pussy every drop of my come, and we can finally relax. I'll take care of you." I toss my head back, roaring a howl as the light of the moon hits me.

I can feel the power, the urge to completely ruin her and fuck her until she's unconscious. Her cries echo alongside my own, except mine are more brutal, more commanding.

Looking down, I pant in delight when I see the shine from her cunt soaking the gray hue of my cock. She's pulled wide, stretched to the max. I push her head down, burying her face in the dirt, and fuck her harder, never taking my eyes from my shaft drilling into her fragile body. I'm not sure when I'll let her take control of me again, but it won't be for a while.

Her muscles clamp around me, and her slick squirts down my long length as she comes. "You're fucking drenching me, Ru." There's so much slick, it drips down my sack and puddles on the ground. If it were any other time of the month, this wouldn't happen, but heats are brutal.

She'll be worn out and sleep for days.

Every huff that leaves me, a rumble lies in the mix.

I lift her onto her knees, wanting a better grip on her body while I pound and take, staking my claim. With a giant hand kneading her breast and one around her neck, I use her entire body as leverage, bouncing it on my cock while I thrust.

"That's it, My Lucky Charm. Take my cock. You love the bite of pain. It's too big for you, isn't it? It hurts."

She's half-way limp, bobbing her head in agreement. Her eyes are glassy but light up again when more slick rushes down me once more.

"Anwyll! Oh, fuck. Yes. Yes!" She tenses, trying to stop me from moving so she can ride the waves of her orgasm. "More. More," she sobs, falling against me. Her shoulders are slick with sweat and glide against my chest. "More, Anwyll. Give me more."

I squeeze her throat until she can't breathe. "You'll take what I fucking give you. No more. No less. What I give you will be enough." I drop my hand to her stomach, my orgasm so close, it steals my breath. "Soon, so soon, I won't be leaving this cunt until you're pregnant."

Just the thought, the pure pleasure of the sensation of experiencing the change of her scent has me thrusting inside her one more time and biting into her shoulder.

"Anwyll!" she screams my name.

My. Name.

And it unleashes something lethal inside me.

I push her onto her stomach again, burying myself as far as I can, letting her cunt drink every drop I spill into her.

Bending down, I lick the bite wound on her shoulder and it heals. I hate that.

I can't wait till she scars, and everyone will know she's taken.

The strength of her heat fades, and I'm left with mourning inside my soul.

Gently, we both groan as I pull every long, thick inch of me free. Her cunt weeps with my come, crying down her thighs, and I sneer, displeased.

I scoop the excess with my finger and force it into her mouth. If it won't seep into her womb, then I'll have to settle for it being in her stomach.

"Mmm," she moans, her tongue licking my finger clean.

"That's it," I croon, knowing how much she needs this right now.

The more she gets, the more she'll be ready for me. I gather more from her other thigh, and she licks down my finger, gathering the come that's puddled in my palm.

"So thirsty," I say proudly, loving how much she needs me to survive.

I never thought I'd have that. Never in a million years did I think anyone in the world would ever need me, but here I am.

I'm so thankful for my mate. She heals me. The wounds that are too deep for anyone to see, but only I can feel, she touches those. And every day, I become a better version of myself.

"Are you okay?"

She gives me a sleepy grin and nods. "Great. Sooo great."

I chuckle, shifting into my werewolf and picking her up.

"We need to get ready to go. Let's get you dressed in fresh clothes."

"I need to bathe."

I snap my teeth together, not liking the sound of that. "I can't have my scent off you. Knowing you smell of me is the only thing allowing me to not lie you on this floor and take you."

"I understand." She cups my face, and her touch has me wagging my tail.

Only Ru could cause my tail to wag.

"How long do I have? Before I need you again?" she asks as I set her down in the cave and she undresses, digging into the magic bag Maven spelled for us. She also grabs a different shirt from the bag and cleans her face off with it, scrubbing away the dirt.

"Maybe another few hours. Maybe even until tomorrow, but by midnight tomorrow, you'll be in full heat. You'll be delirious, needy, desperate."

"Sounds pathetic," she jokes, and I don't know why, but it angers me.

I gather her in my arms and tilt her chin up, forcing those glowing emeralds to meet my own.

"Your eyes are red again."

"I think it's the moon. The mating. The heat."

"But they were black."

"A transition, I think. From green to red. Consider black a neutral state right now."

"You're not neutral then and you're not happy? Or they would be green."

"Because nothing is pathetic about your heat. Nothing is pathetic about you needing me that badly, just as I'll need you." I feel my eyes burn brighter. "Only we can make each other feel better. Only we can ease the ache. Only us.

Together. No one else can do that. Don't ever talk down about yourself or your heat again." My voice rises slowly until I'm panting for breath. I shake my head and try to gather my emotions. Closing my eyes, I settle, and when I open them again, I see the brilliant green irises of mine mirroring from hers. "I'm sorry."

"Don't be. I should know better than to joke right now." She stands on her tiptoes, and I have to bend down so she can kiss my cheek. "Let's go. The...giants?" she asks to see if she's correct.

I nod.

"They are asleep. So we have to hurry."

"We have to hurry when we are there too. It's littered with wolfsbane. I won't be able to be there too long."

"Okay, then let's go." She grabs the bag and hikes it onto her shoulder. "And we need to make note of your eyes. It will help with your brother if he doesn't know."

"What's it matter?" I spit as I march out of the cave, then remember who I am talking to like that. "Fuck, Ru. I'm sorry. I'm an asshole when the moon is high. I've never experienced a full moon with a mate before, and even when I didn't, it wasn't this bad. When I was spelled, I didn't even know when the full moon was near. I was constantly angry."

"You don't have to explain yourself. I know you're still adjusting. You're not mad at me, Anwyll. A lot of emotions are heightened right now due to our situation, but why don't you think it matters? Every little bit helps, right? To know about your kind?"

"Not if we are the only ones."

"Your brother needs to be ready. When he meets his mate. The change in color can be off-putting at first, especially if his mate is human. She'll be terrified."

There are more things I want to say. As in, 'What if he is dead by the time we get back?' or 'What if he doesn't have a mate?'

But Ru is trying to remain hopeful, so I need to do the same.

"We know my eye color changed when I met you, a way to show our souls are tethered. Black means in... transition? It seems the closer we get to mating, the more the red takes over, like..." I think, looking for the right words. "Like I get lost in my instinct."

She steps over a log, and a glowing butterfly lands on the tip of her nose. Ru freezes, then giggles, going cross-eyed to look at it. The wings are blue and the body is pink.

"Do you see this?"

"I do. I'm not surprised. Animals drift to the purest of souls, the ones who can be trusted."

The butterfly flies away, and Ru watches in awe.

"That was beautiful. There are a lot of horrors on this journey, but I can't deny, some scenery is beautiful. The Unwanted Lands, not so much."

"I can't say I find anything beautiful right now," I say honestly. "I haven't paid attention to anything except you. I don't see the good in anything around me like you do, Ru. I love that about you. I admire it, honestly. With everything, including your dad, which I worry about for you."

"Don't." She takes my hand and gives me a reassuring smile. "I can't miss something I no longer have, and it's been a long time since those few good memories I had with my father. Don't waste another thought on it, My Gentle Giant."

"I haven't been so gentle," I correct her.

"No." Her heart rate accelerates, and the sweet scent of her slick fills the air between us. "You haven't."

I grip her by the waist and lift her into the air, her feet dangling as I bring her to my eye level. Her fucking scent is driving me insane, and when she and everything around us turns red, I know I'm losing my control.

"Do. Not. Tempt. Me. Mate." I bite out every word, punctuating each with agitation.

I fucking hate that we don't have the time for me to do all the things I want to her, but the sooner we get through this mess, the sooner I can do the things I want to her. We have to be in a safe place. A place where we won't be disturbed for days. I'm not sure how long the heat and rut will last, but I have to make sure we are okay.

Her feet hit the ground when I lower her. "We get through this first. I won't take you again until I know we are safe. I'm hanging on by a thread, Ru. A fucking thread. It's tattered and shredded. I'm the last single piece of the damn thread waiting to break and being pulled so fucking thin." The words come out as a deep rumble. "I'm so close to losing control. My nature is boiling at the surface, and my instincts are screaming to fuck you without stopping." I prowl toward her, and she steps back the closer I become. "My instincts," I sneer, slamming my fist against my chest. "Are you telling me not to give a fuck about anything else. My brother? He is very close to not mattering to me right now because nothing else matters to me besides being inside you. Feeling your wet, soft cunt hugging my cock—" I roll my head over my shoulders and grit my fangs together. "—It makes me crazy."

She slips on a patch of moss as she backs away from me. She's so much smaller than me. The things I could do...

"The way you gasp, the way you moan, the way you claw at my fucking back when I'm burying myself inside you..." I close my eyes and my skin arises in goosebumps.

"Oh, Ru…" I snag my hand out again, gripping her by her throat, and bend down until my nose is touching hers. "You have no fucking clue," the words slowly thunder between us as if a storm is taking its time raising— bringing its fury. "Do I make myself clear, Ru? Do not test me. Do not joke. Do not tease or taunt me. It *will not* end well for you."

Her heat is growing again, the scent heavy between us. She's not afraid of me at all. Her heartbeat is fast, too fast, but I don't smell fear.

No, my wicked little mate wants to push my bounds. I see the mischief swimming in her eyes. I bet the words are gathering on the tip of her tongue to push me, to see what I would do. She loves to be in control of me—I do too—but this is not that time.

And it won't be until her womb is mine.

Her shoulders ease, and she lowers her eyes, finally giving me submission. "I understand, Anwyll." She stares at my cock, and I don't hide how hard I am for her, but I want to make her wait. I want her to ache as she notices what she does to me.

I *want* her need to hurt.

The sound of a rock skidding across more rocks stops me in my tracks, and Ru spins around, hair fanning over her shoulders.

"What was—"

I stop her from speaking, putting a giant paw over her mouth to silence her, then pull her against my chest. My cock instantly softens, and my hair grows to cover my groin. The fur on the back of my neck stands up, signaling danger.

"Be very quiet, Ru," I whisper into her ear.

She nods quickly as we crouch down behind a few trees. The moon is almost at its highest, and as much as I feel the power, the fear, and worry push it aside. The moonlight and stars give enough light for us to see the giants that the Void told us about.

"Oh my chauns, Anwyll." Ru looks up to me in pure terror, and she has every right to be.

The cliff is made up of four—of what I can see—sleeping stone giants. All around them, even growing on their legs and on the cliff, are hundreds, if not thousands, of the purple flowers we are seeking.

The giants are huge.

"Ru." I make sure to speak so low, I can barely hear myself. "Take this." It's the horn the Void gave me. "It will help you, and if we survive this, I will explain everything later. Trust me."

She nods, gulping, then wraps her hand around the base of the horn.

I don't know how that will protect us.

"We grab one flower. One," she says, lifting a finger. "And we run."

A singular flower.

If only it was that easy for me.

Chapter Thirty-Five

RU

They are the most amazing, frightening, gigantic creatures I've ever seen in my entire life. The cliffs are so high, they seem to touch the stars, and the giants are very easy to see. Their legs seem to be cemented to the ground and hang over the cliff's edge. Moss covers their groins, and their stomachs are chiseled with natural grooves from erosion over the years. Their arms are the size of a tree trunk, and their jaws are literally carved out of stone.

I know Anwyll can't touch the wolfsbane, which is impossible because it's everywhere. We don't have much time.

One of the giants scratches his stomach and groans, the baritone carrying for miles.

As we creep closer, the woods come to a sharp end, and soon the pillowy ground of the earth transitions to stone.

I lift my finger to remind Anwyll of the plan, and he nods, covering his mouth with his paw to not breathe in the scent of wolfsbane. It smells good too, sweet, like candy, but there's a musk to it I can't put my finger on.

My heat—my want for Anwyll—it's forgotten. All I

want us to do is make it out of this alive. I won't lie, burying the lust for him down is hurting my stomach, but it has to wait.

It has to.

We haven't come this far to die.

I'm determined to live the rest of my life with the werewolf I love, and so help me, if anything threatens that, I will fight tooth and nail, even if it kills me.

The pressure gets to me, and the damn panic tears begin to fill my eyes. No. No, I won't cry. I won't let my emotions hinder this situation. There's no time to act like I have no luck.

My luck is my own.

Not scratch-offs. Not jewelry. Not seashells.

I make it myself.

Watching every step I take so I don't step on cracks or kick loose rocks or pebbles, I place my tiptoes down without flattening my foot. Anwyll follows my footsteps, remaining on his hind legs.

When I get to the edge of the wolfsbane, I appreciate it for a second. It's very old and potent, growing on patches of grass lining the rock's surface. It's beautiful in a twisted way. The view overlooking the cliff is gorgeous. I can see most of the Unwanted Lands from here, including the lake that blinded me for a few hours.

It's hard to believe something so gorgeous holds so many deadly things.

Anwyll falls forward, bracing his hands on my shoulders. When I look up, his eyes are glassy and his entire body is swaying. I have to hurry.

With one last look at the giants, I hold my breath and tug an entire bushel of wolfsbane up, roots and all. I shove it in the bag and wrap my fingers around Anwyll's wrist, telling him we need to go.

Rock grinds against rock. A massive shadow falls over us, and my entire body trembles when I realize we are too late.

Anwyll stands in front of me, shaking off the dizzy spell he's under, and roars at the giant.

It's nothing compared to the rolling storm escaping the stone creature. It's as if hurricane force winds smash into us, and Anwyll holds onto me, planting his feet, but it doesn't stop us from sliding across the flower bed of poisonous blooms.

The giant raises his arm, dust and small bits of rock fall from his body, and he swings it through the air. We dive to the right, and Anwyl lands in the thick of it.

"Anwyll!" I shout his name, watching as he has no other choice but to breathe in.

He manages to get up and grab me, rolling me again just as another arm slams on the ground, cracking the cliff.

The giant yells again, but this time, two others flank his side.

"Run, Ru!" Anwyll shoves me out of the way, taking a hit by one of the stone arms, and he hooks his talons into the rock, holding on while the giant tries to shake him off.

I do as he says. I don't know where I'm running. I can't run away because I won't leave Anwyll alone.

The positive thing about these giants, they move slowly due to their size. One bends down, trying to grab me with its oversized hand, and I slip between his legs, remembering the unicorn horn I'm grasping.

I stab its foot, and remarkably, the horn penetrates it as if the stone is butter. The giant bellows, reaching behind itself to grab me again.

Great. I've pissed it off.

Anwyll flies through the air and smacks against a tree, his werewolf form falling limp.

"No!" I scream so loud, so hard, I taste blood in the back of my throat. I sprint to him, leaping over wolfsbane, but one of the giants captures me by the ankle, swinging me in the air. I don't bother screaming for Anwyll. There's nothing he can do.

I'm upside down, staring at the angry face of a giant. I take the horn and stab its hand. Cracks vein across its palm and it lets me go.

I freefall. If I hit the ground, I'm dead.

In a rush of panic, I fling out my arms, and the horn catches the side of the giant. It roars to the heavens as I slice down its side. With both hands, I grip the horn, and I descend until my feet are planted on the ground.

It bellows as it falls apart, and there's a part of me that feels bad. I never want any creature to die, but if it's between me and them, I'll choose me every single time. Survival has no room for regret or guilt; those feelings won't get you out alive.

It groans, parts of its body falling away. Boulders hit the ground as its arm falls away, and it stumbles when its leg crumbles. The giant falls over the cliff. One of the other giants tries to catch its friend but tumbles into the valley with it.

Anwyll is back on his feet, swaying left and right to get to me, but there are two other giants left, and by the look on their faces, they are furious.

I run between them, slicing their ankles with the horn, and a loud crash sounds as they each lose a foot. There's no time for victory. I jump over one foot and run to Anwyll. We have to get out of here.

The ground shifts under me, and I bring my momentum to a stop, stretching out my arms to balance myself. The cliff moves again, breaking away from the main shelf. Anwyll and I lock eyes, and even poisoned, he somehow finds the energy to run to me. He drops to all fours, sprinting, leaping over a giant's arm as it tries to catch him.

The giants crawl to us, deadly gurgles and sneers leaving their mouths.

A gasp leaves me when the cliff gives out from under my feet and I fall. Anwyll roars, and I look up at the sky. Time moves slowly. It almost feels like I'm not even falling.

Anwyll's talons sink into my arm, and I cry out in pain as he catches me at the very last second.

His entire body is hanging from the cliff, minus his other paw. His claws are the only thing holding us.

"Anwyll," I begin, my feet dangling above a rocky valley. "You have to let me go."

"No!" he barks, his talons scraping across the rock, and we are dropped an inch lower.

I shout from the sudden jolt. "You have to. They are getting closer." His grip on me is weakening because he is lying against a bed of wolfsbane as he holds onto me. "I love you, okay? I love you." Tears drop onto my heated cheeks. "You were the adventure of a lifetime, My Gentle Giant. It's okay. Let me go."

"No." He shakes his head, looking over his shoulder. "Letting you go isn't an option."

"Yes it is. Anwyll, damn it!"

"You're my fucking heart, Ru. I'm not letting you go. You can't ask that of me. You can't ask me to let you fall to your death. I won't."

"There isn't another way," I whisper as the cliff shifts again from the weight of the giants crawling closer.

"There is," he says, leaping from the cliff just as a giant smashes the spot he was just in. He flips, wrapping his arms around my body, and pulls me to his chest as we fall. "Either life or death. Together," he whispers into my ear as we tumble to our deaths.

I should be thinking of a hundred different things right now, but I'm only feeling Anwyll. The strong beat of his heart against my cheek has me shutting my eyes as I relax to the sound of it. Death isn't so bad when I hear my favorite song.

I don't look to see where we are going. I can't.

I can't bear it. I hide my face in his chest and inhale him, wishing we had more time together. His scent brings me peace, and I think that's all anyone could ask for when they are about to die.

We hit the ground, Anwyll taking all the force, but we don't stop falling. I scream as we flip and twist into darkness. Every second, we fall faster, and Anwyll takes another brutal hit, protecting me from the force.

His arms fall limp, and I wrap mine around him, holding on tight because there is no way I am dying without being attached to him.

Suddenly, we slam against the ground so hard, I fall unconscious.

I wake with a painful, sharp breath. My vision blurs as my eyesight tries to focus. When it does, for a second, I think I'm in the afterlife.

It's beautiful.

The sun is warm, the grass is green and plush. The trees are whimsical and thick with leaves.

All the beauty in the world couldn't make me forget about why I'm looking over the edge of a crater at all this new scenery.

Anwyll.

I tilt my chin down, ignoring the sharp pain in my head, and see his unmoving body.

"Anwyll?" I bend down, placing my ear against his chest to hear his heartbeat.

I hear nothing.

"Anwyll!" I scream at him, shaking his shoulders. "Anwyll! Wake up. Please!" I sob, clutching onto his fur. Blood drops from his nose and ears while pooling at the side of his mouth. "Anwyll, please." I fall onto him, rubbing my cheek against his chest. "Wake up. It's going to be okay. You'll see. You just have to wake up for me," I say in denial, cupping his handsome face.

He is still in werewolf form. That's good, isn't it? He can't be dead.

"Someone help me! Help!" I bellow as loud as I can, the emotion strangling the words. "Please, someone! Is anyone out there!" I shout, but nothing is returned. I press my forehead against his, and I don't feel the warmth of his breath. It's only mine. I kiss his unmoving lips. "It's okay. We'll be okay. It's okay," I repeat, touching his face, shoulders, and chest. "We will be together. Life or death." The horn is lying next to his body, and I grab it, turning the sharp point to my chest.

It will only hurt for a second. It will be quick.

At least I'll get to be with him.

With a deep breath, I press the tip against my chest. I'm stopped when a hand wraps around mine.

"Don't."

A soft voice has me opening my eyes, and the blurriness from the tears disappears as the salty liquid drips down my face.

"You are okay."

I look at the person in front of me with confusion.

"We are here to help you. We heard you."

I glance around and notice a dozen or so people around me. All with various shades of skin tones, ranging from yellow, pink, red, purple, brown, black, orange, and many others in between. The one speaking to me is light blue with silver veins, and his ears are pointed, like Reuel's.

"You're elves?" I ask, my voice hoarse from the emotion and screaming.

"Woodland Elves," he explains, taking the horn from my grasp.

They look so much like Reuel. They are beautiful. Ethereal.

"Your mate is badly injured. We have to get him to the Ice Prince. He has a warlock who can help you. We would take you to ours, but only princes have warlocks, and the Woodland Elves do not have a Prince. The bloodline was lost," he says sadly. "We are waiting on our rightful Prince."

I don't say anything because I don't understand. I'm confused. I'm tired. I'm sore. I'll do whatever they want.

"How long is the journey? Will he make it?" I watch as the elves create a gurney out of tree roots with their own magic. Flowers line the edge, and I can't help but think of Reuel and how much he loves flowers.

The elf cups my cheek and smiles, the piercings in his ears glittering in the light. "Just a snap of a finger away." He snaps his finger, and the next time I open my eyes, I'm in a castle. I don't have time to understand what is happening.

Sitting on a red throne is a beautiful silver-skinned man with blue eyes and veins to match. His hair is long and white, cascading down to his hips, and two braids frame his face while a crown sits on top of his head.

"Prince Cailian." The elf doesn't kneel but bows his head to the man sitting on an ice throne.

"Freyzan. It's good to see you, old friend." The Prince walks down from his thrown and eyes me, then Anwyll, who is lying on the gurney made of roots. His eyes widen as he walks over to me, then my mate. "A lycan and a leprechaun. It has been thousands of years since I've seen either of you."

"The Lycan is injured. He needs a warlock," Freyzan explains. "They broke through from up above."

"Oh, you're special, aren't you?" His voice booms through the hall, lifting my chin with his cold finger. His eyes swirl, something similar to Reuel's when he is harnessing his power. "What would you do for your mate?" he asks.

I glance over to Anwyll, who is still bleeding from everywhere, and I sob. "Anything. I'll do anything." I lick my dry, cracked lips, wondering if I'm dreaming because this can't be real.

"Yes, I suppose you would. Mates do that to you." He bends down and smells me, then roughly grips my chin. "Where are you from? Why are you here? You smell of something that belongs to me. It's faint."

"Salem. Uh, Earth? I don't know where we are. We are looking for heartsnow."

"For werewolf sickness? You've come to the right place. Welcome to the land where fire meets ice. I'll give you anything, but you'll have to tell your ruler to be expecting me."

"Okay. Anything. Master Monreaux is kind, and his mate Maven—"

"You are from the coven that has a Wildes Witch?" He is in front of me again. "Oh, you are special. No wonder you broke through into this dimension. What is your name, dear?"

"Ru. My mate is Anwyll. Please, you have to help him."

"The full moon is tomorrow night. You haven't mated yet."

I blush, shaking my head.

"You'll be safe here. I'll be sure to alert the plains to let everyone know to stay out of the woods for your mating." He snaps his fingers, and I sway, finding myself in a room full of herbs and flowers.

Freyzan isn't with us. None of the elves are. It's a method of transportation I will never get used to.

It's me, the prince, Anwyll, and a gorgeous woman with sapphire skin and gleaming eyes.

"Prince Cailian," she greets, her voice a soothing echo.

"Raltena." He takes her hand and kisses the top. "These are our guests, Ru and Anwyll. They are injured from a long journey. Can you heal him?"

She runs her hands over Anwyll's body, and the grim expression on her face has my knees buckling.

"Easy, Ru. My witch is very powerful as well. Listen to her." He helps me to my feet and places my hand in Anwyll's. "A mate's bond is very powerful. You'll be surprised at what it can do. You are a warrior, Ru. You do not fall to your knees when there is weakness. That means surrender, and you aren't doing that, are you?"

"No. No, never."

A glowing light emanates from Anwyll's chest as she studies him. "He is barely alive. His werewolf strength is the only thing keeping him from dying at this point." She rushes to examine me next. "A leprechaun. As I live and breathe," she sounds astonished.

Everything is happening so fast. Snaps of fingers and I'm in a different place. Anwyll is lying on a gurney made of fucking sticks, and I have no idea where I am.

Maybe I am dead.

"Your mate will die," she explains. "The injuries are too severe for his werewolf to heal; couple that with the extreme amount of wolfsbane in his system."

"Nothing can save him? Nothing? But I'll do anything. Please. Do you want my soul? You can take it. I don't want it if it means having him."

"Your soul? We aren't evil. I suppose you don't know that. The one thing that could save him is your luck."

"My luck? I don't have any luck. I haven't gotten it."

"Oh, but you're wrong. You've made it this far. Your mate isn't dead. You haven't died. Don't you think that requires a little luck?"

I think about it, knowing we have had a few times that were considered lucky.

"Will you sacrifice your luck to save him?"

"Yes," I say without hesitation. "Take it. I don't want it."

"If I do that, you'll no longer be a leprechaun. When you mate, and he bites you, you'll eventually turn."

"I thought werewolf bites were poisonous."

"Only to vampires. Their bite is powerful. If he bit the prince, the prince would no longer be elven, but a werewolf. Would you change everything about your blood, your DNA, and your soul to save him? That's what would happen."

I look her in the eyes and lift my chin. "Yes," I repeat without waiting for a second. "I'd change the foundation of my bones if it meant keeping him alive." I let the tears fall, grabbing onto Anwyll's hand harder.

"Good because that's what you're about to do, and it won't be easy. Removing luck from your soul is painful. You will wish you were dead."

"I don't care. I'll tiptoe the land of life and death if it means being with him forever."

She smiles, flicking her hand, and another table appears next to Anwyll. The prince is watching from the corner. "Lie down, sweetheart." Her fingers dance slowly, and I'm pulled through the air and slammed on the table.

Ice bands attach to my wrists and ankles.

"To stop you from moving," she explains. "Ready?" She places her hand above my chest, her fingers digging into the bone.

"What are you doing?" My voice shows my fear as it breaks.

"Like I said—" she buries her hand in my chest, and I scream, pulling on the ice restraints as her fingers wrap around my heart. "It will be painful." The more she pushes her hand into my sternum, the brighter the light becomes surrounding her wrist.

My body burns, and the agony is unlike anything I ever felt. It truly feels like someone is inside me, tearing at my organs—which isn't far off from the truth.

"I have it. Your luck. It's going to take time to separate it from the rest of your soul. Thread by thread. Then, I'll place it in your mate."

My cries are so loud, the prince comes and takes my hand, holding it to give me support while every molecule inside me shifts. I feel her cut the first thread, and I sob, losing a centric piece of me. My back arches, and I toss my head back, roaring just like Anwyll does, only without his beast.

"Can't you put her to sleep?" The prince asks with concern. "She's burning up. It's obviously painful."

"No. She has to be conscious."

"How. Many. Threads?" The question is half shouted on a guttural moan.

"Thousands. This is only the beginning." She slices another thread, and I weep, turning my head to look at Anwyll.

For him.

I'll sacrifice every thread of my luck. I'll go through every bit of pain.

If it only means I get to see him open his eyes again.

"You're a brave woman. I hope I find a mate who loves me this much," the prince admits.

Another thread is separated, and a cold sweat breaks out all over my body. I feel like I'm about to throw up.

"Prince? A dragon is here to see you," another voice enters the room.

I tug on the prince's hand and look up at him, knowing I'm a sweaty, ugly mess. "Don't leave! Don't," I whimper, another strike of pain slicing my insides. "Please, don't leave me." I'm sweating. My hair is sticking to my face, and I know I look desperate, but his kindness is helping me through this. I need it.

"Fuck!" I scream again, tugging on the restraints as I lose another thread.

"Tell the damn dragon he can wait," the prince seethes.

"Gladly." The other elf gives me a pitied look before leaving.

"I'm—I'm sorry."

"Don't be. Dragons are dicks."

I would laugh if it didn't hurt so bad to move.

Another thread is cut free, and another jolted bellow escapes me, filling the room with torture.

The screams last for hours until my throat is raw, and when she removes her hand, a light green orb sets in her palm, but I'm not able to stay conscious to see what she does with it.

Night consumes me.

Chapter Thirty-Six

ANWYLL

I snap my eyes open and tighten my arms across my chest to hold Ru, but she isn't there.

She isn't there.

Growling, I jump to all fours and look around the room.

I'm on a bed. It's soft, the air colder than usual, but since I run hot, it doesn't bother me.

Where is my mate?

I inhale, trying to scent her, and I can't. That only pisses me off further. I should be able to smell her. It's so close to the moon. I should be able to smell the intense waves of her heat. I'm sure she's already in pain, crying, needing me.

My talons rip the silk sheets as I jump off the bed. I look around, the walls are made of stone, and there are different shades of blue stained glass to make the windows. As the light shines through the glass, a kaleidoscope of various shades of sapphire, cobalt, and periwinkle glitter on the floor.

Ru would love this.

"Well, Good Morning, Anwyll."

A voice I don't recognize has me launching myself at the

bars that make the door to the room. I slam against them, and my skin and fur sizzle.

Silver.

A rumble of agitation slides up my throat.

This isn't a room.

It's a cage.

"I'm not here to hurt you. The bars are here to protect me and my people, including your mate. You must be feeling many"—he cocks his head—"heightened emotions right about now. You have about twelve hours? Give or take. Before you lose your mind completely. Am I right?"

I slam my body against the bars again, uncaring about the pain or burn the silver does to my skin. "Where is my mate?" I yell at him, showing my fangs.

"Stop being rude. I'm the one who opened my home to you and had my witch save your life."

I think back to what I last remember, but all I remember is falling. "Is Ru okay?" I ask, gaining more control of my temper.

"She's fine. She's resting. She'll need her rest too, for what's coming."

"Who are you?" I ask, staring at the man with silver skin and blue veins. I've never seen hair so white and long. I swear, in the right light, it glistens like ice.

"Prince Cailian, the Ruler of the Ice Elven."

"Ice Elven..." I mutter in complete confusion. "Where am I? Can I see Ru?"

"You're on the planet where fire meets ice. Haven't you been looking for us? You want heartsnow, don't you? I can give you what you need."

"How did we get here?"

"You fell from up above. You slipped through a portal as you fell, and you crashed here. The Woodland Elves found you and brought you to me so I can heal you. You were dying."

"How am I here, then?"

Cailian grips the bars with one hand. "Only one thing could have saved you. Ru sacrificed her luck for you. My witch dug her hand in your mate's chest and cut Ru's luck from her soul, thread by thread. It was painful and it lasted hours, but Ru did that for you. That is an amazing love you have, Anwyll."

"She did what?" I press my palm against my chest, not wanting to believe it. "No. She wouldn't have. She needs her luck. She has to have it. Give it back. Give it back to her!" I clutch the bars with my hands, ignoring the pain. "Please, give it back."

"I can't do that. Her luck healed you, and that took all of its power. She's a human now. A regular woman."

My eyes widen in horror. "No. No, no. She'll be human for the moon. I'll bite her and she'll turn."

"She will, but it was something she didn't care about if it meant saving you."

"She knows?"

"She knows," he echoes.

"Can I see her?" I hang my head, hating what I've cost her. Will she ever forgive me? Tears burn my eyes at the same time a river of lust bends my fucking bones. I catch myself on the wall, digging the tips of my claws into it.

"Not until the time is right."

"I won't be in my right mind when I see her. I can't wait that long. I need to talk to her while I still have my head. Please," I beg him. "And I'm starving. How is this going to work? Are you going to keep me locked in here during my mating? I'll end up killing myself."

"No. Your mating will be safe. I've already let the entire

planet know to stay inside until I say otherwise. Granted, I can't be to blame if the dragons come out. The fire side of this planet doesn't really like listening to me. You'll have your mating. I'll bring food up too. So you're fueled."

"Can I see her?" I ask again. "Please."

"She's asleep, Anwyll. Losing her luck took a lot out of her. She needs to be ready for your mating too."

"The last thing that happened to her can't be painful. She deserves more than that for what's about to happen. Please, let me see her. I'll do anything. I'll give anything."

He sighs, but he nods. "I won't let you free. I'll bring her right where I am standing. That's it."

"Why? Why can't I hold her?"

"Because you won't hold her. You and I both know that. Her scent will overwhelm you, and the moon is almost at its highest. Do you really think you'll be a good boy, Anwyll?"

I snag my arm through the bars, disregarding the smoke coming from my flesh, and wrap my palm around his neck. He doesn't react. He keeps calm and doesn't fight me. His eyes swirl similarly to Reuel's, but then ice begins to travel up my arm, and the limb goes numb. I have no other choice but to let go. My fingers are a dark blue, and when I try to bend them, I can't.

"You might be strong where you come from, but you are no match for me here. Do not take advantage of my kindness, wolf. I will freeze you until you can't breathe and watch the wind blow you over until you shatter to pieces on the ground, then watch the breeze carry you across my fucking planet. Don't ever touch me. I could sentence you to death for that."

I'm finally able to move my fingers and groan in relief when warmth flows back into my hand. "Okay. I'm sorry. Please, don't call me a good boy," I say through tight teeth.

Even the words alone are testing my strength. "Only she gets to call me that."

"Ah, I see. Apologies." He bows his head. "Let me go get your mate. But you'll eat first, maybe it will help ease your... emotions."

I nod, turn around, and let my eyes travel around my luxurious prison cell. I suppose accommodations could be worse. I take a seat on the bed and it gives, rubbing my chest in hopes I can feel Ru's luck inside me.

All I feel is the beat of my heart, which I guess is all the luck I need.

I can't believe she did that for me. I wonder if she feels the same without it or if she misses it. Hours of pain, hours of agony, and she did it for me.

I've never known anyone who would do that for me. I know what torture is like, and I wouldn't want anyone to experience it. Ru chose temporary torture for permanent peace.

How will I ever pay her back?

The smell of chicken makes me turn my head, and another elf is standing there, this time he has dark blue skin and silver veins.

"Your meal." The bars disappear enough for him to push the cart through, and then they slam back into place.

There's an entire chicken on a platter, surrounded by potatoes and green beans. There are buttery rolls and a pitcher of water.

I attack it, tearing the skin and meat from the bone. I'm famished. The meat is tender and juicy, the bones snapping under my fangs as I chew them too. I shove the rolls into my mouth next, then green beans, then chug the entire pitcher of water.

"Well, I guess me bringing my plate to you so we can

eat together was a silly thought." Ru's voice is light and playful.

It has me spinning around, and I run to her, gripping the silver bars and trying to pull them apart. "Ru. You're okay." I grab onto her shoulders and pull her against the bars. "You're okay. You're alive. You're here. Are you safe?"

"Anwyll! Your skin. Stop it. You have to let me go. You're hurting yourself."

"I don't ever want to let you go. Are you okay? Have they hurt you?" I push her back and take a good look at her.

"No, they have been so kind." She presses her hand against my cheek, and I groan at the simple touch from her.

She whimpers as she pulls her hand away, pressing it against her stomach. "I don't think we have a lot of time."

"We don't. It's why I needed to see you. Why did you do it, Ru? Why did you sacrifice your luck?"

She narrows her eyes at me. "Why do you think, Anwyll? To save you. To have a life with you. I didn't want you to die. I wanted more time. So I sacrificed it and I'd do it all over again for you."

"Are you okay? How do you feel?" I dare to ask.

"The same, honestly. I'm not missing it. I'm just glad you're okay." She tries to touch me again, but I pull away.

"I can't handle your touch right now. You need to be ready, Ru. I already want you, and these bars won't be strong enough to keep me back once my humanity switches off."

She slides down the wall and begins to eat her dinner. "I know."

I sit down too, mirroring her position. "Thank you for what you did. For saving me."

"I'll always save you, Anwyll."

"You're *always* the one saving me," I correct her.

She gasps, then moans, the plate clattering to the ground as she falls over. Her heat slams through her, and the scent of it reaches my nose. I growl, my cock hardening, and all of my reasoning flies out the window.

I slam against the bars, snarling and biting at the air to try to get to her while she moans in pain, her cunt craving pleasure. The kind only I can bring her.

"I think that's enough." The elf is back, and with a snap of his finger, he is gone, taking Ru with him.

He took my fucking mate.

He touched what was mine.

I'll kill him.

I roar in anger, continuing to slam myself against the bars. Over and over again, I hurt myself, but I don't feel the pain. My shoulder bleeds as the wound becomes bigger. I do this for hours, ramming my body against the silver, not feeling anything. The smell of her still lingers in the air, and I fist my cock, stroking it to relieve the pressure, but I can't come.

I physically can't come because I'm saving every fucking drop for Ru. Wasting it isn't an option.

I spread my arms out, chest open and wide, and growl so loud the vase falls from its shelf and shatters. The vicious tone echoes, and I know everyone in this fucking realm heard me.

Time is ticking, and when I'm freed, everyone better get out of my way.

Or I'll kill them.

All of them.

The moonlight shines through the window, and blue light scatters across my body. I feel it take over my body. Inch by inch, my humanity slips under my skin, and the power of the moon awakens every instinct I have.

With two hands, I grasp the bars, but this time, my skin doesn't burn, and with a slight shove, the bars are uprooted from their place. I throw them against the wall and drop to all fours, sniffing the air to find my mate. Her sweet scent is like a honeysuckle dipped in a sugary floral scent that has my mouth watering.

A snarl leaves me as I take my first step, and my cock swings heavily between my legs.

It's time to hunt, and there is nowhere my prey can hide.

Chapter Thirty-Seven
RU

A roar vibrates through the palace, and the elf I'm with snaps his fingers, teleporting us to the middle of the woods.

I'll never get used to that.

"You have to run. You're safe. Nothing will harm you, except for your mate, of course. This is all a part of the mating. You want to run, don't you?"

I nod.

"It's instinct. It's a little dance that comes very naturally to werewolves and their mates. You'll be fine." He stops talking when a howl rips through the sky. "Run," he advises one last time before vanishing again, leaving me alone in the forest. I have no idea where to go.

My stomach cramps and burns. I double over in agony and desire. Slick drips down my thighs, and I moan, dipping my hand between my legs.

How am I supposed to run? It hurts. It all hurts but touch feels so fucking good.

Hearing Anwyll growl in the distance shakes me from my stupor, which has me sprinting through the woods. I'm in unknown territory. For all I know, this planet and its creatures will hunt me too. What if they are nice now, only to be enemies later?

My breath comes out in clouds, the temperature becoming cooler with every stride. I plunge through the branches of the trees, tripping over my own two feet. My heat drips down my thighs, and I'm shocked I can see it. It's clear and has a sweetness to it that reminds me of cotton candy. I wipe it off on a tree, then I have an idea.

How bad would it be to throw Anwyll off my trail? I giggle to myself as I wipe my scent on different trees, the further I run into the forest, in all different directions.

The next step I take, my foot sinks into snow, and my breath becomes frozen clouds with every exhale. I stare out in front of me, the scenery white and untouched.

It's beautiful.

"Oh chauns," I moan as more slick escapes me, soaking my inner thighs.

I'm glad it's so cold because I'm sweating. My hair is sticking to my face, my shirt is drenched in sweat, and my shorts don't stand a chance against biology. I need a break. I only want a few minutes to lean against a tree to catch my breath.

Anwyll won't give me the time.

I hear him again, roaring his need to the skies, only this time, he is closer.

I wipe my slick on another tree and start running. Suddenly my stomach cramps so hard, I fall into the snow. Frustration builds, and tears fall down my cheeks because nothing feels good. Not even when I try to touch myself do I feel any relief. If anything, it just hurts more.

Forcing myself to get up, I get my feet under me and start my journey to who-knows-where. When I enter the woods again, the snow is gone.

"What the fuck?" I curse, taking a look over my shoulder to make sure I didn't hallucinate. If I reach my arm out, I'd be able to catch snowflakes, but from where I'm standing, my feet are cushioned in soft grass.

Anwyll's howl pulls me from my thoughts of serenity, and I begin running again, wiping my hand on every tree. I zigzag and double back, wanting to confuse him about where I'm going. When I hear his call for me, my entire body answers. My nipples tighten, my stomach muscles tense, my clit throbs, and my aching hole that will take his knot flutters in agony. Sweat burns my eyes, and it's starting to get to a point where I can't move my legs.

Everything inside me is telling me to keep going. He can't catch me yet. It's too soon. I don't know why I feel that way, but I have to.

Pushing myself from a tree again, I crawl over a fallen log, and the moss glides against my palms. Even that feels good, and I'm not ashamed to say I whimper. More nectar drips from me, just from that, and then I imagine what it will be like when Anwyll finally gets ahold of me.

My pace slows, and my run turns into a drunken walk. My head spins until I lean against another tree. I give in, touching myself when I know it won't help, but I need something. Anything.

I roam my hands down my body, cupping my breasts, and I cry out when my fingers tweak my nipples. They are sensitive and enlarged, almost as if they are irritated. I dip my hand below the waistband of my shorts and plunge three fingers inside me without care. The wet sounds of my slick sound, and I sob in frustration as my want, desire, and lust build to an extreme level.

A bomb is building inside me. All I want to do is

explode. But the more I try to get to that peak, the further away it seems to get, and the desire becomes worse.

"Fuck!" I scream in anger, wishing I could relieve myself. "Damn it! Please!" I weep, circling my clit, and my thighs shake until my legs give out. I fall onto the ground, not wanting to stop. I need to come.

I have to. I'm going insane.

My hand begins to hurt, and I stop. I roll onto my stomach and punch the ground, yelling into the dirt.

"I can't do this," I shake my head, doubling over as another cramp hits. I flip onto my back to stare up at the moon. It's big, wide, and so close I can nearly touch it.

Anwyll sounds again, and this time, the hair on the back of my neck stands up.

He's close.

Very close.

I push myself up again and push through the branches of the trees. The leaves slap against my face, and I hate to say that it even feels good.

Any touch, anything against my sensitive, feverish skin, is heaven.

When I break through the thick of the brush, a clearing of gorgeous flowers comes into view. There are purple, yellow, white, red, and orange. Some even have the edges of the petals tinted blue.

I walk through them, and the soft petals skim against my arms, and glowing specs release into the air. I tilt my head back as they dance to the sky, swaying and circling from the breeze.

The sound of snarling reverberates from the trees, alerting me Anwyll is closing in. The peace the flowers give me is quick, but appreciated, and I begin to move again.

I don't know where I am, which only heightens my

worry about this situation. I'm in heat, which is horrible by itself, but we're on a planet we don't know, surrounded by people we don't know, even though they have been nice.

For now.

I don't have my luck either, and I thought without it I'd feel less, but maybe I don't because I gave it to my mate so he could live. Blood dripping from his ears, nose, and mouth will forever be engraved in my mind.

I'll never forget it. It will haunt me until the day I die.

And if I had to go through hours of torture again while that witch cut away my luck from my soul, then I would.

I'd do anything for him.

Passing another wide tree, I swipe my hand across it, and that's when I notice the carving on it.

Woodland Elves Territory.

I step through, loving how the branches of the trees hang until the tips drag across the ground. The houses are immaculate, like mansion-sized log cabins with moss for roofs. Vines crawl up the sides of their homes, and flowers bloom randomly all over.

Picking up the pace, I cross my arms, and the slight jostle of my breasts sends a pang through me. I bite my lip, holding in a groan.

Their pathway has stones I can walk on, and as I hurry down it, trying to get away, my eyes catch them looking at me through the windows.

They aren't allowed to help me. They can't open their home to me.

Not while I'm in this condition, or Anwyll will kill them.

One of them cracks their window, and I get a glimpse of their baby pink skin, remembering what the Prince said about these elves. They are very strong. Their powers are unlike any other, and if they had a Prince, Anwyll probably could have been saved another way. They bend elements, similar to Reuel.

Tree roots create a platter, and the elf places water and some type of meal on top, then with a swish of a hand, the roots swim to me.

"Thank you!" I call out, and she nods, shutting the window again.

I pick up the bottled water and snag what looks like a drumstick. I groan, not realizing how hungry I am. I toss the bone aside and attack the rest, sucking the meat from the bones, then chugging the water.

An angry howl has the hair on the back of my neck standing up, and I gasp. I've wasted so much time stopping.

I shouldn't have.

I wipe my mouth and begin running again. This time, I feel better, like the haze in my mind has lifted enough for me to fully concentrate on giving Anwyll a hard time.

I'm not sure how long I run for, but I think I'm out of Woodland territory because the scenery is darker, the woods thicker, and I don't see their homes.

A shiver runs down my spine, and this time, the urge to run away isn't the urge to run from Anwyll.

Something is wrong.

I spin around, eyeing the forest, waiting to see what lurks in the darkness, but nothing reveals itself. I listen to my instincts and get the hell out of there; then the haze begins to tinge my mind again.

The heat becomes unbearable, and I stop at the edge of a cliff, needing a second to try to calm my racing heart.

The sky is clear, the stars are out, and the moon is high. The view is breathtaking. I can see the castle Prince Cailian lives in. Everything seems sectioned off in a way. Ice and snow cover his land, the woods are for the Woodland Elves, and then to the left is another castle, surrounded by red sky and flame.

Dragons.

In the distance, I see a few shadows in the sky, and I take a step back, not liking that I'm in the open for them to snatch if they could.

"You smell delightful."

A growling tone has me shaking in fear because it is not Anwyll.

"Cailian shouldn't have allowed you to travel on your own. Our Prince ordered us to stay inside too, but when we heard it was because a woman would be in heat, we couldn't just stay away."

I swallow, turning around to see two giant men standing there with large wings spread out.

"Aren't you just darling?" the one on the right purrs, slithering his forked tongue out to taste the air. "And so sweet."

A gush of slick runs down my legs, and I whimper, not liking the timing.

"Oh, do you like us? You smell like you do." They come closer, and I dodge to the right, trying to run into the woods, but fire stops me.

A wall of it appears in front of me, so close it nearly burns my face.

"Where do you think you're going?"

"My mate will be here any minute and he'll kill you."

"A werewolf against two dragons?" The one with gold wings grabs me by my hair, his talons scraping against my scalp.

I cry out in agony because this man's touch doesn't feel good. It hurts. It causes my entire body to triple in agony.

His sharp teeth snap in front of me before he smiles. "He doesn't stand a chance."

The one with red wings snatches me and tosses me onto my side. I slide across the grass, and he holds my shoulders down while the other tries to hook his talons in the waistband of my shorts.

"You smell so fucking good. God, it's been so long since I've experienced a bitch in heat."

"Get off me!" I try to fight the dragon, but he's too strong.

"Anwyll!" I sob his name as loud as I can, hoping he can hear me.

A dragon's paw silences me by choking my throat, and I gasp.

An answering roar draws near, and relief floods my system just as the dragon manages to drag one side of my shorts down my thighs.

He's knocked off me by a blurring creature, and the other dragon lets me go to save his friend from Anwyll's wrath.

I back away, crawling on my hands and knees to get away from the chaos. Anwyll is in full werewolf form, just as large as the dragons. His eyes glow—burning red as if he's a demon instead, and he rakes his nails down the dragon's chest and stomach.

His intestines unravel onto the ground. He coughs blood from his mouth, and Anwyll roars again in his viciousness before punching his hand through the stranger's chest, then rips out his heart.

Anwyll tosses the red, bleeding organ over the cliff just as the dragon falls to the ground, dead.

The dragon with gold wings tries to shift into his

animal, but Anwyll is there, gripping his wings and tearing them from his back.

"Fuck!" he screams, reaching behind him to feel if his wings are truly gone. "Okay. Okay," he lifts bloody hands. "I'm sorry. We didn't know."

"They knew!" I cry, pointing to him. "They knew about you. They didn't care."

Anwyll swipes the man's face with his talons, blinding him in one eye, and becomes lost in bloodlust. He rakes his claws across the man's chest, but this time he doesn't stop. He rotates his hands, left, right, left, right. Anwyll claws at my attacker until he can't be recognized. His body is useless, a puddle of red and bones.

I've never seen my mate so vicious, so gone in a murderous rage, and even in fear, even watching him, my heat slams into me again. I'm getting turned on by the sight of him protecting me, and he must be able to smell it because he lifts his head to sniff the air.

He snaps his head to stare at me, his nostrils flaring, and he growls, falling onto all fours as he leaves his victim. Every step he takes is bloody. His fur and skin are drenched in red. I manage to stand, my legs shaking and threatening to give out.

Then I turn to run.

Chapter Thirty-Eight

ANWYLL

I taste the blood of the men who tried to take what is mine, and it empowers me. The way that man's heart pumped in my hand before it finally stopped. The way his eyes went wide with the realization that he was going to die— it was history being made.

That's what happens when you put your hands on something that doesn't belong to you.

You die.

My mate, my poor sweet mate, all scared and confused because even though the two men who tried to rape her are dead, she still has me to deal with.

She runs from me, and a jolt of adrenaline pumps through me. I stand on my hind legs, spread my arms out, and victoriously howl to the moon. When I fall to all fours, my vision zeros in on her retreating form.

She can't escape me.

Ru can wipe her scent on any tree to confuse me, but I'll always find her. Her slick has a unique smell, one that's made for me, to call to me, and yes, it will attract others,

Everyone else smells slick and heat.

I smell sugar and honey, two of my favorite things, and once I finally get a taste, it will be a step in the right direction for us to be mated.

Like blood for vampires, her slick is the same for me.

Orienting myself, I give chase, clawing at any tree or bush in my way.

"Anwyll! Anwyll! Stop," she says in terror as she runs. "Let's talk about what just happened."

I laugh at the ridiculous thought. I'm not wasting any more time. "Talking is the last thing I want," I rumble, swiping my paw again to catch her but I miss by an inch.

The ground gives under my feet and hands, the dirt loose as it flings behind me.

She whimpers again, her breathing coming out faster, and her slick begins to leave a trail. I salivate, licking the droplets from the ground, and my cock pulsates, shooting a stream of come on the ground when I get a taste of my fated mate.

I become distracted by the trail. I don't want any to go to waste. I lick every drop, the consistency like honey itself. I clean the path until I realize I can't hear her anymore. Her sweet taste lingers on my tongue, and I fist my cock, every thick inch of it, waiting for her cunt to suck me in and pull me to her womb.

I stand on my hind legs and tilt my head back, inhaling to see where she could be, but her scent is everywhere, and it's confusing me.

"Mate," I growl in warning. "You might as well come to me and make this easier for the both of us because I will have you. I will take you. And I will knot you. Come. To me. Now!" I bellow and it morphs into a roar. The leaves shake on the trees from the brute force.

As I walk by a few trees, I let my claws scrape against the wood, the bark falling onto the ground.

She's close.

I can feel her watching me.

I look up into the trees, letting my infrared vision take over, and search the branches. I continue walking, snarling at every sound I hear. I rip a tree from the ground in frustration and throw it like a spear as if it doesn't weigh anything.

"Ru!" I announce vigorously, my chest heaving from how loud I yelled her name.

I find myself deep in the woods now, following waves of her scent that seem to come at me from all angles, but then I stop when I hear her heartbeat. It's thrumming just as fast as the pants leaving her lips. My ears flicker when I hear something drip.

Turning my head, I see a streak flowing down the tree, dripping to a soft puddle on the ground. A wolfish smile takes over, and I pretend I don't notice it, even though all I want to do is roll around in her nectar and lick the tree until it's clean.

I crouch in a nearby bush, blending into the darkness with my fur and skin, and watch her.

She looks around, unsure if she's free of me.

She'll never be free.

Ru loosens her hold on the branch, and I take that moment to jump, landing on a branch below hers.

She gasps, eyes widening when I dig my talons into the wood, leaving an imprint of my efforts behind.

"Anwyll." She scurries down the branch until it sags, then she falls, risking hurting herself. She lands with a solid thud and fucking runs again.

"Sly little mate," I snarl, jumping from the tree to the ground and sprint.

She won't get far. Not this time.

My breath is warm against her neck, and when we get to a clearing, I tackle her against the ground.

Finally.

I don't wait. I slash her shirt, ripping it from her body, and she yells, a mixture of her own howl into the night.

"Anwyll!"

I flip her over, and her engorged nipples tighten into swollen beads. She needs me so much. Her tits are ready to start producing milk. Her body is aching to be pregnant with my children, and by the end of the night, she will be.

I grip her shorts and tear them from her body, her cunt glistening with her heat.

Shifting into my mid-form, my arms below my elbow stay shifted, and my cock doesn't change either.

"Yes, Anwyll. Please, it hurts. It hurts so much."

"I don't care," I growl, speaking the truth. Her pain means nothing to me.

I thrust my cock in, her drenched walls pouring her heat onto me, making it easier to fuck her.

"Oh chauns!" she screams, her orgasm already running through her, squeezing me tight. "Oh yes, yes, yes."

I wrap a hand around her throat and squeeze. "I'm not done." I fuck her without care, without caress, slamming my hips as hard as I can while she cries out. My fat cock brutally stretches her cunt, the pink lips are opened wide for me, weeping slick.

Her entire body was made for this; her womb has been prepared for weeks now, and now with every thrust, I can see the indent of my cock on her insides. Her stomach bulges with it every time I fill her.

Soon, her stomach will bulge with all the come I'll be locking deep inside her.

"Anwyll. Anwyll, it hurts." Her nails dig into my chest, and pain shines in her eyes.

I feed off it. I lift her by the throat, never missing a stroke while I own and claim her cunt. "I don't care," I sneer, my lips moving against hers. "Fucking take it, mate. You'll give me this cunt. You made me work hard for it all night. Stop complaining."

I shove her down, plundering her cunt the way I want.

She moans, her lips parting as another orgasm hits her. She'll experience a hundred tonight.

"Such a good girl taking my big cock." I spread her legs wider, watching as I sink in and out, her pussy taking every inch of me, something she couldn't do before.

The moon peeks through the trees. I feel my fangs drop, my knot swells, and I glance down, knowing it's almost time, but Ru never makes anything easy.

She pushes me, then uses one of her legs to kick me from her, and I lose my balance, falling backward. My cock slips from her, and tons of slick pours from her.

She tries to run again, but I'm on her before she can take her first step, and we fall to the ground. Ru is on her stomach, her head turned, and her cheek pressed in the dirt, and I fuck my way back inside her from the back.

"For that, I'm going to make you fuck my knot while it's inside you." I plaster my weight against hers so she can't move or get away from me. I hear her crying, but moaning too, the pleasure and pain overwhelming her.

"It won't fit. Please, don't," she begs, sniffling. "I can feel it, Anwyll. Please," she pleads.

I look down, the knot is huge and swollen with my come already. I ignore my mate. "I need to claim you. You're mine. You're all mine. This cunt is mine. Those dragons nearly took you from me." I quicken my pace, fucking her harder. She cries my name, the forest swallowing our pleasure. "Tell me," I nearly rip her hair from her head when I yank her back. "Tell me you're mine. My mate. Fuck. Fuck!" My knot pops into her cunt, stretching it beyond her imagination, and Ru comes, hard, her muscles spasming around me, massaging the knot.

"Yours. Yours!" She claws at the ground to try to get away, but my knot inside her doesn't allow her to move far.

I slice my talons across her back. Five long marks that begin to bleed, and she punches the ground, sobbing with pain.

I've imprinted. She doesn't understand how vital she is to my being. I'll follow her anywhere. Everywhere, but she has to be ruined for everyone else. She can only want me.

I roar as I come, my knot jetting stream after stream of my seed.

Jerking her head to the side, I sink my fangs into her neck. I go as deep as I can without tearing her head from her body, then release.

I feel her blood stitching to my cells, becoming a part of me, and my beast finds peace.

A little peace, but not enough to stop the mating.

While pouring my come into her exhausted body, I roar for the realm to hear. I want everyone to know about my success.

I've mated my mate.

I don't lick the wounds for them to heal. I want them to scar. They will never fade. It's a symbol to me and to all other creatures that she is claimed.

I pick her up and sit down on the ground, leaning against the tree. "Ride my knot until I tell you to stop."

I expect her to fight me, but she doesn't. Her cheeks are wet with tears, but she plays with her nipples and rocks back and forth.

"Oh, fuck. I can't. Oh my chauns, you're huge. I can't."

I thrust up, my eyes lock on her stomach, where I can see the imprint of my cock deep inside her.

My hands slide up her back, gliding easily from the blood dripping from her wounds, and I lean forward, sucking my mating mark.

"Oh fuck, yes," she moans, liking how good that feels.

There's a voice in the back of my head, one yelling at me to be careful, to heal her, but I ignore it. This is how it has to be.

Bloody and painful.

She glances down, lifting her body off my cock until the knot stops her from going further, and I groan when she squeezes her muscles around it.

"You look like you're about to tear me in two."

"I want to." I dig my claws into her outer thigh. "I want you to be in so much pain"—I yank her head back and lick the trail of blood flowing from the mating mark—"you will feel it for days, and the only way you will feel relief is if I'm inside you again."

"I don't think I can take any more."

I throw her onto her back, my cock still lodged in her tight cunt as I flash my fangs. "That's too fucking bad, isn't it?"

Ru's eyes begin to glow and her scent changes, but not in the way I was hoping. She isn't pregnant. Not yet.

Which is the only way this mating will stop.

Fangs drop from her mouth, and her skin erupts in fur before it disappears again.

No.

Not now.

Not yet.

My knot deflates, knowing I need to get away from her so we don't hurt one another in this position. I pull out, sneering when a river of my come floods from her, puddling on the ground.

"Anwyll..." her eyes lock onto mine, and her chest rises and falls rapidly.

I fall to my knees, my cock still painfully hard, and the urge to take her just like this hits me, but I listen to the voice in the back of my head.

"It's okay. It will be over in a minute."

"What's going on? My skin burns," she yells, arching her back as a wave of pain hits.

Her bones break as she shifts, her human skin disappearing.

Tears fill my eyes when her cries of pain slash through me. These are different from the mating pains; these sound like she's dying.

Her back breaks, her legs crack and lengthen, and her human yell changes to a roar as the shift fully takes her.

She stumbles away from me, looking confused as she tries to understand her new body.

I shift too, hoping my werewolf eases hers, and I hold out my hand for her. "It's okay. You're so beautiful, Ru. I've never seen a werewolf like you before." I do my best to let my humanity speak. It's so hard. It's like swallowing nails as the full moon rides my back.

I can't care for much longer. It takes it out of me. This isn't the way of our kind.

Her fur and skin match the color of her hair, a gorgeous strawberry blonde. Her eyes are neon green, the same as mine, because of her. Her breasts are hidden by her fur, and she glances around as if she has no idea what is going on.

She falls to all fours, and her heat slams into me again, then her eyes shift from green to red.

And I know she understands now.

Then, she runs.

Furious, I roar, needing to show my mate who is Alpha.

Chapter Thirty-Nine

RU

I don't have time to concentrate on the fact that I'm a werewolf. My instincts are too strong. All I know is I need Anwyll, but I need him to chase me again. I don't care if I'm a werewolf. I'm happy about it. I can enjoy the moon with my mate. He won't have to howl alone anymore without hearing anything back.

His loneliness is gone.

My paws hit the ground fast and hard. It's freeing and exhilarating. I feel powerful, more so than I ever have.

I leap from tree to tree, then land with a thud on the ground, which wasn't a good idea, but Anwyll slams into me. We roll until he pins me on the ground.

"Shift," he says with a curl of his lips, morphing into his middle form.

I focus on my middle form too, wanting to match his appearance.

"Oh, good girl. Look at you, a professional already."

"I want you," I groan, rubbing my pussy against his cock. "I burn. Oh, chauns. Fuck me. Please."

"It's heightened now." He brushes his lips against my ear. "Everything is heightened now that you're a werewolf."

I choke while I gasp for breath as he wraps his hand around my throat.

"You fucking ran from me again. You had me push my humanity forward for your shift." His head rolls over his shoulders in anger, and his eyes beam in red hues. His fur still holds streaks of dried blood from the dragons. "Unbelievable. Don't make me do it again."

I nod, wanting nothing more than to submit to him.

He forces my legs apart with his knees and rams his cock into me, my cunt soaking wet from my heat, so it's easier, but I'm sore from taking his knot.

I don't know what gets into me, but I slash my talons across his face. He growls, slipping out of me, and I get to my feet, sprinting.

He is quicker, and an arm circles around my waist; he throws me against a nearby tree, my head smacking against it.

"You dare hurt me!" he roars, pinning my hands above my head as he flips me around. "You'll fucking pay for that, mate."

My stomach and aching breasts rub against the bark, scratching me open. He parts my legs and forcefully thrusts his cock in again, controlling my body for his liking. I'm a ragdoll.

My ass smacks against his pelvis as he drives into me, and his teeth sink into my mating mark again. I feel my fangs lengthening again.

"My mate is nothing but a hole for me to fill tonight. You do as I say, do you understand me?" He slaps my ass, scratching my flesh with his talons.

I nod.

"Fucking speak, mate." He slides out until only the head is in, then spits onto his cock, thrusting it inside me.

"Yes," I groan, my claws digging into the tree while he pins me against it.

Every thrust is brutal and rough. It hurts.

We fall into silence, nothing but grunts and moans, while he takes what he wants. He dips his hands between my legs and circles my clit. I'm overstimulated. My entire body is on fire.

"My mate," I growl as I come.

He snarls in reply, shoving his knot inside me again, and I try to climb up the tree from the pressure. We fight. The more I dig my nails into the wood to get away from him, the more it tugs on his knot. Which only steals my breath, making me come again.

His seed is warm, pooling deep inside me, searching for my womb. Every time I try to get off him, he comes more, filling me with so much, my stomach swells.

"Get fucking down here." He pulls me down until my ass is settled against him and he ruts into me, shallow thrusts that drive me into orgasm after orgasm. "You fucking love this. My dirty little whore. That's what you are tonight. Aren't you? My come drunk slut."

God, he's right. I don't even want to fight him, but fighting him turns me on.

His hand drops to my stomach, and he hums in delight when he feels how round I am. All come. He spins me around, and my thighs shake from his knot brushing against my G-spot. I dig my talons into his chest, scratching him as another orgasm crashes through me.

"That's it. Pull my come to your womb, mate. Fucking drink me in." He begins to move again, as much as he can while locked deep, pushing his come further.

Another orgasm hits.

And another.

It's nonstop. Every spasm brings him a step closer to what he wants.

He's all-consuming. This mating is intense, and my body breaks the more we give into it.

Hooking my leg around his hip, his knot deflates, but he doesn't leave me. With a snarl, I push him away, and his come leaks from me with my slick.

He roars at me, eyes red, fangs showing, and I do the same.

We crash into each other, and I slice his skin with my claws while he does the same to me. It's painful, it's beautiful, it's savage.

We roll together, fighting for dominance. I slap Anwyll across the face. Three small lines are left in my wake, and right before my eyes, the skin heals itself.

"Get the hell off me!" I backhand him again, but he doesn't move.

His shoulders rise with rage, and every exhale sounds like a warning.

We fight again, rolling across the dirt until he pins me on my back.

Anwyll bites me, sinking his fangs into my fresh wound as he forces his cock inside me again.

"No! I don't want this anymore. It hurts. Get off—" He silences my denial with his hand so he can't hear me.

He curls over me, fucking me anyway. His long cock rubs against every part of me that no other could.

I try to push him away and cry, his knot too much. I hurt. I need a break.

He growls, biting my mating mark in warning, pinning me harder against the ground, and takes me.

I slice his back with my talons, the scent of blood heavy in the air.

He knots me, pushing the bulge inside me until he can't pull out. The second he comes, I do too, my body reacting.

"You feel so good, mate. I like it when you fight me."

I bite him where his shoulder meets his neck, marking him as mine. I feel him stitch into my soul, binding to my being, and I explode again, coming hard and fast.

He lifts me up and sits down. I wrap my legs around his waist and begin to rock my hips, needing more of him.

It's a constant motion. The energy doesn't lessen. I'm tired, but my body is energized. His hands rub my body, tweaking my nipples, and our mouths clash together. We kiss angrily, needing more and unable to get it.

I want his heart.

I need to feel it beat for me. I press my forehead against his shoulder while I ride him, moaning into his ear. "Fuck, Anwyll. Fuck. Oh chauns, you feel so good. Such a big dick. I want more. Give me more."

"You'll take what I give you." He slaps my ass, and it encourages me to ride him faster.

I tug on his knot with every motion of my hips. My eyes roll to the back of my head from the pleasure, and right as I'm about to come again, his knot deflates, and he slips out of me.

"No! No! Please, give me your knot. I need it. Please," I beg for him this time.

The heat cripples me. I can't breathe. My stomach cramps. I fall onto the ground, and Anwyll gets up, walking away just a few feet and sits down, taking his cock in hand.

"Crawl to me," he says. "Crawl to me and I'll give you what you need. You're at the peak of your heat, mate. You're mindless."

"Anwyll, don't be cruel. Please, fuck me. Fill your mate."

He stomps over to me and lifts my head by my hair. "Cruelty is all I am right now. Crawl to me." He shoves my face in the dirt, humiliating me, but I don't seem to care.

I do as he says.

With every painful cramp plowing my stomach, I grab a fistful of dirt and drag my used, aching body across the ground.

He jerks his cock with his hand, nostrils flaring as he watches me crawl to him like a broken, pathetic... thing. A gush of slick escapes me again, and he stops touching himself. When I get to his knees, I lift myself up.

With a primal grin, he shoves my head down and punches his cock into my mouth. I gag and choke, tasting myself on him.

"That's it, mate. Fucking love that mouth."

My stomach stops cramping while I'm sucking his cock, and I'm able to sense how good he feels through our bond. I hum in delight, liking how I can feel his emotions and pick up the pace. I hollow my cheeks and twist my tongue around the thick head. I can't stop myself.

I grip the knot, stroking the unique base, and rub it. A constant rumble fills his chest, and the more I play with the knot, the larger it gets. My eyes widen, wondering how that fit inside me.

His arms wrap around me, manhandling me by flipping me upside down. I yelp, his cock slipping from my mouth, and drool strings from my lips to the tip of his cock.

"I need to taste you," he mumbles before his lips form to my pussy.

I moan as his tongue slithers in deep.

He stops feasting on me. "I'll only eat your sweet cunt if you suck my cock."

I nod, my blood rushing to my head from being in this position. Reaching for his cock, I guide it to my mouth and suck it again. The crown is soft and spongy, but the rest of him is hard as a rock. I dip my tongue in the slit and he moans into my cunt, the growl shaking my chest.

Twisting his shaft while sucking him, Anwyll's body jerks, and he unexpectedly fills my mouth with his come. I can't swallow in this position, so it leaks from my lips until I choke on it.

He flips me again, and I land on my back. He scoops his come from my mouth and lubricates his cock with it before sliding inside me again.

I lick my lips, still tasting him, and he bends my legs back to my ears. The position makes him slide deeper.

"My mate," he says in appreciation, and something in his tone changes.

I can't put my finger on it.

"Yes. Your mate. Yours. I'm all yours. Give me your knot. I need it." I claw his chest. "My heat is rising. Please, give it to me."

My legs drop to his sides, and he slams himself into me. Brutally, forcefully, and it all feels like punishment.

He digs his talons into my chest, and I cry out as my skin is cut. He carves something, a sick smile twisting his face. There's no sign of his humanity. A memory emerges. He told me he could kill me. He was afraid he was going to rip out my heart, and then he'd rip out his own.

"Do you want my heart?"

He snaps his head up and cocks it, staring at me as if he barely knows me.

"Do you want to kill me?" I ask him next, and his eyes narrow, shaking his head.

He takes my hand and places it on his chest, growling as he pats his chest with my talons.

"Heart," he clips, more wolf than man.

I sit up, wondering if what he was told about mating was wrong or maybe not understood correctly. I crawl onto his lap, his cock still buried deep within me, and I look down.

My lips part in an O when understanding dawns on me.

He carved a heart into my skin, and he wants me to do the same to him. I take his lips with mine, our tongues sliding against one another, and he thrusts into me from below. My nail sharpens, and I dig it into his skin, creating the same mark on him as he did me.

And then a searing pain overcomes the spot, the wound sealed as if it was burned into me. Anwyll doesn't flinch when his heart heals. I touch it, the skin is puckered as if it's years old. How is this possible? They healed faster than wounds normally do.

His eyes burn brighter, and he flips me onto my hands and knees, burying himself to the hilt again. "So wet," he grits through tight fangs. "So fucking wet. I like how it sounds. Mine. Mine. Mine." He thrusts with every word.

My breasts sway with every motion, and he curls over me, kissing my shoulder, and he gently kneads my breast.

His knot stretches me again, punching through my sore, aching cunt, and locking itself for what feels like the thousandth time.

I pass out, darkness creeping in, and I can't help but wonder if maybe he did rip my heart from my chest.

I've died.

Chapter Forty

ANWYLL

I wake with an aching body, my chest pressed against Ru's back, but my cock isn't locked inside her. I bury my nose into her neck and inhale deeply. There's a small amount of heat left, but there's something else, something that has me smiling like a fool.

She's pregnant.

But my happiness is short-lived when I see the massive scars I've left on her back. Five deep gashes from her right shoulder to her left hip are there. They are fully healed, probably from her shifting into a werewolf.

And they didn't disappear completely because wolves can't heal from their mate's talons.

I remember everything I did, only because it was like looking through a haze of anger and lust. I remember her tears. I remember how she begged for me to stop.

I remember how I didn't care.

I sit up and look away, pulling my knees to my chest as we sit in the middle of… I don't even know where we are.

She turns over, mumbling in her sleep. My bite mark on

her neck is perfect. Pride fills my chest, and then I see the heart on her chest.

Pressing my hand against my own, I trace the one she gave me too, and I don't understand why they are there or why I wanted to do that.

I've never heard of mates doing that before.

God, I'm so glad the mating is over. It will never be like that again. She'll have heats, but it won't be that cruel.

I fucked her like I hated her. I treated her like she was nothing to me.

That won't be happening ever again, and I breathe easier. It was because I needed to mark her, and I did.

I fucking brutalized her. Her skin is marred and ruined. I'm so thankful something like this happens once. I will be coherent and in the right state of mind the next time she's in heat. Yes, I'll want her, maybe even chase her, but I won't rape her.

"You're deep in thought," she says sleepily.

I glance down, my heart thumping fast when I look into her eyes. So fucking perfect. She's gorgeous.

"How do you feel?" I ask, my voice hoarse from all the howling, roaring, and snarling I did all night.

She stretches, her breasts lifting, and her nipples tighten from the air kissing them.

How is it possible I want her again? The slightest sweet remains of her heat fill the air, and she gasps, placing her hands between her legs. When she pulls her fingers away, they are wet, but the slick isn't dripping down her thighs like it was yesterday.

"How?" she asks, her breath hitching in her chest, and the smell of arousal fills the air. "I don't think I can take you again like yesterday."

Her words are a stab in my heart, and regret fills me. I

roll on top of her, her legs spreading to accommodate me, but I lie against her instead of filling her.

"I won't ever take you like that again, Ru. I won't be that... brutal." I clutch her hips and shake my head. "I'm so fucking sorry. I'm sorry. I hurt you. I ignored you. I hunted you. I took you when you asked me not to. I'm sorry."

She cups my cheek, and her face softens. "I'm not. I'm not sorry at all. It was amazing, painful, but amazing. And I'm a werewolf. How cool is that?"

I smile, nodding, kissing her palm. "You're beautiful too. Your fur matches your hair. I've never seen anything like it."

"Is that bad? Is something wrong?"

"No, you were perfect. I'm thinking it's because you were bit, not born." I sigh, pressing my head against her stomach. "I'm sorry you had to go through it. You gave me your luck to save my life, and I feel like I've taken yours away from you."

"Away?" she gasps, tugging my arms, signaling she wants me closer.

I move up her body, my hard cock pressing against her entrance, but I don't make a move to enter her.

"You've given me everything. Being a werewolf is more freeing than being a leprechaun. I loved it. It was powerful, and giving myself over to you like that, I wouldn't have had it any other way. I love you, My Gentle Giant. My sweet, caring, gentle, giant." She pets my face with her knuckles.

"But look what I did to you." I flip her over, and she turns her head to look at her back.

"Holy shit," she gasps when she sees the scars. She doesn't seem to care, but they are worse than I thought they would be. "You weren't kidding when you said you'd scar me."

"I'm sorry."

"Are you?" She smirks, trying to ease the tension.

"Of course I am." I frown.

"Anwyll. I don't mind. You did what you did for a reason. I'm marked in every way possible. You warned me. I was fully prepared for anything to happen. Don't be sorry. Don't ruin this for us, okay? Our mating was beautiful, just as it was savage, and I wouldn't change a thing about it."

I blow out a breath and kiss her lips. "Okay. I love you, My Lucky Charm."

"I'm no longer lucky," she says, a little sad.

I take her hand and press it against my chest. "Do you feel that?" The steady beat of my heart bumps against my chest. "It beats because of you. You saved my life by sacrificing your luck. I'd say you're the luckiest of charms. You'll always be that to me."

"I'd go through it all over again. Anything to save you." She leans up and gives me a soft kiss. It's the kind of kiss that's slow and intense. No tongue, but her top lip locks in the middle of mine, and her bottom one hugs under mine.

Such soft fucking lips.

She gasps, breaking the kiss to take in air, then she exhales, and all I can do is breathe her in. I push her hair back. It's still tangled in sweat, blood, and come. I love it.

A faint wave of the last of her heat permeates the air, and I growl at her scent. "You smell so good. It has to be the pregnancy." I inhale again, my cock jerking as I sense our child inside her, along with the traces of her heat fading.

The surprised stutter of her heart has me gliding my eyes up her body until they land on hers. They water and she reaches down to touch her stomach.

Shit. She didn't know. I should have said something

more romantic. I thought she knew because I told her the heat wouldn't stop until she was pregnant.

"So I'm really pregnant? How can you tell?"

I smile gently, looking at her with all the love and devotion I feel for her. I slide down her body and stop at her belly. It's not swollen with my come anymore, which I miss, if I want to be honest. It's fucking sexy to me, knotting her until she's so full, her stomach bulges.

"I can smell it. You probably could too, if you focused. You have a lot to learn still." I can't seem to hide my smile. I'm so fucking happy and excited. My eyes burn, and I press my cheek against her soft stomach, letting the tears flow.

"Anwyll?" She runs her hand through my hair. "Hey, what's wrong?"

"I never thought I'd have this. A family. It was me, just me, locked away for fifteen years. I did heinous things. I hate to think about it, but I remember every second of those years. I remember wanting to die. I didn't want anything good to happen to me. I didn't dare to dream of it. Longing for something I'd never have was more pain than I could handle, but here you are." I rub my hands down her body, her scent becoming slightly stronger from my touch, and desire sweeps through the air. "I still don't think I deserve you, but I'm going to make sure I always earn your love."

"There's nothing to earn, Anwyll. You have it. For free. Always. Life or Death. Remember?"

"I remember." I kiss her stomach, wondering how the hell I got so lucky.

Peppering the same kisses up her body, I palm her tits, and this time I'm able to appreciate just how soft and perfect they are. They fit perfectly in the palm of my hand. My mind isn't crowded with uncontrollable rage and lust. I no longer feel like I want to kill her or ruin her.

I want to take my time with her. Appreciate her.

My hand skims from her ankle, and I watch her skin arise in goosebumps. Her thighs are in ruin. Dried come and slick are all over. Others would probably find it disgusting, but I don't. I see it as a perfect masterpiece, a painting we have created, something only we can experience together to truly understand the beauty of it.

"We've made such a mess," I say, sliding my fingers down her inner thigh, skimming them across until I'm able to slide my fingers through her wet lips. "I think you need me one more time, don't you?"

"Don't you need me too?" she whispers, wrapping her hand around my hard cock and squeezing it until I hiss, the constriction stealing my breath.

"I always need you. More than I've ever needed anyone." I lean down and take one of her nipples into my mouth, sucking the tight bead before flicking it with my tongue.

She hisses when my fang scrapes the fragile flesh, and her claws lengthen, digging into the dirt. I lick up her body, sucking on her mating mark, and her body trembles beneath mine. Lining my cock up to her entrance, I sink in again— for the very last time while she's in heat. It was much shorter than I was expecting, which makes me smug because it means I was able to get her pregnant.

We moan together, and I hook my hands around her shoulders, then plant my knees securely in the dirt, pressing her down while I thrust forward.

"Still so wet, so tight for me, even after taking my fat knot like a good little werewolf."

She cries out as I dig my fingers into the meat of her ass.

"Or maybe you still like to be called my good little slut." My heart pumps with a slight edge of nervousness and anxiety when I call her what I did under the full moon.

Her cunt clenches around me, tightening her grip on my cock, and her strawberry blonde fur sprouts along her arms.

A sliver of the beast I was yesterday slides through my veins and possesses me. "Take my fucking cock. Beg for my knot. Tell me you want me to fill this cunt with it."

She wraps her legs around my hips and flips us, slamming me onto my back with her new-found strength.

Holy shit, I've never been handled like that before.

I want her to do it again.

She presses her hands against my chest, her fangs lengthening as she tiptoes the edge of control and rides my cock.

"I won't beg." She digs ten sharp talons into my chest. "But I'll fuck you. I'll take every inch of your cock." She tilts her head back, her long hair tickling the tops of my thighs.

I grit my teeth together, my orgasm already creeping in. Fuck, this always happens when she's on top. I have the best fucking view. Her tits bounce, and her body snakes, rolling back and forth. Her lips are parted, and I can see the swollen pink clit peeking out as she rubs it against me with every motion.

"I feel your knot already swelling. Are you dying to come in my pussy, *mate*?"

"Yes," I growl, sitting up to take one of her nipples into my mouth, but she shoves me down on my back.

Her eyes glow even brighter, the shade of a green that doesn't exist, beyond bright. She's an alpha werewolf, through and through, but what makes us work is that we know when we need to submit.

"Let me have my way with you. Let me take your cock as deep as I can."

"Fuck yes." I toss my head back, keeping a tight grip on her ass while she fucks me. "That's it. Ru, oh, fuck, you feel so good. That's it, take this cock like a good little slut."

She whimpers and starts to ride me faster, her moans becoming louder. She's dripping again. I feel it dribbling down my sack.

"Ru, I can't...I can't hold on much longer."

"You better. You don't get to come until I do." Her nails threaten my throat. "Don't even think about it when I'm so close. If you come, you won't come again until we are home."

I slap my hands onto the ground and rake my nails across the dirt, tensing my neck and gritting my teeth. My knot is huge, swollen, expanding with more come the harder she slams her pussy down on me.

"What a good boy taking this pussy."

My eyes roll to the back of my head as the wet sounds of her cunt and my sack slap against each other. I growl, biting my tongue until I taste blood to hold back my orgasm.

"You listen so well to me. Give me your come and tell me what a good boy you are." Her mouth drops open, and she screams, her orgasm finally crashing through her.

I ram my hips up, shoving my knot into her little hole, holding her against me while I roar in painful sweet bliss, one of the strongest orgasms of my life.

"I'm your good boy," I rumble. "I'm your good fucking boy giving you all my come just like you asked."

She falls against me, grabbing my face in her hands, and kisses me deeply. Our breaths are wild and entangled, her sweet little sounds slipping down my throat.

Ru's hand fits between us and gives my knot a good squeeze.

"Fuck!" I shout, pouring myself into her again as she massages my knot with her hand and cunt. "You have to stop. You have to..." She squeezes me again, causing me to pinch my eyes shut and nearly fucking sob in pain and pleasure when another hot burst leaves me.

"I want to fucking milk every drop this fat knot has to give me." She keeps at it, torturing me as her muscles tighten around my shaft and her fingers dig into my knot. "I feel it, you know. So hot." She nibbles my earlobe. "And so much of it." She kisses across my cheek and sucks my bottom lip into her mouth. Ru's fangs nip the flesh, and then she licks the blood away. "All that come trying to find its way to my already occupied womb. Aren't you so proud of yourself? I thought heats lasted days, and here you are cutting my one-time experience short. I should punish you for that."

"Ru," I moan her name, my entire body spasming from her constant abuse of my knot. "Stop. Oh, fuck. You have to stop."

I don't think I can make it.

Chapter Forty-One

RU

I dig my nails into his neck, pricking the skin with five individual dots for five sharp claws. Sweat beads along his temples, and I lick the salty liquid off, tasting a sliver of the hunger clawing at my insides for him. "Shut the fuck up and take this pussy like a good boy so I can feel your come inside me," I seductively whisper, loving every hot jet of his come. "Last I remember, you didn't stop when I asked you to. So fucking take it, Anwyll."

Tugging on his knot on purpose, I lift and push down, and the bulge rubs against my G-spot again.

"Oh god, oh fuck, you feel so good. It hurts. Ah, damn it, damn it!" He keeps cursing. A wrinkle forms between his brows, and if I'm not mistaken, his eyes water.

The climax of my orgasm climbs higher as I twist my nipples.

"I can't," he grunts, gripping my hips. "I can't take any more." I shove his hands off me and then cover his mouth with my palm. "You can and you will." I continue to rock back and forth, slower this time because another orgasm looms. It seems that once I've started, I don't ever want to stop. "Give me one more, My Gentle Giant. One more." I move faster. "One more," I whimper, increasing speed, chasing the orgasm that's right there. "Fuck, give it to me, Anwyll."

He places his hands on my waist again, and I grip them, slamming them above his head while I use his cock and knot for my own pleasure. His handsome face is scrunched in bliss and agony. I almost want to take pity on him.

Almost.

Reaching down, I play with the base of his knot stretching me, and he groans, filling me with another feral spurt of come. I tip over the edge one last time, collapsing on him while I ride my high, then use my talons to scratch his shoulder, lower neck, and chest.

I don't know why, but I needed to mark him like he marked me. Five gashes begin to bleed, and his eyes glow a vibrant red. Losing my battle for power, he flips me to my back and buries himself further inside me, licking and sucking at my mate mark.

"You're a savage little werewolf, aren't you?" he asks just as his gashes stitch together and scar.

I trace them with my fingers, the burning inside me finally satisfied. I feel the exact moment the remains of my heat disappear, and both of us let out a relieved breath. His eyes drift to green again, and his knot deflates, leaving me empty.

"I'm your little savage." I nip at his lips, and he smiles. "Will you be able to knot me while I'm pregnant after this?"

He nods, laying on his side, and I press my head against his chest. "Whenever I want now," he replies. "It's recommended because sometimes..." he sounds nervous, tapping his fingers across my shoulder.

"Sometimes..." I urge him to continue.

"The babies are big, and sometimes there is more than one."

"More than one..." I keep a hand pressed to his chest and stare at him, unblinking. "Like two?"

"Or three," he mumbles.

"Three!" I yelp, pressing a hand against my stomach. "Well, what happens when we get to the point where we don't want more kids? What happens during heats? We can't have twenty werewolves running around, Anwyll."

"I know. There's an herb, something easily available to us. I'll have to ask Maven about it, but as long as we take it during your heat, then we will be safe."

"Both of us?"

"It's the only way it will work," he explains. "If you only want one, I'll be happy. I just want a family with you."

My worry dissipates, and I kiss the middle of his chest. "I want that too." My stomach growls, interrupting the sweet moment, and his laugh is loud, boisterous, and echoes through the woods.

"I think it's time I feed my mate. Let's get back to the castle?"

"I don't have clothes," I point out. "Someone tore them from my body."

"And I'd do it again," he rumbles, helping me to my feet.

I sway, my legs weak and shaking. "Whoa."

Anwyll steadies me, then his hand covers my mating mark, his large palm covering the side of my neck while his thumb brushes my cheek. "You'll feel weak for a few days. It would be best if you shifted. Your werewolf is stronger. Her form will cover all the places I don't want others to see with her fur. Do you know how to shift into that form?"

I shake my head. "I barely remember how I did it before."

"It's because you were new and had no control over it. It's simple. Watch me, look at my form, then imagine that form. Soon, it will be as easy as breathing." He shifts in front of me, his entire body stretching, growing taller and wider. His snout elongates, and his tail thumps against the ground, excited for me to shift.

Smiling, I close my eyes and picture my werewolf, asking her to come forward.

Her green eyes glow in the back of my mind, and suddenly, with a sharp intake of breath, I feel her take over.

My body morphs, and there's no pain this time. I stagger under much larger legs and feet before gaining my balance. Anwyll nuzzles my snout, then licks my face. He holds me, and his massive arms are still so much bigger than my own. I love how I still feel small in this form compared to him. The size difference makes me feel safe.

"Ready?" He falls on all fours. "Follow me. I'll keep you safe."

I mimic his stance, and we take off running through the woods.

He howls, telling the entire planet how happy he is.

I howl too, replying with my own joy.

He'll never have to run alone again.

I'll follow him anywhere.

And everywhere.

Chapter Forty-Two

ANWYLL

The journey is quiet and uneventful but perfect at the same time.

Ru playfully tackles me, and we nip at one another, rolling down a hill. Our heads bump together; then she tugs on my tail. I pin her shoulders down to the ground, and that's when I notice how long her eyelashes are. Goddamn, she's beautiful in this form.

"I'm glad to see you're having so much fun when you killed two dragons, and I have their asshole Prince demanding retribution."

A shadow falls over us, and by the scent, it's Prince Cailian.

"They attacked my mate during the chase, during the hunt, and they touched her. They would have raped her. I did him a favor getting rid of dragons that would do such a thing. I'd do it again too. If he doesn't care about that, he's an asshole, and I don't have a problem going to kill him myself."

"He only sent a message by one of his couriers. I've actually never met the man, but I don't blame you. Is that true, Ru? Did those dragons try to harm you?" His ice-cold eyes land on her, and she nods, glancing away as if ashamed.

I take her hand and bring her to her feet. "There's nothing to be ashamed of. They didn't listen to Prince Cailian and didn't stay inside. Maybe their prince should have better control of his people," I growl, fury rising in my chest the longer I think about it. "Maybe I want retribution. Maybe I want to challenge him."

"You don't want to do that, friend," the Prince warns. "You were able to take two dragons on during the full moon, but without that power, you don't stand a chance. Plus, the dragons you encountered were young; they weren't of royal blood, which makes a big difference too." He spins around, sophisticatedly dressed. He's wearing form-fitting trousers with a white blouse nearly all the way unbuttoned. His long hair is pulled back from his face, showcasing his sharp features and calculating eyes. His pointed ears are pierced from top to bottom, dashed in silver.

Makes me shiver.

He looks over his shoulder. "Are you coming? I believe I have something you want."

"I want to go home," I grumble under my breath, wondering how the fuck we are supposed to get there.

Do we have to go through all that again? I don't know if we'd survive.

We follow the Ice Elven Prince, flanked by his security guards, as we walk across the ice bridge. It's cold under my feet, and below us is a flowing river. Their grass is more like icicles, small, thin, individual blades, and the flowers are ice too, yet blooming in different colors.

The magic here is odd.

I don't like it.

It begins to snow, and the white flecks stick to my fur. I huff a sound of annoyance, but then Ru slides her paw into mine, and I look down as she looks up at me, and I feel at ease.

It's all okay.

When we step inside his castle, the door slams shut, and the smell of food makes me groan.

"We will have dinner soon. I've prepared your room for you to go shower, then I'll give you what you need, and we can talk about how you are going to get home."

"Do we have to go back the way we came?" Ru asks.

One of the elves stares at Ru too long, and I snap my teeth at him. Cailian sighs, pinches the bridge of his nose, and slaps his elven friend on the head.

"They are newly mated. Stop staring, or I'll allow him to rip your ears off."

"Apologies," he bares his neck. "I've never seen a werewolf her color before."

"You've seen other werewolves?" I step forward. "When? Where?"

"It's been years. Way before your time. I'm sorry," he says with sincere sorrow in his tone.

My shoulders sag. "I see. It's fine. I think it's because she was bitten, not born."

"Very unique. Be very careful wherever you go. Hunters would kill for a werewolf hide that color."

I growl at the thought, and all of the elves step away, except for Cailian. "I'd like to see them try. I'll skin them first before they ever lay a hand on my mate."

"With how easily you took down two dragons, I believe that." Prince Cailian snaps his fingers, and we're in another room.

Ru yips, losing her balance, and I catch her.

"A warning would have been nice," she grumbles. "I hate being transported like that."

He winces. "I'm sorry. I forgot you're not used to it. This is your room. Get ready, shower, and come down for dinner. I have your heartsnow."

"You do?" I sound surprised.

"It grows in abundance here, right where my territory and the dragon's territory meet. I actually keep a bushel in the castle for medicinal purposes. It's amazing for the libido too."

I hear Ru intake a sharp breath, and when I stare at her, even in her werewolf form, she's blushing.

"I don't think we have issues in that department, Prince."

He chuckles, clicking his tongue before rubbing his chin. "No, you don't. The whole realm heard you two."

"Oh chauns." Ru buries her face in her hands.

"Yes, that was heard as well," he teases.

Ru hides her face in my chest, and I can't help but laugh too. We were very... vigorous last night.

"I'll leave you be. I'm sure you're ready to get home, but I suggest a good night's rest, in a bed for starters."

"I don't know," I say, scratching behind my ear. "My brother has been with sickness for a while. He's probably lost it by now. I'm worried that if I wait another day, he might be dead."

"He won't be. He won't be all there when you see him again, but one day won't hurt anything."

"How do you know?" The question isn't meant to sound so harsh, but it does.

"Well, a long time ago, this planet was shared by werewolves. They were Wind Werewolves, very unique. They could create wind with their howls. It came in handy when the dragons got carried away. But it was my kind, the dragons, the woodlands, and the winds. On the other side of the planet, we used to have water creatures. Times have not been kind. We no longer have the winds or the water."

"Wait, it all sounds very elemental," Ru speaks, curious and interested.

Cailian smiles, bowing his head. "You're right. This planet is Elementalu. The planet of elements and their creatures."

"That's so cool."

"I suppose it is... Cool," he replies. He sounds like he has never said the word before. "Okay, I'll leave you to it. It's been..." he pauses searching for the right word. "Nice having guests. Not many come here."

"Why not?"

His eyes shift to Ru. "Not many know we exist."

Ru makes a face of disbelief, pinching her lips together. "We know elves exist because of Reuel. He is the elf in our coven."

Cailian steps in front of her, gripping her shoulders.

I snarl in caution, and he removes his hands.

"What kind of elf is he?"

"We don't know. He's beautiful though."

I rumble in discontent. I don't like hearing she finds another good-looking.

She slaps me in the chest. "Stop it. He's otherworldly. Sharp features, white eyes like you, but he has dark hair. He doesn't know either. He was raised by werewolves, if I remember the story correctly."

He inhales. "I'm coming with you to your home. We will leave at dawn." Cailian swiftly walks away, but Ru grabs his arm.

She hisses when she realizes he is cold to the touch. "Why?"

"Because I have questions that need answers." With that vague statement, Cailian closes the door behind him, leaving us confused.

My stomach grumbles. I can't remember the last time I ate.

Ru shifts into her human form, and I follow. "What do you think he wants with Reuel?"

"No idea, but we will find out soon. Let's shower. I'm starving."

"Me too." She slaps my ass as I walk by, and I wrap my arms around her, swinging her around in a circle. "It's just so plump. I had to give it a smack."

I toss her over my shoulder, laughing as she playfully slaps my ass while I head to the bathroom. The tiles that make the floor appear to be ice, but as I step on them, they turn orange and warm. They don't melt under my feet, but they feel good after running through the forest.

"Don't make me knot you again, mate."

Her scent changes with lust and apprehension. She rubs her hands up and down my cheeks, then spreads them, blowing on the puckered star only she has ever dared to see or touch.

I jump, startled, and set her down, then blush.

"You didn't like it?"

I shrug my shoulder as I turn on the shower, not wanting to look at Ru just yet. There are so many ways she makes me feel inexperienced. I've finally gotten down how to please her and make her orgasm. Anything else, I'm afraid I'd be bad at.

"I can't help that I want to own every part of you." She saunters up to me, reaching her arm behind my body, skimming her index finger up and down the cleft of my ass.

I swallow, my face heating with uncertainty and inexperience. My heart pounds against my chest. I'm not sure what to do. I want to do anything that makes her happy, but this is different. It's intimate in ways I never thought I'd be with someone. It's more forbidden than regular sex. I don't have an issue with it, but what if it hurts?

Hurts?

I roll my eyes at myself. I've experienced pain.

"If that's what you want," I answer, thinking that was the right thing to say.

Ru's eyes soften and her lips curve slightly into a sad smile before she steps into the shower. She holds out her hand, and I lift my leg over the lip of the tub to join her. It's been a while since I've felt so vulnerable. The last few weeks of me being in a very protective mode and letting my alpha werewolf roam free has felt nice, but things are getting back to normal. Ru is ready to take over again, and I don't mind. Being in control all the time is exhausting. I'm glad I have a mate who likes to take over sometimes, then submit when I need her to. It's the perfect dynamic.

The warm water splashes down my back, and I hang my head, letting my muscles relax from weeks of stress. Ru's small palms meet my chest, the tips of her toes touching mine while she steps closer to me.

"Anwyll, I want to make you happy. I care about what you want. Do I want to explore every inch of you? Yes." She rubs her hands down my body, then wraps them around to my ass to grab it. "And I'd love to give you pleasure I thought you'd never want, but never does that mean you give me this part of you because you want to do it for me. Ever. Only when you're ready."

"I just"—I lick my lips and the warm water hits my tongue—"I'm nervous."

"Why? I'd never do anything to hurt you."

It's a funny statement considering we just scratched our scars into one another. It's different now. We aren't crazed.

"What if I'm bad at it? Or I don't like it." I sound ridiculous.

"You can't be bad at it. All you have to do is lie there or stand. And if you don't like it, you tell me, and I'll stop." She glances around, looking for something. "Where's the shampoo and body wash?"

I look down to see frozen cubes. One jar is labeled S with purple cubes, while the other two are clear and labeled with B and C. "Here." I point to the shelf, thinking about what she just told me.

I do want to try it with her.

"Oh. Neat." She grabs a cube and it melts in her hands, releasing its scent. It reminds me of lavender. She suds up her palms and begins to wash me, days of dirt, sweat, and blood tint the water. I watch it go down the drain, but then I witness her fall on her knees, lifting my left leg off the ground. She washes it, scrubbing the skin with her fingernails. She gets every inch, including where the crease of my thigh meets my groin.

She moves to the other leg, grabbing another ice cube, and it melts again. She does the same, cleaning me, then taps my thigh. I spin around, leaning my arms against the wall while she cleans me. The water plummets against my neck, and I exhale, the stress releasing from my body. Her hands on me awaken my cock somehow, even though I'm tired. I'm not sure if I have the energy to come again. The more she rubs me, the greater the ache in my dick becomes though.

Ignoring my ass, she scrubs my back, then my arms. When she reaches for a new cube, I snag her wrist, guiding her to my backside.

"Anwyll?"

"I'm curious," I say through a dry throat.

"You're sure?" Her voice darkens to a raspy husk.

I eventually nod my head but not with confidence. There's no way this is going to feel good. Maybe now isn't the best time, but I want it now. I want to always try new things with Ru.

"Spread your legs for me, My Gentle Giant."

I gulp, doing as she says, and I'm so glad she can't see my face because I'm embarrassed.

"Anytime, I'll stop. There's no pressure."

"I know," I croak, my voice breaking as if I'm fourteen years old all over again. I clear the frog in my throat. "I mean, I know. I know I'm safe."

"You are. You're always safe with me." She strokes my back with her hands, kissing each shoulder, relaxing me until I'm not so tense. She continues to adorn me with her affection, her fingers smooth as silk while she caresses my sides. Ru kisses down my back, her nails tickling the sensitive flesh of my cheeks before grazing the back of my thighs.

God, this feels good.

If she kept doing this, the barely there touches and the slightest of kisses, I'll come eventually. Her hands on me are the only type of heaven I've ever experienced, a peace that lightens my soul, and I'm dependent on her now.

If there were a day that I had to be without her, for any reason, a piece of me would go missing.

"You're being such a good boy for me, Anwyll. I love it when you're good."

I whimper, rolling my forehead back and forth along the wall, squeezing my eyes shut as her praise zips through my system. I've gone my entire life being bad, so being good is a feeling I've experienced only with Ru. I always want this from her.

I'll always be her good boy-her *best* boy.

She reaches around, palming my cock, but with no pressure. It's easy, almost lazy, as if she has all the time in the world, and I have to catch my breath. She touches me in ways that prove how much she cares about me. Someone like me, deprived of touch, experiencing it is like a balm on the wounds hell inflicted on my soul.

"The best of boys. I'm so lucky to have a mate so caring, so giving, gentle, smart, and who listens. No one's boy is as good as mine. No one's." Her praise makes my cock jerk, and I whimper, fisting my hands together as she licks her tongue down my clean crease.

Words of affirmation are apparently a big turn-on for me too. I love hearing how much I please her. I'm worthy.

I'm finally worthy.

"Are you okay?"

I nod.

"Use your words, Good Boy." She spanks my ass playfully.

"Yes, I'm okay."

"I want you to keep telling me that as we go. Without me asking. Okay?"

"Yes, My Lucky Charm."

"Good." The word is breathed on a warm puff of air, and a tingle spreads down my spine.

She releases my cock, spreads my cheeks, and hums

when she sees my virgin hole. "So pretty. I'm going to take care of you." Her tongue lashes me, and I yip, standing on my tiptoes from the unexpected lick.

"I'm okay," I rush out before she can ask.

"Oh, the best boy. I'm going to give you a reward." Her tongue flicks my star, and I moan when she continues, the pleasure mind-numbing.

It's better than I thought it would be.

She moans into my ass, plunging her tongue into the rim.

"Fuck!" I shout, my talons extending and scratching the ice. "Oh, fuck. Ru, goddamn it. Don't stop." The cool sheet of ice the shower stall is made of cools my cheek while she feasts on me.

I reach down to stroke my cock, and she slaps my arm away. "Anwyll, don't be bad. You want to come like this, right?"

I whine. "Yes, please. I'm sorry. You make me feel so good."

"I'll forgive you this time." She blows against my hole before plundering her wicked tongue inside me again.

My mouth parts, and I pant, staring at the throbbing pulse at the base of my cock. Even without being inside her, my knot swells.

"I'm going to insert one finger, okay?"

"O-okay," I stutter nervously, her finger rubbing over the rim.

"Look at you. You're fluttering for me. I bet you'd let me fuck you, wouldn't you?"

I just might. I'm not ashamed.

"Yes," I admit, wondering how that would work, but I'll try anything with Ru.

She'll make sure I'm safe.

She inches her finger in, and I clench, gasping from the spike of pain.

"Relax for me. Push out, good boy."

I breathe through my nose and do as she says, taking her finger to the knuckle. She reaches around again, stroking my flagging cock.

"I'm okay," I tell her, the words she needs to keep going.

My cock hardens again, and as she strokes me with a tight grip, she begins a slow pace with her finger. It becomes easier with every motion, but then she curls her finger and presses against something inside me that sets off rockets behind my eyes. My knot pulsates again with come, filling with so much seed. Once I'm allowed to orgasm, I'll make a mess.

"Fuck, Ru. Do it again. Oh my god," I chuckle at how ridiculous it sounds. I never thought I'd like this, but now I know I'll want more.

She kisses my right cheek, keeping the pace on my cock the same as she finger fucks my ass. I'm nearly climbing the walls.

"That's your prostate making you see stars," she informs.

"No, it's you," I gasp, my knees weakening as my orgasm builds. "Only you. Ru, I'm going to come. Please, can I come?"

She rams against my prostate over and over again, my body trembling as every nerve fires.

"Good Boy for asking. Yes, you can come."

She clutches my knot, massaging it with large rotations, and with another punch against my prostate, my shout is mixed with a lethal roar, shaking the ice around us. I unload the come, spraying it against the wall with an amount made to fill her cunt so I can watch her drip of me.

"Oh, so good. That's it. Come for me. What a mess. You're clenching around me so tight. Good Boy, so good for me." She kisses me again, slowly sliding her finger in and out while grasping my knot, milking it of every drop.

I sag against the wall when I'm done. I tremble as if an earthquake has gone off inside me, shifting everything I knew about pleasure.

"Give me a minute. I'll lick that pretty pussy."

"No. I wanted that to be about you. I wanted to care for you."

"That doesn't seem fair."

"You were a good boy. Good boys get rewards." She turns me around and stares into my tired eyes. "I'm fine. Okay?"

That makes me feel special. She wanted to do that for me, show me something new, and now I have time to wrap my head around it and think about what else I want.

We finish showering and get dressed in the clothes the prince left on the bed.

I'm relaxed and it's all thanks to my mate.

RU

Anwyll doesn't understand how relaxed I feel after giving him pleasure. It pleases me. I don't even need to orgasm because of how good I made him feel. I buzz with it. I feel his pleasure in my veins still as we walk down the hall to head to dinner with Prince Cailian. Through our bond, his peace, relaxation, and happiness are pure energy. It fuels me.

As we walk hand in hand down the hall, I catch him smiling. It's goofy and adorable. He's in his own submissive headspace right now, and that, right there, is worth more than any orgasm I've ever felt.

"How do you feel?" I ask him, my hand gliding down the freezing rail.

"Amazing," he exhales on a relaxed breath. "Thank you. I...really needed that."

"I know." I squeeze his hand. "I'll always know what you need."

He cuts his eyes to me, his normal ones, the maple hues gorgeous under the reflection of the ice chandelier. It seems like ages since I've seen his human form, truly have seen it, instead of it being rushed between forms.

I see the relief in him, and he kisses the top of my hand, the tips of his wet hair dampening the material of his plain white shirt around his shoulder.

"Ru. Anwyll. Please, follow me." One of Cailian's men guides us to the dining hall, but first, we have to walk through the living room, which has tons of space. There are a few elves lounging across couches, and I make a sound of surprise.

"Did you expect ice?" Our guide asks, peeking over his shoulder with an amused, raised brow.

Embarrassed, I look away from the men, hanging out in sweatpants as they watch TV.

I don't know why I thought they wouldn't have TV, but I suppose it's more modern than I thought.

"I'm sorry. That was so rude of me."

"It's okay. Yes, we love ice and to stay cool. We're connected with it, but we love comfort as well. I have a large down feather comforter on my bed with silk sheets." He kisses the tip of his fingers and pops them in the air. "Perfect. It's so soft and warm."

"Warm?"

"Well, we like to be warm too. When we want, of course."

I feel so close-minded. Of course, they like to be warm. Being warm feels good. We pass lavish curtains made of black silk cascading from the ceiling to the floor, but they aren't covering the windows that overlook the forest.

What I love about this place is how certain parts are cold and snowy while other parts remain clear and green. Such a unique place. I love it.

Minus the dragons.

I don't like them at all.

We enter the dining room, and the table is a long, hand-carved natural table made from a gorgeous tree. I've never seen anything like it.

"Wow," I gasp, running my hand over the wood.

"It's rare, taken from the valley where fire meets ice. Heartsnow grew in a large white oak," The Prince explains, rubbing his palm across the snow-white top that has flecks of embers in it. "It's said that having a table made of heartsnow cures bad energy and makes a happy home. Please." He gestures. "Take a seat."

We pull out the chairs, and I like that no one else does it for us. He is a Prince but keeps independence and responsibility in his castle.

"Well, it's beautiful. I can see the embers. It's almost as if they are burning." I bend down to get a closer look. I swear, fire is moving in this wood.

"You're correct. These embers will burn forever, but they are frozen just like this. They won't ever catch fire."

"So cool," I say with awe.

The chef, I assume, with his team in matching uniforms, brings out silver platters. "Dinner is served, Prince Cailian."

"Thank you, Chef Yaliax. It smells wonderful," Cailian genuinely thanks his chef.

"Are they paid?"

"Yes, they are paid," he answers.

Fuck.

I said it out loud. I didn't mean to do that.

"I'm so sorry. I'm so used to royalty being greedy with servants. That was so rude of me."

"Your curiosity is valid. I pay all my people. Everyone

has fair wages so they can live how they like to live. Especially with the portals open again, many like to travel."

The chefs lift the lids of the platter, and a gorgeous fish filet sits in the middle of a bed of rainbow arugula with a brown sauce drizzled over it that smells like spicy maple syrup. I've never seen arugula so vibrant before. I'm excited to try this. There's a basket of rolls accompanied by a bowl of soup that smells divine and has chunks of potato in it.

"I hope you don't mind, Anwyll, but I told the chefs to cook you something different," Cailian says.

The chef lifts Anwyll's lid, and a huge steak takes over the entire plate. There's nothing else on the plate. The steak hangs over the edges and drips juice onto the table. It has to be at least seven inches thick.

Anwyll growls, practically drooling when he stares at the steak.

His fangs descend, and his eyes glow from toffee to green.

Cailian laughs, lifting his glass filled with water. "Dig in."

I cut a piece of my fish and get a little bit of sauce and arugula, then moan as I chew. It's so good.

Anwyll doesn't use utensils. He stabs the meat with his talons and feasts, snarling and growling as if it's live prey he is taking down. He's making a mess, but Prince Cailian doesn't seem to mind.

"I have another prepared for you just in case, Anwyll. Really, there's more where that came from." Cailian watches him in amusement.

"Thank you," Anwyll grumbles as he chews, blood dripping from his chin from the meat that's perfectly red in the middle.

We sit in silence as we eat, and when I'm done with the

fish, I pour myself a ladle of soup and grab a piece of bread. It's soft and fluffy, perfectly flaky. I dip the bread in the soup, and the salty broth bursts across my tongue.

I feel like I haven't eaten in ages.

"Congratulations, by the way," Cailian states, sipping his drink. "On your mating and the pregnancy."

"How did you know?" I wipe my mouth with the softest napkin I've ever felt.

"It's an aura about you. I can tell. You're literally glowing in my eyes. Plus, I know enough about werewolf mating's to know they don't end without pregnancy. There's the tiny heart on your chest too. I see it peeking through next to his name. He really did a number on you."

I blush a little, hiding my face as I eat my soup. "Do you know what the hearts mean?"

"Does Anwyll not?"

I shake my head. "He was under a spell for most of his life. He is learning about werewolves along the way."

"Oh, I'm sorry to hear that. That has to be difficult. Well, the hearts signify strength and loyalty. You know that if a werewolf has sickness and if it's bad enough, he will hunt down their mate and rip out their heart, then his own. The heart on either of your chests represents safety and strength. Your heart is officially guarded by the other. No other werewolf can touch you. No other can have your heart and it can't be ripped out. But once the other dies, the heart scar will break, and your actual heart will be open to so much pain, you'll die from it because you won't have the guardian of your heart anymore."

I sit there for a minute, digesting his words. "That's sad yet really beautiful that their kind loves so viciously."

He agrees, lifting his drink to his mouth. "They are vicious creatures, but like you said, beautiful as well."

I rub the spot where he carved a heart into my chest. "And you?" I ask him. "What about your mating habits? How do you know when you find your mate?"

A saddened expression flashes across his face. He leans in his chair, elbow on the armrest, as he stares out the window. "I'm thousands of years old, Ru. As much as I would love to find my mate, I do not think he or she exists. Only my mate can melt my ice, meaning, any power I hold to freeze, they can stop it. A quick touch of their hand on my arm and my cold veins will turn warm."

"I'm sorry, I didn't mean to upset you."

"It's okay. Selfishly, it's another reason why I want to go with you tomorrow. I want to meet this elf, but also, when you first arrived, you had a scent on you. It was old, distant, but it called to me." He waves his hands away. "Or maybe that's just wishful thinking." He sighs, lost in the dreams and hopes of his mate. "As for mating, the ends of our hair will intertwine, binding and sharing all of our emotions, childhoods, dreams, and fears. It's a link to the mind. We transfer everything of who we are like that and then, of course, we mate to seal our souls. It's very pleasurable."

"It sounds beautiful."

"I wouldn't know. My kind haven't found mates in a long time. It's why many are traveling to other dimensions. They want to find their mate."

"Understandable. I wish them the best, and you too. Maybe when you come to the coven, you'll find her or him."

He gives me a crooked smile. "Maybe."

The chef sets down another steak for Anwyll, and my mate digs in, eating another huge piece of meat.

"How do we get home? Actually, I don't know if it is possible, but I promised someone who helped us on our journey. His name is Irving, and he lives in the Unwanted

Lands, which used to be called Gleminor. He lives in the lake there, and I promised him I'd bring him and his kind to Salem because the Unwanted Lands are too unstable for them. Is there a way we can keep my promise?"

He gives me a slow, considerate, and thoughtful nod while placing his hands in a steeple position. His elbows hit the table while he ponders. "I don't see why not. It will be tricky. We aren't exactly close to Gleminor, but that doesn't matter now that portals are available. We will get you two home first, and then we will bring Irving to you."

I blow out a breath, happy I get to keep my word. "Great. Thank you. He helped us out so much. I'd hate to leave him behind."

"It's honorable. I like a person who can keep their word."

We're interrupted by Anwyll picking up the plate and licking the steak juices off it. I kick his leg under the table.

He startles. "What? Oh." He sets the plate down and licks his lips. "Sorry. It was really good."

"You have no table manners," I tease, chuckling. "But I love it." He eats food like a true wild animal.

"I don't care. It's a compliment. My chef is fantastic." He pushes away from the table, tucking his hands in his pockets. "Did your elf give you anything before you left? Anything special?"

I shake my head, but then it dawns on me. I can't believe we forgot. "The powder," I whisper. "It's in the bag Maven made us, the coven witch. It's sunset magnolia powder. To help us transport from one place to another." I turn to Anwyll and grip his hand. "Do you know how easy this trip would have been if we remembered that damn powder?" I laugh ironically, then give my attention back to the prince.

He is hunched over, gripping the table, smiling as he whispers to himself.

"It has to be," he mumbles. "It has to be him. No one knows of that powder or flower besides Woodland Elves. No one. It comes naturally to them like common knowledge, breathing, they just know these things. I have to bring him home to his people. I think he's the prince. I think he is the last of the bloodline."

I flinch thinking about Reuel leaving. "He won't leave the coven. That's his home. He doesn't know the Woodland Elves. You can't bring him to a place he doesn't want to be in."

"Of course, I won't. But I can bet he doesn't feel like himself. That something is missing. He's half of himself. That isn't fair to him. If I fail to bring him here, so be it, but I have to try. If it's him. I could be wrong." He begins to walk away. "Get rest. We leave as soon as the first snowfall."

Anwyll stands. "Is that like dawn? What time is that here?" he shouts but doesn't get an answer.

I'm left with a twisted stomach, wondering how we are on this journey to save one family member, only to

Chapter Forty-Four

ANWYLL

The next morning is quiet. Ru's been lost in her thoughts about Reuel. I like the elf and I'd hate for him to leave, but at the same time, I understand if it's his responsibility to come home. If he is feeling like only half of himself, then that isn't fair. I know what that's like, to feel like a piece of you is lost and you don't know where it went.

Ru slips on a long green dress that ties around her neck and back. It's beautiful and form-fitting, the color is the perfect contrast against the cool tone of her strawberry blonde hair and fair skin. I bend down and kiss her shoulder, wrapping my arms around her as we look in the mirror in front of us.

"Are you ready to go home?"

"More than ever, but we still need the heartsnow," she replies.

"We will get it. When we get home, everything will go back to normal." My hand flattens along her stomach, and I can already feel bonds forming between me and my young. I growl, but it's with peace and contentment. Kissing her neck, I step away. "Come on, Ru. Let's finally go home," I hold out my hand, and she slips hers into my palm, slinging the bag over her shoulder to keep it safe.

That poor sack has been through so much. It's filthy.

She peeks her gorgeous green eyes at me through her light lashes. Exhaustion hangs underneath, coloring shadows on her angelic face.

I grip her chin and press a kiss to her pink, silken lips. "I'll always take care of you. When we get home, you're all mine."

"I'm always yours Anwyll, whether we are home or not."

"Through life and death?"

"I promise," she whispers, leaning her cheek against my palm.

She seems so tired, so exhausted. I don't even want to travel because I know it will only heighten how she feels. I swing her into my arms, and she laughs, wrapping her arms around my neck.

"What are you doing?"

"Carrying you. You're tired. I want you to rest. Don't argue with me." I let the werewolf come out to play, to warn her to listen, and she nods.

She doesn't even fight me. Ru rests her head against my shoulders, and I open the door to walk down the hall, then down the steps to the lobby of Prince Cailian's castle.

He's standing there with a bag of his own.

"You're in charge while I'm gone, Zyrl. Okay? Keep the dragons at bay until I return. They can be pissy all they want. They are the ones who decided to interrupt a mating and tried to rape a werewolf's mate. Remind them of that or freeze them, then have them delivered to the Prince of Dragons himself. I could really fucking care less."

"You won't have to worry about a thing, brother. I have everything under control."

"I know you do. I wouldn't trust anyone else. Make sure the Woodland elves are okay too. I know they are fine, they constantly remind me, but I want to make sure they have everything they need."

"You're their prince too until we can find them one."

"Don't tell them that," Cailian smirks, then stops the conversation with his brother when he sees us coming down the stairs. "Is she okay?" His knuckles brush against her cheek, and small veins of icicles spread along her jaw.

She sighs in relief as if the cold feels good.

"She'll probably sleep for the next few days. The exhaustion of the heat and mating is getting to her, and pregnancy is quick with werewolves, so she's probably already experiencing symptoms. It's a good thing we are getting you two home today."

He opens the front doors of his castle, the ice slabs grinding against the floor, and we step outside. I'll never get over the beauty of this place.

"I have your heartsnow." He opens his bag and shows us the flowers that look similar to wolfsbane. Half the petals are white, the other half burn with embers. "We get this to your witch, your brother will be fine."

Yeah. If he isn't dead.

A loud roar echoes from the distance, rumbling the ground under my feet. It's a threat, and while I keep Ru close, I shift. Her tiny body disappears in my arms, but I roar to the skies in return, daring this fucking dragon to touch my mate.

"Hell no. Not today." Cailian digs in his pocket and tosses the powder through the air, creating a hole in the universe.

Sunset Magnolia powder.

"Think of your home," he shouts over the whirling wind. "Hurry. Before he gets here."

"Who is that?"

"It's the Prince of Dragons!" He holds his hand above his eyes to block them from the debris flying through the air. "He hasn't shown his face. I've never met him, and I don't plan to now!" Cailian grips my shoulder. "Think. And jump." His eyes cast toward the sky, and a dragon spreads his wings, blocking so much of the sky, and roars. "Now, Anwyll! Now! For fuck's sake! Before we turn to crisp."

I jump into the portal with Cailian having a tight grip on my shoulder. I expect it to be like going through the portals on land, basically nearly dying before coming out the other side, but my foot lands in soft grass instead.

The sunflower field is in front of me, and the house is just there, on a slight hill, and I've never been more relieved in my life.

I collapse to my knees, tired, thankful, and hold my mate tight while she rests.

"We're home, My Lucky Charm. We're home. We made it." My eyes blink away tears.

Cailian strolls a few feet ahead. A massive scratch is on his shoulder.

"Prince—"

"I'm fine."

He doesn't sound too happy, but that's when I see the veins around the wound. They aren't blue, but a dull orange, as if he is warm.

"Cailian," I whisper when I realize the magnitude of the situation.

The Ice Elven Prince and the Fire Dragon Prince are

mates. They have never met, but from what I understand, they do not like one another.

"I don't want to talk about it. I barely escaped his clutches. Let's be glad he didn't come through the portal too." He glances around and breathes in. "It is beautiful here. I see why you call it home. What are those?" He points to the flowers.

"Sunflowers. Maven keeps them alive all year with her magic."

"I like them. I want to take them back with me. Can I do that?"

"Uh, I don't know. Maybe Maven can help with that."

He stares at the house and chews on his bottom lip. "What if they attack me?"

"Alexander would never allow it. He is a fair Alpha."

"Covens have masters, no?"

"Yes, but for my kind, he is an Alpha."

"I see. Well, standing here won't change your brother, will it? Let's save the day, or all your efforts will be for nothing. Plus, you want to get her to bed. She won't be waking anytime soon."

"What about Irving?"

"I'll do that when everything else is taken care of. He needs a water source first, something else I would need to talk to your Coven Witch about. Do I look okay? I've never met a coven witch. It's like meeting royalty. I'm a little nervous."

"You look... fine? Maven is pretty laid-back. You don't need to worry." She's quite the celebrity; everywhere, in every dimension, people know of her.

I begin the short track home, and my beast is at ease at last. I push past the sunflowers as we walk through them, breaking a few stems, but Cailian stops to sniff nearly every single one. It's funny. He comes from a gorgeous planet. Others would argue the things seen there would be impossible, yet he is enchanted by a sunflower.

The closer I get to home, the quicker my legs move. Until all of a sudden, I'm running, racing the setting sun. I don't know where I get the energy, but I am. Tears are spilling down my face. My heart slams against my chest.

Family.

I'm so close to my family. The relief, the happiness of not dying on that journey, and then it's the thought of seeing my pack.

I break out of the sunflower field, gasping for air, sweating, the cool evening air doing nothing to decrease my excitement.

Someone stands from the porch swing. "Anwyll?" He doesn't even run to the steps. He jumps over the porch rail, a huge smile taking over his face. "Holy shit, Anwyll. It's really you." Greyson sprints to me, and I shift into my human form, showing Ru in my arms, and he slows his pace, but his chest thumps against mine as he wraps his arms around me. "Fuck, it's good to see you," he whispers. "It's so good to have you two home." The words break as he talks, and I bury my face against his shoulder, blinking away the tears.

Home.

We fucking made it.

"I'm so fucking glad to see you." My shoulders shake, and my knees give out as pure exhaustion takes over. The adrenaline is gone. There's no need to be savage. No need to be on alert.

I can be at peace.

"I got you. Shh, I got you." Greyson takes my weight on one side while I shift Ru to my shoulder.

"I can take her," Cailian says, holding out his arms. "I won't harm her."

Even at my most vulnerable, my weakest, I'm not sure if can trust anyone else's arms around her.

The front door slams open, and I lift my head, my entire body suddenly sore.

"Anwyll?" Alpha says in shock. "Anwyll has made it back! With Ru! They are home!" he shouts, and the entire pack comes running out onto the porch.

Through the pack bond, I feel the love, the happiness, the excitement, and the relief to know we are safe. I pull away from Greyson, stumbling forward, and Alpha catches me.

"Oh." Alexander Monreaux shakes as he cups my face. "It is good to see you again. We have all been worried." He glances down at Ru and holds out his arms. This time, I don't hesitate.

I hand her over to him.

"Is she okay?" he asks, brow furrowing in concern. "She's sleeping and feels warm."

"She's in heat hibernation. It's what female werewolves go through after a...rigorous mating," Cailian states.

I blush, and my pack giggles and laughs.

"Thatta boy!" Luca slaps my arm. "I knew you had it in you." He messes with my hair next and hugs me. "It's good to see you. The coven hasn't been the same without you."

Alexander eyes Cailian, fangs descending, and the moonlight glitters from the lethal weapons. "Who are you?"

"I'm Prince Cailian. Prince of the Ice Elven. I'm here for selfish purposes after finding out information from Anwyll, but all that can wait. Let's get them settled and prepare the treatment for his brother."

"My brother," I gasp, kicking myself with how I almost forgot. "How is he?" I look around and notice Maven isn't around, and neither is Luna. "Where is Maven?"

"You came home just in time. The twins were born this morning. Luna is there healing Maven with Reuel. She's doing well. I can't wait for you to meet them. Let's get inside."

"My brother," I remind him.

Everyone falls silent, including Zaffre, Gullivere, Amberella, Amory, Drayce, and Dottie.

"What's wrong?" My voice roughens with emotion.

"He's hallucinating. He's been reliving the time you both spent under a spell. We already have his blood because he's been pulling on the silver so much, puddles of it have been pooling on the floor," Alexander explains.

"Oh." I take Ru back, needing the comfort of her body against mine, and mind-numbingly walk up the steps to go inside.

The moment I'm inside, I hear him in the catacombs, roaring and banging against the wall, but then upstairs, I hear the cries of newborns.

I'm standing in the middle of life and death.

"How is Severide?"

"Still spending his time with Atreyu." My Alpha is bitter.

Dottie walks up to me and gives me a hug out of nowhere, and the glow of her beast takes over her body. I still can't tell what she is.

The moment Cailian steps into the house, he inhales, staggering so much, Greyson has to catch him. His veins turn orange, and I look around to see who it could be.

"Anwyll!" Rarity shouts from the top of the steps.

"Rarity." I've never been more relieved to see my best friend.

She sprints down the steps and wraps her arms around my neck, holding me tight. "It's so good to see you. Oh my god. You're here." She pats my shoulders, feeling me to see if I'm really here. "You're home." Tears flow down her face, and a watery smile is on her face when she sees Ru in my arms. "You're mated, right?"

"Yeah," I croak, tightening my grip. "Finally."

"I'm so happy for you—" She pauses, sniffing the air. She glances over my shoulder and pushes by me.

We all watch as she stands in front of Cailian. "Who are you?" She asks, her veins turning blue.

Cailian's eyes drift over her, from head to toe; it's like he can't believe what he is seeing.

"Cailian," he answers, lifting his hand to her cheek. "My mate."

"Beloved," she whispers. "You're really here."

"Beloved?" Alexander's tone reminds me of a big brother. "Fuck, there is so much going on."

"You are a vampire, but somewhere you are Ice Elven," Cailian explains. "Somewhere. I can feel the ice, the cold, and the freeze. You are beautiful. I've never seen anyone like you." He presses their foreheads together, and we all watch as the tips of their white hair dance and sway toward one another, like magnets, but Cailian pushes her away. "As much as I would love to do that with you, I think it's best if we wait for a better moment."

"I don't know what you mean, but okay," she answers, watching as Cailian throws his hair into a messy bun.

"Just for now. There are other matters we have to focus on."

"Yeah, like how you say my sister is ice eleven but has two vampire parents. It's impossible."

"She's different. She's always been different, and you know it," Cailian spits, closing the front door behind him. "You have powers you don't understand. Your touch can be cold, right?"

She nods.

"A witch must have bound ice elven blood to you somehow. I don't know how, but that's the only way."

"Can we talk about this later?" Alexander pinches the bridge of his nose. "We have a werewolf to save, and I have to get my beloved out of bed to make this mixture for Aziel. It won't be easy for her, so please, can we focus on that?"

"Of course." Cailian grabs Rarity's hand and kisses the top. "I am forever yours, My Snow. We will have plenty of time to talk, Rarity. Such a beautiful name."

Rarity leans into him, and Cailian already looks different.

Warmer is the only way I know how to explain it.

"Okay. Meet in Maven's library. I'll bring her down."

"Yes, Alpha." First, I lie Ru on the couch and cover her up with a blanket. She's out cold, sleeping deeply. "So proud of you, mate. I love you," I whisper in her ear, slipping the bag off her shoulder.

Everyone follows me into Maven's library. There's a table in the middle, herbs in different-sized bottles scattered everywhere, and her spell book is open. The pages are worn, but the ink is fresh.

It's the treatment ingredients for Aziel.

A breath catches in my throat, and I close my eyes, focusing on Aziel. I'm exhausted, but this needs to be done as soon as possible. He's currently talking to himself; the sickness has its fingers wrapped around his soul.

He's suffocating.

"Kill everything. Kill everyone. Everyone is the enemy."

He switches tactics, pulling from the nightmare of when we were spelled and making up his own scenario.

"Anwyll is stupid. A sorry excuse for a pup. His mate is mine. I'll kill her in front of him, rip her heart and lungs from her body, then squeeze them to pieces in front of him." Aziel hysterically laughs. *"Yes, I'll do that. I'll feast on her bones, lick her clean from my talons. Maybe I'll fuck her first. Show her what a real werewolf is like. I'll skin her flesh from her, then use it as a blanket. Oh, the coven will be mad. So mad. I don't care. I'll kill them too. I'll swim in the lake of blood I create from their bodies."* He cackles and then it turns into a manic howl.

Everyone hears the call he gives, and a tear drips down my face. "If this doesn't work, I'll have to kill him. I promised him. I promised."

"It will work." Rarity presses her head against my shoulder. "You have to have faith."

I listen in on him again, but this time, he is crying.

"I wouldn't dare. I wouldn't. I love them. They are my family. I'd kill myself before I did something like that." Then, like a switch, the sickness grabs him again. *"They make you weak. They are pathetic. You will kill all of them. Anwyll isn't your brother."*

I bend over, clutching my stomach, the blow of his words knocking the breath out of my lungs.

"Anwyll," Maven's voice makes me straighten up.

Tears fall freely as I run up and hug her. "Maven. Thank you for taking the time away from your newborns. I'm forever in your debt."

"Nonsense. We are family. I'm happy to help." She's slow to walk to find her place in front of her spell book.

"Your brother deserves peace. He isn't well. He is skin and bone. He won't live much longer if we don't do this."

"He's going to be an uncle. We have to save him."

"Oh, Anwyll. Congratulations. I'm so happy for you. Don't be sad. I need you to hold on to hope. Energy matters with a spell like this. The more positive vibes I get from nature, the better the outcome. Tune the poison out that your brother is spewing. It isn't him. Okay?"

I nod, trying to agree, but there's doubt creeping in. I hand Maven the bag she gave us, and she grins, unzips it, then waves her hand. A dull yellow glow appears, and the contents she needs float from the bag.

Purple wolfsbane, check.

Unicorn hair, check.

Clover, check.

"We have vampire tears." She grabs a vial from the table and lifts it in the air. The liquid travels back and forth, shining against the candlelight, and the pearl hues of the tears glow. "And we have the vial of werewolf blood we collected while you were away." She checks the inventory and frowns. "Where's the heartsnow?"

"Oh, I have it. I'm sorry." Cailian pulls the heartsnow free of his bag and hands it to Maven. "It's an honor to see a Wildes Witch perform magic."

Maven winces and grabs the edge of the table, suddenly looking pale.

"We don't have to do this. You just had twins. We shouldn't be doing this. Go rest, Maven," I argue, taking the vials from her.

"No. I don't know what you have been through, but I bet it was horrible. I can handle a little pain for this." With the color drained from her face, she grabs her small cauldron. She pours vampire tears first. "They are from Lex when our children were born," she whispers. "Don't tell him I told you."

I chuckle. "Your secret is safe with me."

She adds three heartsnow petals, three purple wolfsbane petals, three of the unicorn hairs, and one six-leaf clover, then she pricks her own finger, adding one drop of powerful blood.

"It's muddled, then shaken, not stirred," she says, crushing the ingredients together. Fire blooms in the cauldron, smoke sways, and then a sheen from the vampire tears glistens just as the concoction settles.

She pours it into a glass, covers it with her hand, then shakes it.

"When this is over, I hope to meet the twins," I say, not wanting to make the moment about me. I don't want her to feel like I'm using her.

"Whenever you want. Enver and Esmeray are beautiful. They have been waiting for their Uncle Anwyll."

Uncle.

I love that.

"Enver and Esmeray. Beautiful names."

"We wanted to name our daughter after Alexander's mother, but with a twist."

"Very unique."

"Well, when it comes to names, we had to keep the tradition." She sets the glass down with a cheeky grin.

"Okay, it's ready." She presses a needle into the liquid, pulling the syringe until it's full. "This should do it."

The last two weeks have been amazing and horrible. I never want to relive that experience. I hold the syringe and stare at it. Chunks of clover float, and the vampire tears add a shimmer to the red of the blood.

This holds all the answers and hope. My entire world is

in this syringe. I wouldn't know where to begin if it didn't work. I have never lived in a world where my brother didn't exist. If I had to kill him, I wouldn't know how to live the rest of my life.

"Can someone please keep an eye on Ru while I go to the catacombs? I don't like it when she is out of my sight right now. She's too vulnerable to leave alone." I roll my head over my shoulders as I shift, fur sprouting over my entire body as I grow taller, wider, and stronger.

Rarity takes my paw. "I'll watch her. Don't worry."

I breathe easier knowing my friend will watch her. "Thank you."

"I'll go down with you," Greyson offers. "You need someone to have your back. He's more werewolf than human since the last time you saw him."

Curling my fingers over the needle, I take a second to gather myself. I have no idea what I'm about to see. "Thank you. Thank you to everyone who waited here while Ru and I went on the journey. You all took care of Aziel while we were gone. I'm so thankful. I know it hasn't been easy."

"Anything for family, Anwyll." Luca pats my back, and as I walk out the door, every member of my pack gives me reassurance with some form of touch.

I stop at the couch, bending down to give Ru a kiss. "I'll be back to take you to our room. We're home now, Ru." I comb my talons through her hair. "We're home."

"I have her. I promise." Rarity sits at the end of the couch, and Cailian is behind her, following his mate everywhere.

Leaving Ru is so difficult. Her being in heat hibernation calls to my animalistic side. I want to lie with her in our bed and hold her while she rests, but I don't have that luxury right now. I have to go save my brother.

Staying in my strongest form, the talons clip the floor as I walk to the door in the library that leads to the catacombs. Alexander opens it, and a darkened tunnel is all there is. Greyson is next to me, then leads the way.

Maven's black roses still pulse in the middle to give light. Greyson opens the next door, leading down another tunnel. We don't speak to one another. The further we get, the more I feel the chill in the air, and my brother's sickness taints every breath I try to take. I feel the sting of his illness in my lungs, and my eyes water.

Greyson comes to the trapdoor in the floor, flinging it open, and that's when my brother's psychotic break echoes freely. The hate he spews are knives in my heart.

"Are you ready?" my friend asks just as a maddening cackle from Aziel sounds.

"No," I say honestly, jumping through the trapdoor. I land on my hind legs, dust kicking up into a cloud.

Greyson jumps next, and the hysterical laughter of my brother makes a whine escape from me.

"He isn't the same as when you left. I need to warn you. You can't hesitate when you see him. You have to inject this treatment."

"You don't think I know that? I've spent the better part of two weeks fighting for my life for the shit in this syringe. I'm not going to fail now." The catacombs look the same as when I left. There are cobwebs in the corners, but other than that, it's clean.

When I come to the end of the hall, before taking the turn right, I stop, needing a minute to gather any strength I have left. So much bad shit happens down here. Atreyu is still in a coma, trapped in a cement coffin, and Severide never leaves his side. He is dying slowly because he barely eats, barely spends time with his family, but I think it goes beyond his worry for his comatose son.

I think he misses his mate, and now that they are back from the in between, because the portals are active, life without her is too hard to live. I can't blame him. I couldn't live without Ru.

"I smell you, brother," Aziel's words are sardonic with a hint of humor, as if he finds it funny. "I smell your fear and hesitation. You've always been weak!" he roars, the chains rattling while he tugs on them. "I hate you. I hate that my life is ruined because of you. And you're the one who gets the mate."

I press my head against the wall, shutting my eyes as he spews his venom. Greyson's presence helps me, but it doesn't fix me; it doesn't give me the energy I need to take on my older brother. I've looked up to Aziel my entire life. He holds bravery and selflessness to a level I've always wanted to achieve, but I know I'll never get there.

"It's all your fault, you know. That we were under that spell. It's your fault I'm like this. I'll never fucking forgive you." A sick clicking sound follows, and I peek my head around the corner to see his head moving in ways that remind me of a body taken over with possession. "Waste of fucking space. I should have let the warlock kill you when I had the chance!" he yells.

"It isn't him talking," Greyson reminds me. "You have to remember that."

"I know." I do know that, but in this moment, that doesn't seem to matter.

"When I'm free, I'm going to kill you. I'm going to rip your heart out and feast on it. Then, I'll kill your pregnant mate. I can smell it on her. I can smell the pathetic runt of a pup growing inside her. It doesn't deserve to live. I bet her pregnant blood tastes sooo good too."

Growling in anger at how he speaks about my mate, my child, I jump from my hiding spot, and roar at him. Spit flies from my mouth, and I charge at him, blinded with rage.

I want to kill him.

I don't care about saving him anymore.

"It isn't him!" Greyson grips my wrist, our strength colliding as he tries to stop me, and I try to pull away from him. "Anwyll, remember," he says. "Remember the day you found him, begging you to kill him if it got too bad. Remember the kindness your brother holds. The sickness is slowly murdering that inside him. "I know what he is saying is hard to hear but—"

"Shut the fuck up, you bloodsucker," Aziel sneers, his arms wide as he tugs on the warded chains. "You don't know anything. I'm going to pluck your fangs from your mouth and stab you in the eyes with them, watch as your tears run bloody."

My own tears fall as I get a good look at the werewolf who used to be my brother. He's skinny. Patches of fur are missing from his skin. I can see his ribs. He's foaming at the mouth, and his eyes are clouded with white.

Is he blind?

He sniffs the air and his eyes round. "Anwyll?" He looks around for me, but he can't tell where I am at. He truly can't see me. "Anwyll, is that you?"

I run to him and nod frantically, forgetting he can't see me. I grip the back of his neck and press our foreheads together. "It's me, brother. It's me. I'm here. I'm back."

He breaks, sobbing in loud wails that tear at my heart. "Please, kill me," he begs. "Kill me. You promised. You promised me. I can't hold it back much longer. I can't. It's so hard. Please, I'm begging you. Kill me."

I wrap my arms around him, my tears dripping onto his bony shoulder. The rivulets of his spine press against my paws, digging their sharp points into my skin. One squeeze, one powerful chokehold on him, and I could put him out of his misery.

"Do it," he says. "Do it. I love you. I love you. It's okay."

I press the needle against his neck.

"Fucking kill me, you coward!" His sickness breaks free, and I stab the needle into his skin, injecting him with a myth that can cure him.

"I can never kill you." My voice cracks while he falls limp in my arms. "You're too much a part of me, brother. I'll find a thousand different ways to save you, but killing you, never."

"You promised," he slurs, lifting his head with trembling efforts. "You swore."

I watch the white clouding his eyes spark to flames.

"I'm killing the poison inside you, that I promise," I say just as his eyes clear, but then they roll to the back of his head, and he falls unconscious. He lies on the ground, unmoving, but I can see the slow rise and fall of his chest.

"What now?" Greyson asks, squatting to get a closer look at my brother.

I drop the syringe, and it breaks against the ground. "I don't know."

Chapter Forty-Five

RU

I wake on a gasping breath. I'm warm, sweating, and feel disoriented.

"Ru, you're okay. You're home." Anwyll's voice is right next to my ear as I struggle to keep my eyes open already.

I don't want to fall back asleep. I want to know what's going on.

Pressing my cheek against Anwyll's chest, I sigh, fighting the slumber trying to pull me under. My eyes blink open, and I'm surrounded by the coven.

"What's going on?" I manage to ask through a rough, sleepy voice. "The treatment. Your brother."

"It's all taken care of, Ru. You've been sleeping for thirty hours," Alexander informs, and I flinch, thinking back to the last thing I remember.

"Thirty?"

"Heat hibernation. It happens after a mating like you had," Cailian explains, who is sitting next to Rarity.

"Oh." I flip around and look up at Anwyll's human face. He has a few days' worth of scruff on his face, but it's the dark circles under his eyes that have me worried. "Your brother?"

"Don't know yet. He's been unconscious since I gave him the treatment," my mate explains. The sadness in his tone has me pressing a kiss against his cheek.

"We don't know what happens next. No book says. He might not wake up. We don't know. We have to give it time. He's in his room now. He hasn't fought. He is very still, but I still put silver chains on him. I have newborns to protect now. I can't take any chances." My Alpha holds his son, wrapped in blue. He looks just like Alexander. Maven holds a pink bundle, and I'm reminded about the fact that we are related.

That's my niece and nephew by blood.

"Not to change the subject, but I've waited longer than I've liked, Master Monreaux. I need to see Reuel. The elf."

"Why?" Rarity and Alexander ask at the same time.

"It's okay," Reuel finally comes out of his room for the first time since we have arrived. "No need to get defensive. I should have spoken to the prince when he first arrived, but I wasn't ready," he explains, coming down the steps.

That's when I see the hint of silver glowing in his veins, and I grip Anwyll's hand with every ounce of strength I have.

Cailian stands from the couch as Reuel comes closer. They are similar in height, tall, lithe, yet muscular.

"How can I help you, Prince Cailian?" Reuel asks, never breaking eye contact.

"Maybe we can go somewhere private and talk."

"What you have to say, you can say in front of my coven."

Cailian darts his eyes around, landing on a few curious

faces before meeting Reuel's unwavering glare. "I believe you are the lost bloodline of the Woodland Elves. You are their prince. They have been without leadership for many years, and they are weak without you. I don't know how you are here or have wandered so far away from home, but I can take you back."

"This is my home," Reuel's voice darkens. "I don't know what a Woodland Elf is. I wasn't raised by elves. I was raised by werewolves."

"This is my home," he repeats. "This is what I know."

"And what you know is killing you. You want to do more. You feel it, don't you? You're meant for more. Meant to be more."

"I don't want to be more!" Reuel shouts, and it takes all of us by surprise. He's always calm and collected, even-tempered. The babies cry, and his shoulders sag. "I'm sorry to disappoint you, but I'm not the royalty you're looking for." Reuel turns away, and Cailian snags his arm. The ice travels up Reuel's veins, but then the ice drips from Reuel's body, and small green vines begin to wrap around Cailian's arms.

"Don't touch me."

"That is how I know you're of royal blood. Only royalty can overcome my power, but Woodland Elves are special. They are fierce and powerful, Reuel. The strongest of all elves. You're getting stronger, but there is nothing here for you. Your people need you."

"These are my people." Reuel's vines sink into his skin, and he takes a calming breath.

I've never seen Reuel control vines like that before. It's... amazing.

"I can't help you. I'm sorry you wasted your trip here."

"It isn't wasted," Cailian states, turning to Rarity. "But I won't give up on bringing you home."

"I am home, Prince." With a snap of his fingers, Reuel disappears, and Cailian curses.

"Fuck," he groans, spinning around to face my alpha. "He will continue to deny himself, but his power will grow. He is meant to lead his people. You know what that's like. He doesn't belong here, no matter how much that hurts you and everyone else. He needs to be with his kind."

"He is my family. My coven member. If he doesn't want to leave, then that is his decision. I won't force him away."

"Then you are a pathetic leader," Cailian hisses.

Everyone stands, and vampires hiss at the elf for being rude to Alexander.

Alexander places his son in Luca's arms and stands nose to nose with Cailian. "You will not disrespect me in my home, or I'll make sure your elves do not have a leader at all. Do I make myself clear?"

Cailian snarls before vanishing before our eyes, leaving Rarity staring at air.

"Lex, I'm so sorry. I..."

"You don't have to explain the poor actions of your mate, Rarity. You two don't know each other yet. I can feel how upset he is. He feels strongly about helping the Woodland Elves. I can't fault him for that."

I yawn, and everyone turns to me when it's louder than I expected.

"You're hiding something," Amberella says, tilting her head to the side. "You don't want to say. Your aura is muggy with truths needing to be told."

I love it here, I do, but the special abilities some of them share drive me crazy sometimes. "It can wait. We've had enough going on, don't you think? It can wait."

"It can't. Not when it has to do with Maven."

"Come on," I groan, swaying with dizziness as I sit up. "We just got home. Cailian pissed off Alexander. Maven just had twins. Aziel is sleeping off the sickness with the treatment we nearly died getting. I'm pregnant. I'm fighting to stay awake due to this hibernation that's apparently a thing, and now you want me to get into this? Can't we have a moment of peace?"

"Sure, when the truth is told. That's the only time peace truly exists." Amberella is unbothered as she sits there with her legs crossed, appearing as sophisticated as ever.

"Fine." I toss the blanket from me and hold my stomach when it rolls.

"Ru." Anwyll steadies to me.

"I'm okay." I lock eyes with Maven, her soft smile giving encouragement just as the gothic black grandfather clock chimes behind her. "When we were in the Unwanted Lands, the place on my home planet where leprechauns go where they don't get their luck—"

"—You don't have yours," Maven gasps. "That's what is different about you. It's gone. I don't sense it. What happened?"

"I gave it to Anwyll to save his life. Anyway, that's not important. While we were there, I met a man and a young woman. I knew him. He was my father. I was always under the impression he was sent to the Unwanted Lands because he never got his luck, but that wasn't the case. He had a ring that allowed him to be a dimensional traveler, even when the portals were closed, and that's how he met my mom, then yours, then Pearl's, the young woman with him. We're half-sisters. And he told me..." I swallow when I see tears swell in her forest-green eyes, but she doesn't seem shocked either. "He said your mother died a long time ago.

She gave you her magic before she opened and closed the portal for herself. She was getting away from Brenden, but the lack of her magic slowly killed her. I'm sorry. I'm so sorry."

Maven rocks her daughter, giving her a watery grin just as a tear falls. "I figured she was dead, but to know I have sisters is wonderful. I'm happy you told me, and I knew we kind of looked alike," she jokes, taking my hand in hers. "What's our father like?" She seems dissociated, her tone soft but robotic.

"Horrible and selfish. He whored around the universe knocking up women," I say a bit too bluntly. "You aren't missing anything. I unlinked my luck from his, so I'm not considered his daughter anymore."

Esmeray coos, wrapping her small hand around Maven's index finger. The Coven Witch stays quiet, thinking about everything I said, and everyone senses the slight tension.

"And our sister? Pearl?"

"I don't know. She's with our father."

"I'll have to find her then and bring her here."

"With him? No, Maven. No, that's a horrible idea. He isn't good. He isn't a good person. He is bad for you."

"I don't care about him. Only her. She deserves to be with people capable of love. I'm going to go lie down with the twins. I think I've had enough for the day. I'm exhausted."

"Of course, Beloved. Let me help you." Alexander takes his son from Luca and blurs Maven with their daughter up to their room.

I sigh, feeling like I've ruined everything. Why didn't I stay asleep?

"I think it's best if we try calling it too, My Lucky Charm. We need rest. All of us do. It's been hectic here."

"Agreed," Luca concurs, stretching his arms over his head. "Tomorrow is a new day."

And I can't wait to leave this one behind.

Chapter Forty-Six

ANWYLL

"I'm going to need you to wake up because the tension here is way too thick." I try to make a joke as I speak to my brother. He's lying there in the middle of the bed, still in werewolf form, and the bed swallows him.

My big, mighty, strong, deadly, and protective brother is gone. I'm left with someone broken, small, and ill. His cheeks are sunken in, and his arms remind me of a child.

I lean my elbows on the bed and grab his hand, a horrified choke leaving me. I can feel every bone, see every vein, and even his talons are dull. Gone are the shiny onyx talons that can tear through flesh like butter, and instead, yellow, chipped claws take their place.

"Please," I plead with him, holding his hand to my forehead. "I can't lose you. I can't. Please, wake up."

He doesn't move.

"Aziel, I can't do this without you. I don't know how to be a father," I admit on a whisper, hoping it magically wakes him up so he can slap me upside the head.

But he lies still.

"I'm excited. I don't want you to think I'm not. I am. Bu

is my entire life. You're really going to like her. She's strong-willed and smart, god so smart. My favorite quality about her is something you two share. She's so selfless." I swallow, thinking of the two people in my life who have sacrificed so much for me. "Like you, she didn't hesitate to save me. I don't understand why. I don't know what's so special about me that you two would do that, but I'm thankful. It's your faith in me that keeps me going." The silver chains keep him weighed down on the bed, not that they are needed. He wouldn't have the strength to attack anyone. I can see the middle of his sternum through the dull skin of his hide.

"She's perfect, Aziel. I'm not good enough for her, but I try to be. I try to remember everything you taught me before being spelled by the warlock. I want you to meet your niece or nephew. You'd be so happy. I just want my brother back. I did everything." My shoulders shake with defeat as I sob. "I did everything!" I raise my voice, forgetting not to wake everyone. "I traveled dimensions for you. I killed. I almost died. My mate almost died. You have to survive, or so help me, I'll keep my promise and I'll fucking kill you."

I watch him, waiting for him to smirk, to pat my hand to tell me I worry too much, but damn it, he just lies there.

"Do you remember when we hid under the floor? That warlock had just killed our pack. You placed your hand over my mouth because I was breathing hard. I was so scared, and you— you were so strong during that entire time. Even when he found us and he threatened me, you didn't blink. You gave him what he wanted. For me." I talk to myself since he isn't able to reply, but it feels good to get this off my chest. "I don't know if I ever thanked you for being there for me. Even while we were under the spell, you somehow still protected me. I'll never forget everything you did for me. I just...I really need you back, okay? I need you to fight like you never have before. I need you to come back to us because this life is so good, brother. It's good. It's the best life we have ever had, and I need to experience this next step in my life with you. I'm going to be a dad. I need you to teach me all the things so I can teach my son or daughter. God," I chuckle. "What if I have a girl? We won't let anyone get near her. I don't even feel bad. No man or werewolf or shifter, elf, or any other creature will ever be good enough for my daughter. I bet you'd let her braid your fur." I chuckle at the thought of him in werewolf form, a grumpy look on his face as my daughter braids his hair with bright, colorful hair ties. He might even have makeup on.

"Oh, that's a funny thought. Maybe she'd even paint your talons bright pink. You'd allow her to." I plop back in the chair and sigh, wanting that to happen more than ever because I know Aziel would let my daughter do whatever she wanted.

I drop his hand and stand, becoming angry at him for lying there, leaving me wondering if he is dying. With a roar, I kick the chair across the room, and one of the legs snaps off when it hits the wall.

"You're supposed to be here for me!" I yell at him, stomping to the side of his bed, then lean over him until the tip of my nose touches his. "What the hell is wrong with you that you're not!" I grit through tight teeth, waiting for his eyes to flutter open.

Nothing.

I grip his fragile shoulders and shake him. "Wake up, Aziel. Wake the fuck up! You've been through worse. You've experienced worse. You can beat this."

But he continues to be deathly still.

I slide the second chair from the small table, pulling it across the floor until I'm seated again. I hold my brother's hand and nod when I realize that everything I want, he can't give me.

"It's okay," I reassure him. "I'm not mad at you. It isn't your fault. It's okay. It's all okay."

His chest rises and falls so slowly, his lungs wheeze, and his heart beats so slowly, I'm not sure if he'll make it through the night.

"It's okay," I say again, realizing the time with my brother might be cut short. "It's okay if you can't fight anymore. It's okay to be tired. I love you. I miss you."

"Anwyll?" Ru's voice comes from behind me.

I startle, not expecting to hear anyone this time of day. "I'm okay. Go back to sleep." I came into my brother's room while everyone in the house was sleeping, vampires included. It's daytime, and it's been another twenty-four hours since Ru and I have come home.

"I can't sleep without you. Especially right now."

"Right. The hibernation." I don't mean to sound guilty, but I feel like I've ruined her life. She's stuck with dangerous heats, violent mating's, and now hibernations that I didn't even know about. I didn't get to warn her about them because I didn't know. What else don't I know? On top of all that, she changed herself for me.

She has no luck.

I don't think I'll ever be able to accept what she sacrificed for me.

"He'll wake up, Anwyll. I have faith." Her hand grabs my shoulder, and I release a breath.

"He looks... terrible. He looks like he's on the verge of dying. What if we are too late? What if we did more harm than good? I should have killed him. I promised I would, and I didn't. And now he's... this."

"It's better than him screaming and crying out nonsense, right? This is a step, Anwyll. You have to give his body time to heal."

"I just need to know if he is in pain."

"I can help," Luna pokes her head in, and I quickly wipe my face of tears. I don't want anyone to see me crying. "I already know you're in pain. It woke me up."

"I'm sorry, Luna."

"You feel so much guilt, and you shouldn't." She rubs her eyes as she sits on the bed next to my brother. "I'm unable to heal him. His sickness, his type, it doesn't allow that."

"I understand. I just need to know if he is okay."

Luna presses her hand against his chest. She closes her eyes and concentrates. A confused expression pinches her face. "I-I don't know." She removes her palm, massaging the middle of it to bring it to life again. "I can't see anything. It's just dark. I feel nothing. I'm sorry, Anwyll."

"Nothing? Like no pain or literally nothing?" Ru is forceful with her questions.

"Nothing. He's alive, but that's all I have for you. I'm sorry. It's probably the treatment blocking me. If I were you, I'd go to bed. Check again tomorrow. You being here doesn't help because I don't think he can sense you, Anwyll. Go hold your mate."

Luna touches me, relieving some of my guilt, and I feel lighter.

"Thank you, Luna. You didn't have to do that."

"Please," she snorts. "I don't want the waves of guilt wafting from you, waking me up again." Luna leaves us, and I gently lay my brother's hand on the bed.

She's right.

I have to stop fussing over what I can't change.

I gather my mate in my arms and with one last parting look, I close the door behind me, leaving my brother alone.

Aziel

I'm right here, Anwyll. I can hear you. I'm right here. Why can't I move? Why can't I speak? No one can hear me, but it hurts.

Flames lick my entire soul. Pain, unlike any other, engulfs my body. Every molecule, every cell, becomes reborn.

I scream at the top of my lungs, but I can't move. I'm paralyzed. I can't move. I can't cry for help.

Waves of fire and ice pour through me, burning out the sickness as I lie here, unable to ask for help.

I'm dying. I have to be.

Looking in, I bet everyone sees peace, but looking out, I'm trapped in a broken body, roaring in agony I've never felt before.

Someone help me.

Someone hear me.

Someone please...

Kill me.

Chapter Forty-Seven

RU

It's been three days with no change in Aziel's progress. He's still lying there, but I think he looks different. It's subtle. His fur looks healthier.

Maybe.

Or maybe I'm hoping for something that it isn't there.

Whiskey, Maven's grandpa's familiar, whines as if he can sense my unease. I scratch behind his ears.

"Such a good boy. Aren't you?" I tell him just as Esmeray cries from the nursery, and Enver follows right behind her.

Whiskey runs to their room, so protective of the babies.

"I know. I know," Master Monreaux tries to soothe his children. "You want your mom. I want her too. She's beautiful, but she's making a water haven for our new guests with that Cailian guy. I don't know if I like him. Okay, that's not true. I do like him, but our power collides too much. He needs to go back home, but he is a man of his word and is going to bring some of Anwyll and Ru's friends here."

I peek my head into the nursery and place a hand against my stomach when I see a very powerful vampire holding each child in his arms, bouncing as he walks to calm them down. It's adorable.

Leaving them to have their privacy, I head downstairs, and Reuel is staring out the window, watching Cailian and Maven talk.

"Are you okay?" I ask him.

He doesn't say anything at first, then moves his hands behind his back. "What were they like? My...I mean, the Woodland Elves."

I think back to the short interaction I had with them. "They saved us, me and Anwyll. We had fallen from a cliff because of stone giants, and we fell. And fell...fell so fast we ended up entering a portal to their planet. Anwyll took the hit. He hit the ground so hard, I swear I heard every bone break. I called for help, cried, horrified he was bleeding everywhere, and the Woodland Elves showed up. They took us straight to Cailian."

"Why didn't they save you? Why go to him?"

"Princes are immensely powerful, but only princes have access to warlocks and witches. Since the Woodland Elves don't have that, they couldn't heal him."

"So, if I am the Prince, I could help them with that too."

"There's no pressure."

"All there is, is pressure." He vanishes in front of me, going who-knows-where, and I step outside, heading toward Maven and Cailian.

I wonder what Reuel will decide, and if he chooses to leave, will we ever see him again?

"I'm thinking it has to be deep." Anwyll tries to explain to both Maven and Cailian what we saw in the Unwanted Lands. "The issue is that it needs to be big. They need enough room to swim. You know?"

"We have plenty of land for that. I can make secret

passageways underwater too, to other places they can go. I'm so excited to have an oasis for them. Is it that bad there?"

"The water is toxic. It blinded me for two hours." I approach them unexpectedly, and Anwyll runs up to me, hauling me into a big hug.

He swings me around. "How are you feeling?"

"Better since I got to cuddle you for a few days." I press my hand against the tiny swell of my stomach. "I can't believe I'm showing already."

"Werewolves only have three-month pregnancies, so it will be over before you know it."

"Three months. I'm so jealous of you right now. My twins didn't come until three days after their due date."

"What about elves?" I ask Cailian, and sadness creeps over his face as he stares at the house. Something happened between Rarity and Cailian. I haven't seen them together in a few days.

"Six months," he says wistfully before looking away and staring at the ground. "Anyway, this is the perfect place. We should get started. The sooner I can retrieve Irving, the better, and then I can go back to my people." Cailian places his hand on his hips and rolls his shoulders, sweat breaking out over his skin. "It's too hot for me here." The tops of his shoulders are red, and he rubs the back of his neck, clearly overheated.

It's the middle of winter too. It's a warmer day, and it's clear he isn't used to it. Now that I think about it, it is much colder there. The atmosphere is different. The air is thinner where Cailian is from, but easier to breathe somehow.

"What about Rarity?" I daringly ask, taking Anwyll's hand in mine.

He stands underneath the shade of a tree and kicks the

ground. "She's upset with me for how I treated her brother. I'm not sure if she'll come with me. I realize it would be hard for her to leave. I won't force her."

"You'd be surprised by how far an apology can go," Anwyll suggests.

Cailian is about to reply when the gurgles of screams echo. Maven groans, and Anwyll rubs his temples.

"You've got to be kidding," he mumbles.

"What is that? It's horrible." I cover my ears, and Maven presses her hand against the ground, mumbling something under her breath.

The wind sways, the leaves pull from the trees, and water begins to seep from the ground.

"I suggest everyone move toward the house." Maven lifts her hand, and a pulse of energy shoots from her palm, acres of land changing from lush woods to blue waters. The woods stretch, and a few trees stay deep within the new lake.

All of us hurry back, trying to beat the water sloshing, and we make it, just as the lake waves splash against the grassy shore.

"Wow. That was the most impressive thing I've ever seen," Cailian says, dipping his finger into the water only for it to freeze. "Feels good. I might stay out there for a little bit to cool down."

The screams come again, and I turn my head to see where the god-awful sound is coming from. I rub my eyes when I see motorcycles appear and disappear in the blink of an eye. They remind me of the Void from our journey. "What is that?" I ask again.

"Hell's Harvesters. You're about to meet the Four Horsemen. We haven't seen them since Halloween."

Anwyll told me about Halloween, but we have only

talked about it once. It was a horrible experience for everyone, and poor Finnick hasn't been the same since.

"What are they doing here?" Cailian asks, splashing his feet in the water as he sits on a rock.

"I don't know." Maven wipes her hands on her jeans. "But it can't be good."

"Well, on that note. I'm going to go find Irving. I'll see you guys soon." The Ice Elf tosses a handful of sunset powder, giving us a quick finger wave before walking through the portal.

The demons park their bikes made of bones. Their boots clink with every heavy step, and all of them are wearing leather jackets.

They are giant, bigger than Anwyll in his werewolf form.

"It's good to see you again, Maven."

"Abaddon," she greets. "War, Death, Famine," she nods to the others. "Still no Conquest?"

"He's almost done repairing himself in Hell."

"What are you doing here?" Alexander asks from the porch.

"Nothing bad." The demon, Abaddon, lifts his hands in innocence. "The creatures we rescued from the carnival—they would like to come here." His eyes look out to the new lake Maven just created. "The siren and the kraken would like that very much."

"All of them?" Maven asks.

"All," Abaddon nods.

I lean against Anwyll, feeling the need to hide behind my mate.

Abaddon's eyes land on me, and he smiles, showing his sharp teeth. "No need to be afraid, little wolf. I won't hurt you."

"I'm glad my friend could help you," Death speaks to us. "You met one of my Voids."

"He calls me Spot," Anwyll grumbles, and I have to do everything I can not to laugh.

"Lorcan always was a pain in the ass. Don't mind him."

"Thank you," I add quickly, not wanting to piss off Death. "For the help."

"Any friend of Maven's is a friend of ours," he says.

"We came to say congratulations," War announces. "The twins have been born. Your werewolf is pregnant. We wanted to celebrate."

"Why don't I believe you?" Luna questions from the front door. "You shouldn't have come at all. We don't need you here."

Luna runs into the house, and War sprints to her. "Luna, wait. Luna!"

Reuel steps in front of War to stop him from chasing after his friend. They argue, and Death takes that second to come up to me and Anwyll. He touches our shoulders, and a coldness drips into my veins, something dark and sinister.

His touch is very unwelcome, but again, I won't tell Death that.

"Your brother is on a very thin line," he informs us. "He is in the balance of life and death. I sense him."

"He's dying?"

I rest my head on Anwyll's shoulder and rub my hand up and down his arm.

"No. He's lost. He can't find his body. He's lost in a very dangerous plain where creatures worse than demons would gladly feed on his spirit. It's why your friend can't sense him in his sleep. The treatment worked, but he is trapped now. His physical body is stuck here, but his soul is elsewhere."

"Well, get it back. How can we get it back?" Anwyll rushes. "I'll go there. I'll help him. Take me there."

"I can't."

"You can't or won't? You're Death. You can do anything."

"I can't do anything. I have to respect the balance."

"How long do we have? Until he can't be saved."

"His spirit has until the lunar eclipse. If he can't find his way back by himself, he'll be stuck there forever."

Anwyll heaves, losing control of his temper, and bursts into his werewolf form, sprinting away from all of us. He roars to the night sky, running off his sorrow.

"How can we get him back?"

"I don't know," Death states sadly. "I've never seen anyone overcome it before. Being stuck between plains is painful. The sickness had already transported his body to the other side for me to take, but the treatment saved him from me. All he needs is his soul in his body."

"So it's similar to Atreyu being in a coma."

"No," Death shakes his head, a crowd gathering around us while he explains. "Alexander's brother is in a coma. His spirit is asleep. For instance, Alexander's ghost didn't wake up until Maven stepped foot in the house. Aziel's spirit is awake, and he is fighting for his life in a place where I put the worst of the worst."

"But he can't hear us," I add. "We try to talk to him, and he doesn't respond."

"He can hear you, but he can't move. He can't speak. His body is frozen. And the pain... the pain is surreal. The heart-snow is twisting the sickness in his body, healing his phys-ical form so when his spirit finds a way back, he will be healthy. His spirit form isn't sick."

"He's suffering," I say with realization, and a few members of the coven begin to cry. "In both forms."

"Yes, but if I have to reap him, I'll make sure everyone has a chance to say goodbye."

"But you're a god, right? Or similar? You're one of the most powerful beings. Can't you break this rule? Fuck balance. Bring him back."

"I can't do that," he snarls, showing his true form for a split second, and fear possesses me.

Large wings spread from his back, and half of his face is sewn with human skin, while the rest looks monstrous. He has two long horns, one twisted like a spiral while the other is curved.

"I change fate, then Fate herself will correct every domino effect. I save Aziel, so many other people will have to die. I can't change Fate."

"Well, bring her down. I'll bitch her out then," I yell at Death, trying my hardest not to shove him. I know how pathetic I sound, but I'll do anything. Anwyll will be ruined if anything happens to his brother.

"Fate doesn't answer calls," Famine drawls in a southern accent. "She's too busy making sure all you lot get mates." He pinches his nose, reminding me of someone thinking an animal is cute. "Ain't that just adorable? She don't have time to go cleaning up after your messes."

I growl at Famine, letting my werewolf slip through.

"Oh, I'm so scared." He trails over to me, cocking his head in amusement. "I could make you choke on your own blood. Don't you know I could wipe all of you out with one little disease? Maybe I'll start with the werewolves and give you heartworm like the dogs you are."

A lethal roar soars from above me, and Anwyll tackles Famine to the ground.

"Anwyll! No!" I scream just as Abaddon lifts Anwyll from his brother, tossing him to the side.

"Enough," Abaddon states just as Anwyll chokes, then begins to cough up blood.

"Anwyll?"

He falls to his knees, then forward onto his hands, more blood flying from his mouth with long strings that he gags on.

Worms.

"Stop it! Stop! Please. I'm sorry, okay. Don't. Please," I beg, holding onto my mate while he struggles to breathe.

"Famine," Abaddon warns.

"You suck the fun out of everything," he drawls, waving his hand in the air.

Anwyll inhales, the blood gone, and the worms vanish. I hold my mate in my arms while I stare up at Famine.

"You're a monster."

"I'm a Horseman. Learn your place."

"Enough," Abaddon bellows so loud the power causes the trees to bend, and clouds darken in the sky. "We are here to make friendships. Our futures are intertwined. We have to work together. If we are at each other's throats, we won't ever be able to help each other. Now, we are so close to finding where Brenden decided to rest, but Azazel has so many people working for him in purgatory. It's us against them, and I'd rather us win, understand?"

Everyone nods, but the silence is awkward.

Dottie's creature emerges again, this time, a bright orange surrounding her entire body like armor, and for the first time, I see sharp, pointy ears. The rest is still a blur.

"I haven't seen one of you in a very long time," Abaddon says. "I wasn't sure at first, but now I know."

"You know what I am? Tell me, please—"

"—I can't. If I do, I'm as good as dead, and I'd rather not be the reason you earn a—"

Famine slaps Abaddon to keep his mouth shut. "You're sayin' too much."

Dottie shouts in rage, her creature exploding from her body. Lightning bolts shoot across the sky and thunder claps. Dottie hurries inside the house, Drayce hot on her heels.

"That was mean," I say, brushing a piece of Anwyll's hair out of his face.

"I wasn't trying to be. Her kind is rare, but she has to find out for herself, or her creature won't emerge." The demon crouches, presses his hand against my stomach, and I squeeze my eyes shut, waiting for pain. "You're having triplets, by the way. They are strong. Would you like to know the sexes?"

"No," I say quickly, just as Anwyll says he does.

Abaddon grins, his image fading to show his form, but I'm not as scared now. "They are healthy. Feisty. Lucky," he adds with a friendly smile. "They are very lucky." He stands, and I can't help but wonder what he means.

A splash of water sounds, and everyone turns to see a portal open. A head pops out from the water, and I wave. "Irving!"

"Ru!" He swims to the shore just as a few of his kind dive into the water. "Thank you for keeping your word. I'm forever in your debt."

I introduce him to Maven and Alexander, then the Horseman, but I can't help but notice how Famine is looking at Irving.

Is he interested or curious?

Maybe everything will be okay. Everything is coming

together. Irving is safe. Apparently, more creatures are coming here too, then they will be safe.

The only person left to be saved is Aziel. We will save him too. We will find a way.

"Three," Anwyll whispers, lifting me into his arms as he rushes away from the chaos of people.

"Irving is here. We can't be rude."

"The hell we can't. I just found out my mate is having triplets. I have to claim her again. Irving can wait. He has plenty to keep him busy."

In one jump, he leaps up the stairs and sprints to our room, then tosses me on the bed.

"But we need to talk about—"

"—Nothing." His eyes glow, and he shifts to his midform. "I don't think you understand how much I don't want to talk." He locks the door, then prowls toward me, then his claws skim across my ankle. "The only thing I want is to get lost in my mate's moans."

He climbs on top of me, diving his tongue into my mouth. "I'll love you always," he mumbles between kisses, rubbing my entire body with his hands. It's like he has no idea where to touch but wants to feel me everywhere.

"Life or death?" I moan as he nips my ear.

"In life *and* death," he corrects me. "Nothing will keep me away from you. You are mine. In all forms, in all realms, in all fates."

"Promise?"

Epilogue

ANWYLL

"Ru needs help upstairs, Anwyll." Alexander holds his son while watching the new members of the coven in the fields and lake. "Something about something heavy," he yawns. "I can't believe we have a minotaur."

"Don't forget a kraken," Luca adds.

"And a siren and a mermaid," Greyson tacks on.

"Oh, and the lake monster, Irving," Finnick mumbles over the rim of his coffee. "Just what we need." He sounds grumpy, per usual.

A wail makes all of us cover our ears, and Alexander's son Enver cries.

"Let's not forget the banshee." I shake out the ringing in my ears.

"She's practicing. Give her time," Reuel says. "It isn't easy throwing around frequencies like that."

"Well, we need to soundproof the house. I have newborns. It's hard enough to get them to sleep. Ouch—" Enver sinks his fangs into his father's chest. "I am not your mommy. I don't have what you need, Enver. Let me take you to her— Ow." Enver bites him again.

I grin, wondering what my children will look like. What did Abaddon mean when he said they would be lucky? In general? It's only been a few days since the Horsemen came, and things have changed for the better, some for the worse.

Reuel is still here, but Cailian is not.

Rarity is, and she's more depressed than ever. She never leaves her room.

Alexander is worried and has debated on kicking her out of the coven to force her to be with her mate.

Severide has come up more from the catacombs to spend time with his new grandchildren, and he even seems healthier. He's holding Esmeray right now, smiling down at her like she is the answer to the universe.

There's good here and bad.

Balance.

Just like Death said.

My brother is still stuck, but his physical form is healed; all I need to do is snatch his spirit from where he is stuck.

I don't know how, but I will.

"If you need anything, holler. I'm going to go help my mate," I tell Reuel, hurrying up the steps.

When I get to the room, Ru is there.

Naked.

Wearing something very intimidating.

I lock the door so no one can come in and swallow.

"You've been a good boy, Anwyll. Such a good boy lately. I want to try something new with you. Are you wearing your toy?"

I shift my weight, the butt plug hitting my prostate again, and I bite back a groan. "Yes, I am."

"Show me," she says, lubing a strap-on cock with a small knot at the base. It's something we have been working toward. Every night, my mate plays with my ass, and every night, I spill my come inside her because that's where she wants it.

Her stomach is already getting round, but not too round to interfere with what we are about to do. I undress quickly, kicking off my shoes, then drop my pants, my heavy cock slapping against my stomach.

"Spin," she orders.

I do as she says and bend over, spreading my cheeks so she can see the plug.

"Oh, so good. You look so fucking hot, My Gentle Giant. Do you know what I'm going to do with you today?"

I shake my head, reaching down to stroke my cock.

"I'm going to fuck your ass until that knot swells with so much come, you sob, and then you're going to flip me over and fuck me, not wasting a drop of it. You'll knot me too."

"You want to flip?" I ask, a little surprised.

"Yes. On the bed. Face down. On your knees."

I listen eagerly, knowing she'll make me feel better than ever. It's a good thing all the bedrooms are soundproof because my mate makes me shout and groan, noises I don't want anyone to hear.

She stands next to the bed, and the small cock she has strapped onto her doesn't impress me, but I know it will be a challenge to take since I never have before. It can't be more than five inches, and the knot is the size of half of a small fist. Maybe I'm not intimidated because it's purple with pink glitter.

Ru probably did that on purpose.

She drifts her fingers down my back, then teases the crease. "So beautiful. You're my beautiful boy, aren't you?"

I turn my face away from her, not wanting her to see how embarrassed I am when she calls me that. Her hand slaps my ass, and it burns, spreading across my cheeks like a wildfire.

"Anwyll. Look at me."

I face her and nod. "I'm your beautiful boy."

She's pleased, wrapping her fingers around the base of the butt plug, pulling and twisting it, then plunges it forward.

"Fuck," I groan, biting the blanket.

"Does that feel good?" She continues the pattern, moving the butt plug in circles, and it brushes against my prostate every time.

My cock leaks with precome, and I watch the length hang large and ready between my legs. I'm not allowed to touch it. I have to follow the rules, or I won't be considered good.

She turns my face and kisses me ruthlessly, our tongues fighting and teeth clinking. Right as I'm about to lay her flat and pound into her, she stops, pulling away until she is settled behind me. Ru hums when she gently tugs the toy free, and I whimper from being empty for the first time today.

"Such a pretty hole that I plan on making mine." She bites my right cheek, gripping the other with her hand. "I'm addicted to your ass."

"I know the feeling." I feel the same way about hers.

A click of the lubricant bottle sounds, and I hiss when it dribbles down my crack. "Okay?"

"Yes." I grip the comforter in my hands and shout when she pushes two fingers inside me. "Fuck! Oh, fuck." I arch my back, giving my pleasure over freely to my mate.

"I love you, don't hold back. I love that I get to hear you." She slides a hand between my legs and squeezes my full sack, tugging it until it hurts.

More precome leaks from me, wetting the blanket under us.

"Your knot is already swelling. So eager." Ru traces the growing swell with her finger, the slight tickle adding to the sensations building my orgasm.

"Ru," I whimper, wanting her to make me feel good. She's the only reason why I haven't broken into a million pieces since we have been back.

I'm fragile.

She's solid.

I don't have the strength to be in control.

She takes the lead, letting me surrender it all to her.

Giving up control, being submissive sometimes, makes me feel stronger, more put together. It's like every time I heal a little more inside.

Ru does that for me.

She's my treatment after self-inflicted sickness.

In my life of chaos and pain, she's serenity and pleasure.

"I know," she croons, pulling her fingers free and then thrusts the dildo between my cheeks.

I gasp, excited and nervous. We've never done this before. We've never gone this far.

"Breathe," she reminds me.

I let it out, relaxing just as she pushes the tip inside.

"You know what's great about this strap-on? Every thrust, it rubs against my clit. I'll probably get to orgasm before you," she rubs in.

I clench down, the burning causing me to forget to breathe again.

"Push down. You're doing so well." She strokes my back, easing me, comforting me, and I do as she says, taking her to her fake knot.

We both groan. I feel so full, which I'm not comparing

to when I'm inside of her, but the new feelings make my legs shake. I readjust my stance, and my knee hits a small puddle of precome.

She curls over me the best she can, kissing the middle of my back while she wraps a hand around my cock, then fucks it with her fist.

"Fuck. Fuck! Ru. Stop. It's too much. Don't, no. Keep going." I sound insane, but it's everything I want and don't want at the same time.

She pulls out, then thrusts back in, pegging the spot inside me that makes me see stars. I growl, tearing the blanket with my claws as she picks up the confidence to fuck me.

In and out, in and out, she drives into my ass, claiming it as hers like she's always wanted. She's marked it too. Three small gashes from her talons are scarred on my right cheek.

We have to stop doing that, or we will have scars all over.

It's a werewolf thing. We have issues with control sometimes.

She whimpers as the toy presses against her clit, and she fucks into me faster, picking up the pace. She grabs my ass, using it as leverage to pound into me.

"Yes, harder, Ru. Fuck me harder. That's it. Oh, fuck, yes," I groan long and loud, reaching above my head to grip the headboard.

My toes curl. Sweat drips down my spine. My vision becomes a haze. My knot swells to its biggest size, and all I need is permission to come.

"Oh, feels so good. I can't stop. I'm so close," she whines, her hips stutter with their pace. "Anwyll! Fuck,

About the Author

January Rayne is a paranormal fantasy romance author who lives in Buffalo, NY with her husband, son, two dogs, and two leopard geckos. Buffalo is freezing, but January loves when it snows as it gives her the perfect atmosphere to write a book for you to get lost in.

Scan here for easy access to follow me on social media:

Anwyll!" she cries, slamming into me so hard, the small knot pops inside and tugs against my rim and prostate.

My cock jerks, and a stream of come shoots from the tip to the bed. I tightened my grip around my length to stop myself, but then the raggedy breaths that leave me turn to broken huffs and snarls.

I'm losing control of being submissive, and now I want to put my mate in her place.

She pulls out of me, and I don't waste another second. I rip her strap-on off, then slam her against the nearby wall. Wrapping her legs around me, I ram into her soaking wet cunt, primed and ready for my knot.

Licking her mating mark, her entire being vibrates with pleasure.

"That's it, mate. Take my cock that's too big for your little pussy." I nibble her neck, wanting to mark her again. "I bet everything inside you is imprinted with the shape of my dick. All mine."

"Yours. I'm yours." I drive into her hard and unforgiving, but it isn't enough. I toss her on the bed and mount her from behind, gripping her hips like she did mine.

I still feel the bite of her efforts in my ass, and it spurs me on.

The large scar on her back stares back at me, and a smug, prideful smirk takes over my face while I pummel my cock in and out.

Yes. She's ruined for all others.

And that makes me feel so good.

"You wish you could fuck me like I fuck you, but you'll never be able to fill me like I fill you." I slam into her, threatening to stretch her opening with my knot. "I smell your jealousy, and it's delicious." I toss her onto the bed, push her head into the mattress, then pin her down while I rut and use her cunt.

I glance down, her nectar dripping down me again.

Flipping her over onto her back, I spread her legs to watch myself disappear between her legs. With one talon, I press against her swollen clit, the sharp point threatening to break the skin. Ru orgasms, her nipples tightening and leaking with milk already.

Another werewolf thing.

I bend down and lick the milk from her body, the sugary sweetness, my new favorite drink. Needing more, I wrap my lips around the tight pink peak, sucking deep, and milk drapes over my tongue. It's like liquid gold. Releasing the morsel with a loud pop, I lick my way over to the other while my fingers pinch the one I just paid attention too. I shift my tongue, letting it slither around her nipple, milking it for my own greedy thirst. I watch as the white liquid drips, and I attack, feeding from her swollen tit. I'm so jealous of my children, and they aren't even born yet. I knead, suck, and bite, filling myself with her, and it still isn't enough. I try to suck her entire breast into my mouth, aching for more of the milk. Her other nipple drips onto my hand as my fingers play around the sensitive flesh. Not wanting a drop to go to waste, I lick my palm clean.

So fucking good.

Her taste sends me over the edge.

With one final thrust, I force my knot inside, and she screams, another orgasm ramming into her. My knot releases thick, full batches of seed into her occupied womb, and I rub my hands over her swelling belly. My nostrils flare as I stare down at her. My bite mark is visible. Her nipples are red and swollen from my attention. Milk is leaking freely and dripping down her breasts to her stomach. Her belly is full of my seed, growing triplets, and her cunt is stuck on my knot. I love watching her pink and abused hole stretch to take my knot. She struggles but always manages to fit me.

What a fucking sight.

She is flushed from our hard fuck. Ru looks used and claimed.

Owned.

Fuck.

She's all mine. Always.

My mate. *My* children.

Mine.

Gently, I wrap my arms around her and suck on her nipples, soothing them with attention while I sip her milk. There isn't much, enough to make her sore, and when I take it, she is relieved.

It isn't a hardship. I enjoy it. I love it.

"My Gentle Giant," she sighs while I'm still locked in her body.

With one hand cupping her stomach, protecting everything important to me, I kiss up her body until I take her lips in a soft kiss.

I'm finally worthy.

We roll onto our sides, and I pull the blanket over us as I wait for the knot to go down. "I got you something," I say, reaching for the nightstand.

I hand her a stack of them.

"Scratch-offs?" She jerks and shouts with so much joy, it pulls her away, and we both make a sound of pleasure and discomfort.

"You make your own luck, right?" I remind her.

She holds the tickets to her chest, and I move her hair from her shoulder, her smile warming my heart.

"Thank you for trying to keep my luck alive by remembering how much I love these."

"I'll always remind you." I kiss her shoulder and hold her.

"What if we win big? How cool would that be?"

"I've already won."

"Cheese ball," she teases, intertwining our fingers. "I love it."

I don't care if she scratches a thousand of these and we never win. She's given me everything.

"Oh, and I talked to Reuel. He'll be bringing Mannix here. Tomorrow."

She squeals and rolls over until she's on top, pressing her cheek against my chest. Her tears splash against my skin. "Thank you. Thank you so much. I'm so excited. I can't believe he will finally be here. I bet he is worried sick. Oh my chauns, he is going to freak out when I tell him I don't have my luck anymore."

"Yes, you do." I hold her hand against my heart so she can feel why it beats as strongly as it does. "It's right here thanks to you."

My pain finally got lucky.

ACKNOWLEDGEMENTS

I'd like to thank all of my patient readers for waiting for this book. I'd love to write more and give everyone more books faster, but life happens, and I do have a big girl job that takes a lot of my time :(. One day, I'll be able to give you everyone's story in a timely manner.

Thank you to the alpha readers and arc readers for helping me make this as perfect as it can be. I'm horrible at catching my own mistakes.

A big thank you to my amazing friend Dallas Ann Designs for this amazing cover and for always helping me with everything. Literally. Carolina, you're amazing. Thank you both for believing in me.

To everyone who helps make my dreams come true. I love you and I am so thankful to all of you.

Hubby, my ginger, thank you for your faith in me.

www.ingramcontent.com/pod-product-compliance
Lightning Source LLC
Chambersburg PA
CBHW040328020826
48978CB00013BC/943